AN UNOFFICIAL GRAPHIC NOVEL
FOR MINECRAFTERS

QUEST *for the* GOLDEN APPLE

MEGAN MILLER
NEW YORK TIMES
BESTSELLING AUTHOR

Acknowledgments

The images in this book were created with the amazing Minecraft animation program, Mine-imator, developed by David Norgren. You can download Mine-imator and find out more about it at Stuffbydavid. com/mine-imator. The mods, Biomes O' Plenty (by Glitchfiend), and The Twilight Forest (by Benimatic) were used to create the fantasy worlds that Damon and Dixie visit in chapter 2. You can find out more about these mods at Minecraftforum.net. Finally, big thanks to my brother, Andy Miller, for building the marvelous monastery shown in chapters 7 and 8.

Sky Pony Press books may be purchased in bulk at special discounts for sales promotion, corporate gifts, fund-raising, or educational purposes. Special editions can also be created to specifications. For details, contact the Special Sales Department, Sky Pony Press, 307 West 36th Street, 11th Floor, New York, NY 10018 or info@skyhorsepublishing.com.

Sky Pony® is a registered trademark of Skyhorse Publishing, Inc.®, a Delaware corporation.

Visit our website at www.skyponypress.com.

10 9 8 7 6 5 4 3 2 1

Library of Congress Cataloging-in-Publication Data is available on file.

Special thanks to Megan Miller

Cover design by Brian Peterson
Cover image credit Megan Miller

Print ISBN: 978-1-5107-0410-7
Ebook ISBN: 978-1-5107-0411-4

Printed in the United States of America

Editor: Julie Matysik
Designer and Production Manager: Joshua Barnaby

INTRODUCTION

If you have played Minecraft, then you know all about Minecraft worlds. They're made of blocks you can mine: coal, dirt, and sand. In the game, you'll find dungeons and pyramids, skeletons and zombies. You can also find villages inhabited by strange villagers with bald heads. You may think you know these villagers, but you don't. These villagers call *you* miners. They call the worlds you mine on miner worlds. That's because the villagers have their very own special and magical worlds that you have never visited. And between the magical villager worlds and your own miner worlds, they've created a protective string of border worlds, all to stop miners from finding the magical, hidden worlds.

And that's where this story begins, on the small border world of Xenos, where there is one girl who doesn't quite fit in with the other villagers . . .

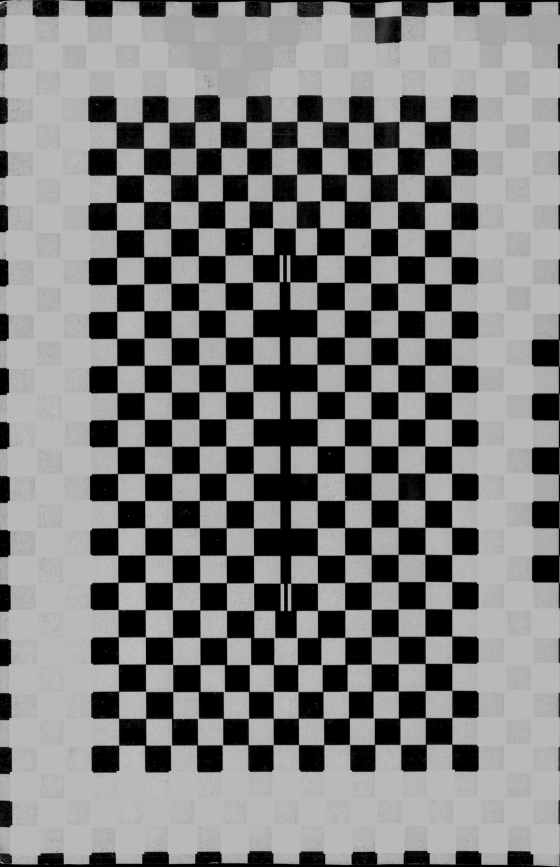

CHAPTER 1
THE FOREST

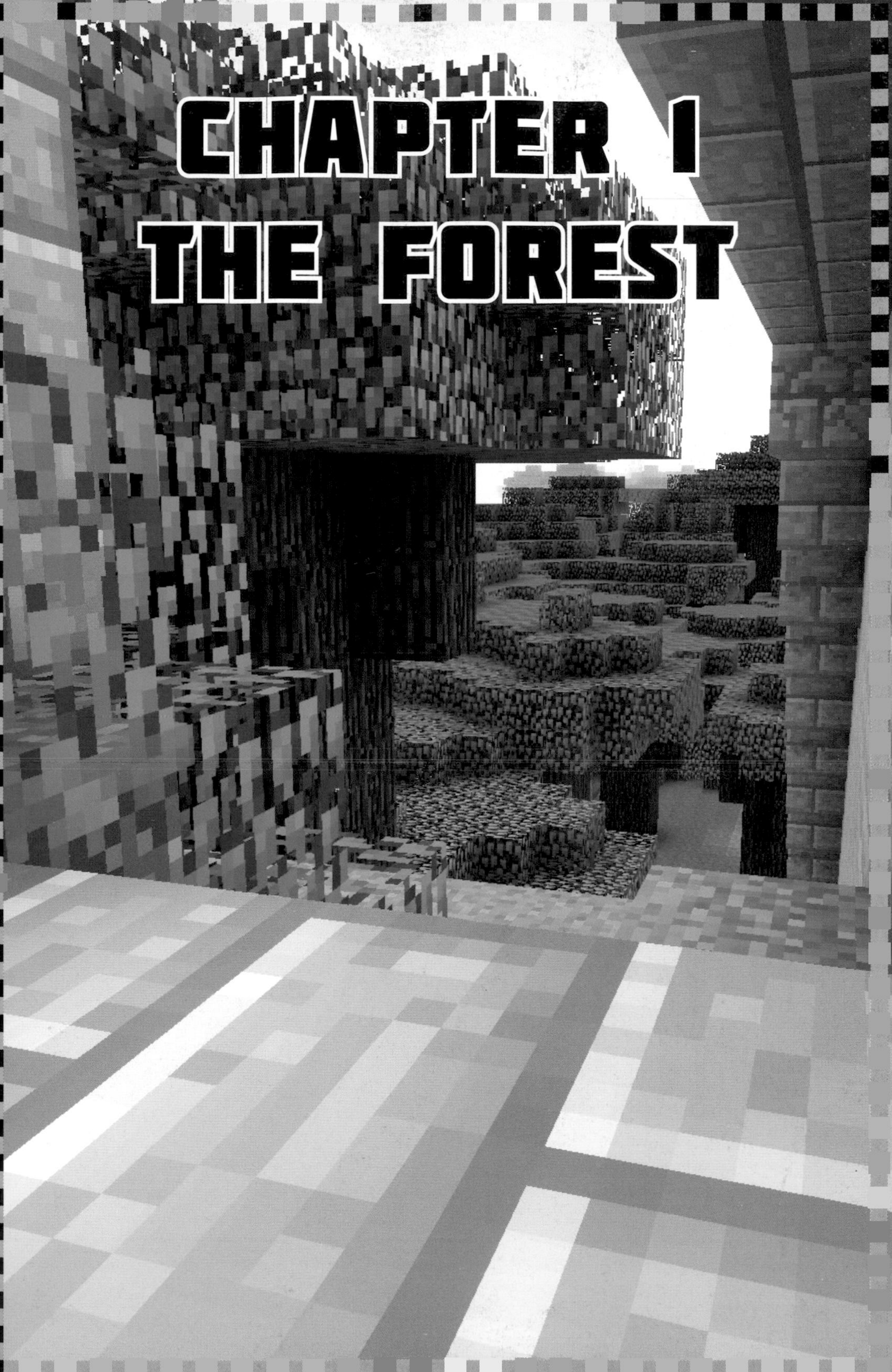

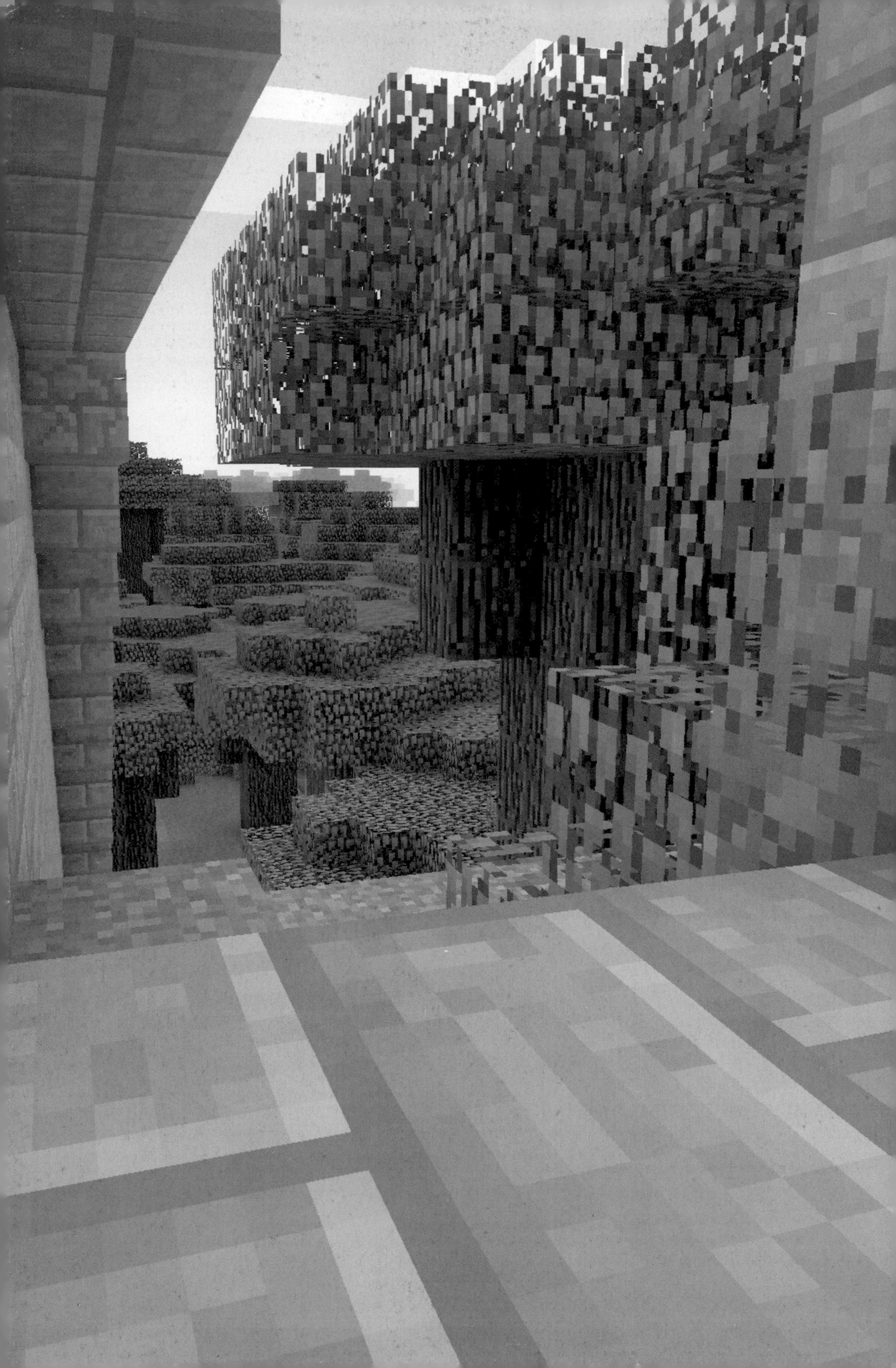

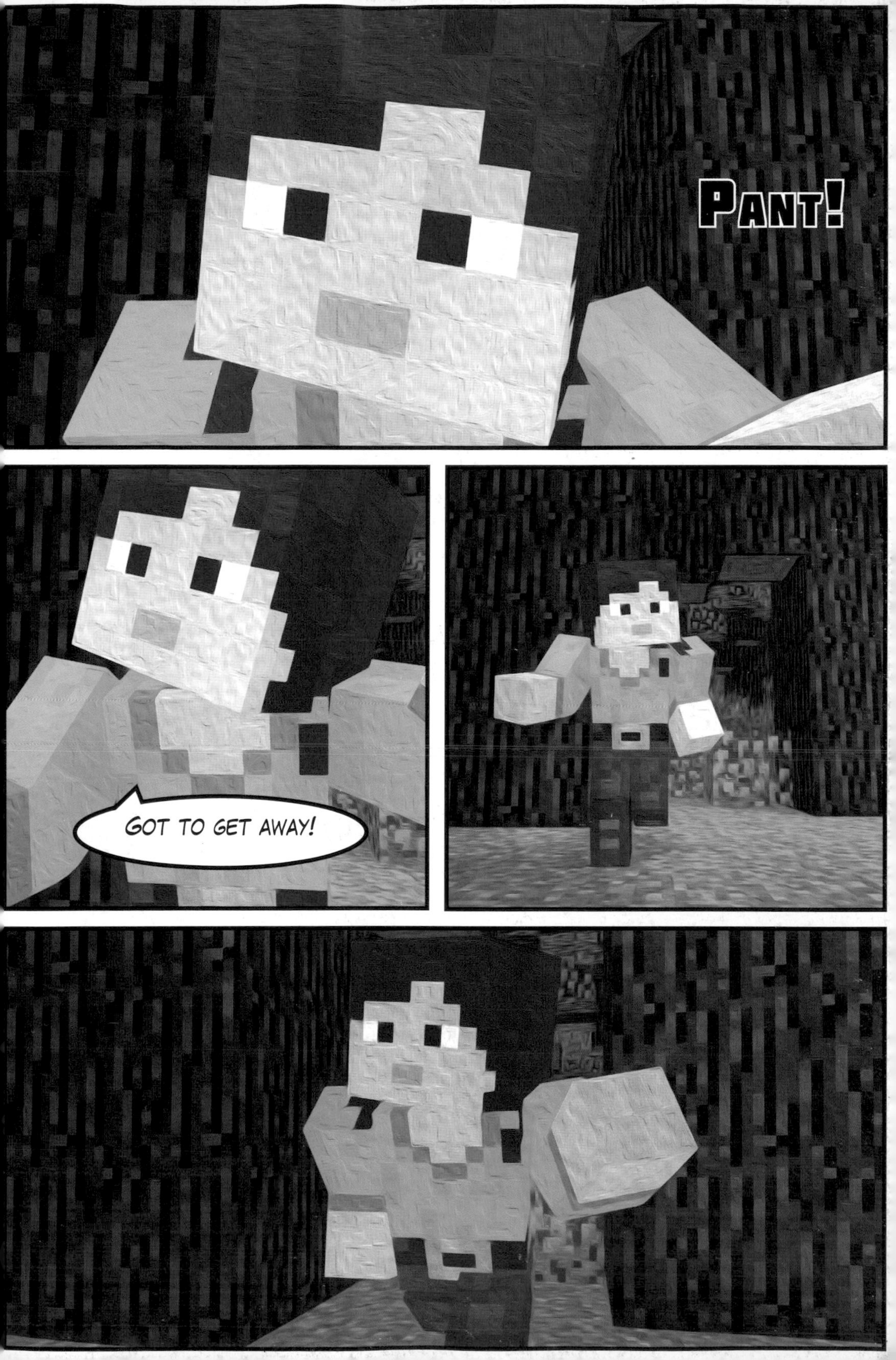
PANT!
GOT TO GET AWAY!

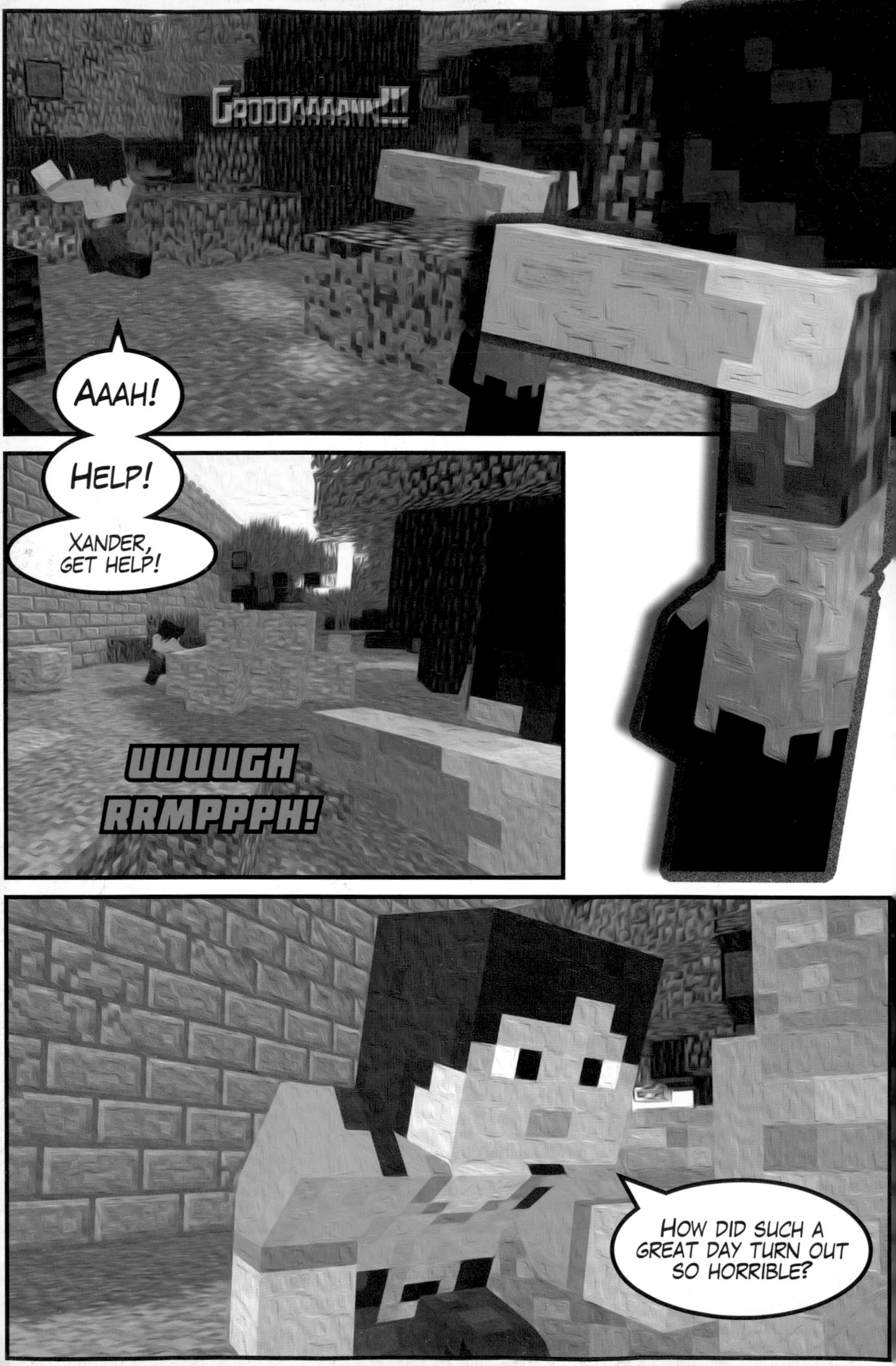
GRODDAAAANN!!!
AAAH!
HELP!
XANDER, GET HELP!
UUUUGH RRMPPPH!
HOW DID SUCH A GREAT DAY TURN OUT SO HORRIBLE?

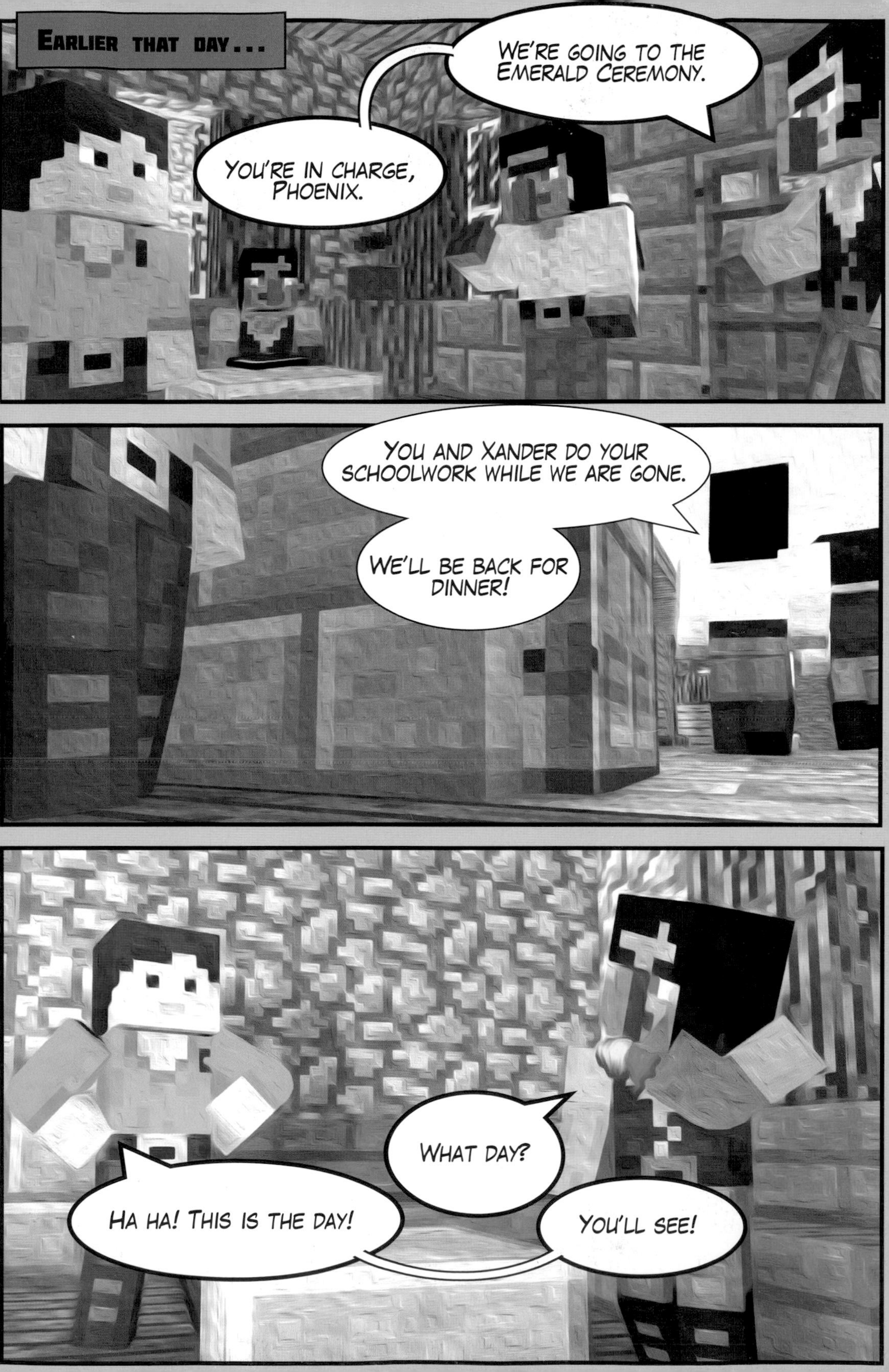
EARLIER THAT DAY . . .
YOU'RE IN CHARGE, PHOENIX.
WE'RE GOING TO THE EMERALD CEREMONY.
YOU AND XANDER DO YOUR SCHOOLWORK WHILE WE ARE GONE.
WE'LL BE BACK FOR DINNER!
HA HA! THIS IS THE DAY!
WHAT DAY?
YOU'LL SEE!

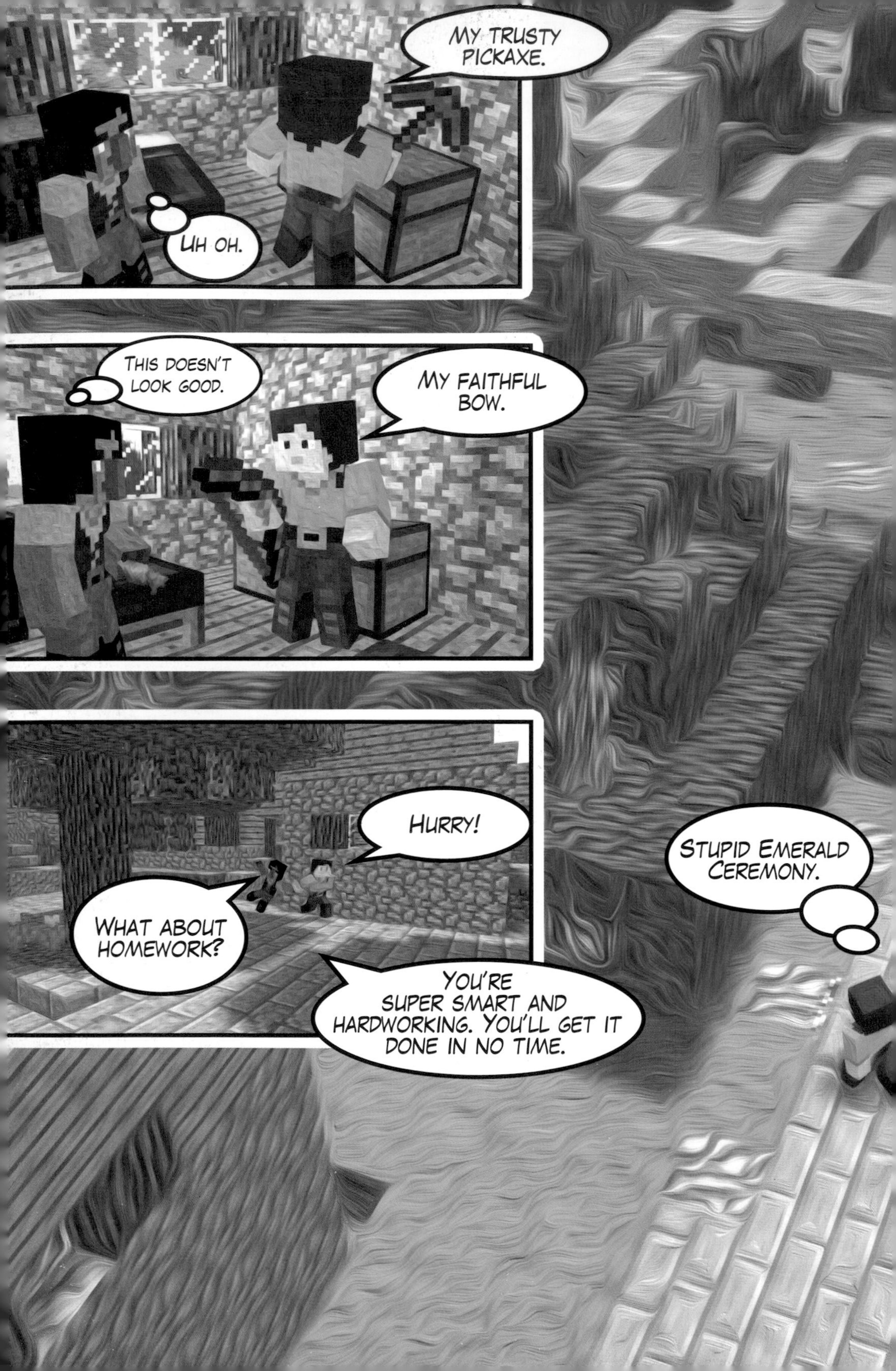
MY TRUSTY PICKAXE.
UH OH.
THIS DOESN'T LOOK GOOD.
MY FAITHFUL BOW.
HURRY!
WHAT ABOUT HOMEWORK?
YOU'RE SUPER SMART AND HARDWORKING. YOU'LL GET IT DONE IN NO TIME.
STUPID EMERALD CEREMONY.

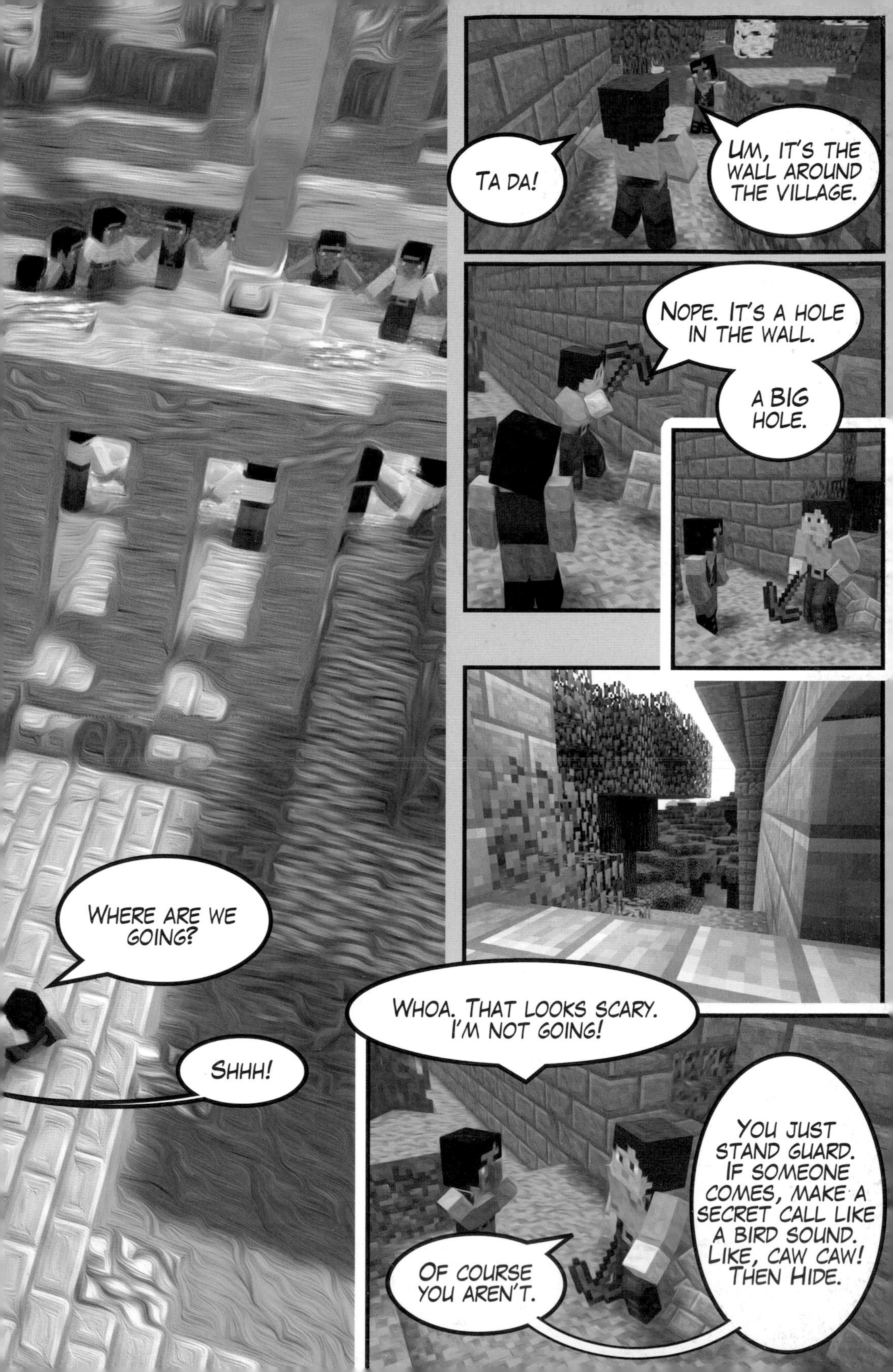
TA DA!
UM, IT'S THE WALL AROUND THE VILLAGE.
NOPE. IT'S A HOLE IN THE WALL.
A BIG HOLE.
WHERE ARE WE GOING?
SHHH!
WHOA. THAT LOOKS SCARY. I'M NOT GOING!
OF COURSE YOU AREN'T.
YOU JUST STAND GUARD. IF SOMEONE COMES, MAKE A SECRET CALL LIKE A BIRD SOUND. LIKE, CAW CAW! THEN HIDE.

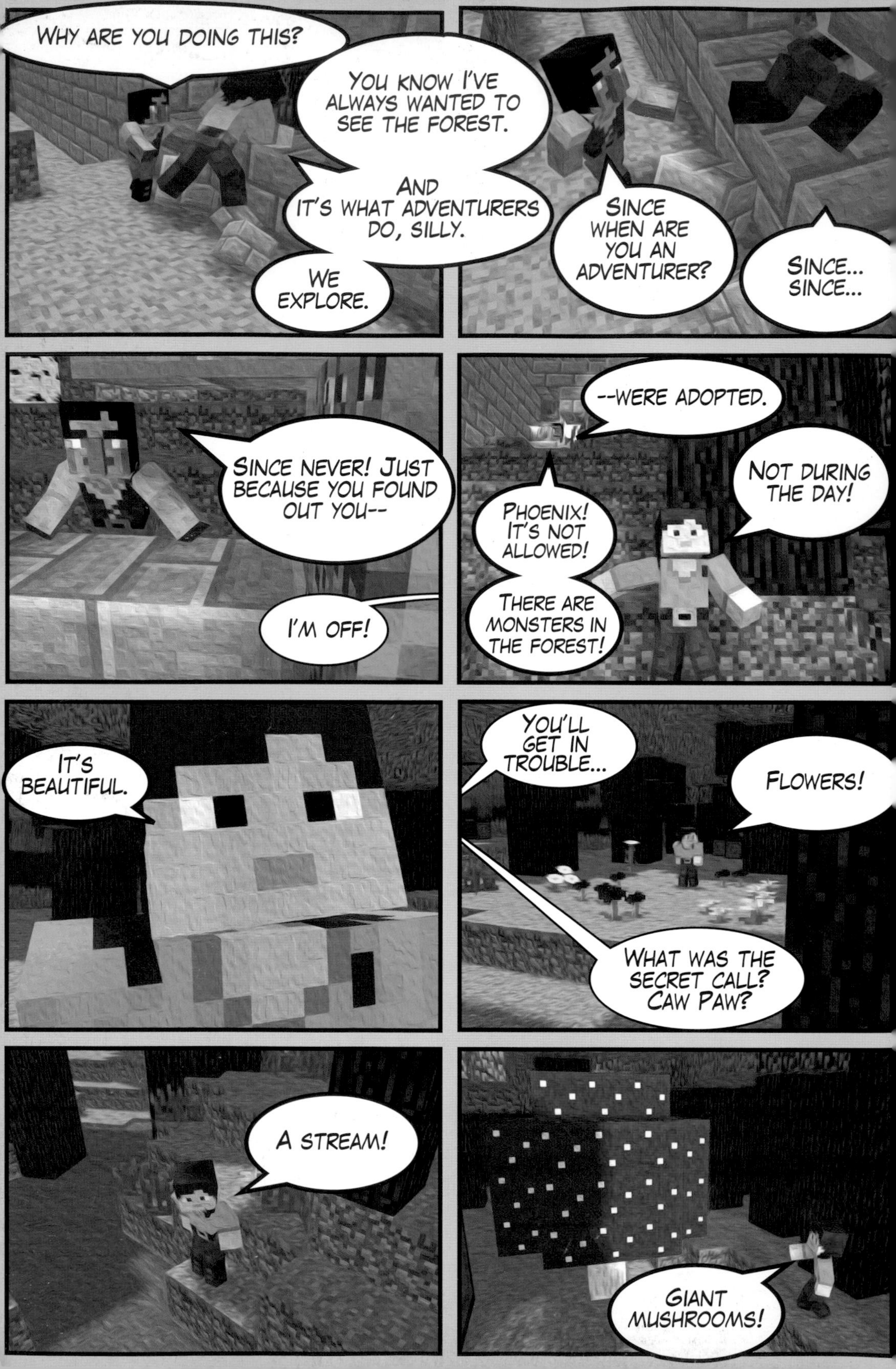
WHY ARE YOU DOING THIS?
YOU KNOW I'VE ALWAYS WANTED TO SEE THE FOREST.
AND IT'S WHAT ADVENTURERS DO, SILLY.
WE EXPLORE.
SINCE WHEN ARE YOU AN ADVENTURER?
SINCE... SINCE...
SINCE NEVER! JUST BECAUSE YOU FOUND OUT YOU--
I'M OFF!
--WERE ADOPTED.
PHOENIX! IT'S NOT ALLOWED!
THERE ARE MONSTERS IN THE FOREST!
NOT DURING THE DAY!
IT'S BEAUTIFUL.
YOU'LL GET IN TROUBLE...
FLOWERS!
WHAT WAS THE SECRET CALL? CAW PAW?
A STREAM!
GIANT MUSHROOMS!

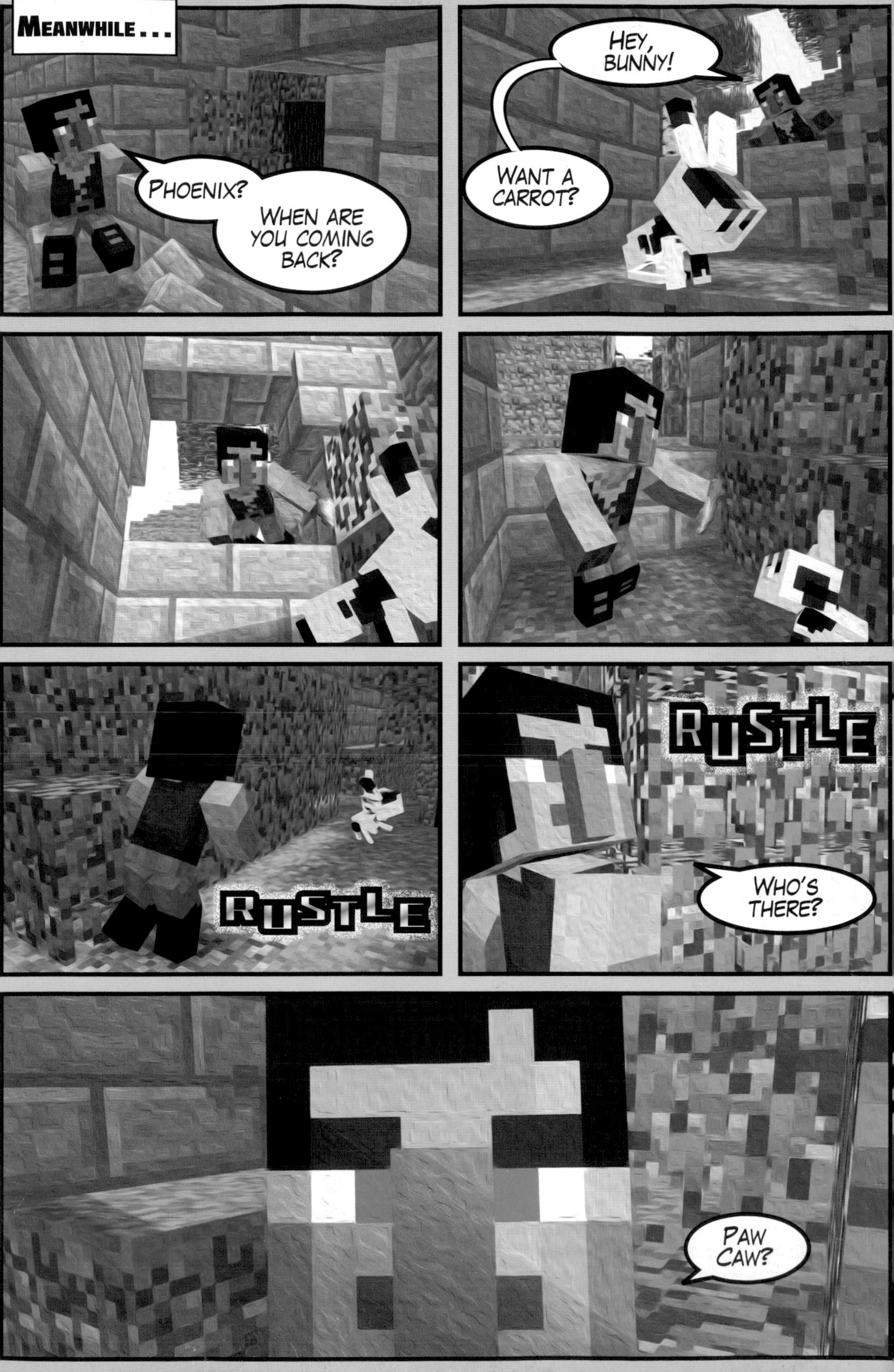
MEANWHILE . . .
PHOENIX?
WHEN ARE YOU COMING BACK?
HEY, BUNNY!
WANT A CARROT?
RUSTLE
RUSTLE
WHO'S THERE?
PAW CAW?

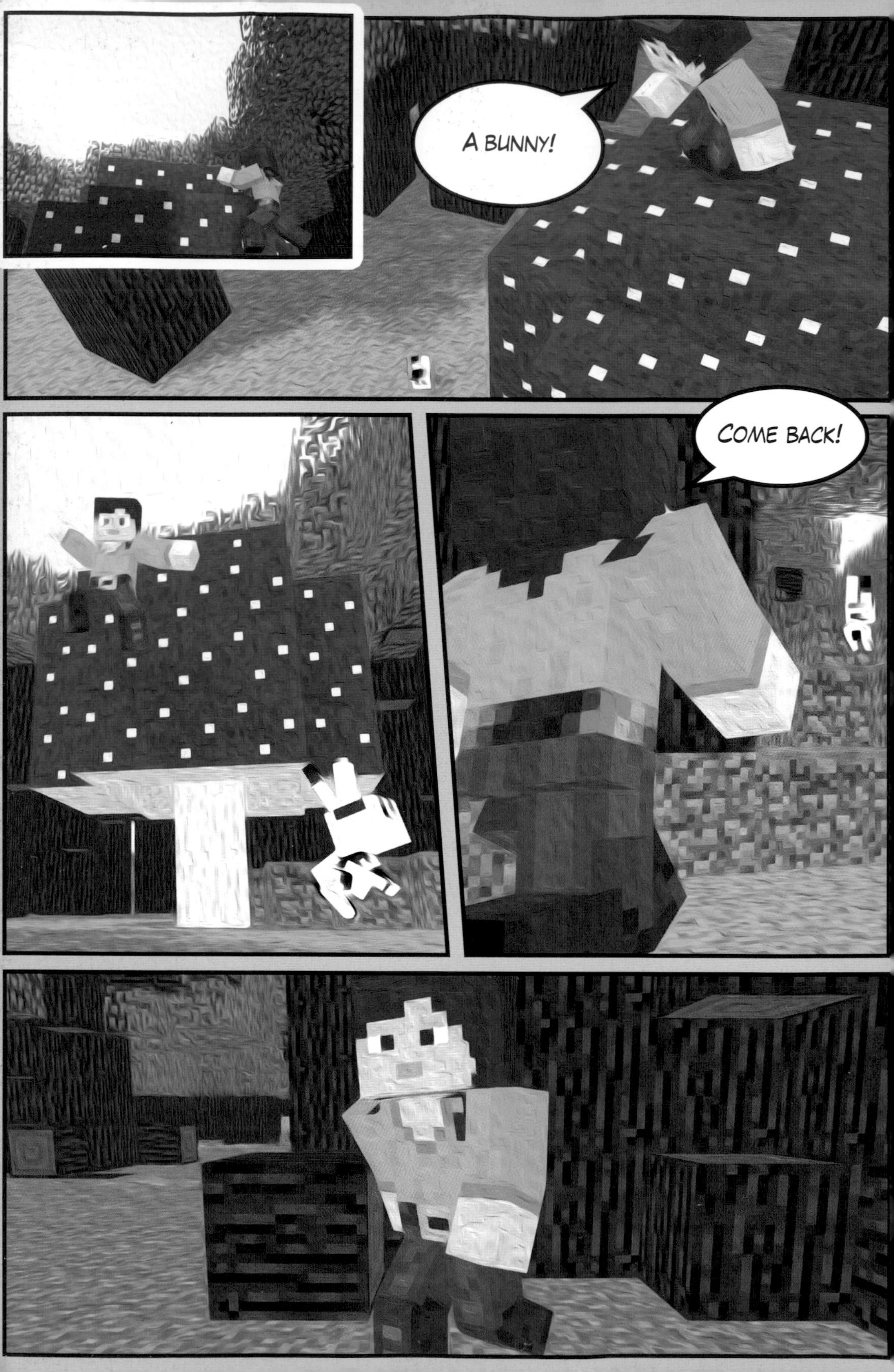
A BUNNY!
COME BACK!

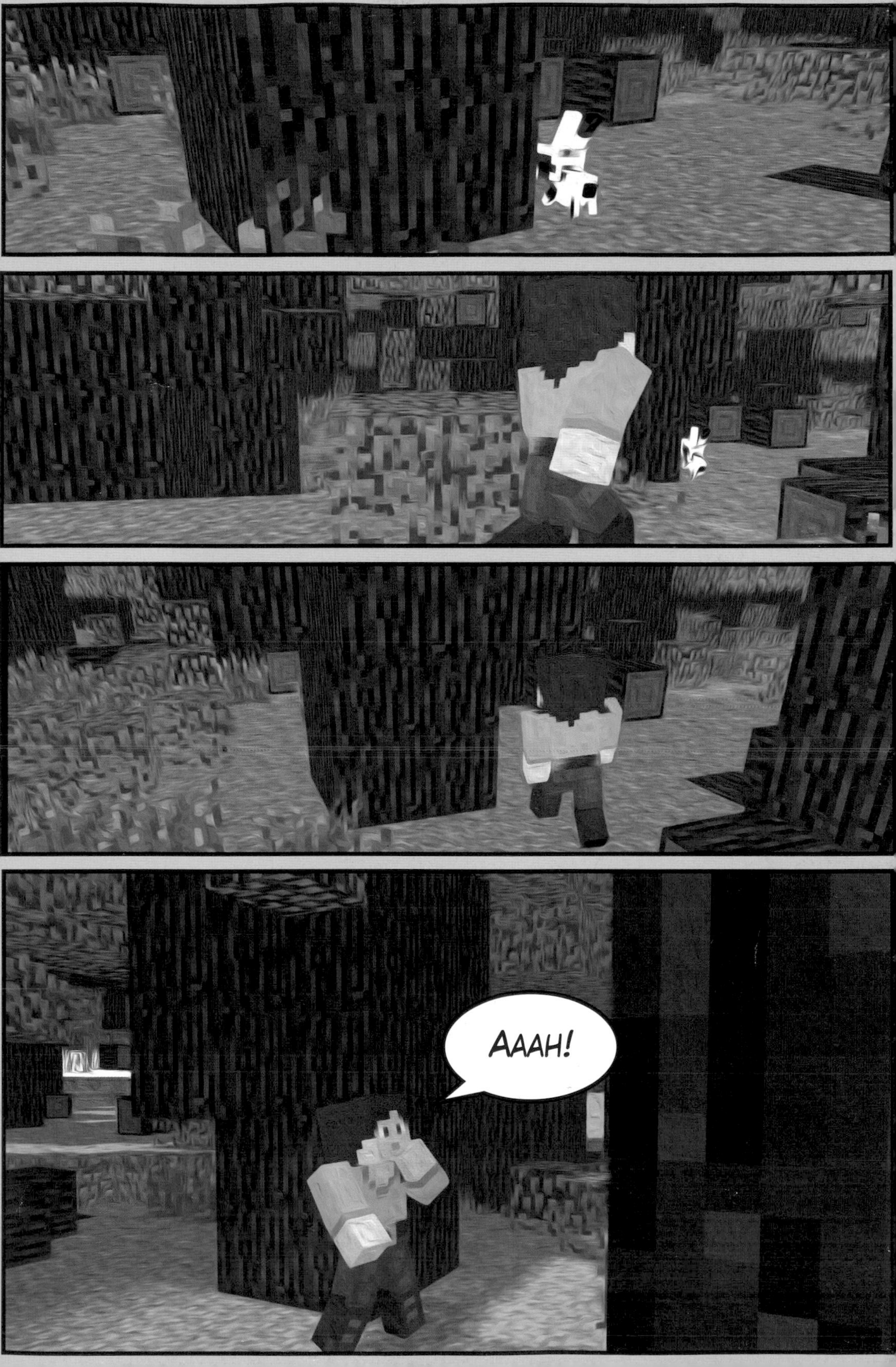
AAAH!

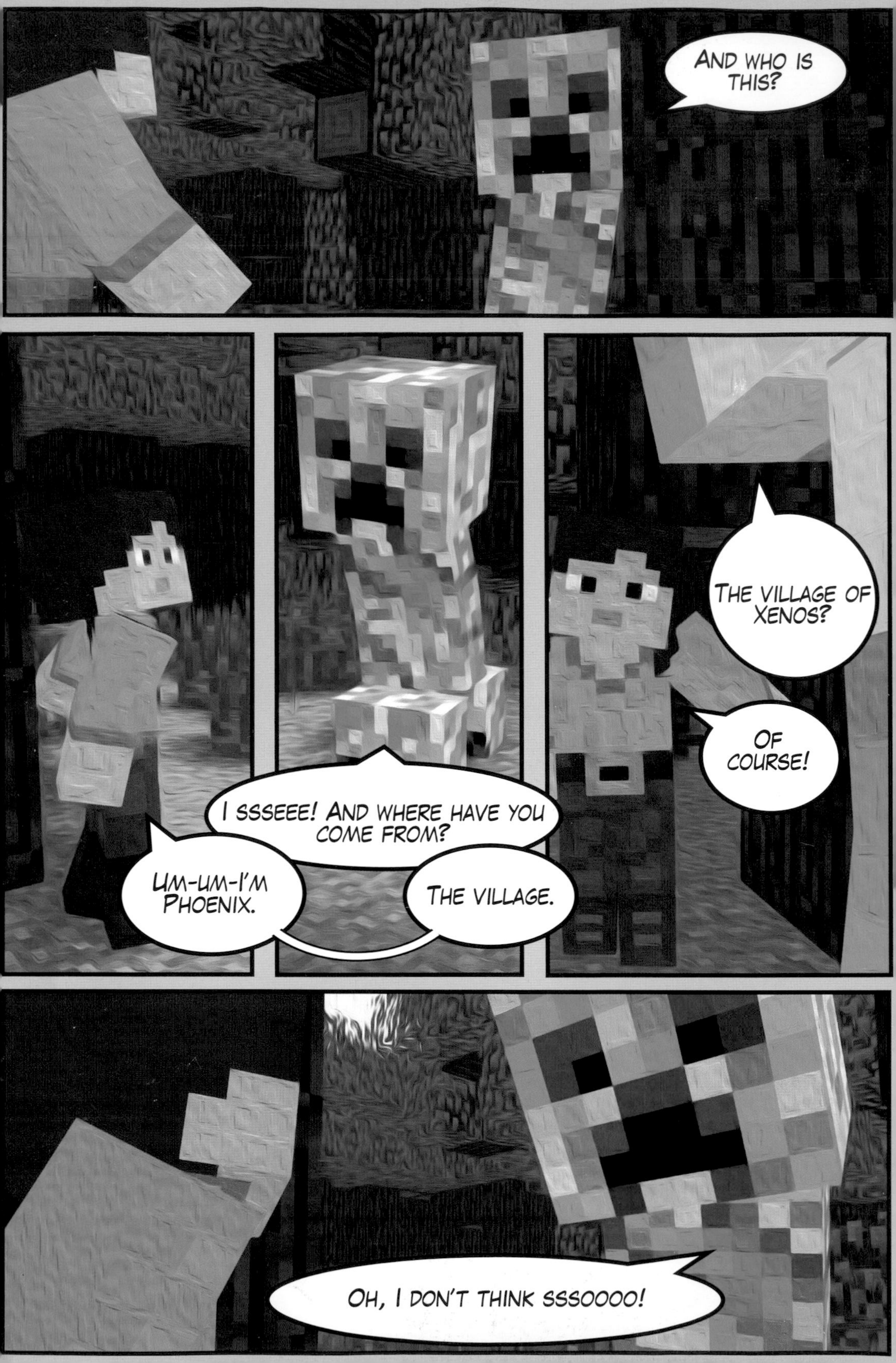
AND WHO IS THIS?
I SSSEEE! AND WHERE HAVE YOU COME FROM?
UM-UM-I'M PHOENIX.
THE VILLAGE.
THE VILLAGE OF XENOS?
OF COURSE!
OH, I DON'T THINK SSSOOOO!

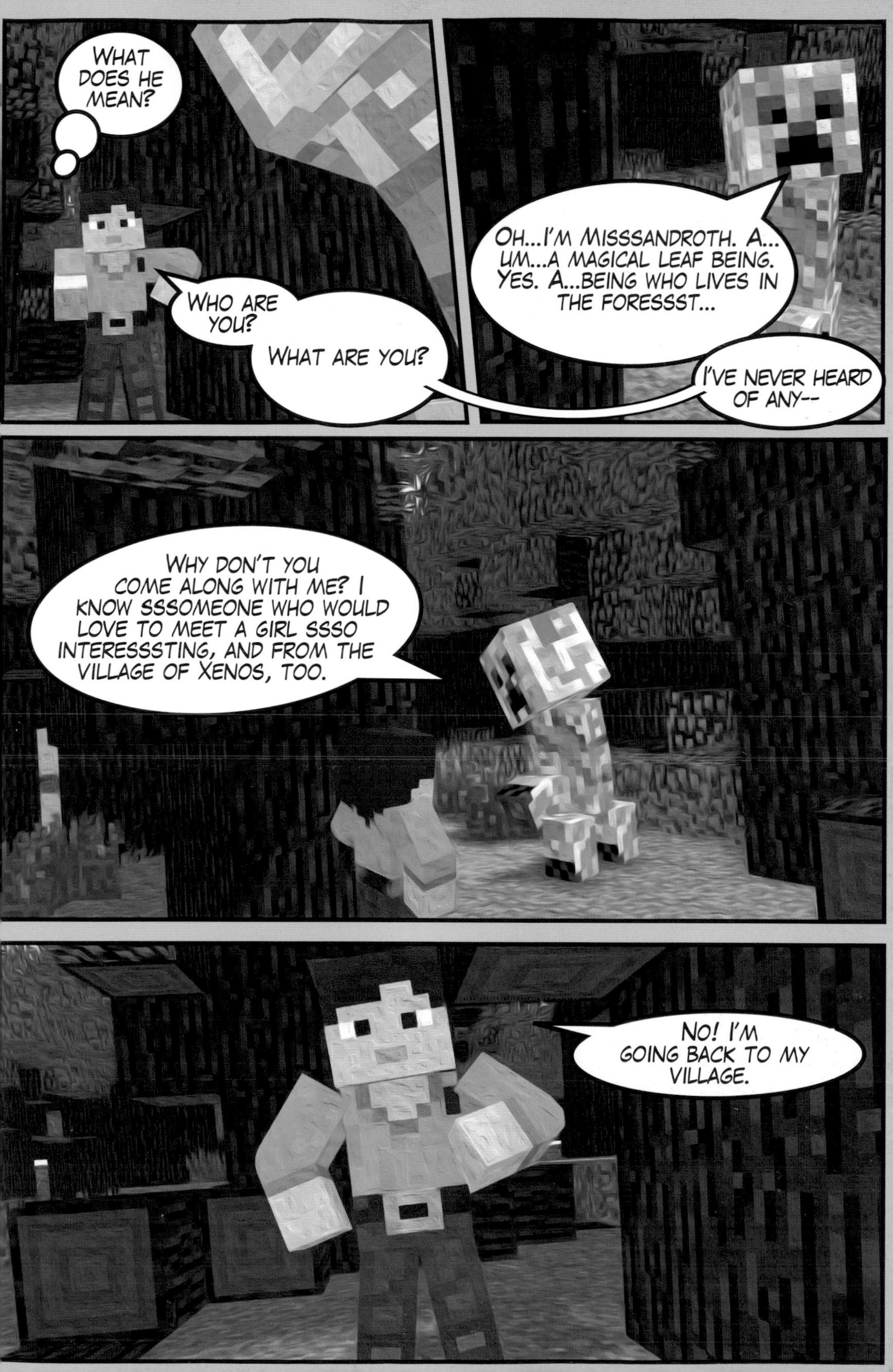
WHAT DOES HE MEAN?
WHO ARE YOU?
WHAT ARE YOU?
OH...I'M MISSSANDROTH. A... UM...A MAGICAL LEAF BEING. YES. A...BEING WHO LIVES IN THE FORESSST...
I'VE NEVER HEARD OF ANY--
WHY DON'T YOU COME ALONG WITH ME? I KNOW SSSOMEONE WHO WOULD LOVE TO MEET A GIRL SSSO INTERESSSTING, AND FROM THE VILLAGE OF XENOS, TOO.
NO! I'M GOING BACK TO MY VILLAGE.

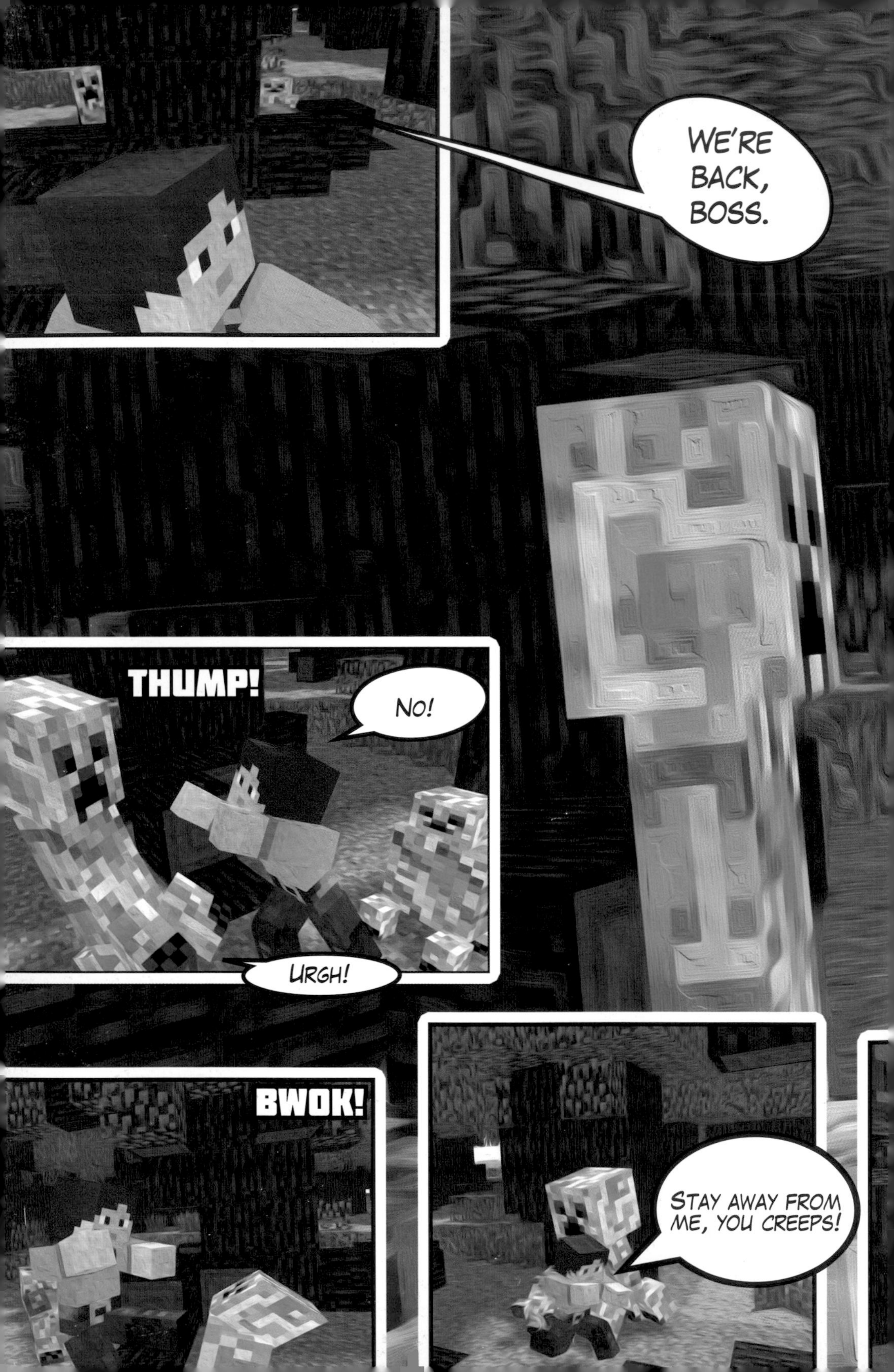
WE'RE BACK, BOSS.
THUMP!
NO!
URGH!
BWOK!
STAY AWAY FROM ME, YOU CREEPS!

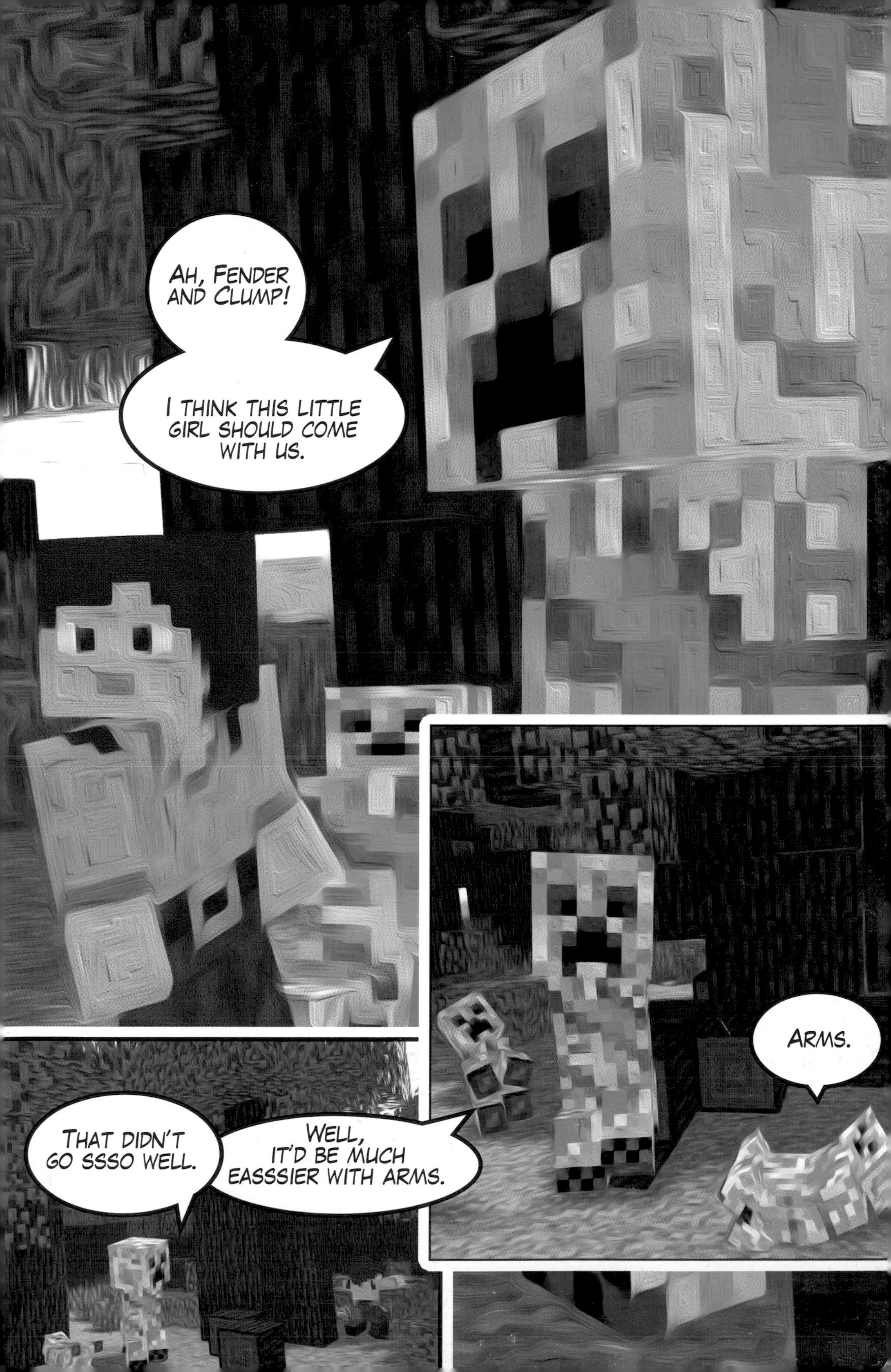
AH, FENDER AND CLUMP!
I THINK THIS LITTLE GIRL SHOULD COME WITH US.
ARMS.
THAT DIDN'T GO SSSO WELL.
WELL, IT'D BE MUCH EASSSIER WITH ARMS.

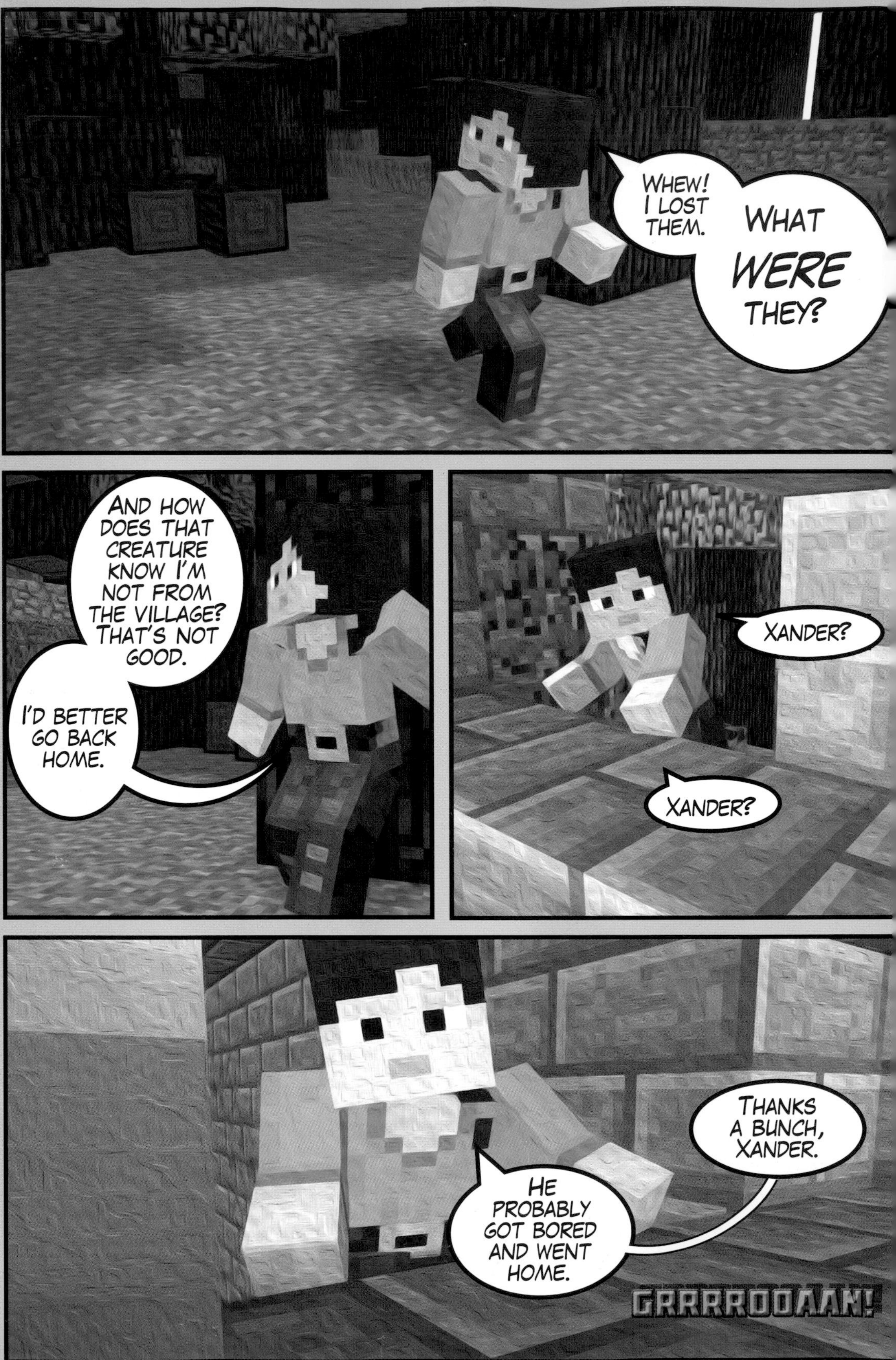
WHEW! I LOST THEM.
WHAT *WERE* THEY?
AND HOW DOES THAT CREATURE KNOW I'M NOT FROM THE VILLAGE? THAT'S NOT GOOD.
I'D BETTER GO BACK HOME.
XANDER?
XANDER?
HE PROBABLY GOT BORED AND WENT HOME.
THANKS A BUNCH, XANDER.
GRRRROOAAN!

IS THAT YOU, XANDER?

URGH!

GROOOAN!

AAAH!

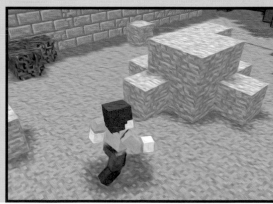

YES. A BEAUTIFUL WALK HAD TURNED INTO A TERRIBLE DAY.

I'VE BROKEN THE RULES,

I'VE LOST XANDER, AND...

I'M ABOUT TO BE KILLED BY A ZOMBIE!

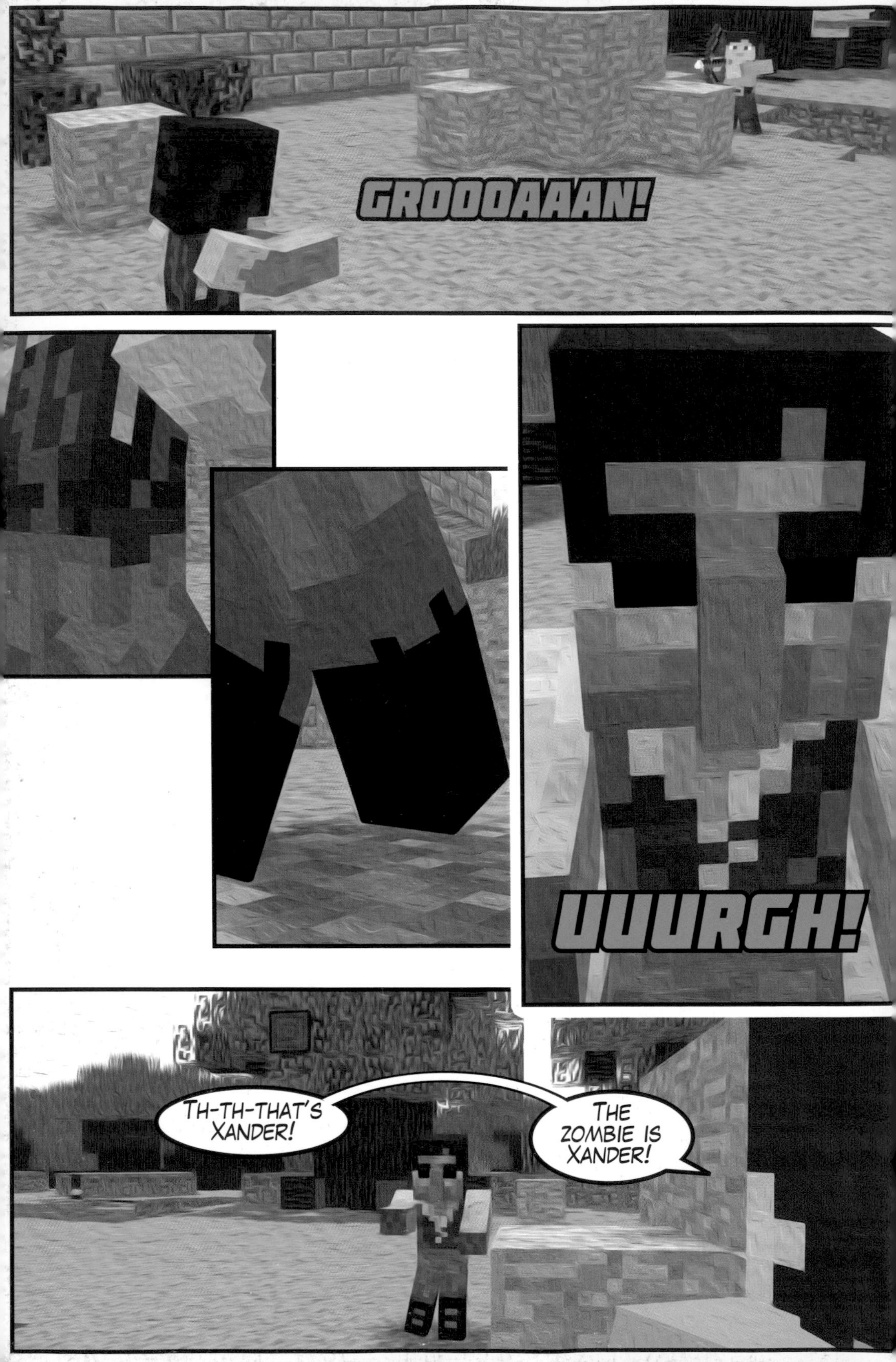
GROOOAAAN!
UUURGH!
TH-TH-THAT'S XANDER!
THE ZOMBIE IS XANDER!

CHAPTER 2
A DISTANT WORLD

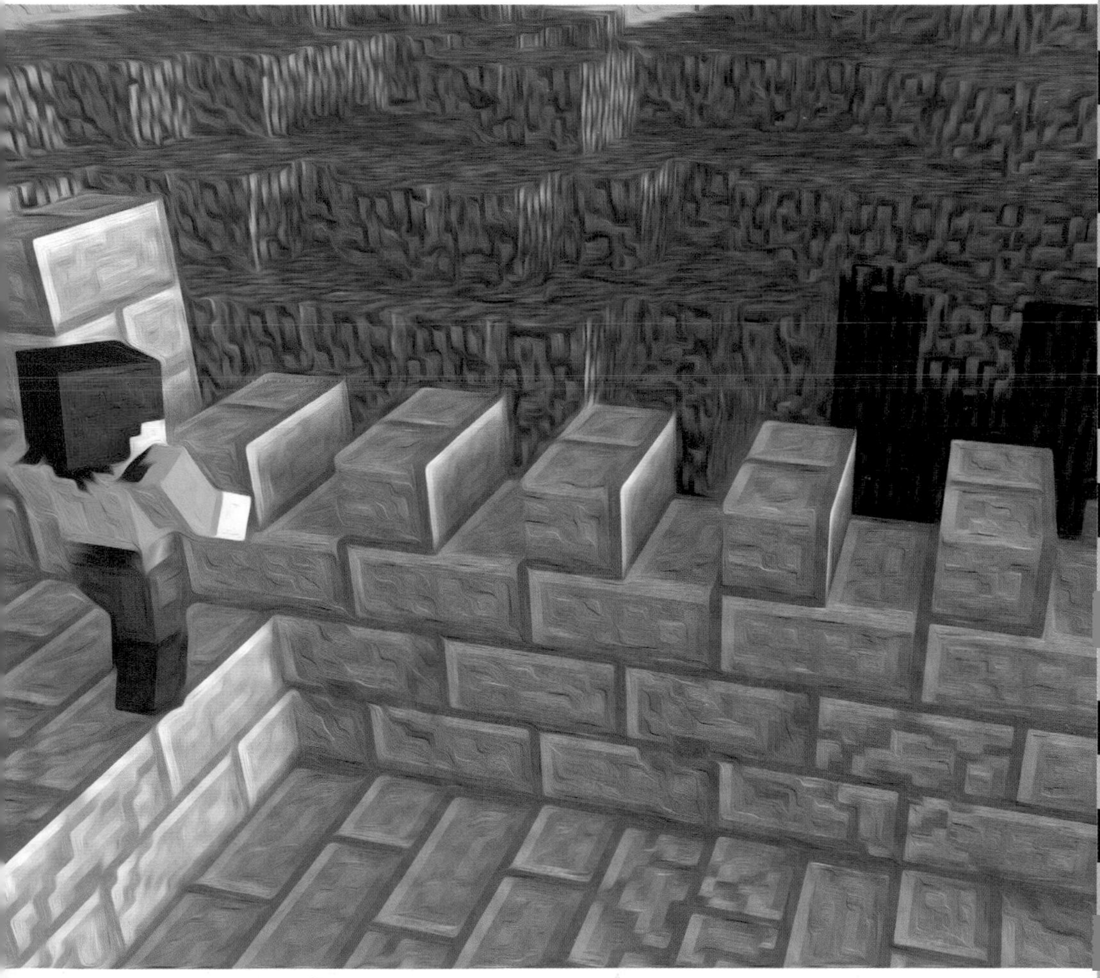

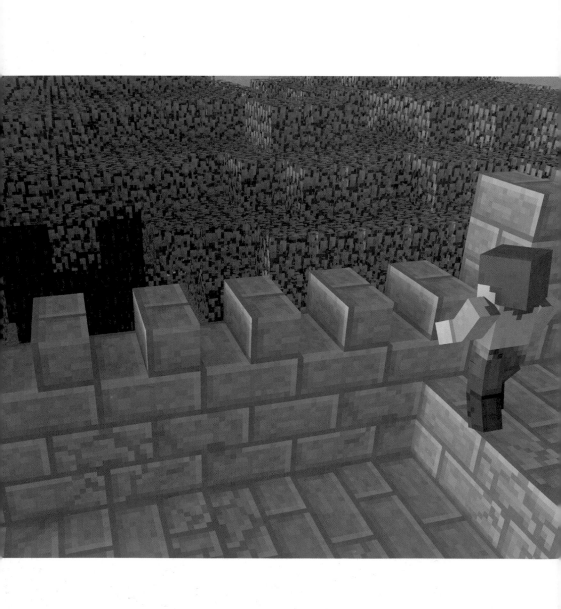

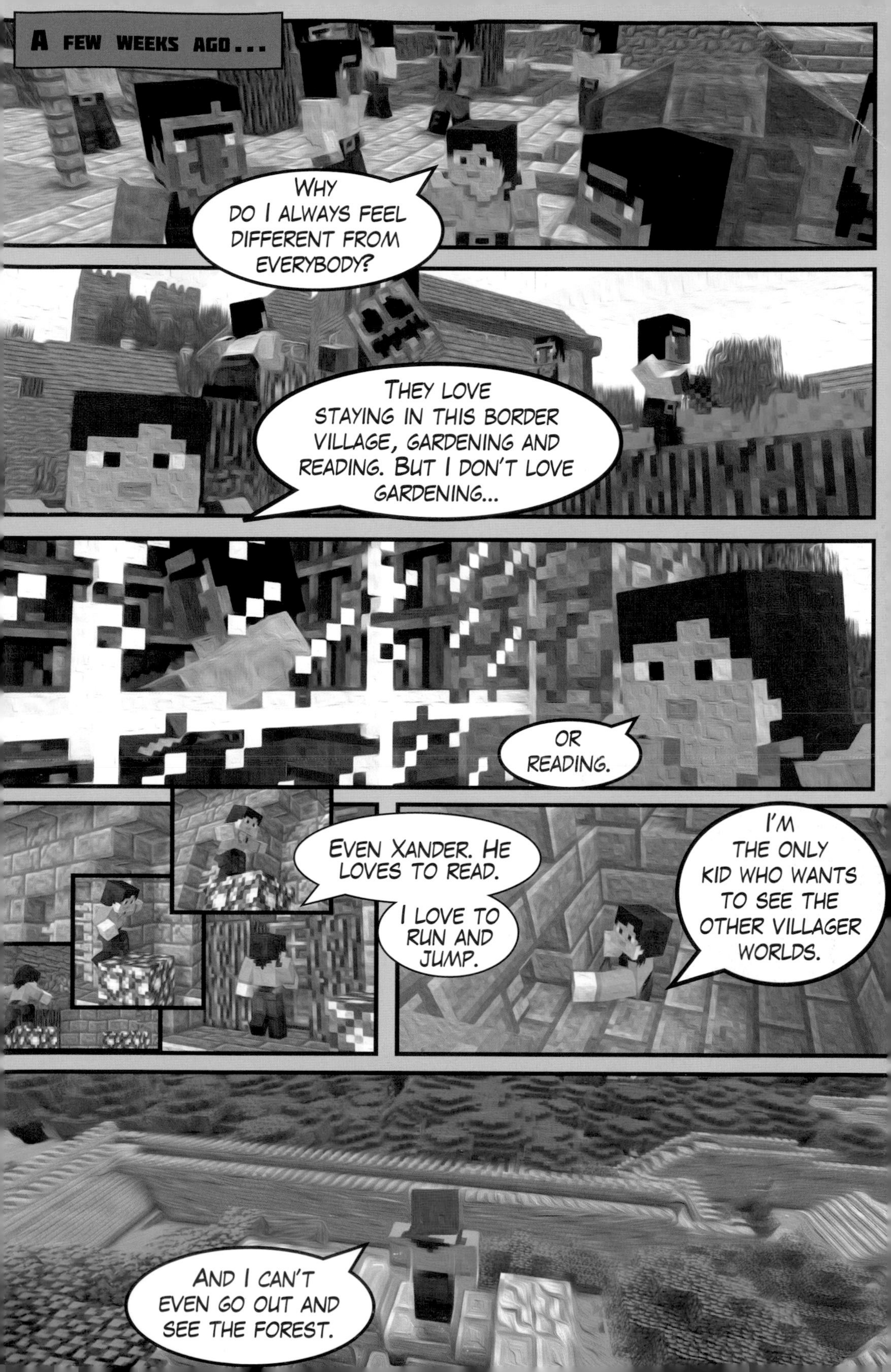
A FEW WEEKS AGO...
WHY DO I ALWAYS FEEL DIFFERENT FROM EVERYBODY?
THEY LOVE STAYING IN THIS BORDER VILLAGE, GARDENING AND READING. BUT I DON'T LOVE GARDENING...
OR READING.
EVEN XANDER. HE LOVES TO READ.
I LOVE TO RUN AND JUMP.
I'M THE ONLY KID WHO WANTS TO SEE THE OTHER VILLAGER WORLDS.
AND I CAN'T EVEN GO OUT AND SEE THE FOREST.

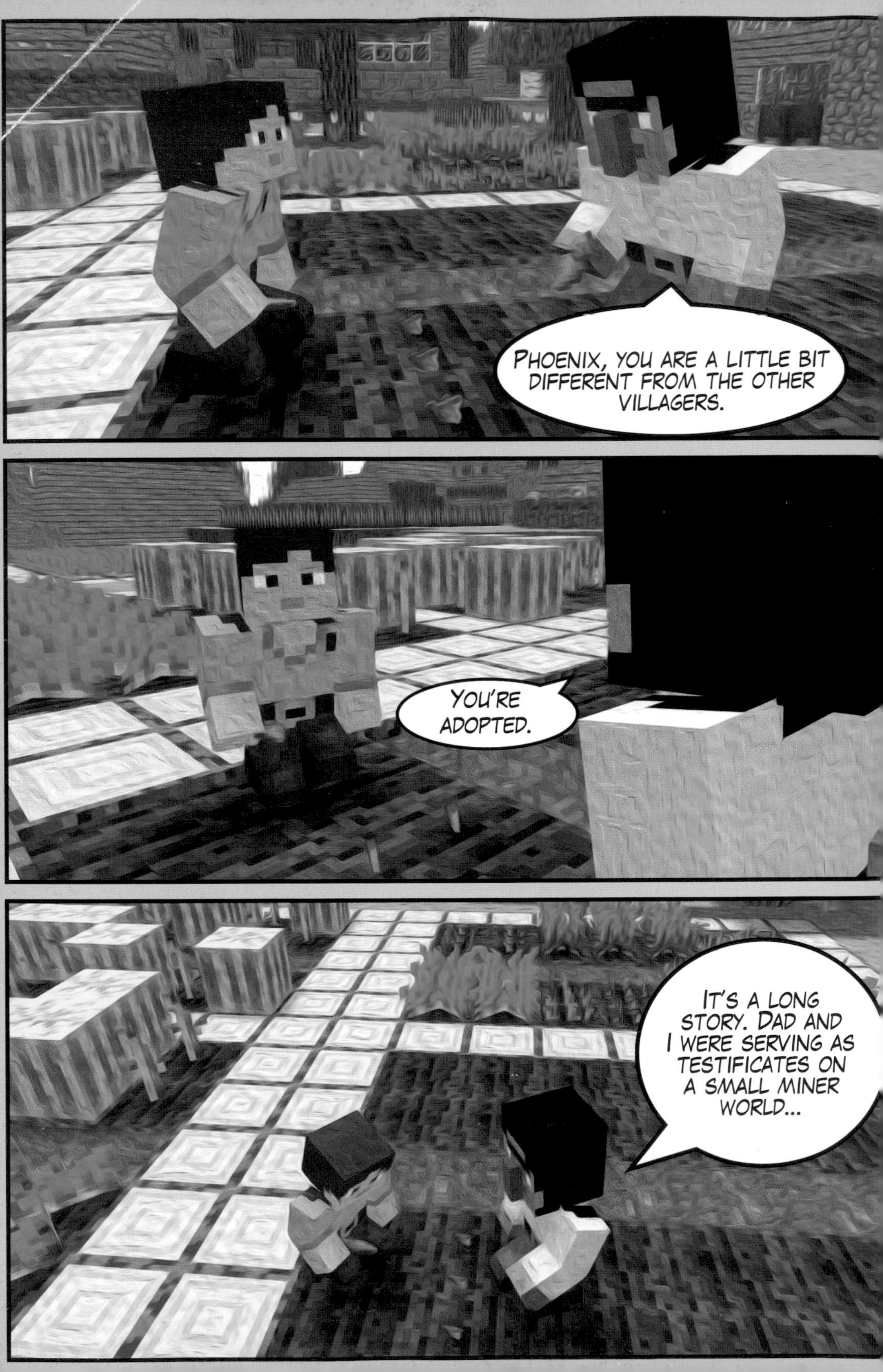
PHOENIX, YOU ARE A LITTLE BIT DIFFERENT FROM THE OTHER VILLAGERS.
YOU'RE ADOPTED.
IT'S A LONG STORY. DAD AND I WERE SERVING AS TESTIFICATES ON A SMALL MINER WORLD...

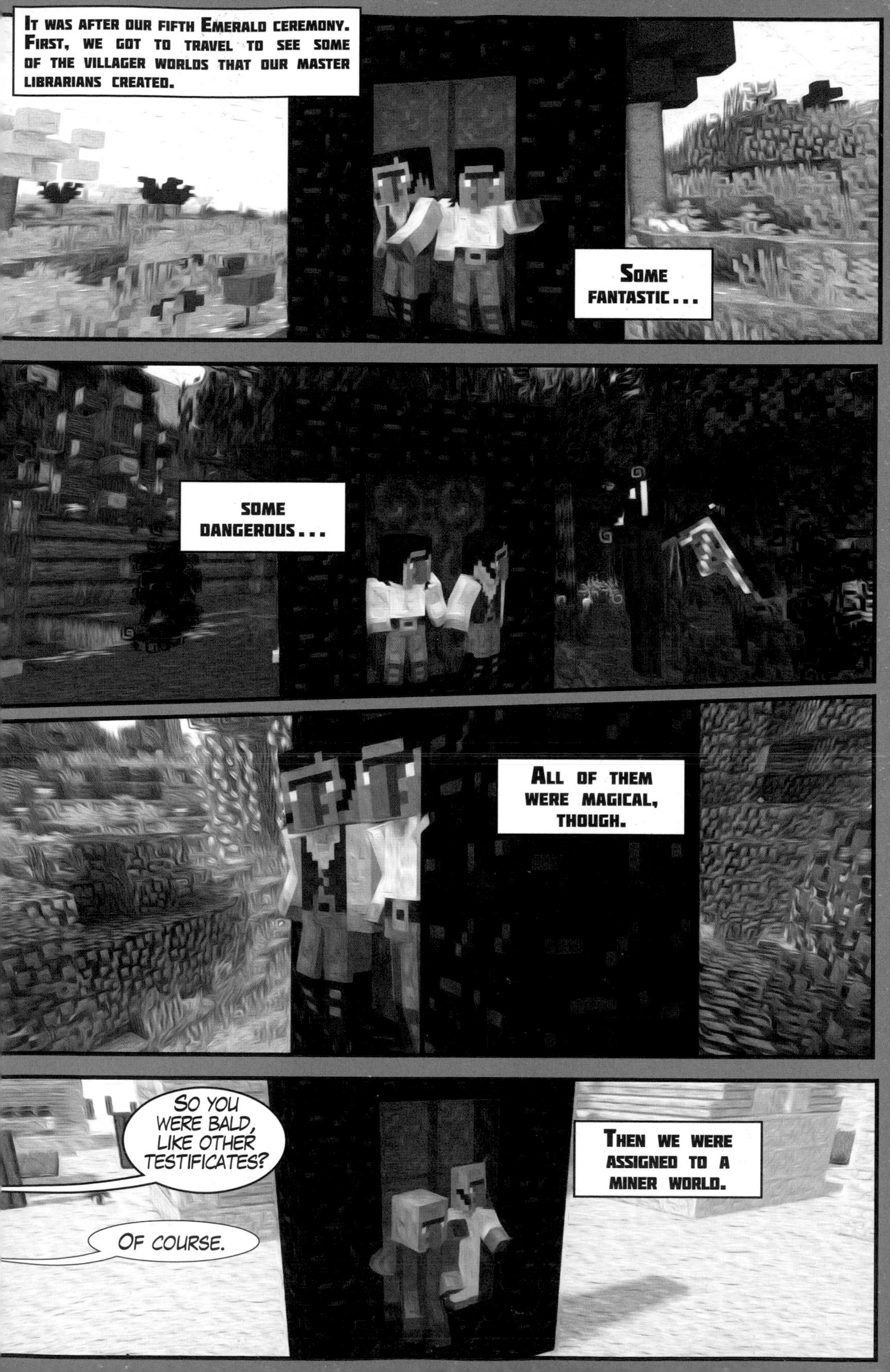
It was after our fifth Emerald ceremony. First, we got to travel to see some of the villager worlds that our master librarians created.
Some fantastic . . .
Some dangerous . . .
All of them were magical, though.
So you were bald, like other testificates?
Of course.
Then we were assigned to a miner world.

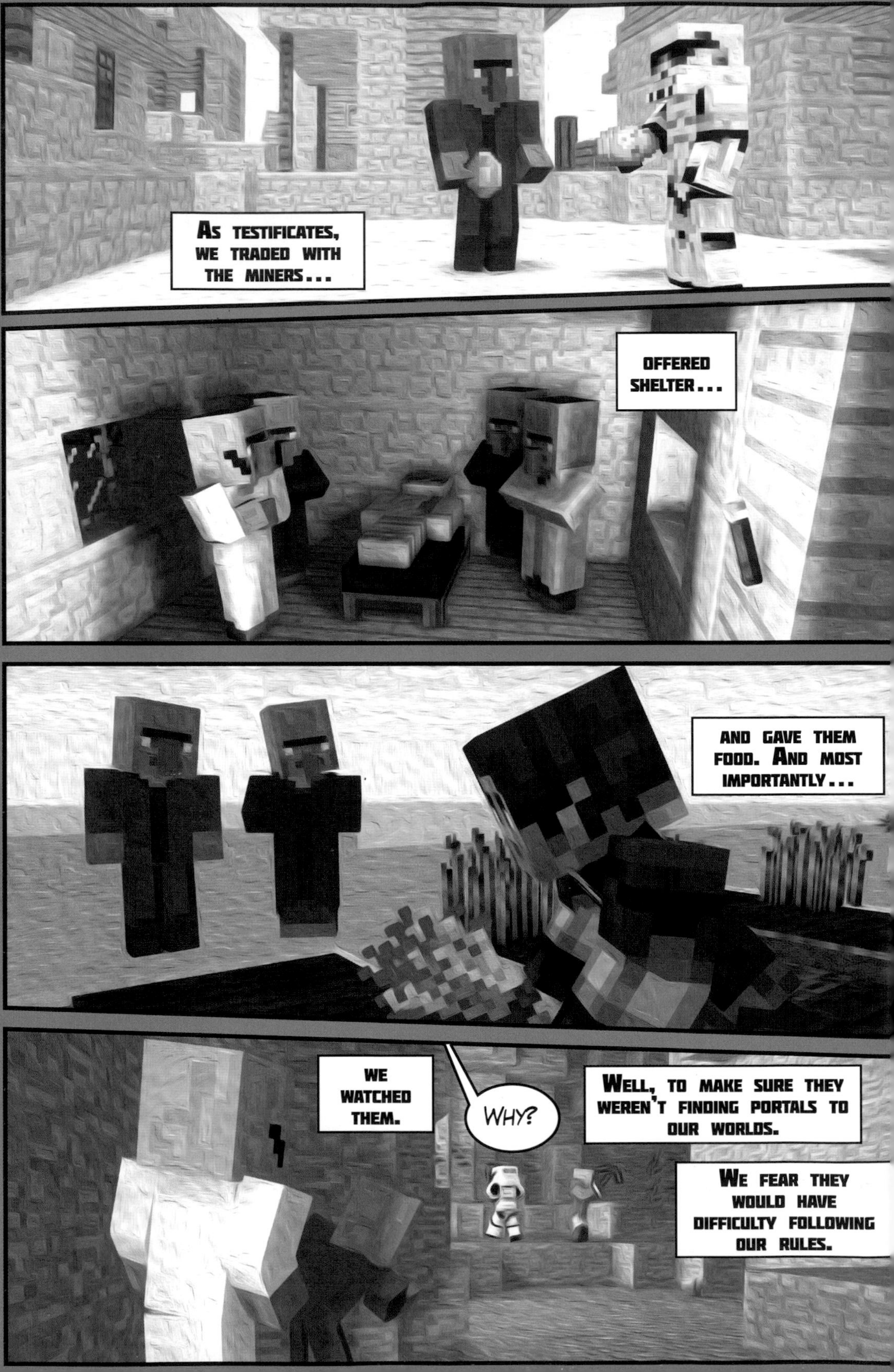
As testificates, we traded with the miners...
Offered shelter...
And gave them food. And most importantly...
We watched them.
Why?
Well, to make sure they weren't finding portals to our worlds.
We fear they would have difficulty following our rules.

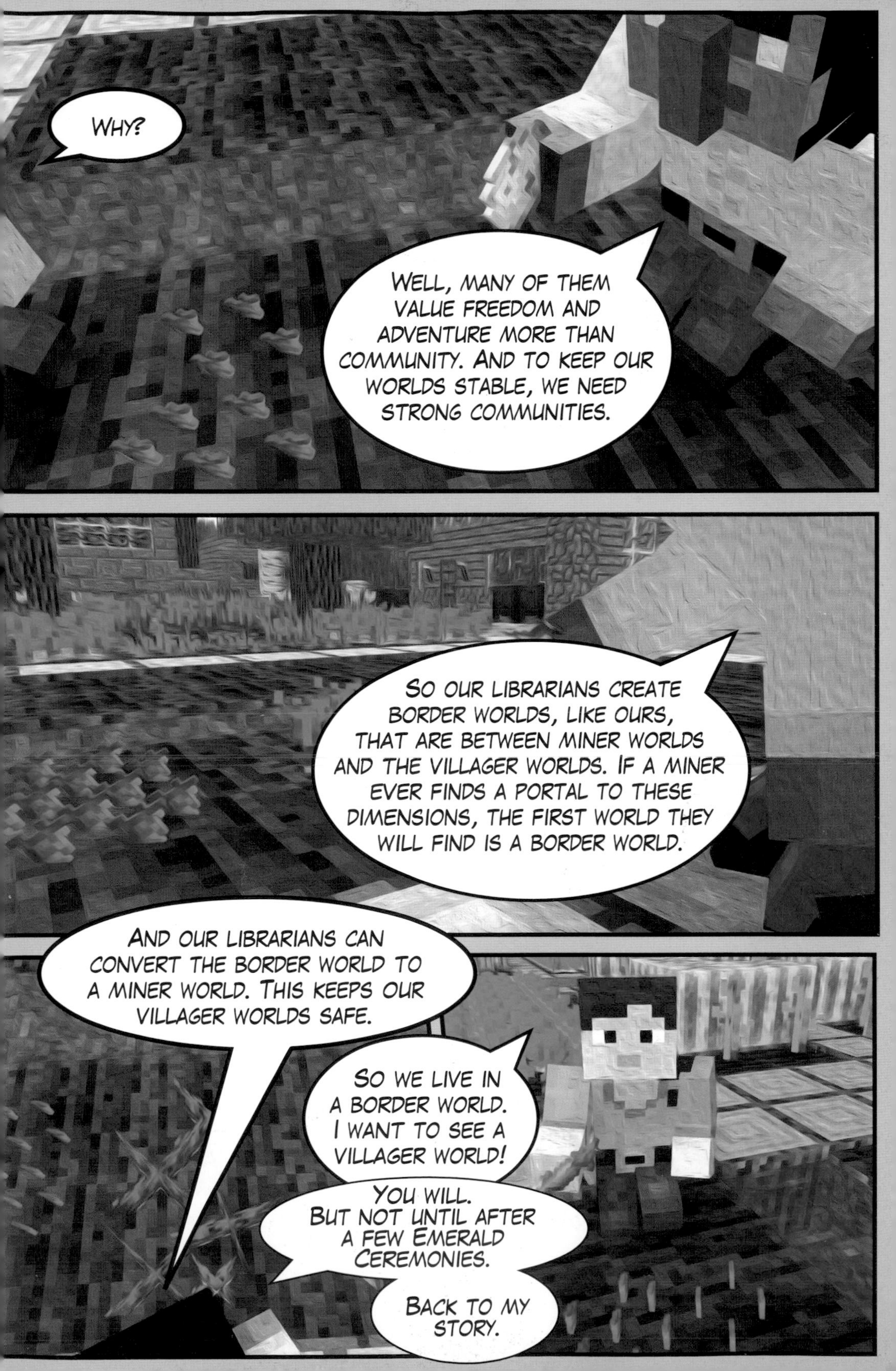
WHY?
WELL, MANY OF THEM VALUE FREEDOM AND ADVENTURE MORE THAN COMMUNITY. AND TO KEEP OUR WORLDS STABLE, WE NEED STRONG COMMUNITIES.
SO OUR LIBRARIANS CREATE BORDER WORLDS, LIKE OURS, THAT ARE BETWEEN MINER WORLDS AND THE VILLAGER WORLDS. IF A MINER EVER FINDS A PORTAL TO THESE DIMENSIONS, THE FIRST WORLD THEY WILL FIND IS A BORDER WORLD.
AND OUR LIBRARIANS CAN CONVERT THE BORDER WORLD TO A MINER WORLD. THIS KEEPS OUR VILLAGER WORLDS SAFE.
SO WE LIVE IN A BORDER WORLD. I WANT TO SEE A VILLAGER WORLD!
YOU WILL. BUT NOT UNTIL AFTER A FEW EMERALD CEREMONIES.
BACK TO MY STORY.

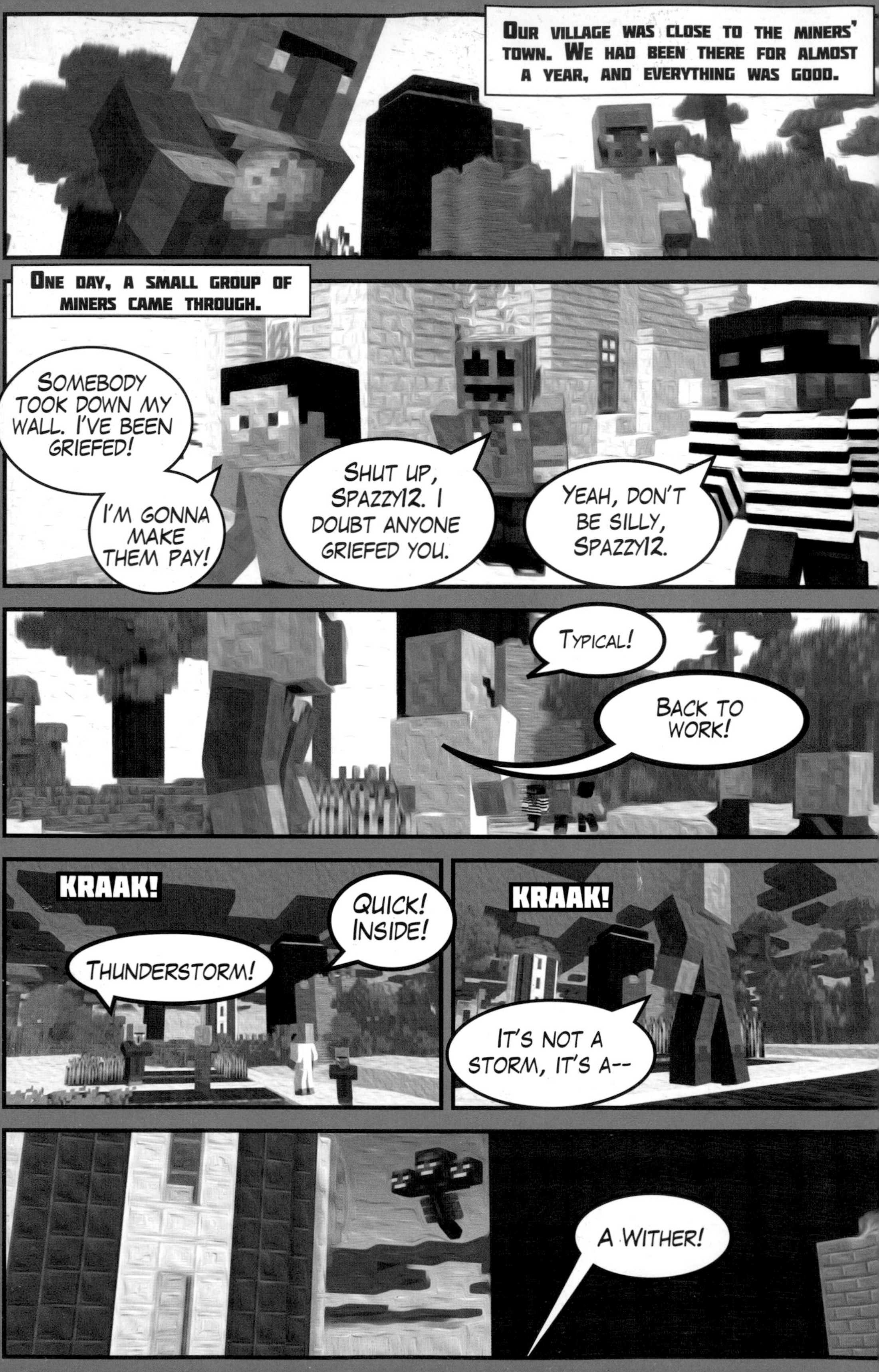
Our village was close to the miners' town. We had been there for almost a year, and everything was good.
One day, a small group of miners came through.
Somebody took down my wall. I've been griefed!
I'm gonna make them pay!
Shut up, Spazzy12. I doubt anyone griefed you.
Yeah, don't be silly, Spazzy12.
Typical!
Back to work!
KRAAK!
Thunderstorm!
Quick! Inside!
KRAAK!
It's not a storm, it's a--
A Wither!

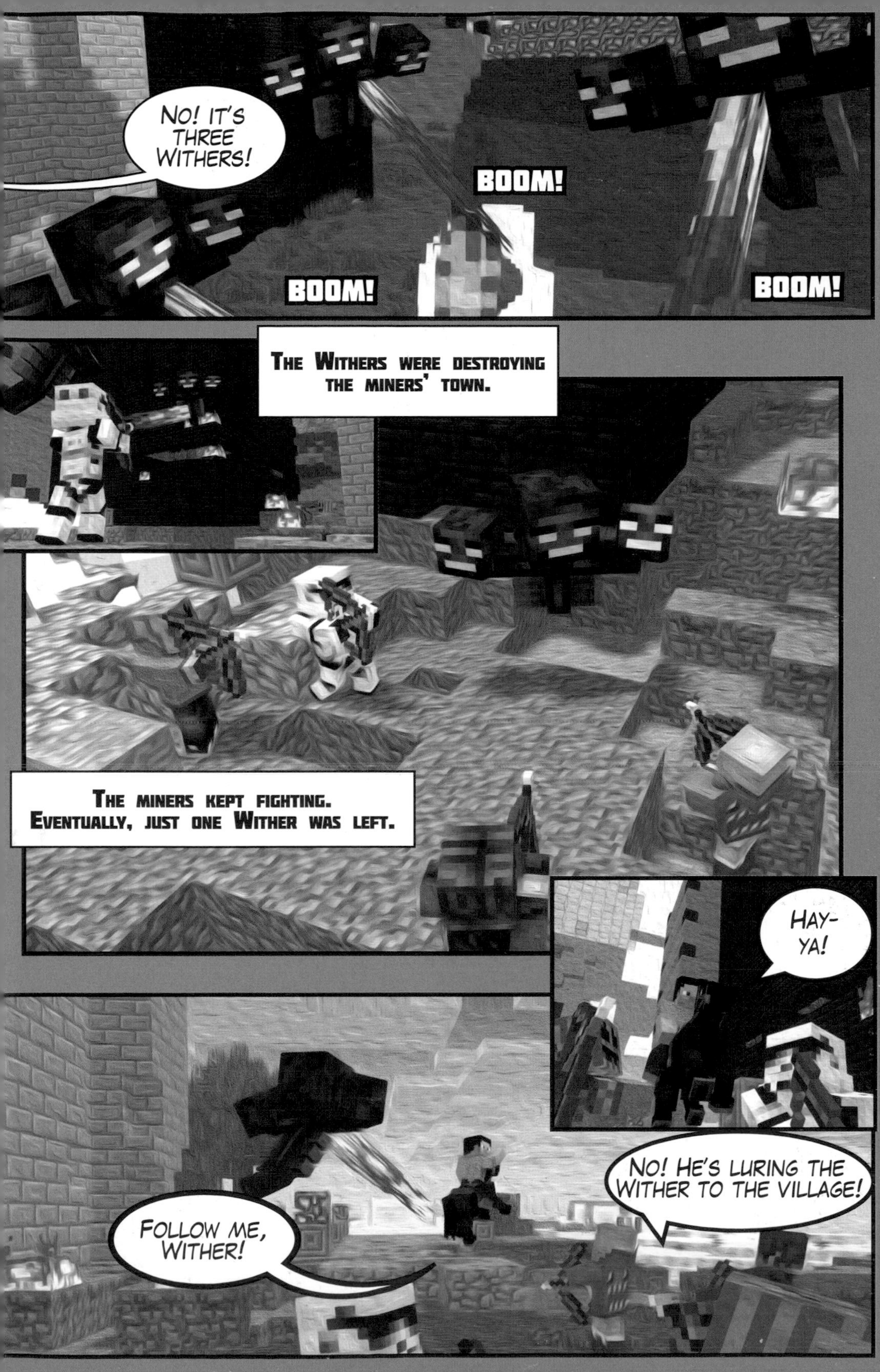
NO! IT'S THREE WITHERS!
BOOM!
BOOM!
BOOM!
THE WITHERS WERE DESTROYING THE MINERS' TOWN.
THE MINERS KEPT FIGHTING. EVENTUALLY, JUST ONE WITHER WAS LEFT.
HAY-YA!
NO! HE'S LURING THE WITHER TO THE VILLAGE!
FOLLOW ME, WITHER!

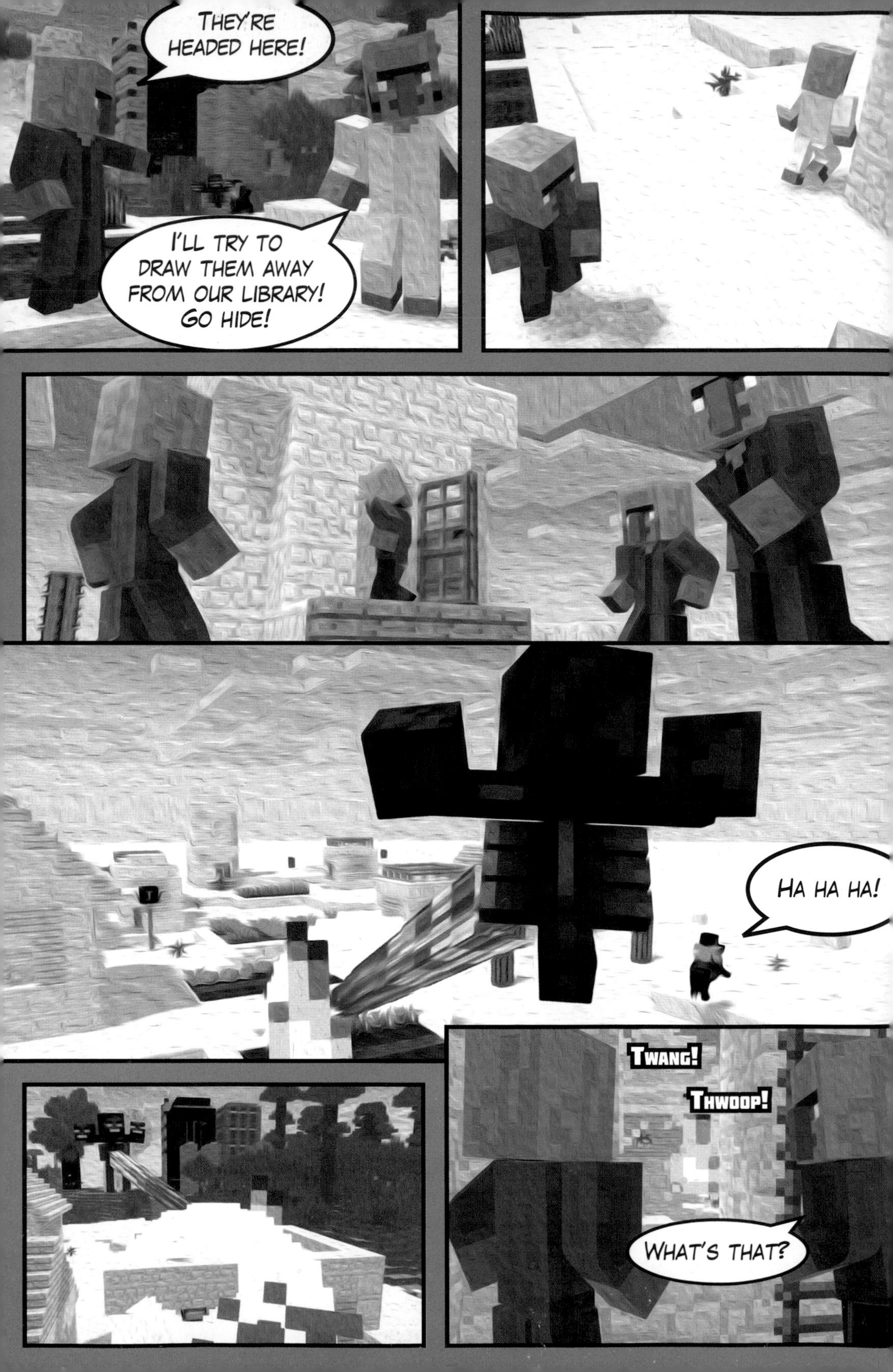
THEY'RE HEADED HERE!
I'LL TRY TO DRAW THEM AWAY FROM OUR LIBRARY! GO HIDE!
HA HA HA!
TWANG!
THWOOP!
WHAT'S THAT?

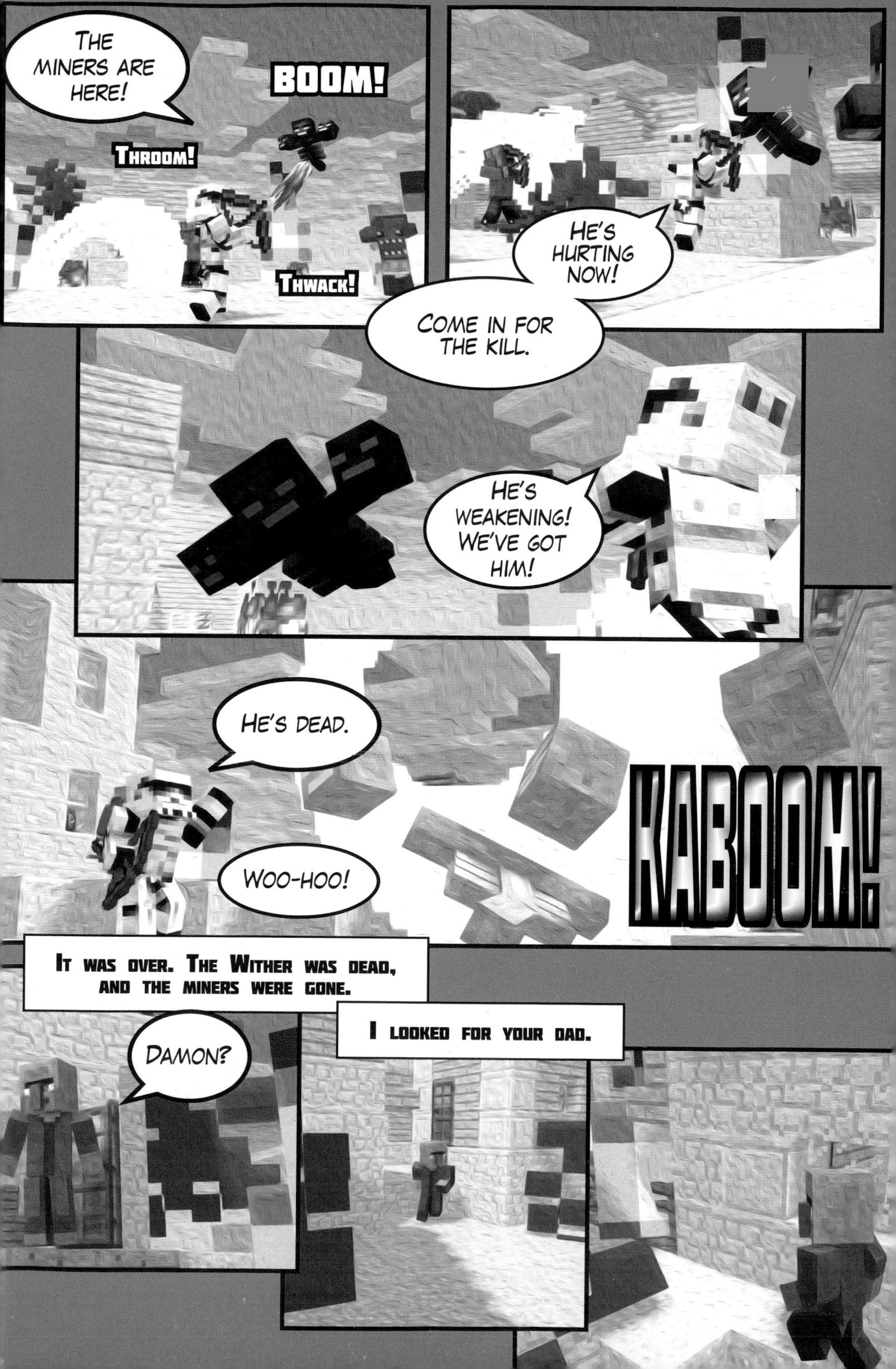
The miners are here!
BOOM!
Throom!
Thwack!
He's hurting now!
Come in for the kill.
He's weakening! We've got him!
He's dead.
Woo-hoo!
KABOOM!
It was over. The Wither was dead, and the miners were gone.
Damon?
I looked for your dad.

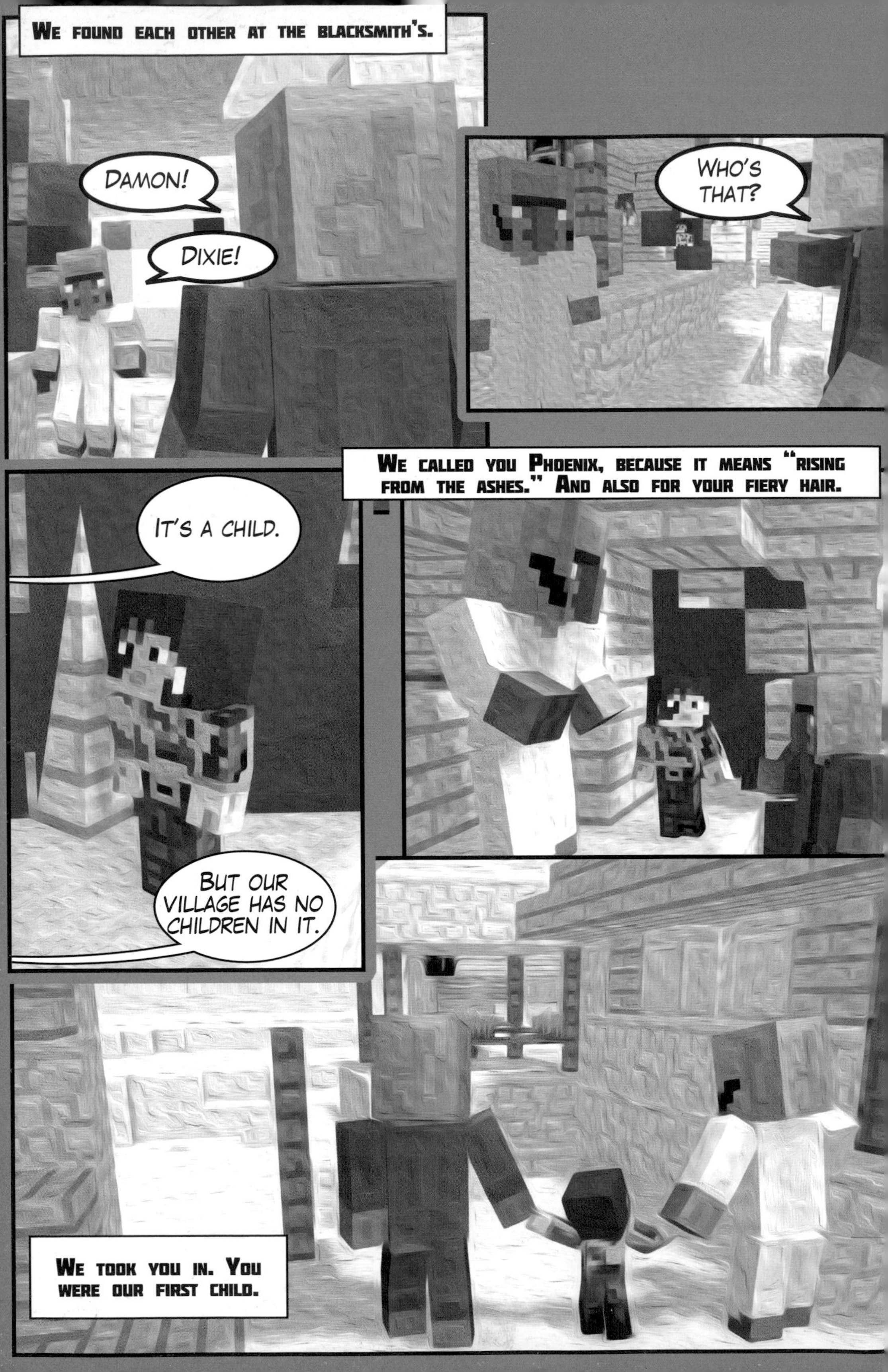
WE FOUND EACH OTHER AT THE BLACKSMITH'S.
DAMON!
DIXIE!
WHO'S THAT?
IT'S A CHILD.
BUT OUR VILLAGE HAS NO CHILDREN IN IT.
WE CALLED YOU PHOENIX, BECAUSE IT MEANS "RISING FROM THE ASHES." AND ALSO FOR YOUR FIERY HAIR.
WE TOOK YOU IN. YOU WERE OUR FIRST CHILD.

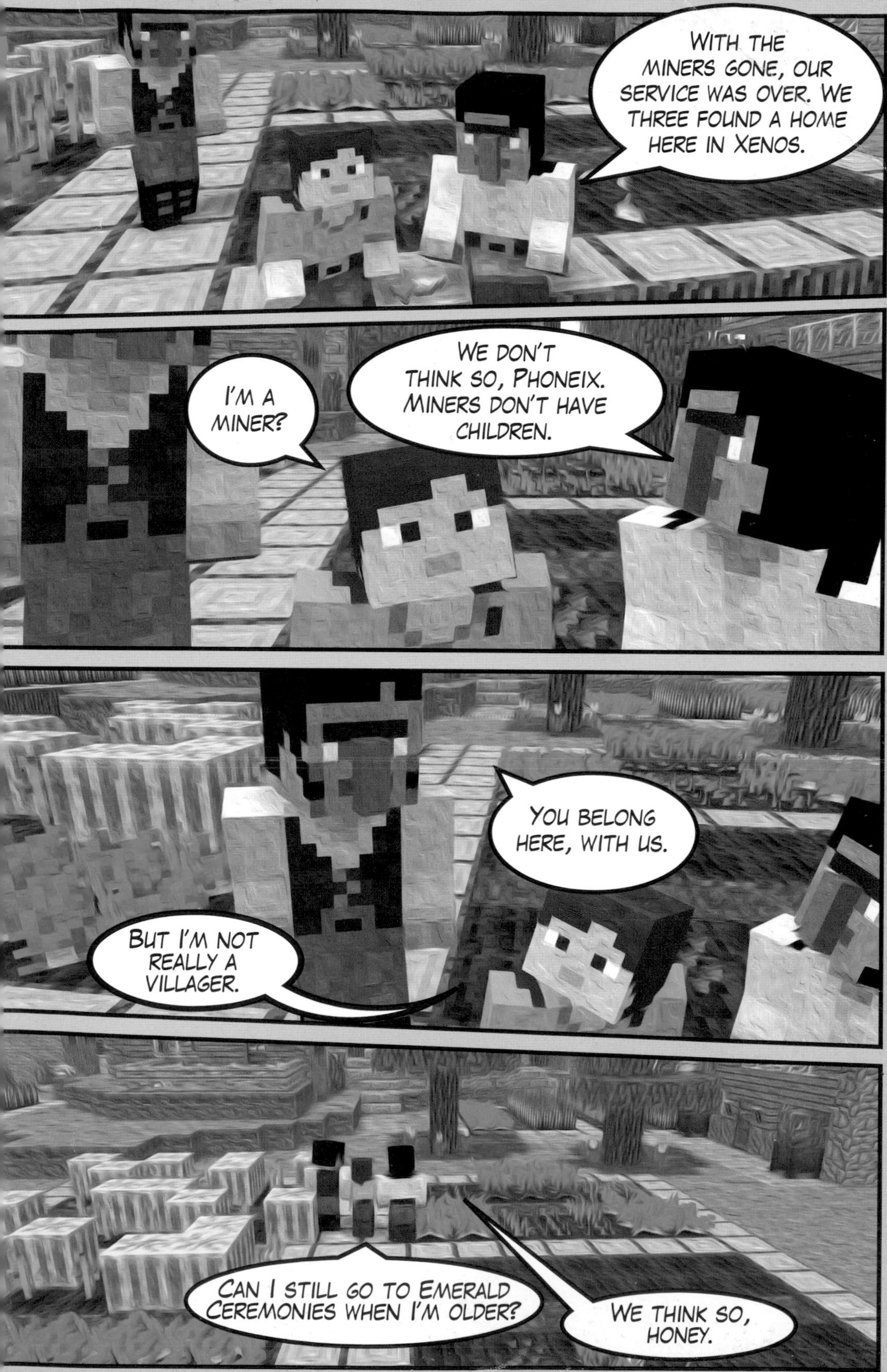
WITH THE MINERS GONE, OUR SERVICE WAS OVER. WE THREE FOUND A HOME HERE IN XENOS.
I'M A MINER?
WE DON'T THINK SO, PHONEIX. MINERS DON'T HAVE CHILDREN.
YOU BELONG HERE, WITH US.
BUT I'M NOT REALLY A VILLAGER.
CAN I STILL GO TO EMERALD CEREMONIES WHEN I'M OLDER?
WE THINK SO, HONEY.

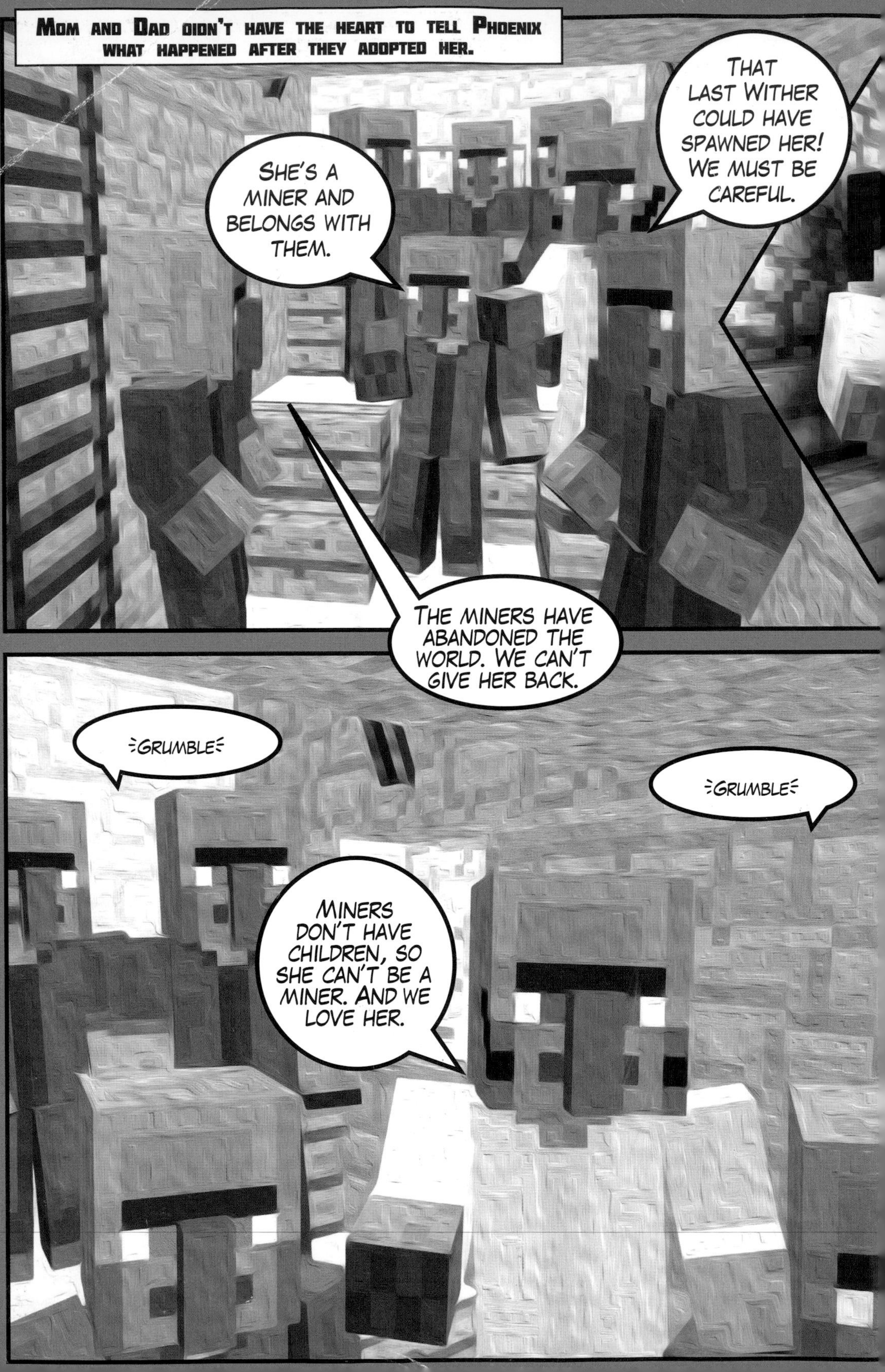
MOM AND DAD DIDN'T HAVE THE HEART TO TELL PHOENIX WHAT HAPPENED AFTER THEY ADOPTED HER.
SHE'S A MINER AND BELONGS WITH THEM.
THAT LAST WITHER COULD HAVE SPAWNED HER! WE MUST BE CAREFUL.
THE MINERS HAVE ABANDONED THE WORLD. WE CAN'T GIVE HER BACK.
GRUMBLE
GRUMBLE
MINERS DON'T HAVE CHILDREN, SO SHE CAN'T BE A MINER. AND WE LOVE HER.

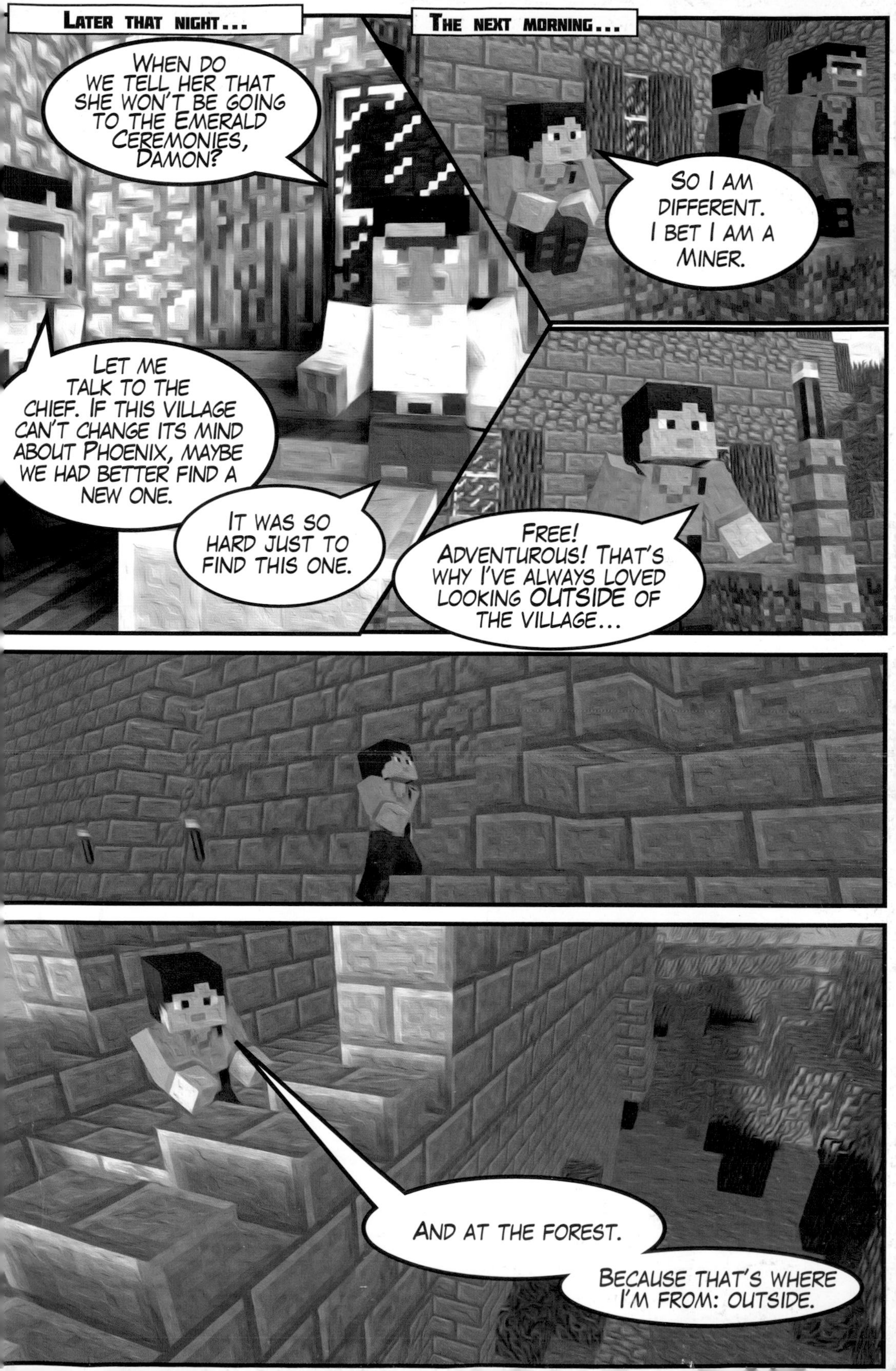
LATER THAT NIGHT...
WHEN DO WE TELL HER THAT SHE WON'T BE GOING TO THE EMERALD CEREMONIES, DAMON?
LET ME TALK TO THE CHIEF. IF THIS VILLAGE CAN'T CHANGE ITS MIND ABOUT PHOENIX, MAYBE WE HAD BETTER FIND A NEW ONE.
IT WAS SO HARD JUST TO FIND THIS ONE.
THE NEXT MORNING...
SO I AM DIFFERENT. I BET I AM A MINER.
FREE! ADVENTUROUS! THAT'S WHY I'VE ALWAYS LOVED LOOKING OUTSIDE OF THE VILLAGE...
AND AT THE FOREST.
BECAUSE THAT'S WHERE I'M FROM: OUTSIDE.

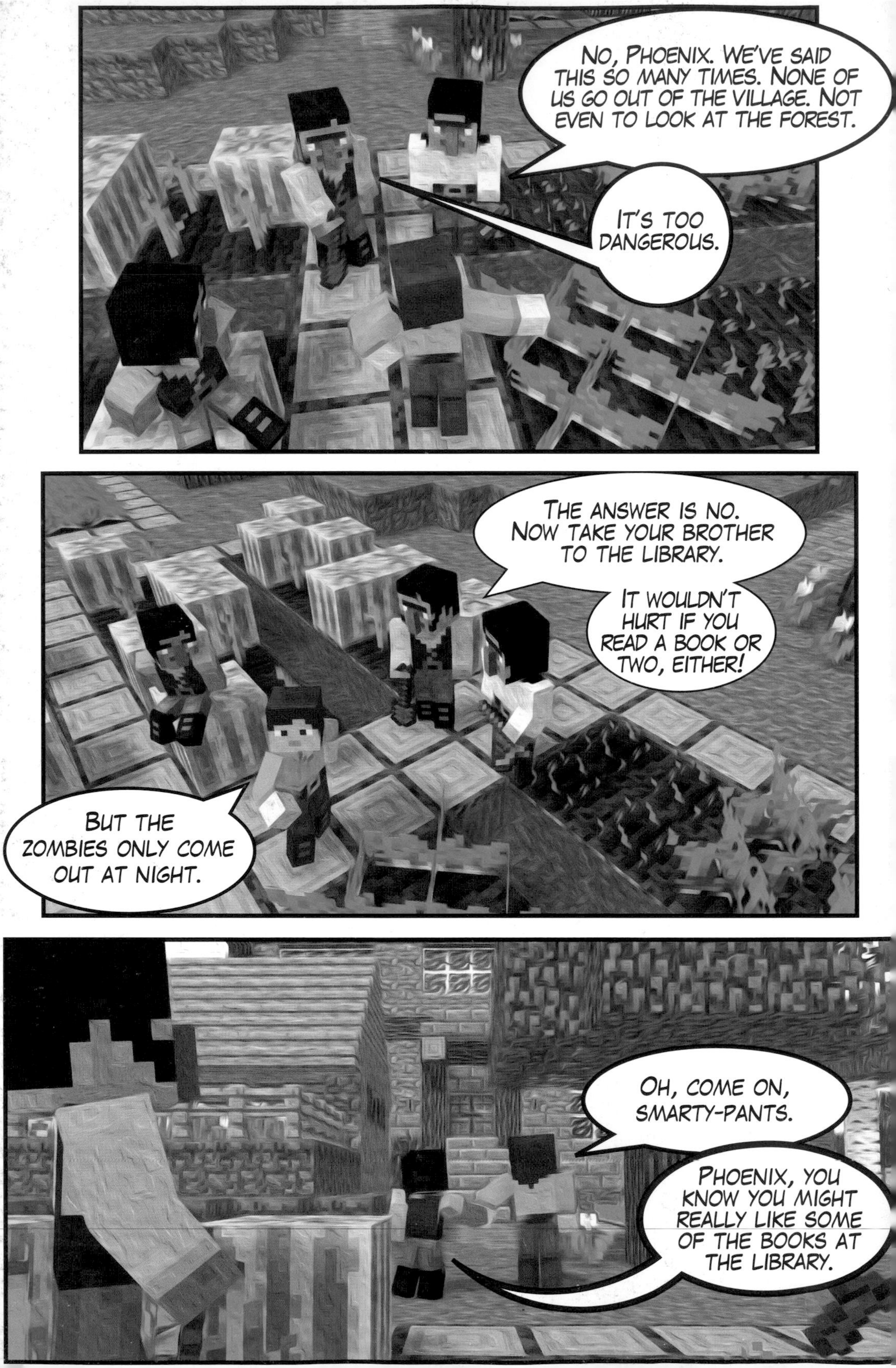
NO, PHOENIX. WE'VE SAID THIS SO MANY TIMES. NONE OF US GO OUT OF THE VILLAGE. NOT EVEN TO LOOK AT THE FOREST.
IT'S TOO DANGEROUS.
BUT THE ZOMBIES ONLY COME OUT AT NIGHT.
THE ANSWER IS NO. NOW TAKE YOUR BROTHER TO THE LIBRARY.
IT WOULDN'T HURT IF YOU READ A BOOK OR TWO, EITHER!
OH, COME ON, SMARTY-PANTS.
PHOENIX, YOU KNOW YOU MIGHT REALLY LIKE SOME OF THE BOOKS AT THE LIBRARY.

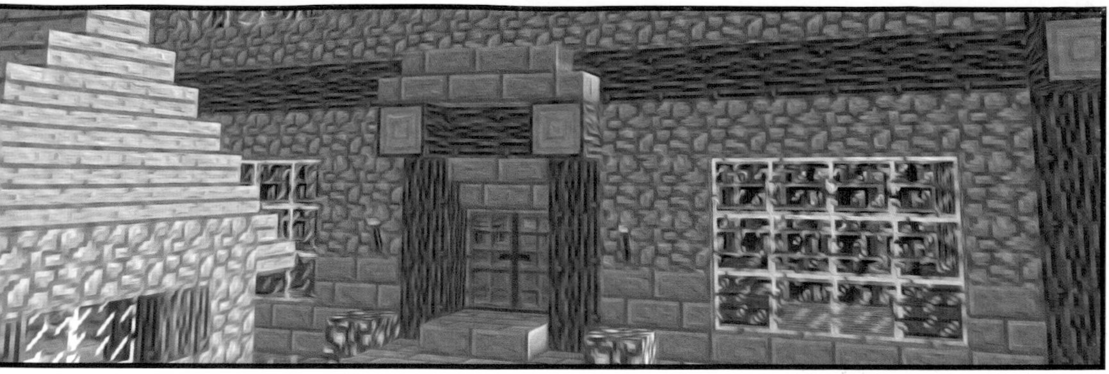

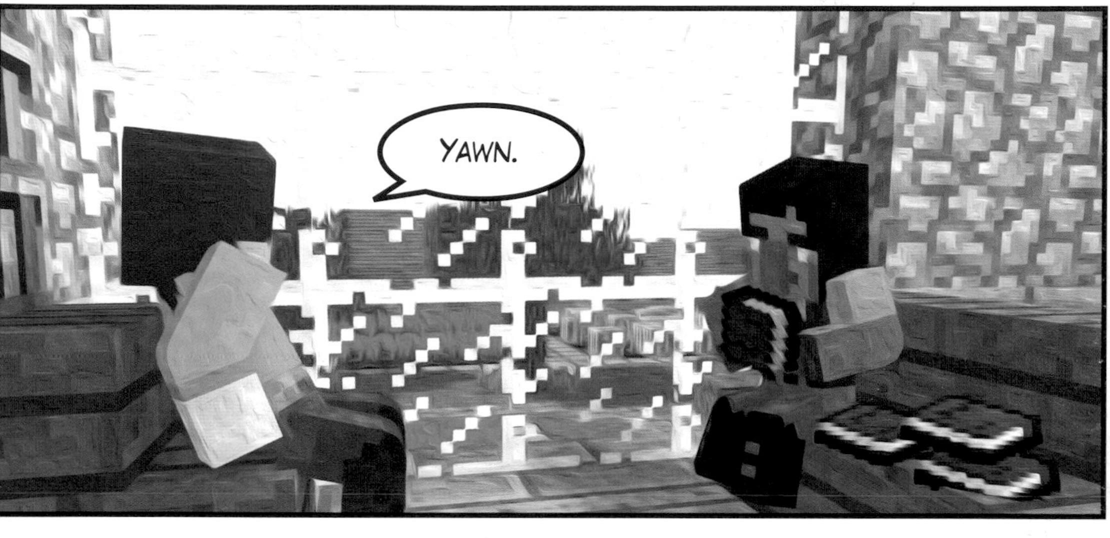
YAWN.

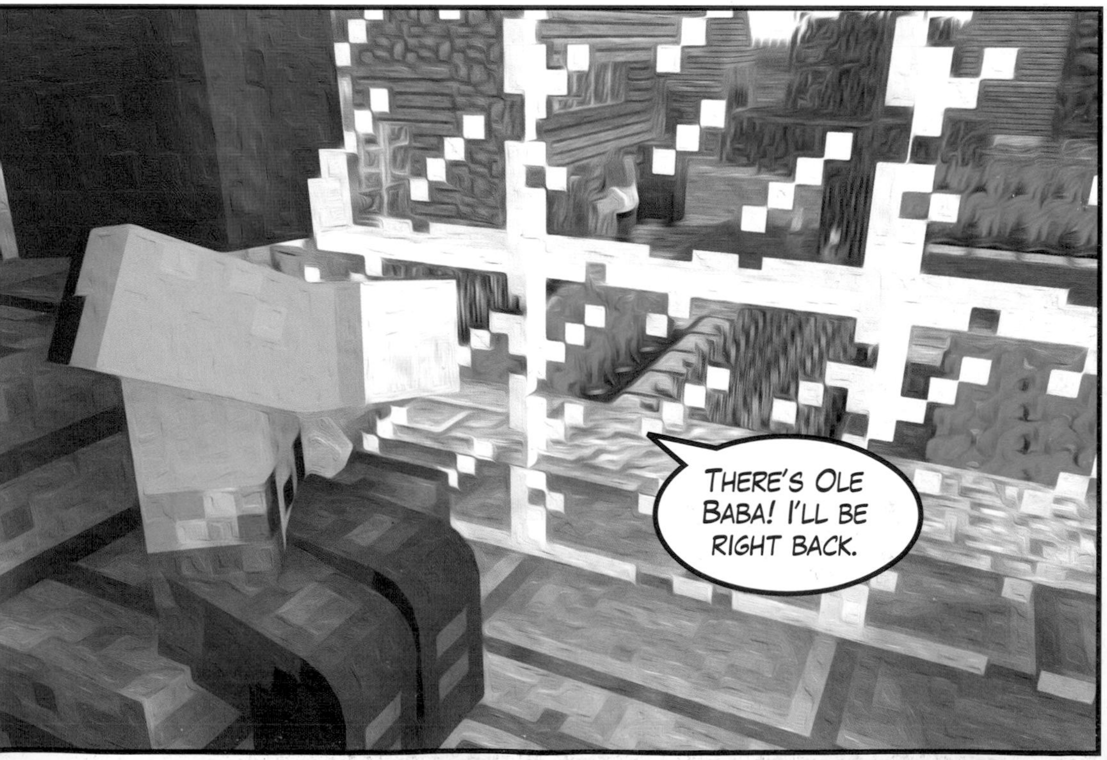
THERE'S OLE BABA! I'LL BE RIGHT BACK.

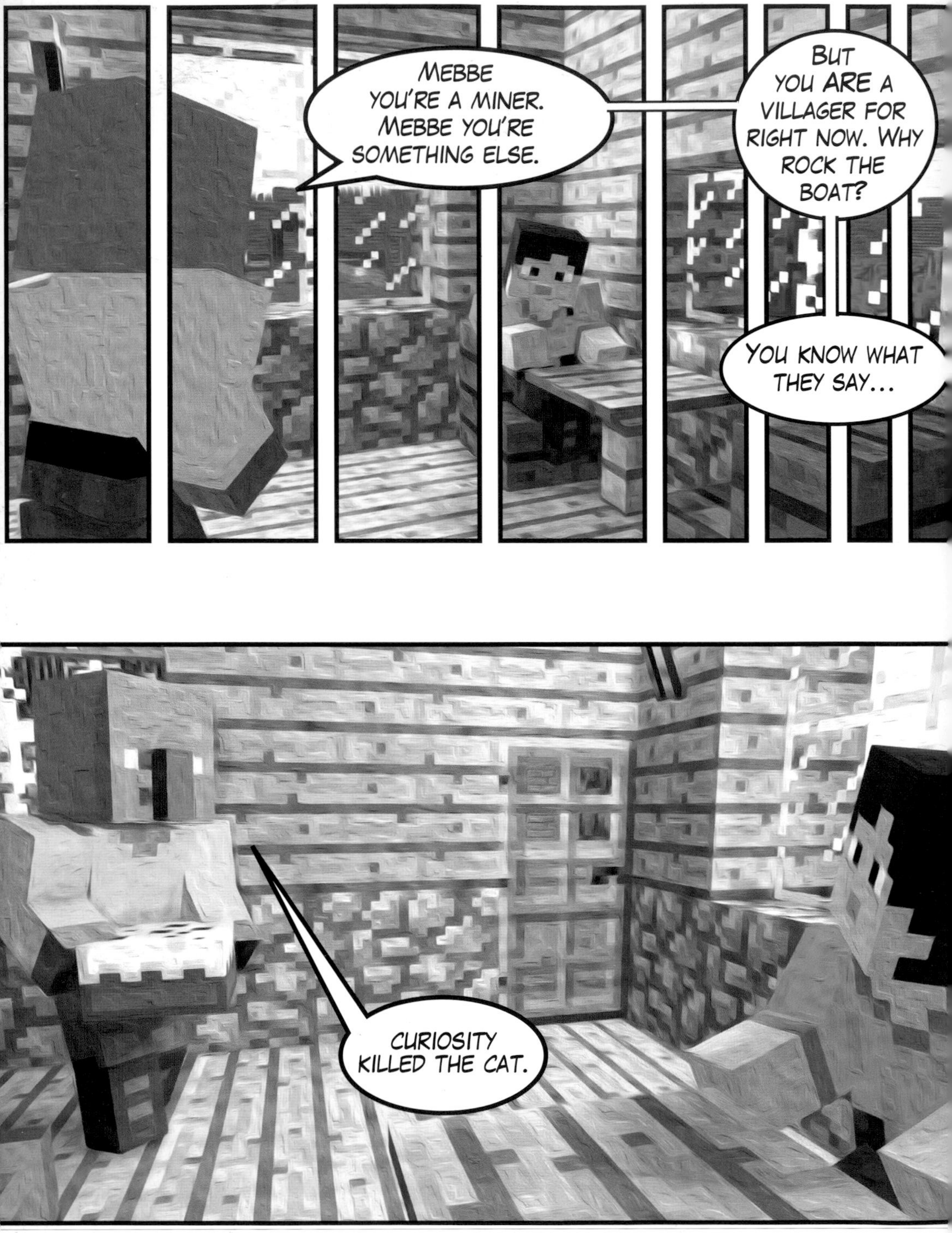
MEBBE YOU'RE A MINER. MEBBE YOU'RE SOMETHING ELSE.
BUT YOU ARE A VILLAGER FOR RIGHT NOW. WHY ROCK THE BOAT?
YOU KNOW WHAT THEY SAY...
CURIOSITY KILLED THE CAT.

CHAPTER 3
A DECISION

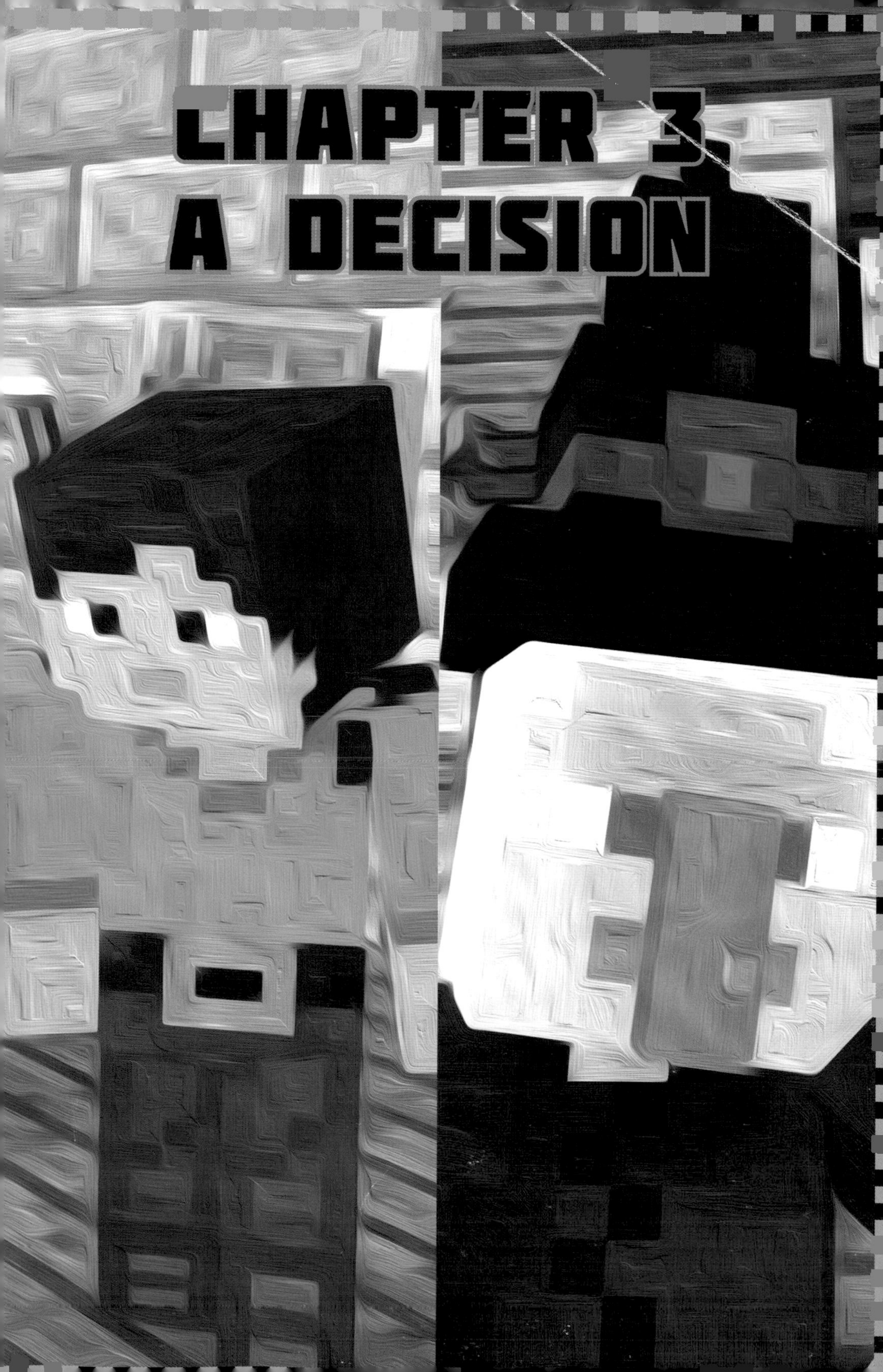

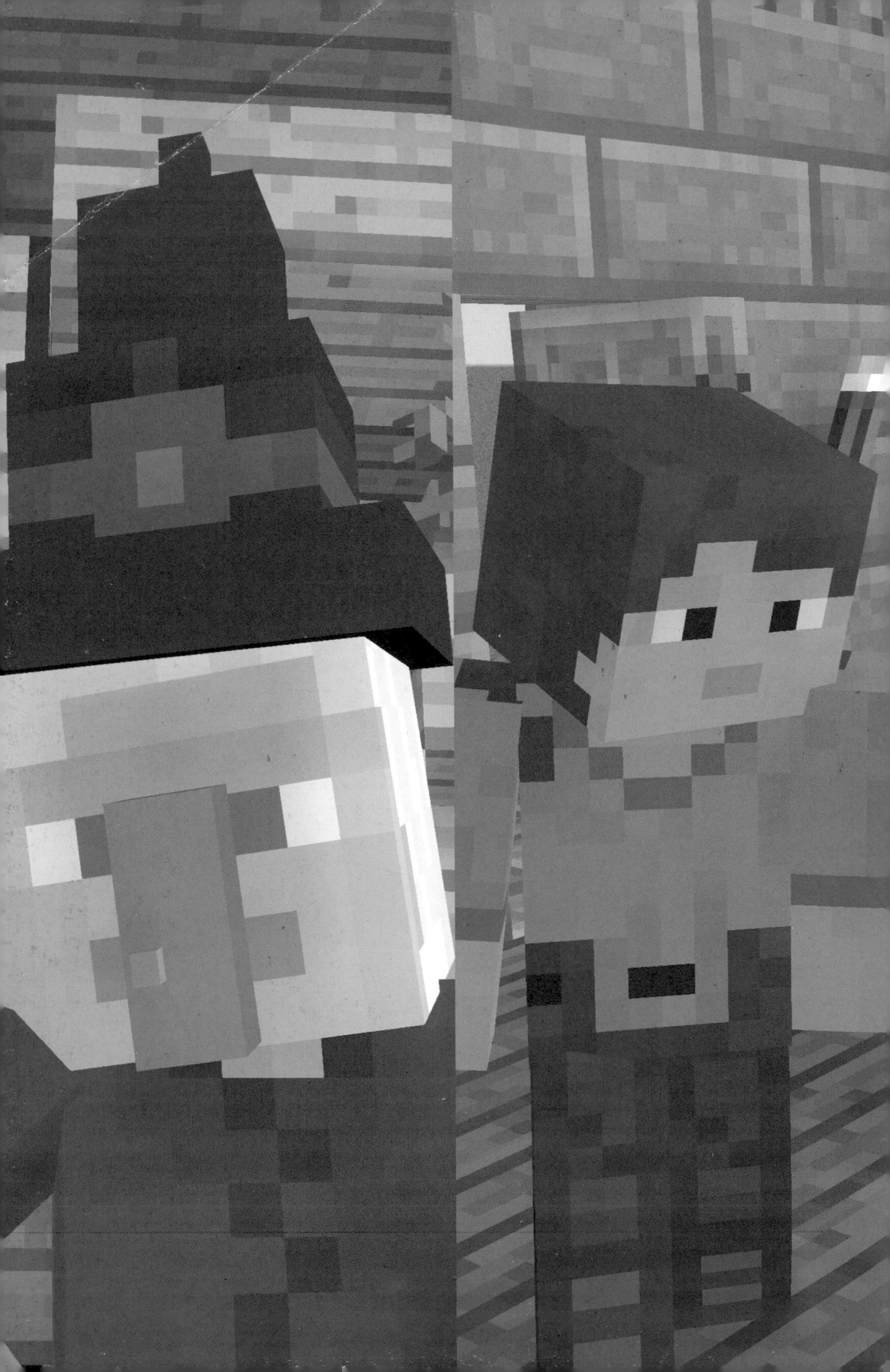

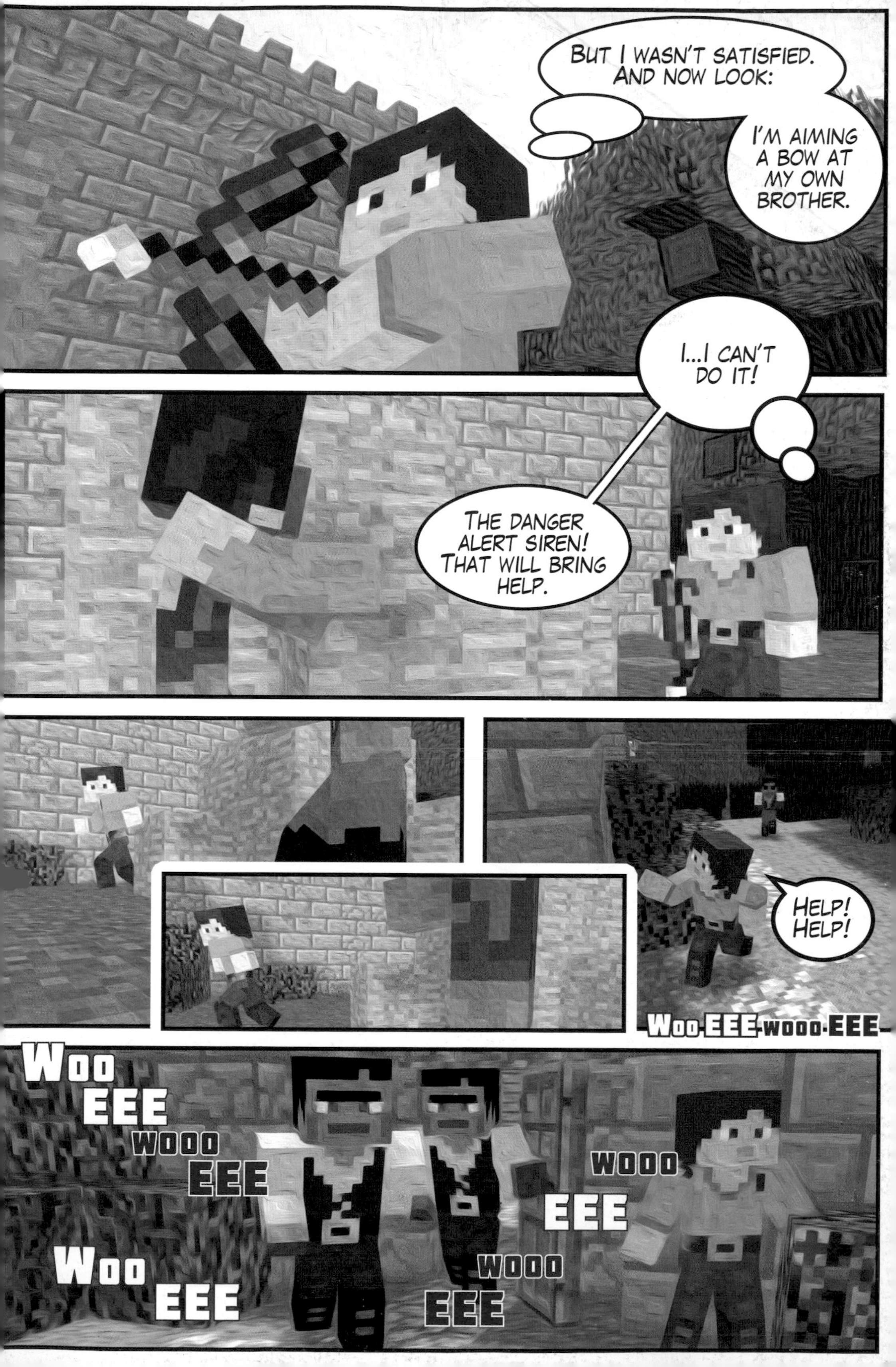
BUT I WASN'T SATISFIED. AND NOW LOOK:
I'M AIMING A BOW AT MY OWN BROTHER.
I...I CAN'T DO IT!
THE DANGER ALERT SIREN! THAT WILL BRING HELP.
HELP! HELP!
WOO-EEE-WOOO-EEE
WOO EEE WOOO EEE
WOO EEE
WOOO EEE
WOOO EEE

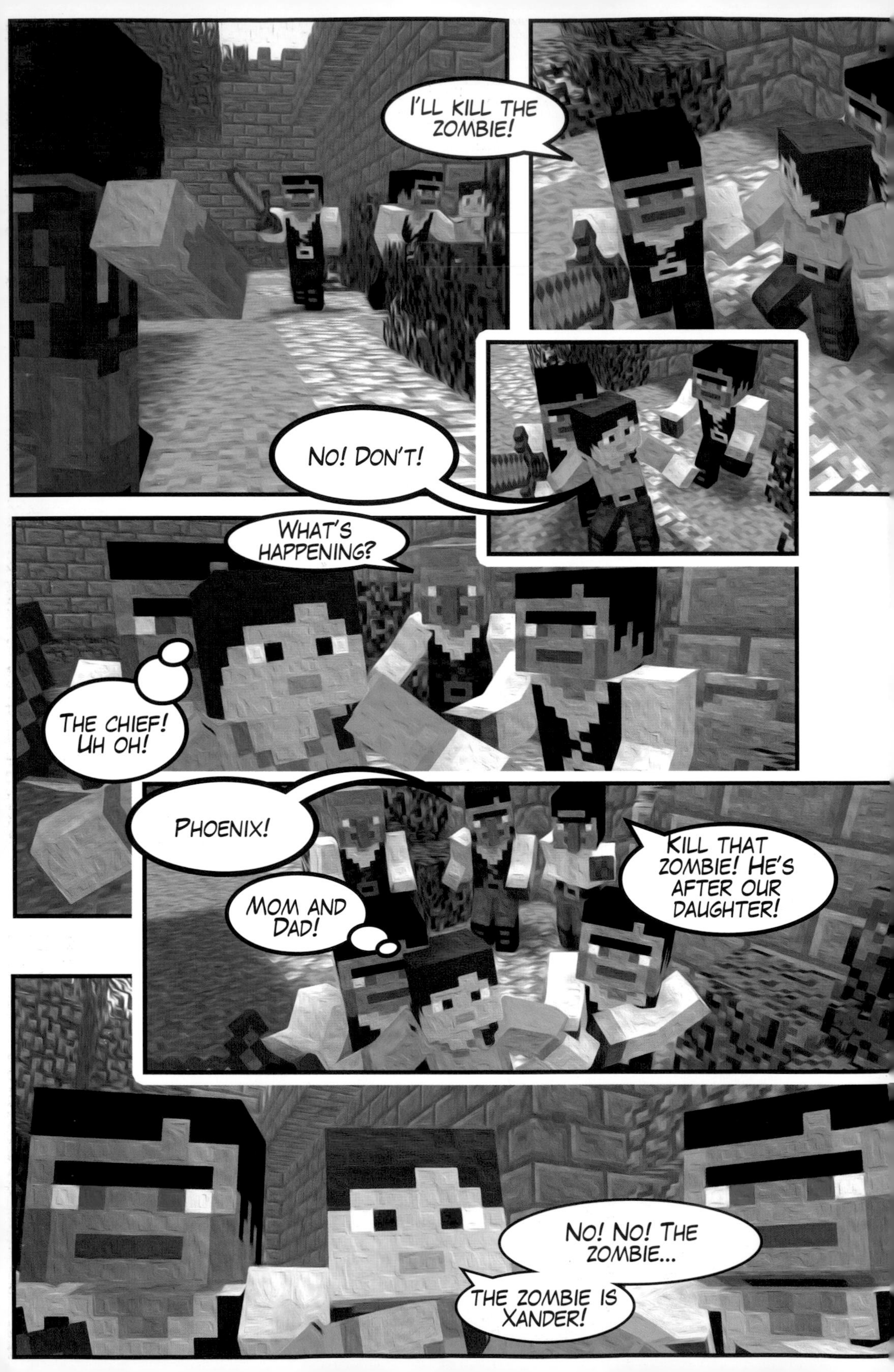
I'LL KILL THE ZOMBIE!
NO! DON'T!
WHAT'S HAPPENING?
THE CHIEF! UH OH!
PHOENIX!
KILL THAT ZOMBIE! HE'S AFTER OUR DAUGHTER!
MOM AND DAD!
NO! NO! THE ZOMBIE...
THE ZOMBIE IS XANDER!

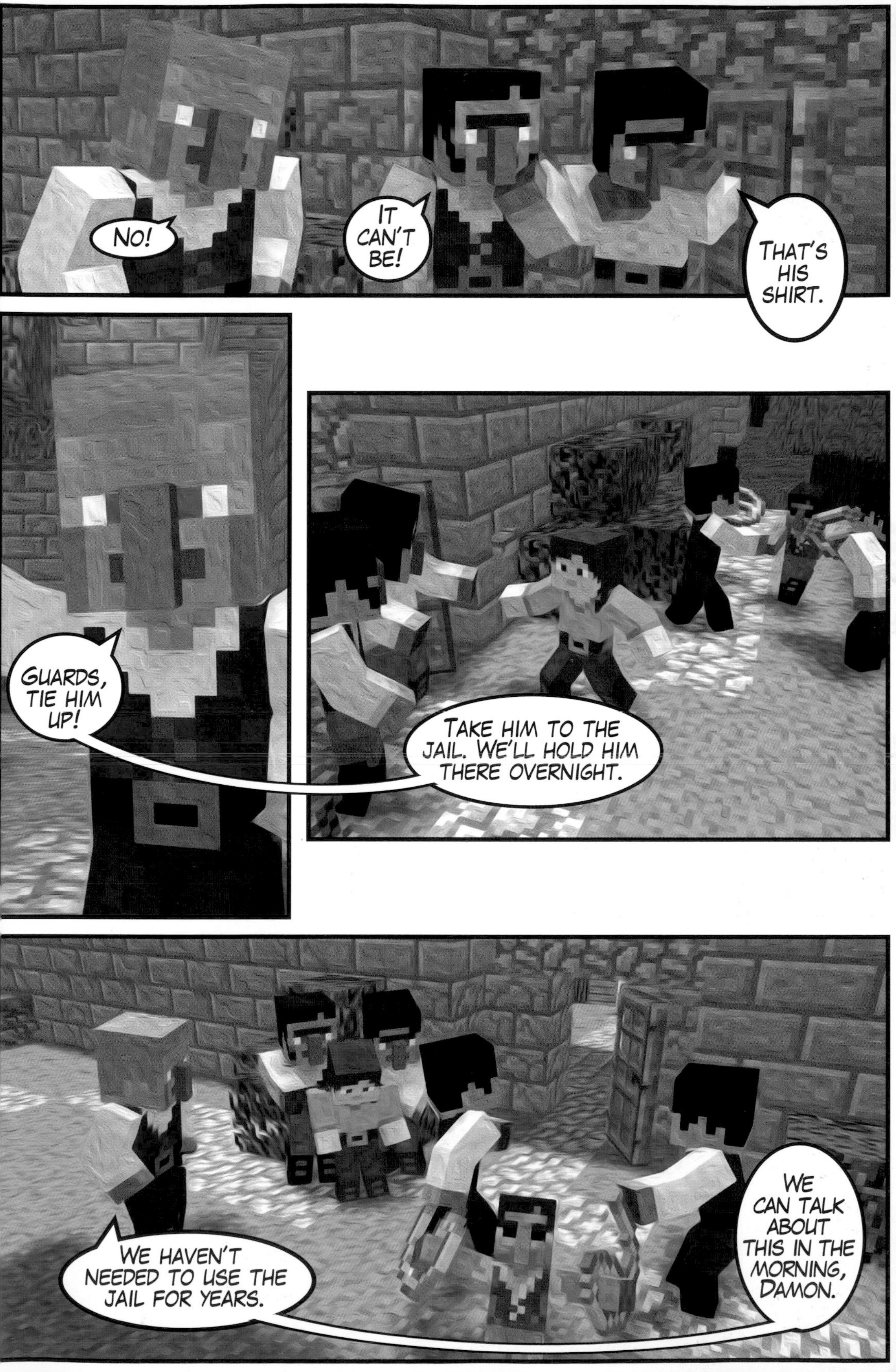
NO!
IT CAN'T BE!
THAT'S HIS SHIRT.
GUARDS, TIE HIM UP!
TAKE HIM TO THE JAIL. WE'LL HOLD HIM THERE OVERNIGHT.
WE HAVEN'T NEEDED TO USE THE JAIL FOR YEARS.
WE CAN TALK ABOUT THIS IN THE MORNING, DAMON.

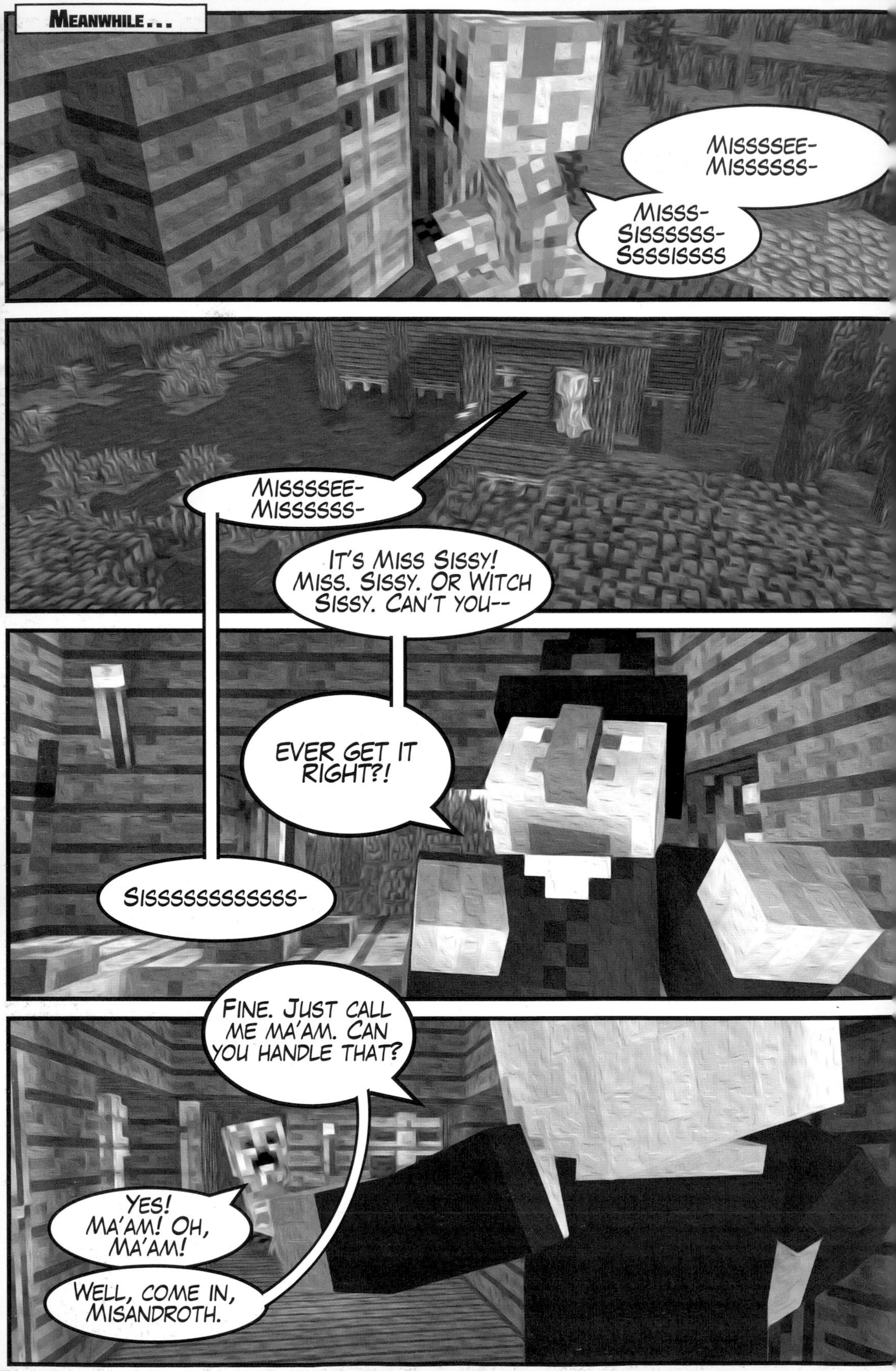
MEANWHILE . . .
MISSSSEE-MISSSSSS-
MISSS-SISSSSSS-SSSSISSSS
MISSSSEE-MISSSSSS-
IT'S MISS SISSY! MISS. SISSY. OR WITCH SISSY. CAN'T YOU--
EVER GET IT RIGHT?!
SISSSSSSSSSSSS-
FINE. JUST CALL ME MA'AM. CAN YOU HANDLE THAT?
YES! MA'AM! OH, MA'AM!
WELL, COME IN, MISANDROTH.

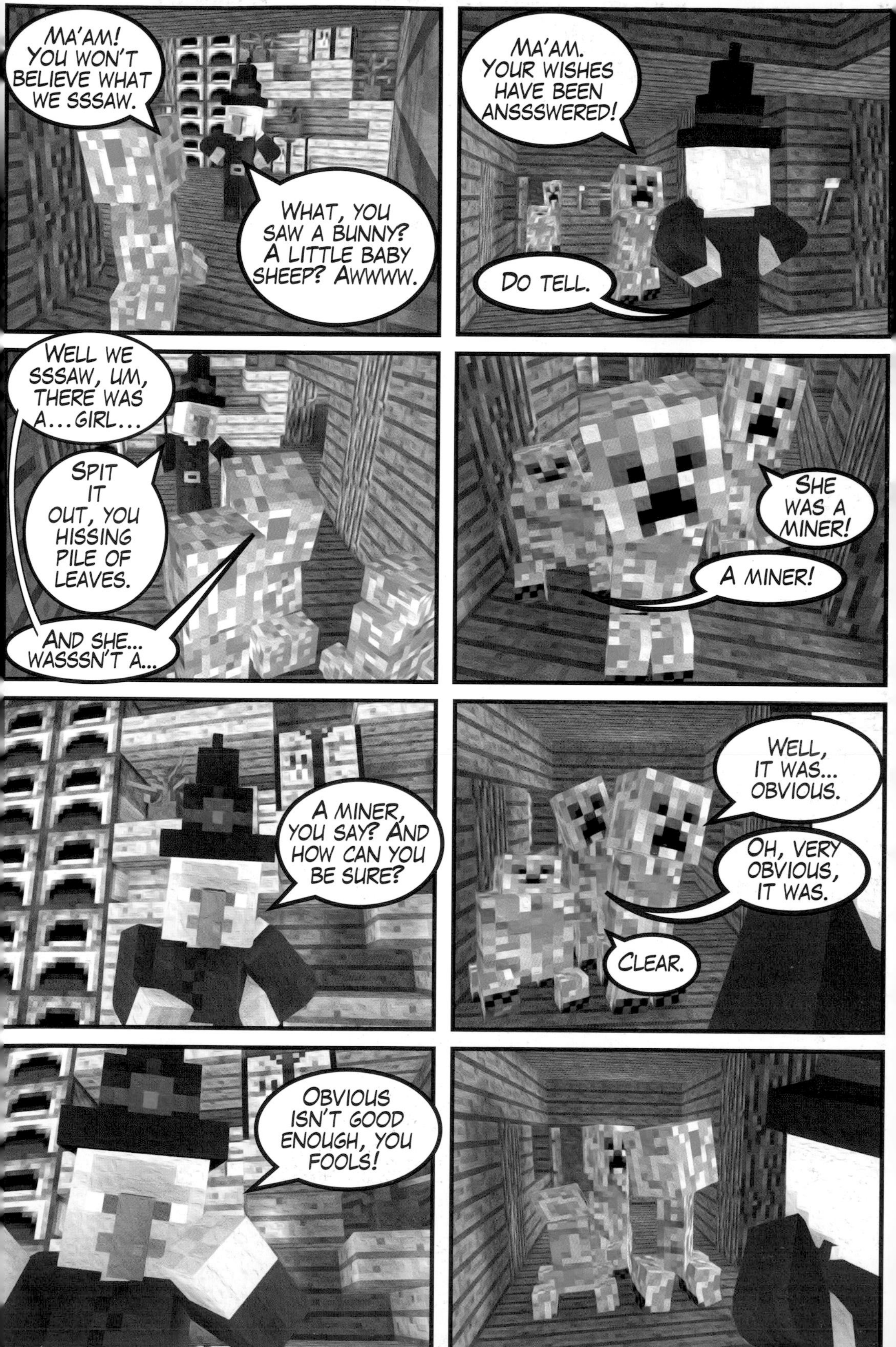
MA'AM! YOU WON'T BELIEVE WHAT WE SSSAW.
WHAT, YOU SAW A BUNNY? A LITTLE BABY SHEEP? AWWWW.
MA'AM. YOUR WISHES HAVE BEEN ANSSSWERED!
DO TELL.
WELL WE SSSAW, UM, THERE WAS A...GIRL...
SPIT IT OUT, YOU HISSING PILE OF LEAVES.
AND SHE... WASSSN'T A...
SHE WAS A MINER!
A MINER!
A MINER, YOU SAY? AND HOW CAN YOU BE SURE?
WELL, IT WAS... OBVIOUS.
OH, VERY OBVIOUS, IT WAS.
CLEAR.
OBVIOUS ISN'T GOOD ENOUGH, YOU FOOLS!

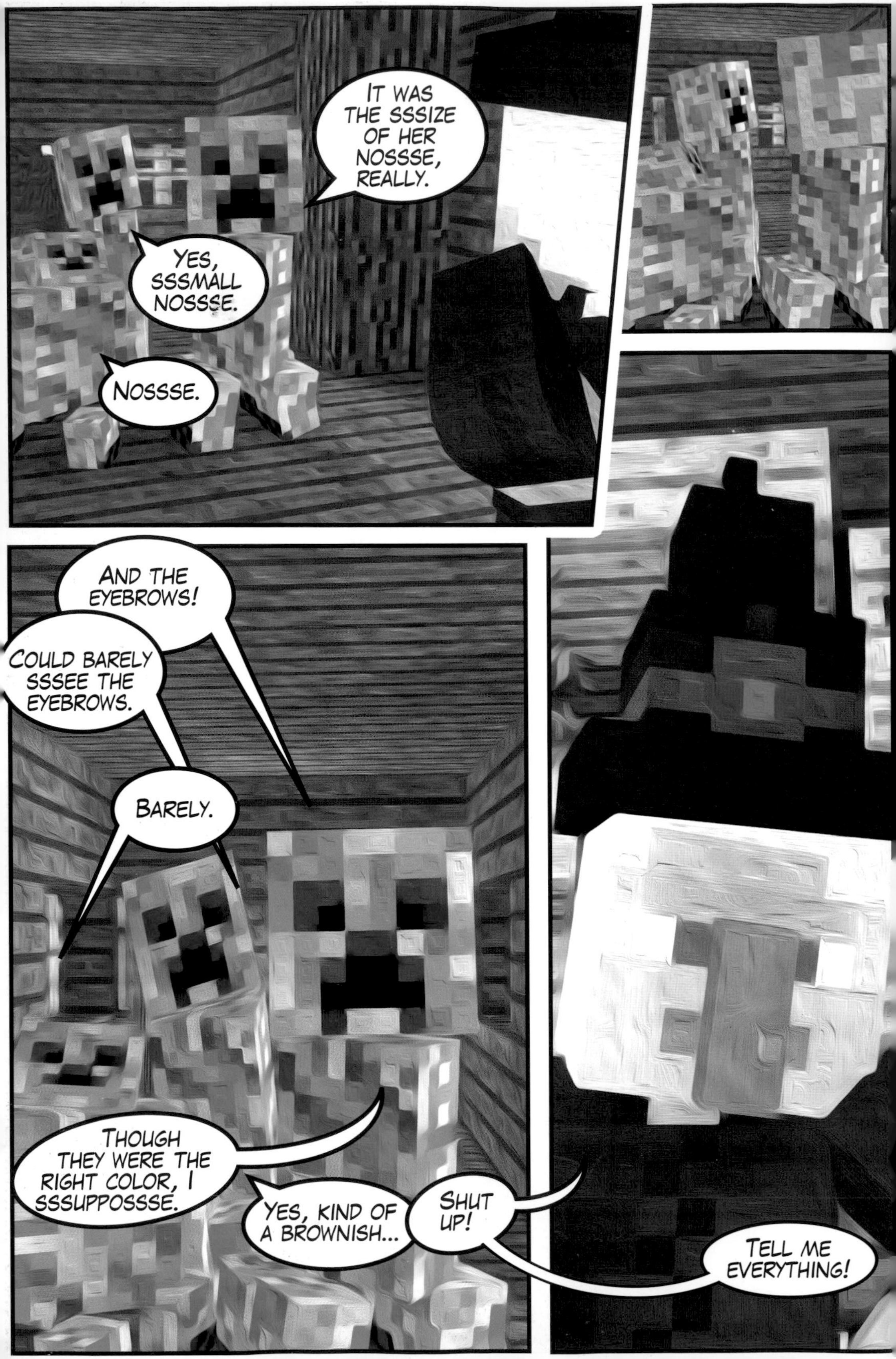
IT WAS THE SSSIZE OF HER NOSSSE, REALLY.
YES, SSSMALL NOSSSE.
NOSSSE.
AND THE EYEBROWS!
COULD BARELY SSSEE THE EYEBROWS.
BARELY.
THOUGH THEY WERE THE RIGHT COLOR, I SSSUPPOSSSE.
YES, KIND OF A BROWNISH...
SHUT UP!
TELL ME EVERYTHING!

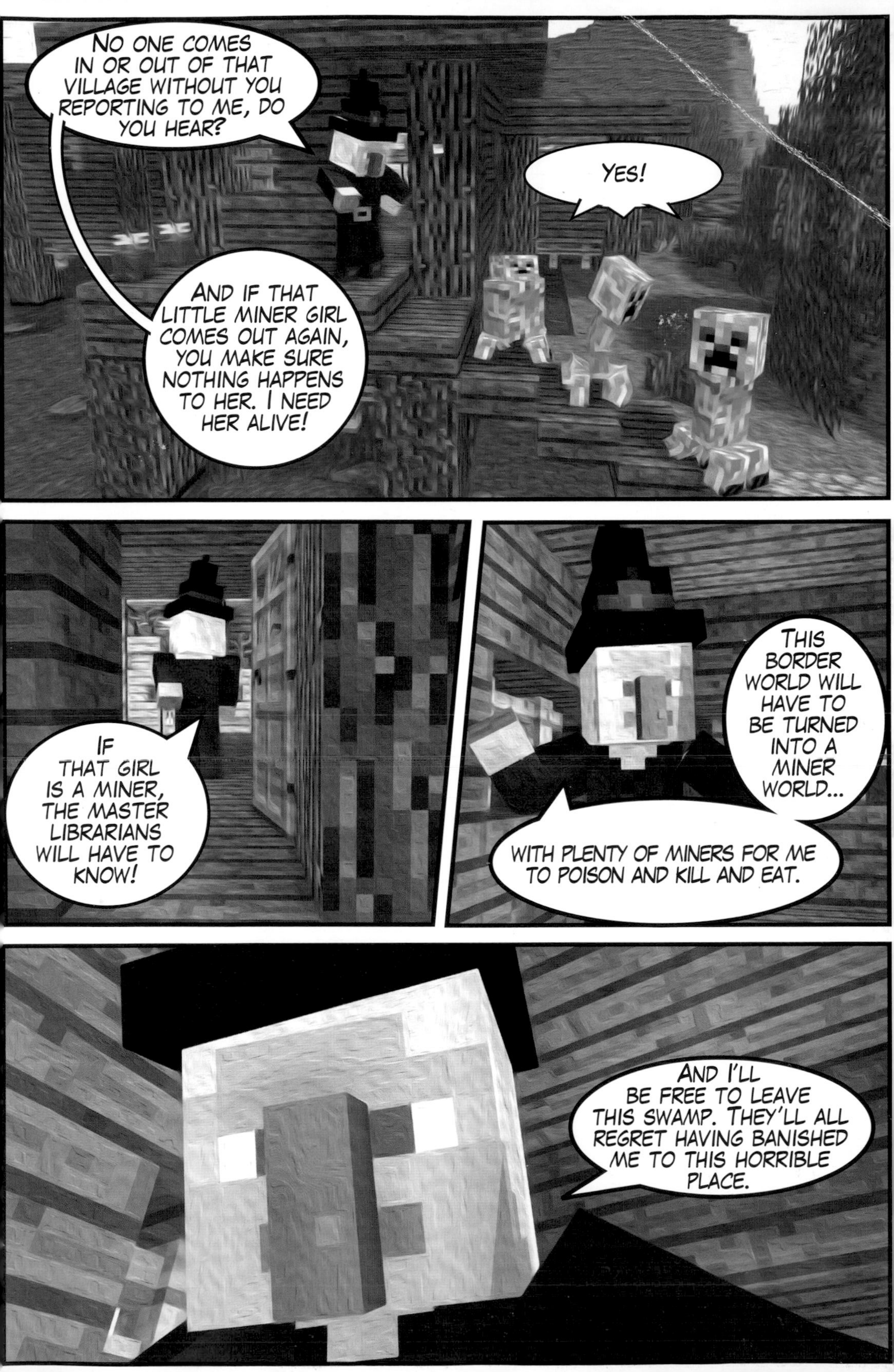
NO ONE COMES IN OR OUT OF THAT VILLAGE WITHOUT YOU REPORTING TO ME, DO YOU HEAR?
YES!
AND IF THAT LITTLE MINER GIRL COMES OUT AGAIN, YOU MAKE SURE NOTHING HAPPENS TO HER. I NEED HER ALIVE!
IF THAT GIRL IS A MINER, THE MASTER LIBRARIANS WILL HAVE TO KNOW!
THIS BORDER WORLD WILL HAVE TO BE TURNED INTO A MINER WORLD...
WITH PLENTY OF MINERS FOR ME TO POISON AND KILL AND EAT.
AND I'LL BE FREE TO LEAVE THIS SWAMP. THEY'LL ALL REGRET HAVING BANISHED ME TO THIS HORRIBLE PLACE.

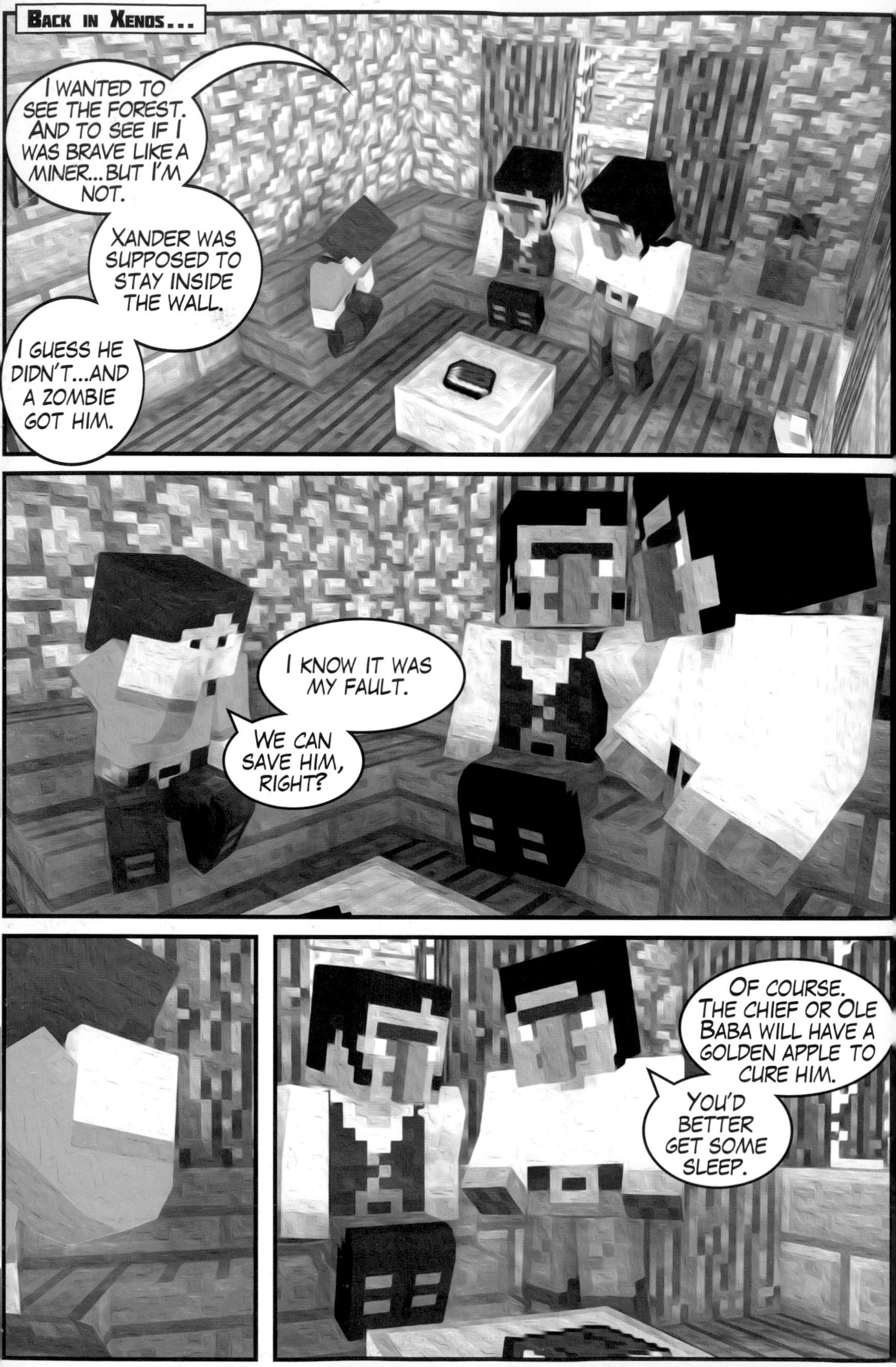
BACK IN XENOS...
I WANTED TO SEE THE FOREST. AND TO SEE IF I WAS BRAVE LIKE A MINER...BUT I'M NOT.
XANDER WAS SUPPOSED TO STAY INSIDE THE WALL.
I GUESS HE DIDN'T...AND A ZOMBIE GOT HIM.
I KNOW IT WAS MY FAULT.
WE CAN SAVE HIM, RIGHT?
OF COURSE. THE CHIEF OR OLE BABA WILL HAVE A GOLDEN APPLE TO CURE HIM.
YOU'D BETTER GET SOME SLEEP.

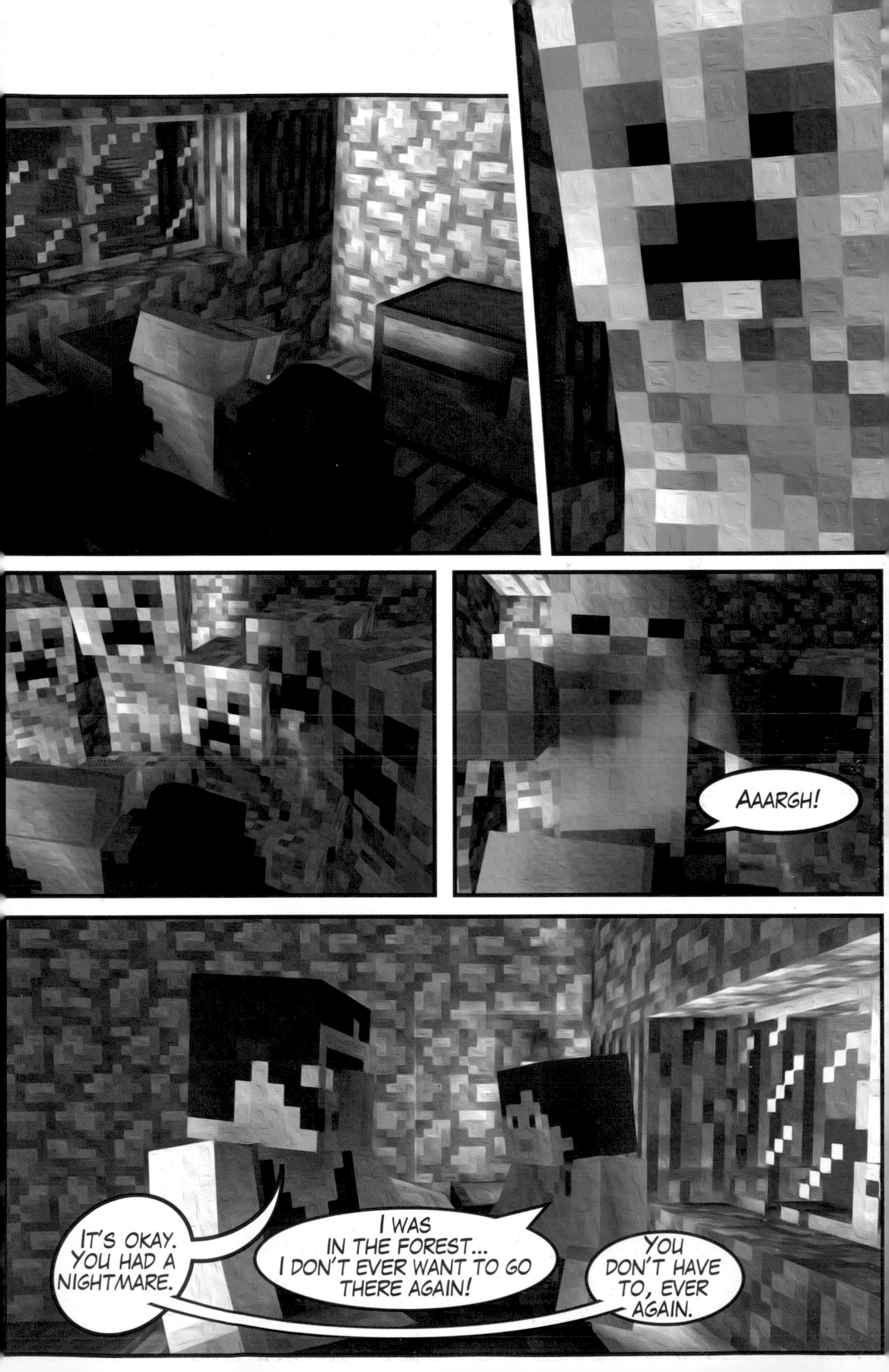
AAARGH!
IT'S OKAY. YOU HAD A NIGHTMARE.
I WAS IN THE FOREST... I DON'T EVER WANT TO GO THERE AGAIN!
YOU DON'T HAVE TO, EVER AGAIN.

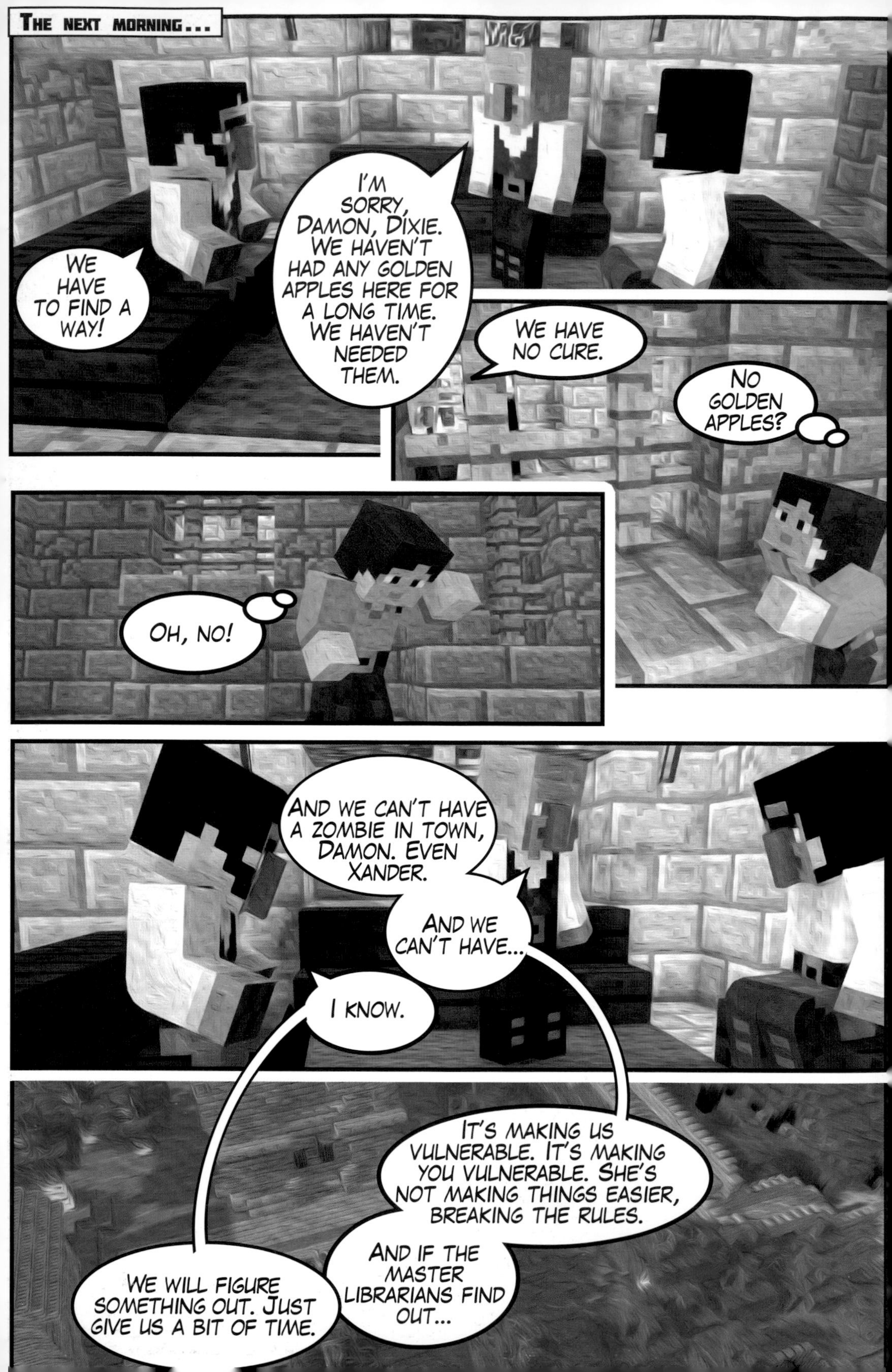
THE NEXT MORNING...
WE HAVE TO FIND A WAY!
I'M SORRY, DAMON, DIXIE. WE HAVEN'T HAD ANY GOLDEN APPLES HERE FOR A LONG TIME. WE HAVEN'T NEEDED THEM.
WE HAVE NO CURE.
NO GOLDEN APPLES?
OH, NO!
AND WE CAN'T HAVE A ZOMBIE IN TOWN, DAMON. EVEN XANDER.
AND WE CAN'T HAVE...
I KNOW.
IT'S MAKING US VULNERABLE. IT'S MAKING YOU VULNERABLE. SHE'S NOT MAKING THINGS EASIER, BREAKING THE RULES.
AND IF THE MASTER LIBRARIANS FIND OUT...
WE WILL FIGURE SOMETHING OUT. JUST GIVE US A BIT OF TIME.

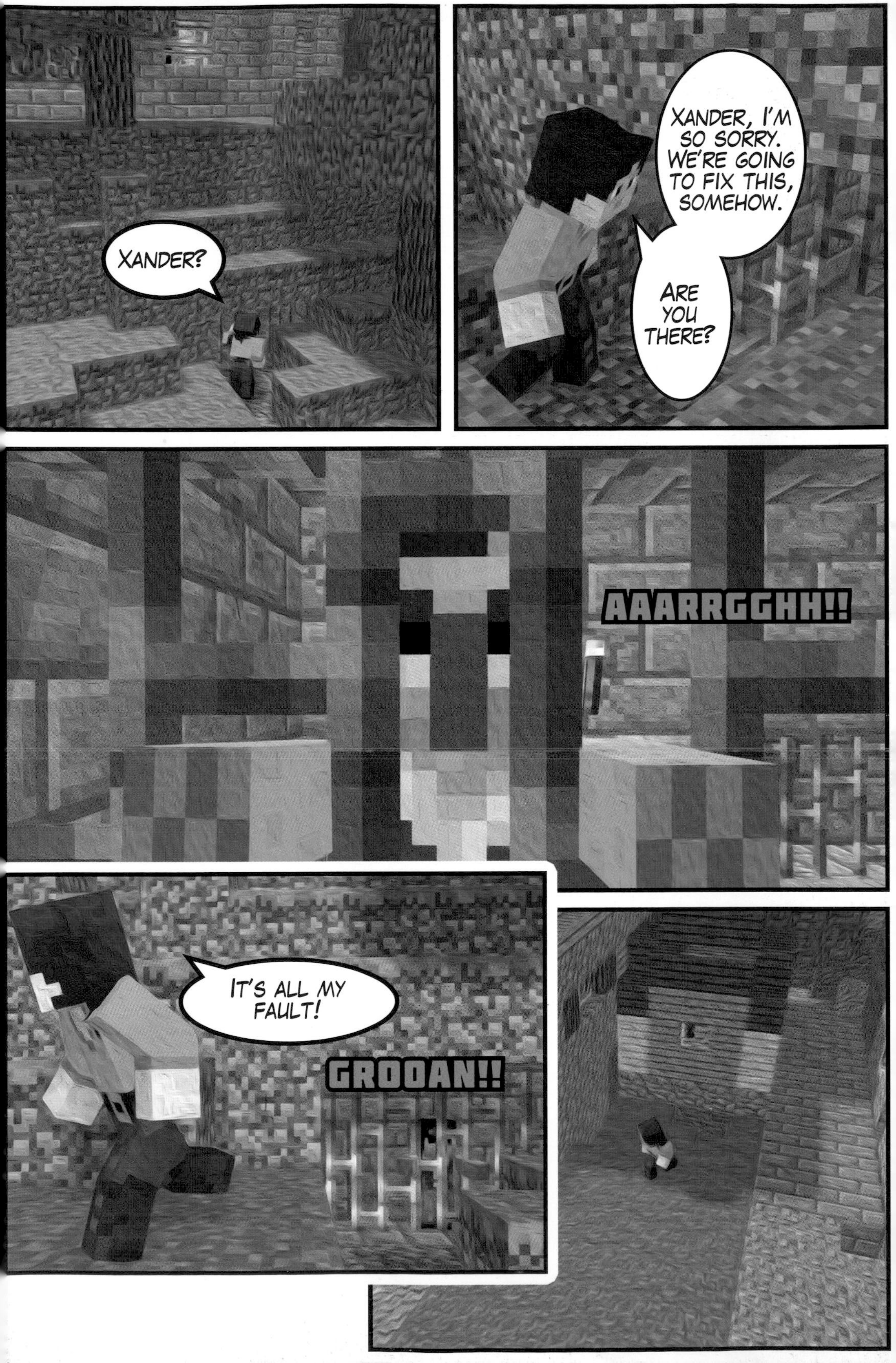
XANDER?
XANDER, I'M SO SORRY. WE'RE GOING TO FIX THIS, SOMEHOW.
ARE YOU THERE?
AAARRGGHH!!
IT'S ALL MY FAULT!
GROOAN!!

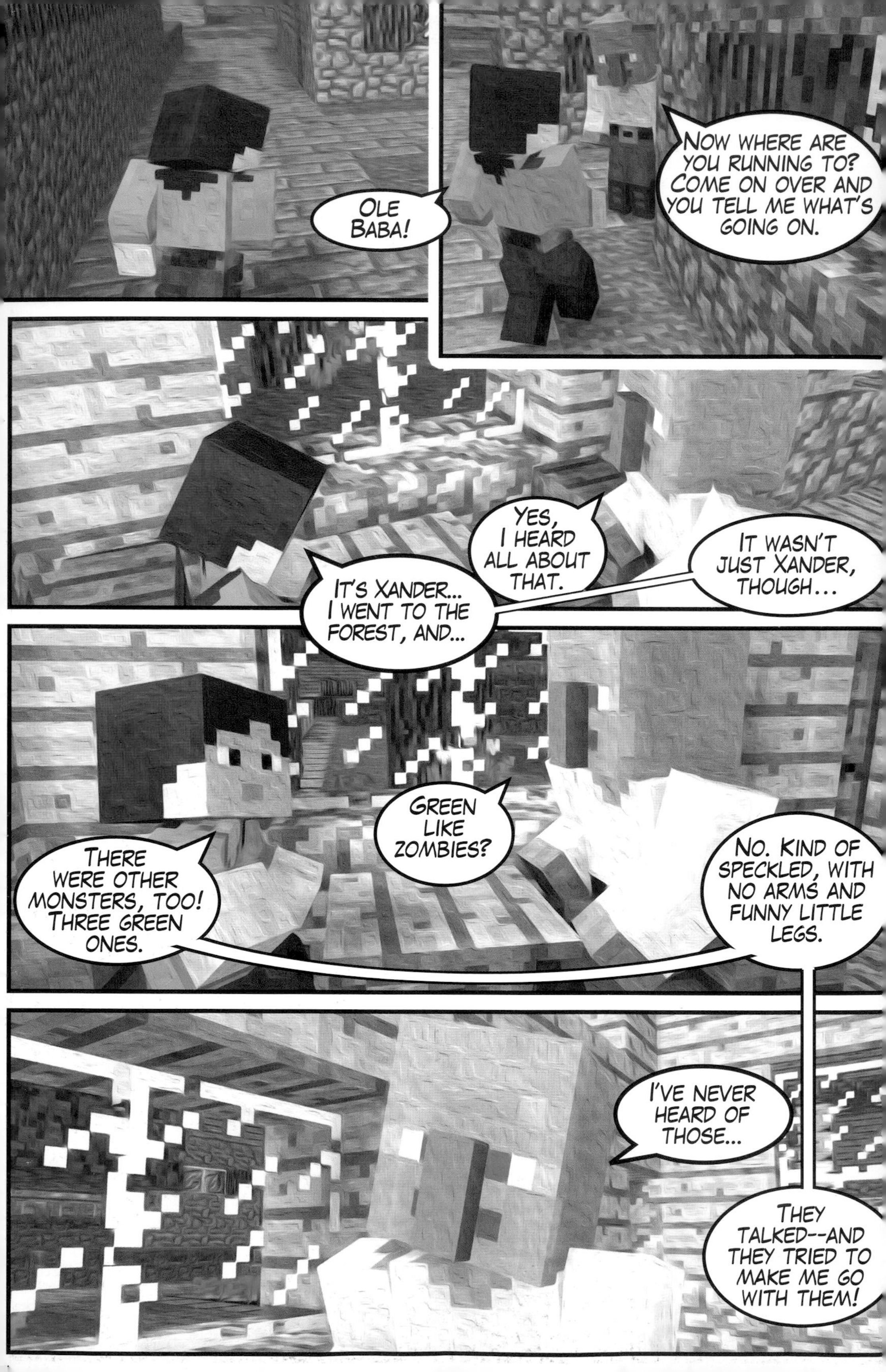
OLE BABA!
NOW WHERE ARE YOU RUNNING TO? COME ON OVER AND YOU TELL ME WHAT'S GOING ON.
IT'S XANDER... I WENT TO THE FOREST, AND...
YES, I HEARD ALL ABOUT THAT.
IT WASN'T JUST XANDER, THOUGH...
THERE WERE OTHER MONSTERS, TOO! THREE GREEN ONES.
GREEN LIKE ZOMBIES?
NO. KIND OF SPECKLED, WITH NO ARMS AND FUNNY LITTLE LEGS.
I'VE NEVER HEARD OF THOSE...
THEY TALKED--AND THEY TRIED TO MAKE ME GO WITH THEM!

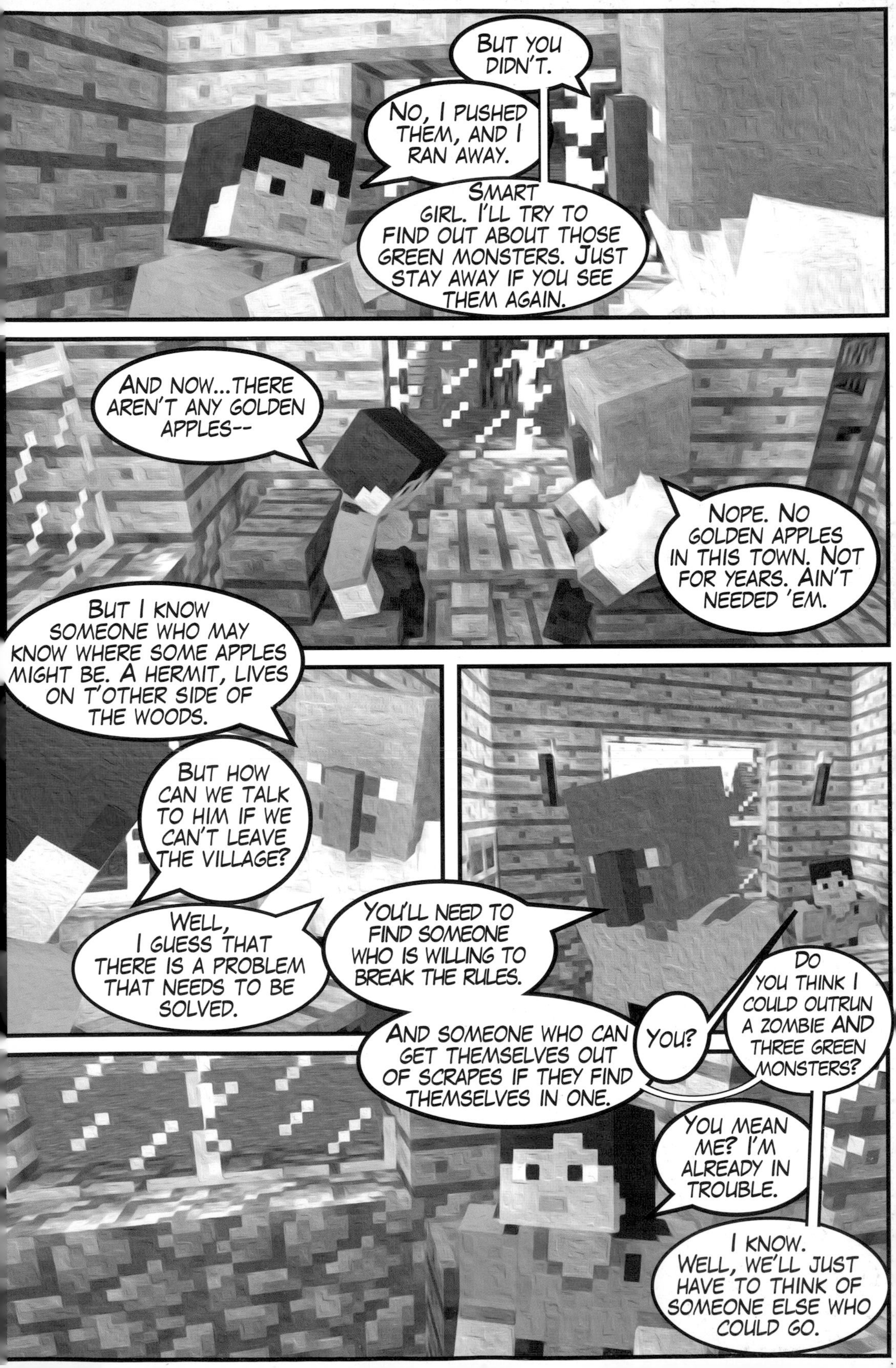
BUT YOU DIDN'T.
NO, I PUSHED THEM, AND I RAN AWAY.
SMART GIRL. I'LL TRY TO FIND OUT ABOUT THOSE GREEN MONSTERS. JUST STAY AWAY IF YOU SEE THEM AGAIN.
AND NOW...THERE AREN'T ANY GOLDEN APPLES--
NOPE. NO GOLDEN APPLES IN THIS TOWN. NOT FOR YEARS. AIN'T NEEDED 'EM.
BUT I KNOW SOMEONE WHO MAY KNOW WHERE SOME APPLES MIGHT BE. A HERMIT, LIVES ON T'OTHER SIDE OF THE WOODS.
BUT HOW CAN WE TALK TO HIM IF WE CAN'T LEAVE THE VILLAGE?
WELL, I GUESS THAT THERE IS A PROBLEM THAT NEEDS TO BE SOLVED.
YOU'LL NEED TO FIND SOMEONE WHO IS WILLING TO BREAK THE RULES.
AND SOMEONE WHO CAN GET THEMSELVES OUT OF SCRAPES IF THEY FIND THEMSELVES IN ONE.
YOU?
DO YOU THINK I COULD OUTRUN A ZOMBIE AND THREE GREEN MONSTERS?
YOU MEAN ME? I'M ALREADY IN TROUBLE.
I KNOW. WELL, WE'LL JUST HAVE TO THINK OF SOMEONE ELSE WHO COULD GO.

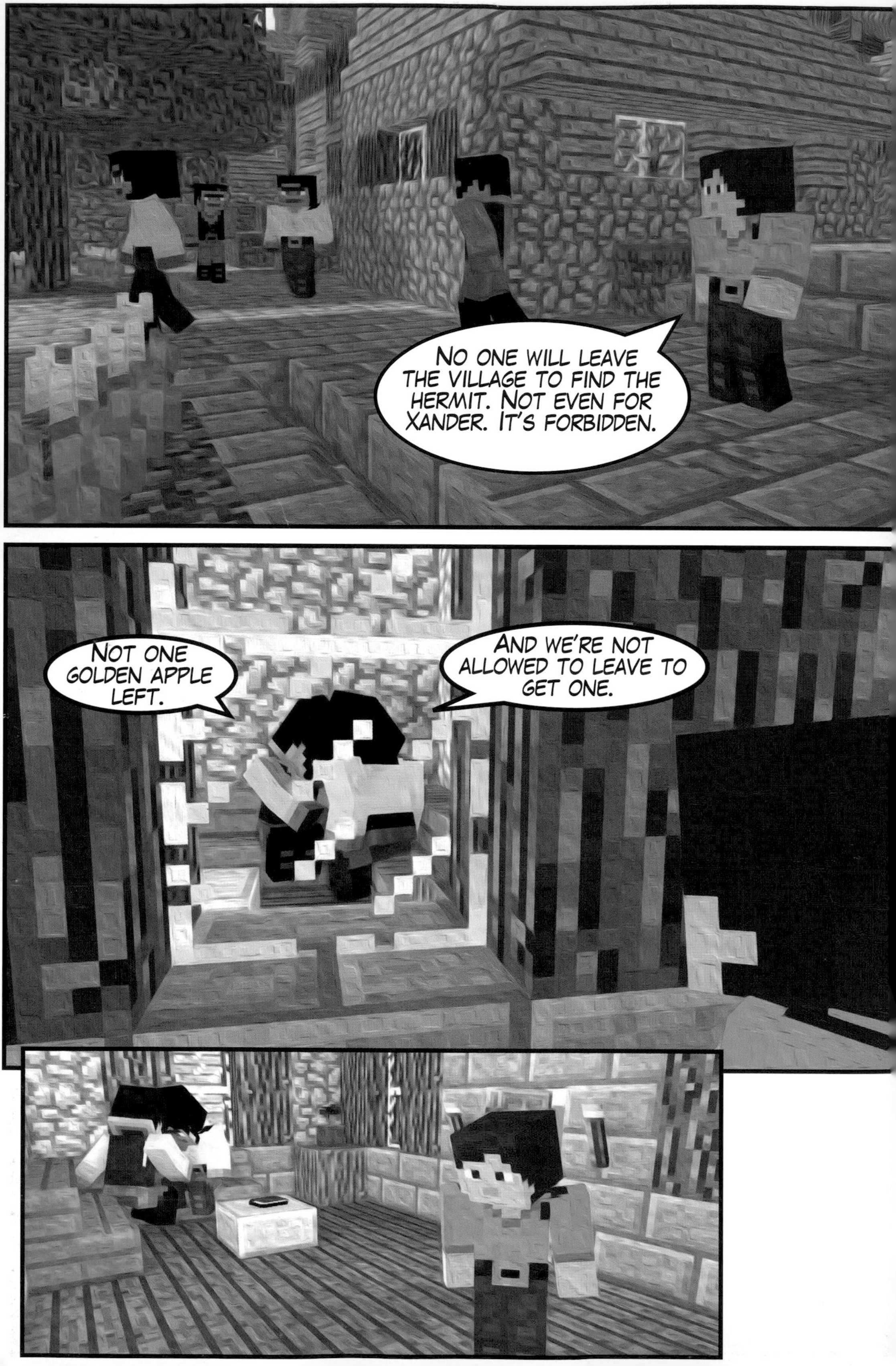
NO ONE WILL LEAVE THE VILLAGE TO FIND THE HERMIT. NOT EVEN FOR XANDER. IT'S FORBIDDEN.
NOT ONE GOLDEN APPLE LEFT.
AND WE'RE NOT ALLOWED TO LEAVE TO GET ONE.

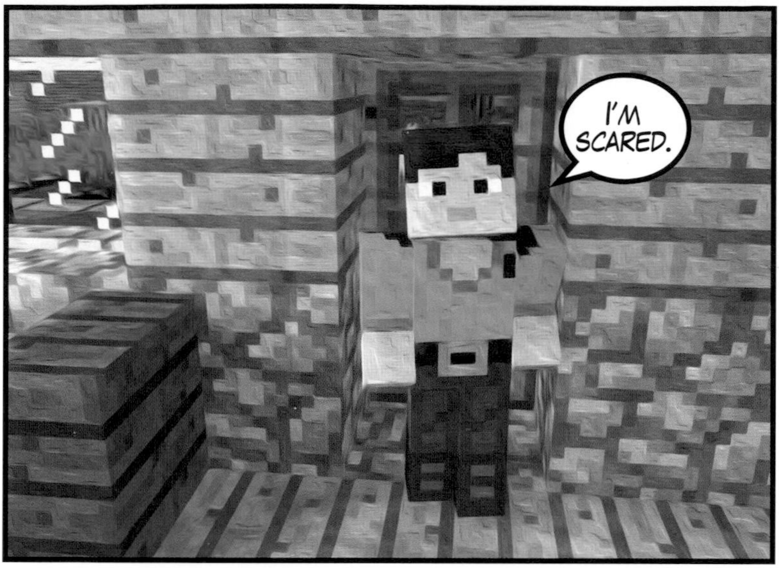
I'M SCARED.

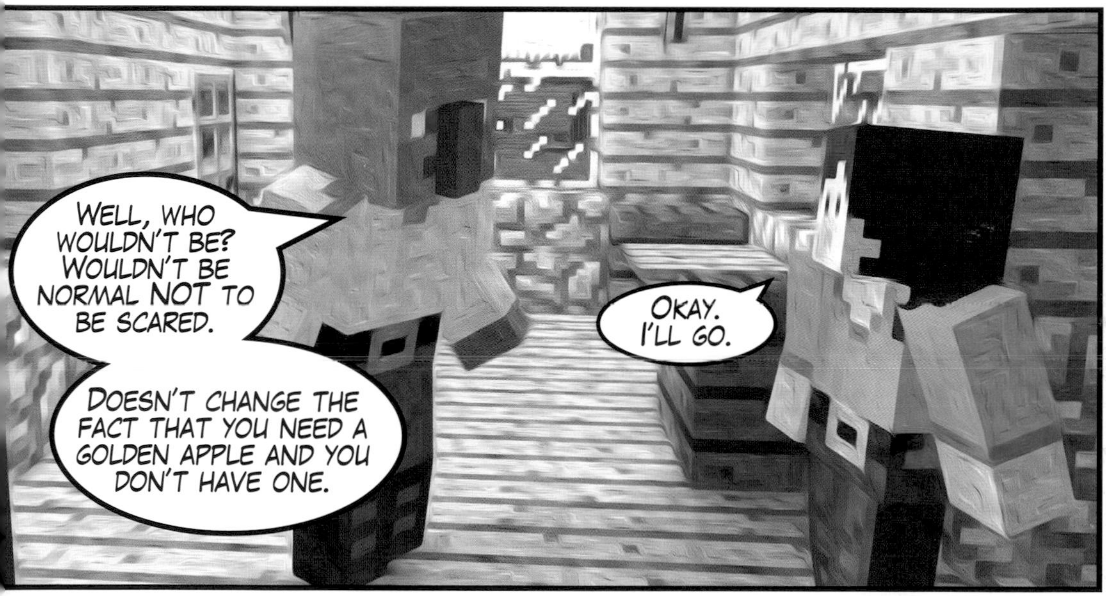
WELL, WHO WOULDN'T BE? WOULDN'T BE NORMAL NOT TO BE SCARED.
DOESN'T CHANGE THE FACT THAT YOU NEED A GOLDEN APPLE AND YOU DON'T HAVE ONE.
OKAY. I'LL GO.

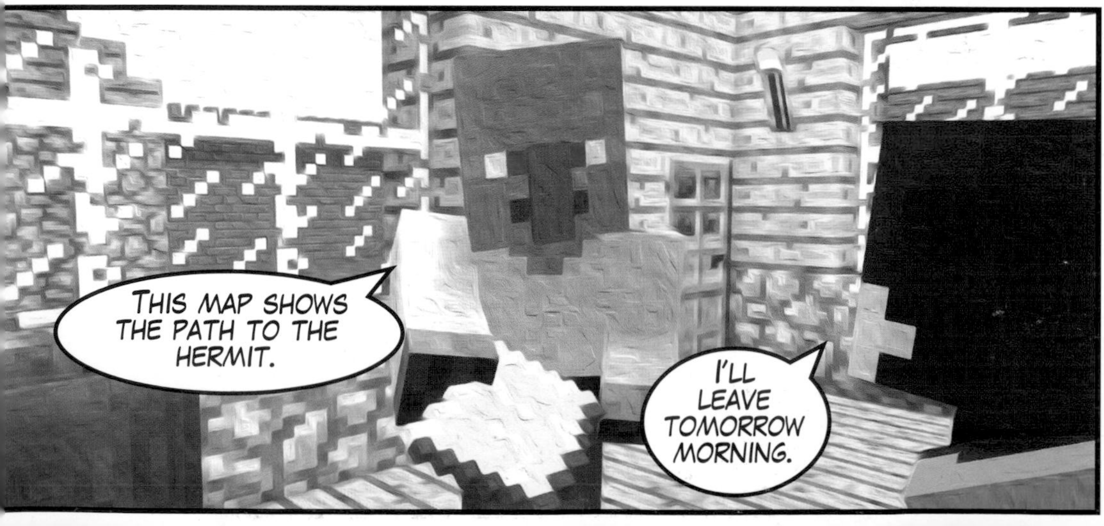
THIS MAP SHOWS THE PATH TO THE HERMIT.
I'LL LEAVE TOMORROW MORNING.

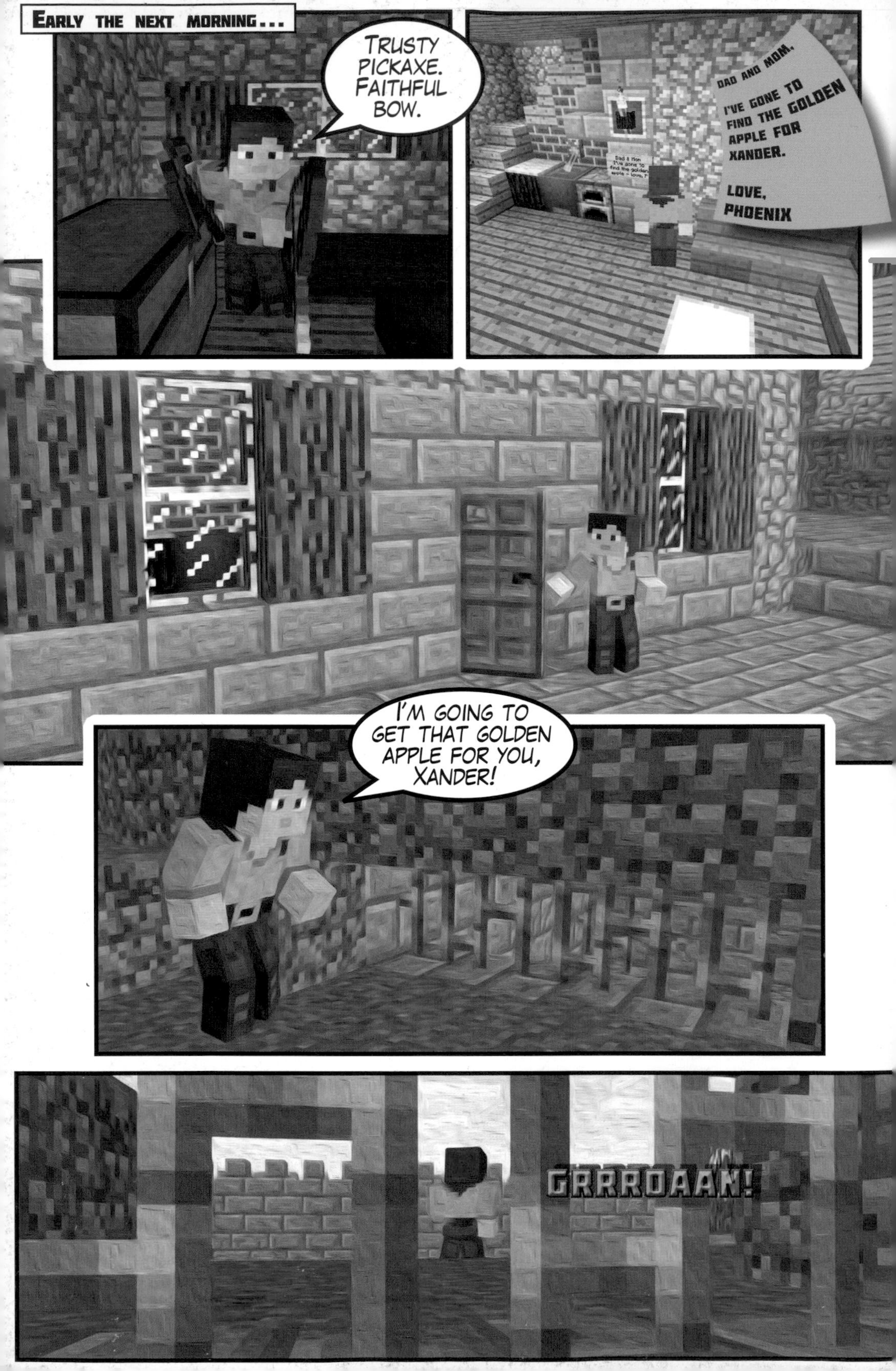
EARLY THE NEXT MORNING...
TRUSTY PICKAXE. FAITHFUL BOW.
DAD AND MOM,
I'VE GONE TO FIND THE GOLDEN APPLE FOR XANDER.
LOVE, PHOENIX
I'M GOING TO GET THAT GOLDEN APPLE FOR YOU, XANDER!
GRRROAAN!

CHAPTER 4

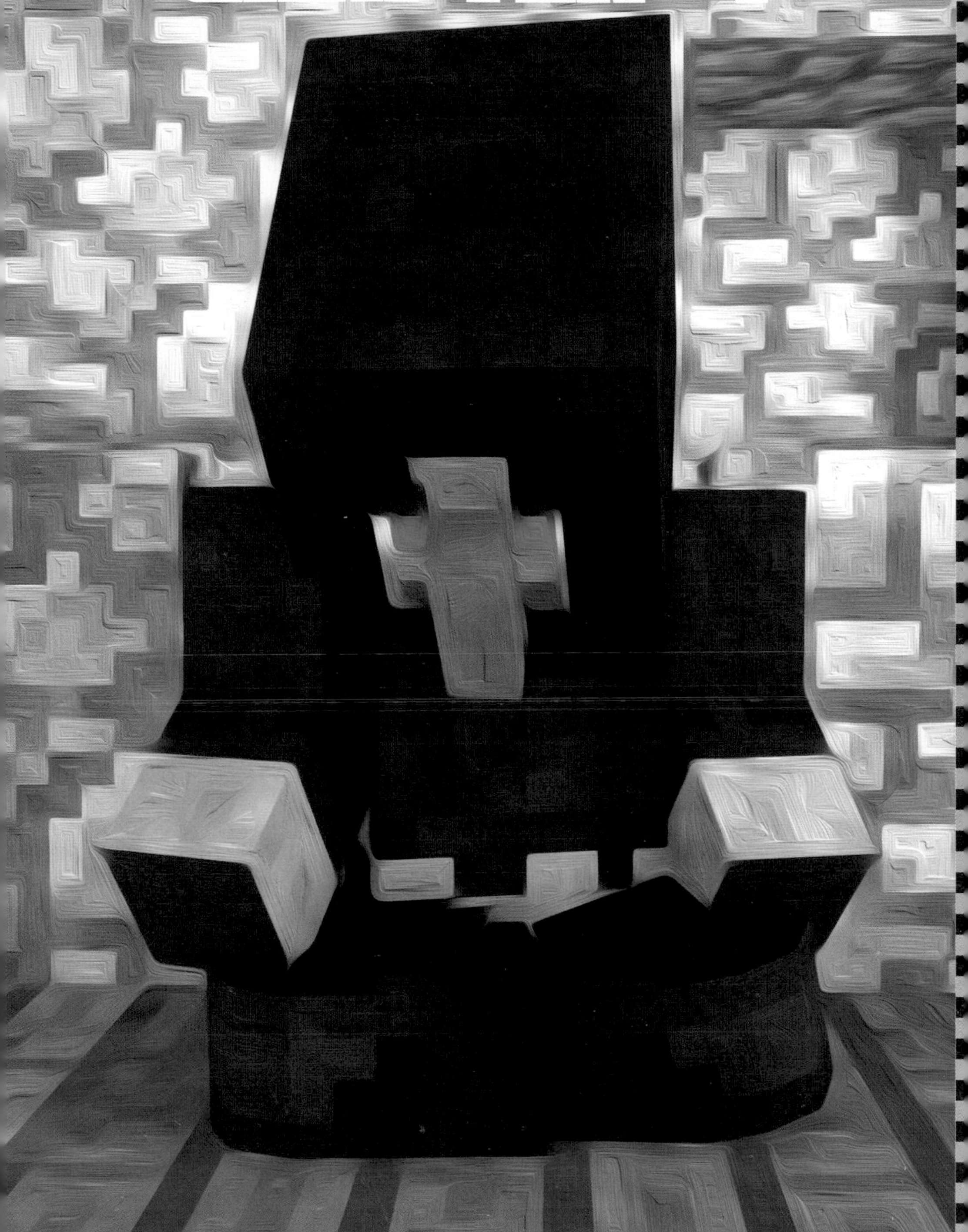

THE HERMIT

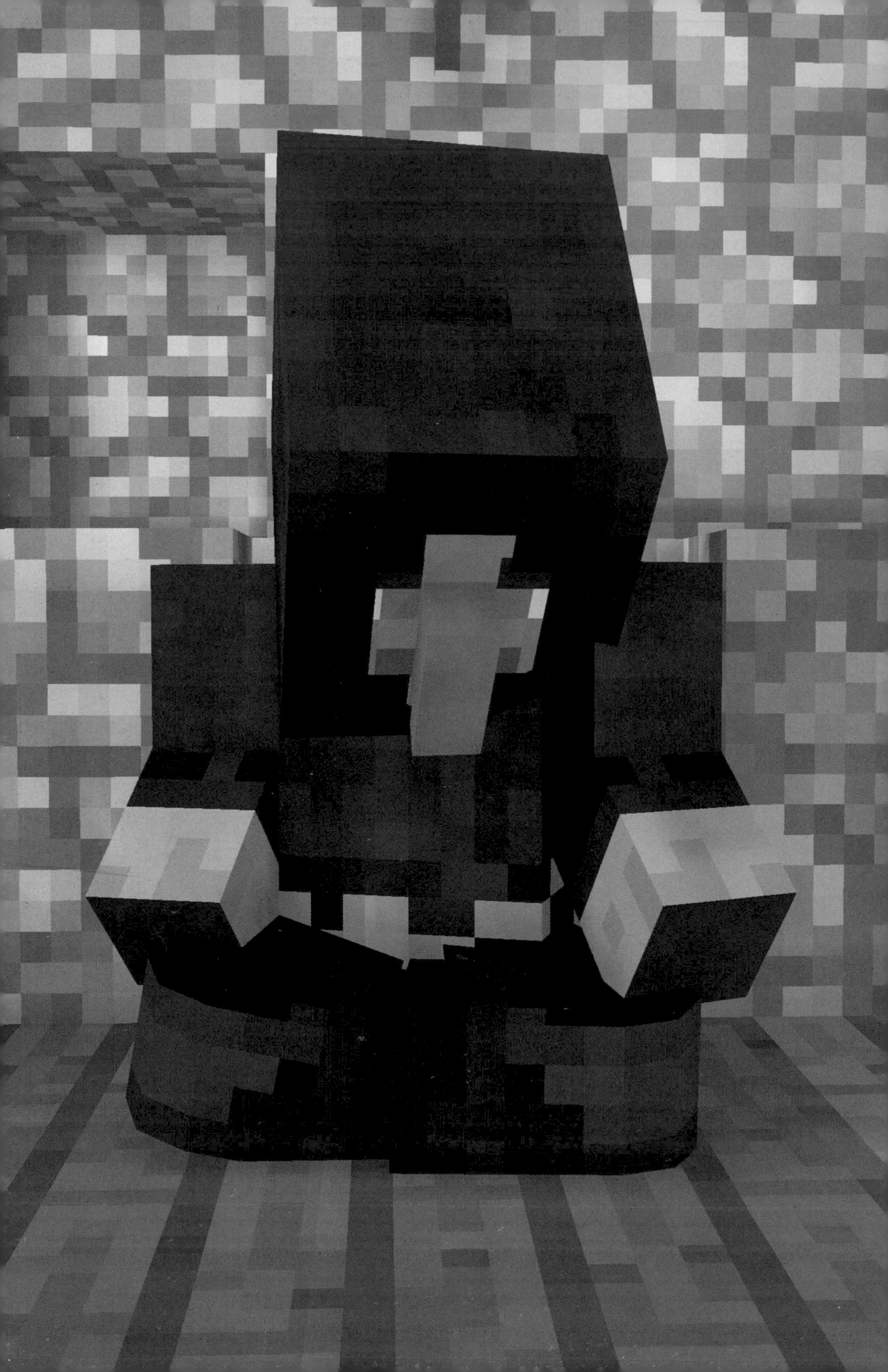

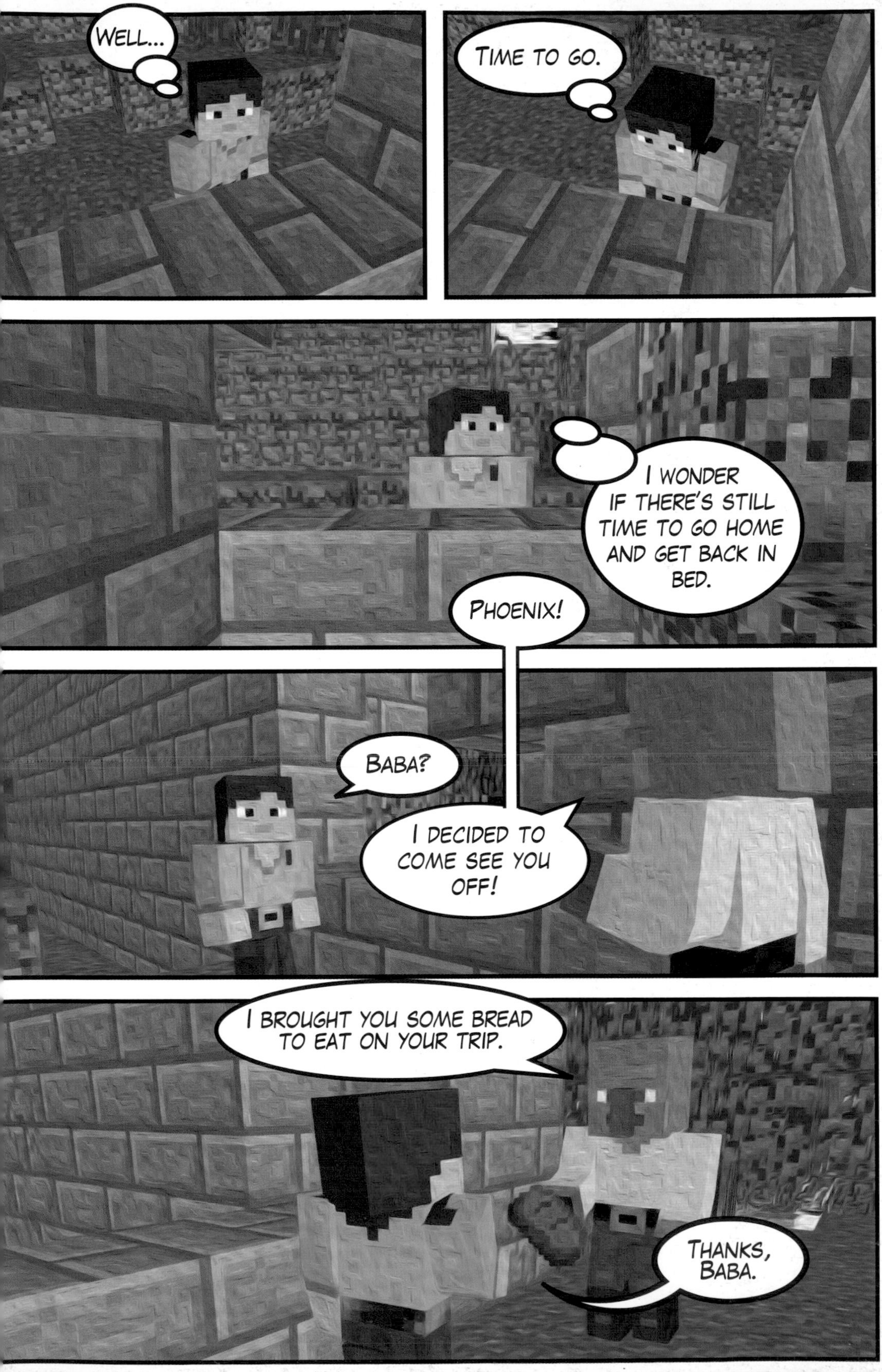
WELL...
TIME TO GO.
I WONDER IF THERE'S STILL TIME TO GO HOME AND GET BACK IN BED.
PHOENIX!
BABA?
I DECIDED TO COME SEE YOU OFF!
I BROUGHT YOU SOME BREAD TO EAT ON YOUR TRIP.
THANKS, BABA.

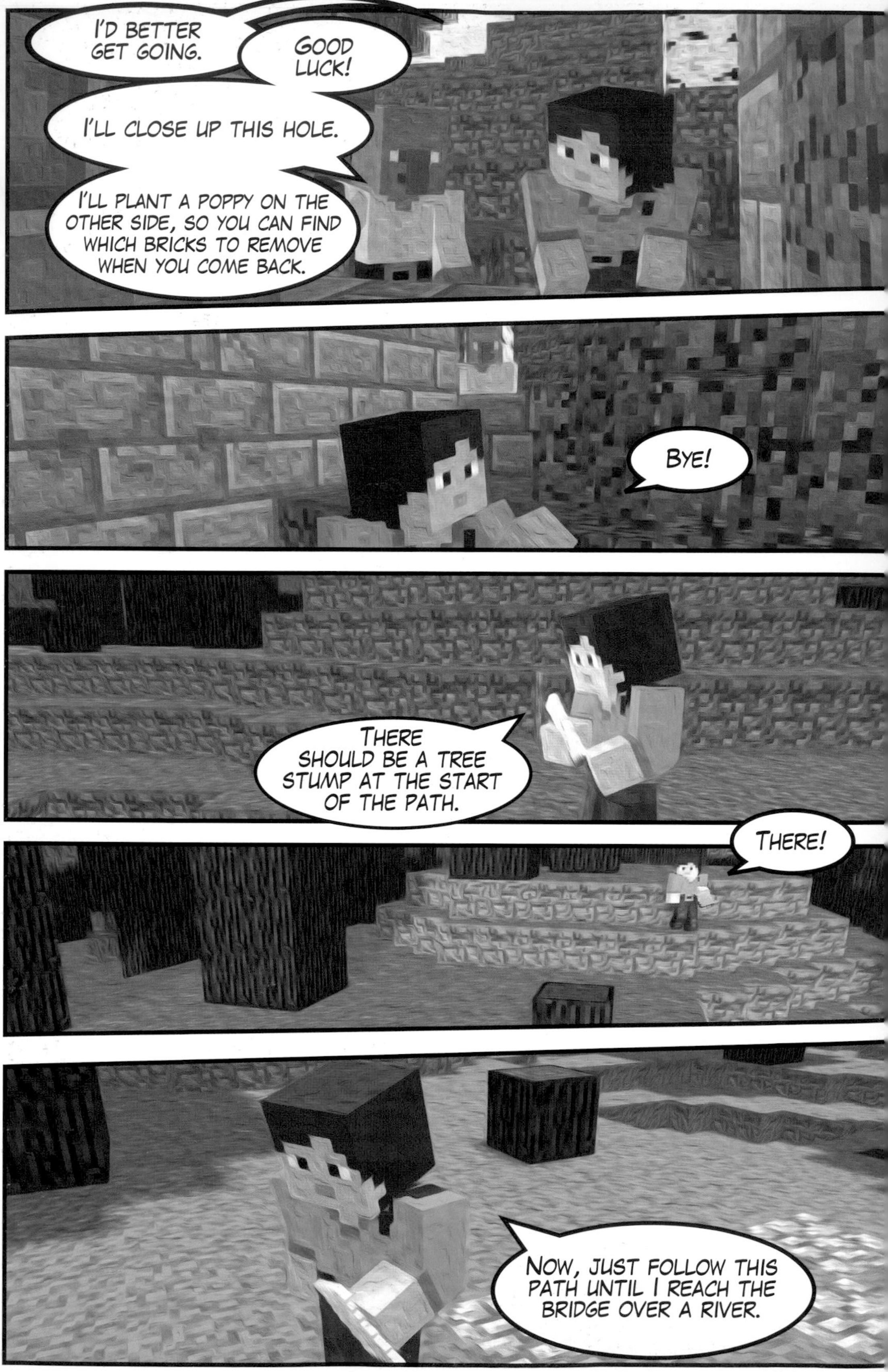
I'D BETTER GET GOING.
GOOD LUCK!
I'LL CLOSE UP THIS HOLE.
I'LL PLANT A POPPY ON THE OTHER SIDE, SO YOU CAN FIND WHICH BRICKS TO REMOVE WHEN YOU COME BACK.
BYE!
THERE SHOULD BE A TREE STUMP AT THE START OF THE PATH.
THERE!
NOW, JUST FOLLOW THIS PATH UNTIL I REACH THE BRIDGE OVER A RIVER.

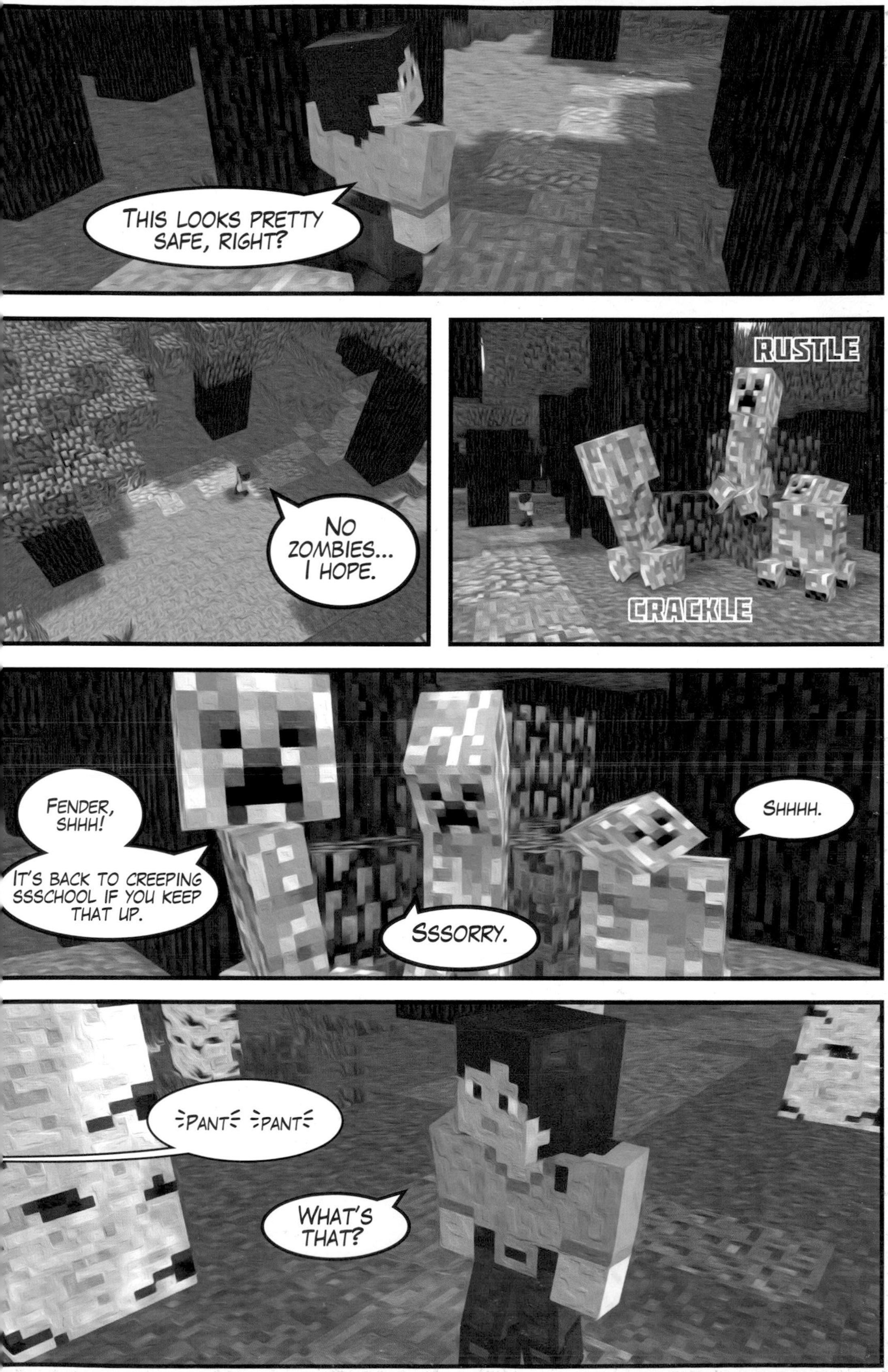
THIS LOOKS PRETTY SAFE, RIGHT?
NO ZOMBIES... I HOPE.
RUSTLE
CRACKLE
FENDER, SHHH!
IT'S BACK TO CREEPING SSSCHOOL IF YOU KEEP THAT UP.
SSSORRY.
SHHHH.
PANT PANT
WHAT'S THAT?

AAAH!

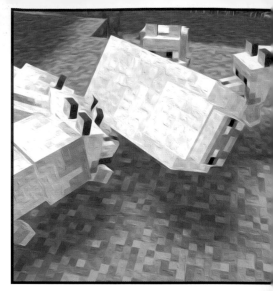

GRRR

THE LAST THING I NEED--

A PACK OF HUNGRY WOLVES!

HURRY! WE HAVE TO KEEP UP!

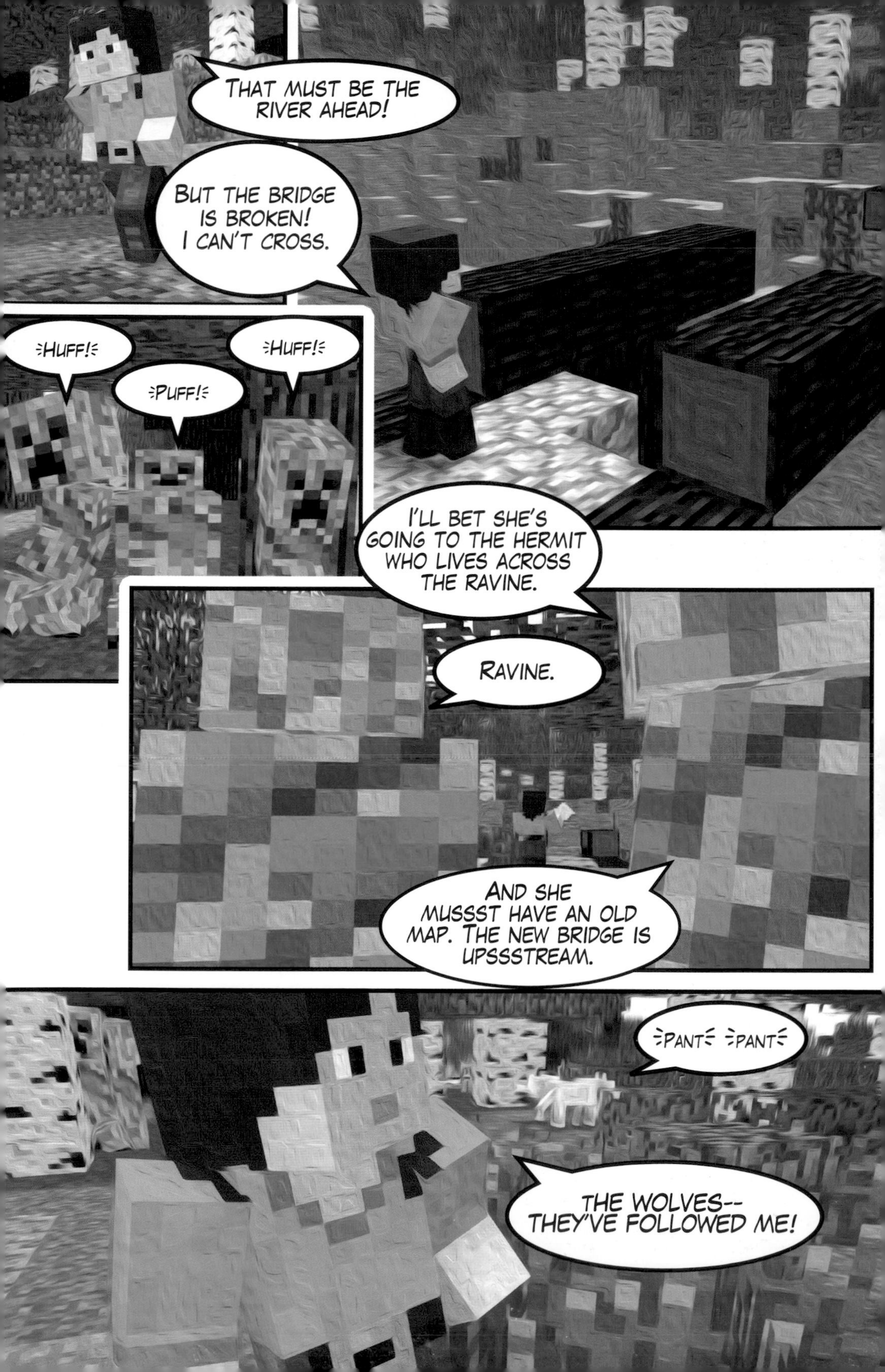
THAT MUST BE THE RIVER AHEAD!
BUT THE BRIDGE IS BROKEN! I CAN'T CROSS.
HUFF!
PUFF!
HUFF!
I'LL BET SHE'S GOING TO THE HERMIT WHO LIVES ACROSS THE RAVINE.
RAVINE.
AND SHE MUSSST HAVE AN OLD MAP. THE NEW BRIDGE IS UPSSSTREAM.
PANT PANT
THE WOLVES-- THEY'VE FOLLOWED ME!

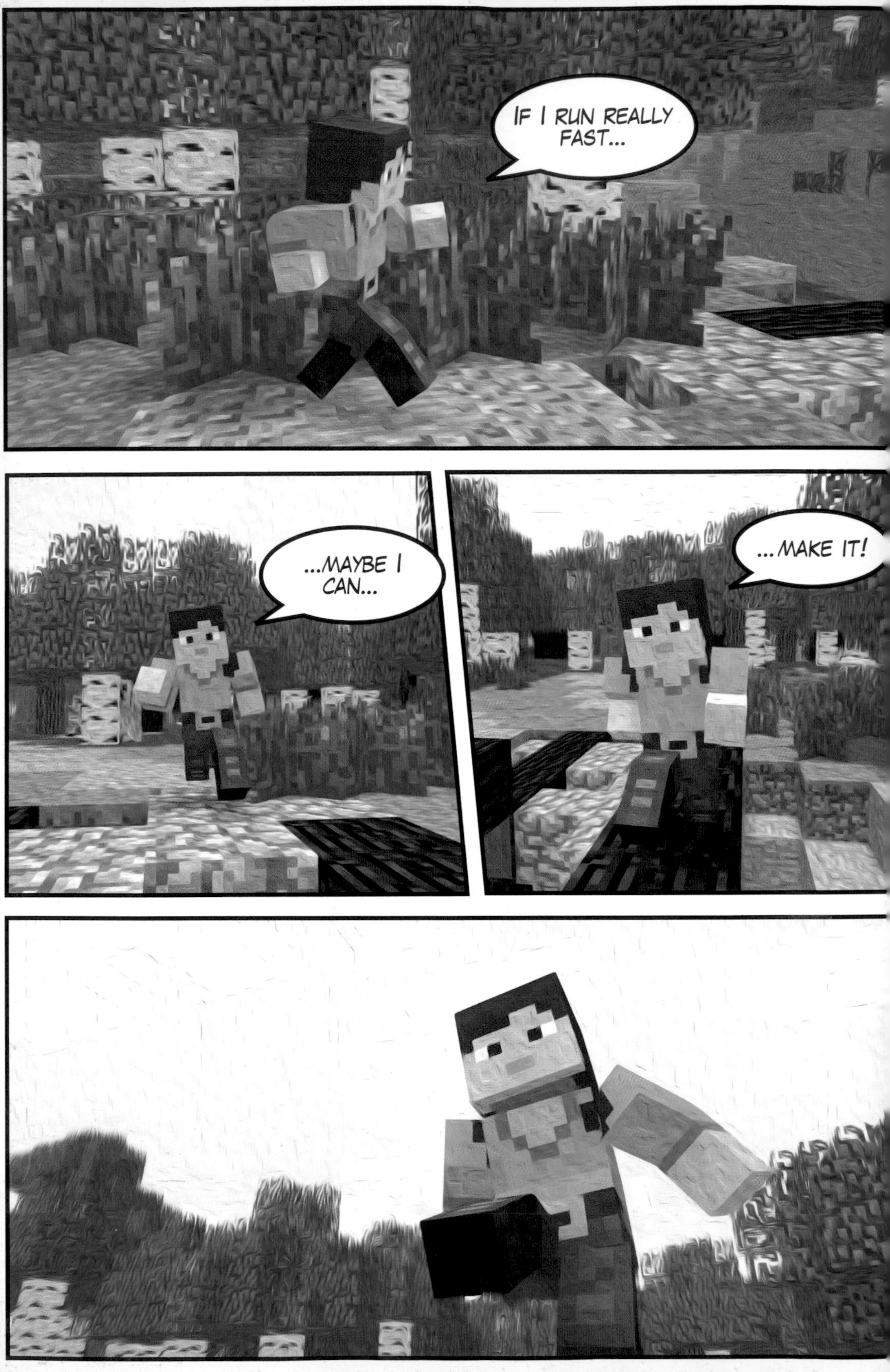
IF I RUN REALLY FAST...
...MAYBE I CAN...
...MAKE IT!

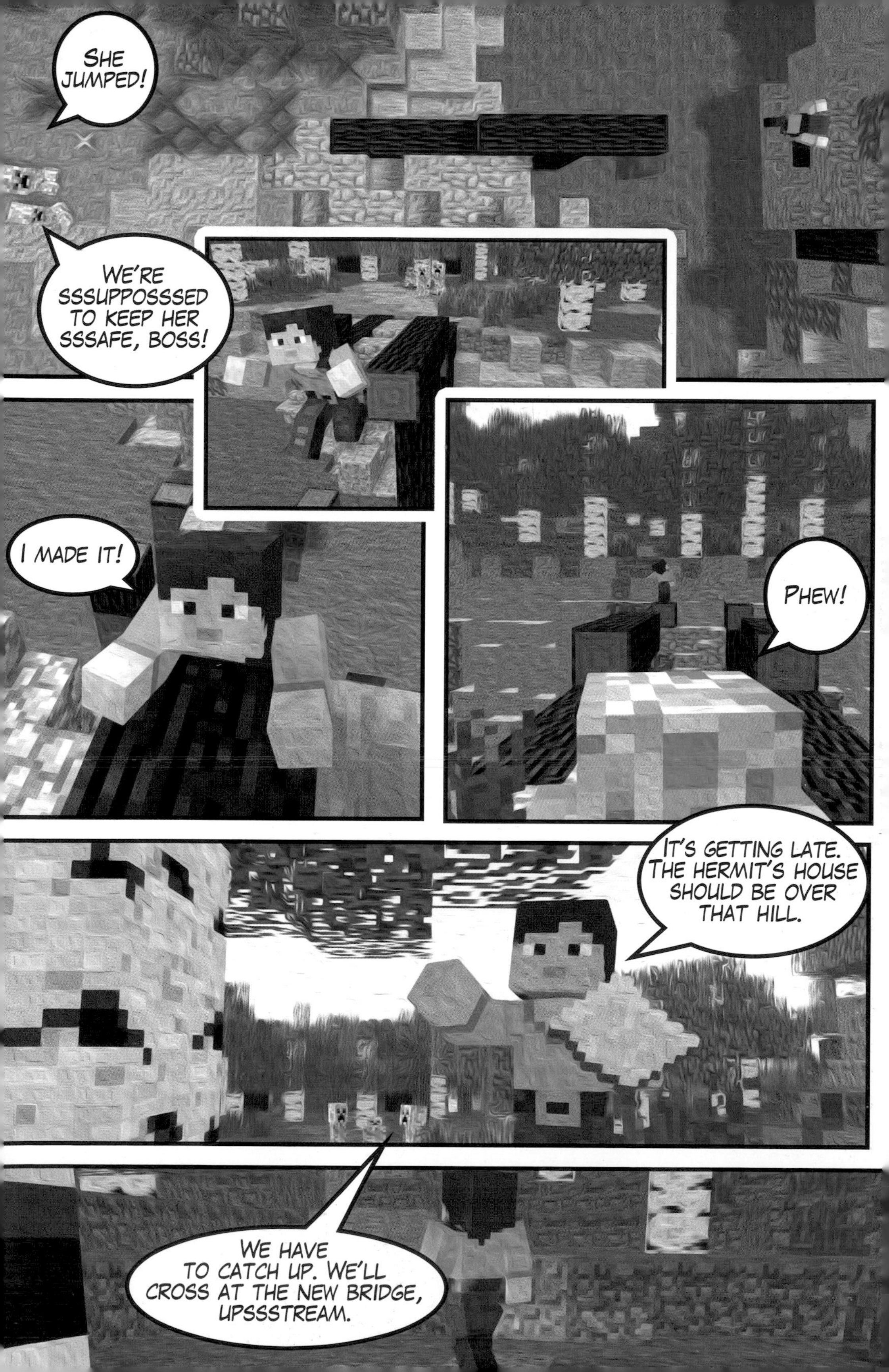
SHE JUMPED!
WE'RE SSSUPPOSSSED TO KEEP HER SSSAFE, BOSS!
I MADE IT!
PHEW!
IT'S GETTING LATE. THE HERMIT'S HOUSE SHOULD BE OVER THAT HILL.
WE HAVE TO CATCH UP. WE'LL CROSS AT THE NEW BRIDGE, UPSSSTREAM.

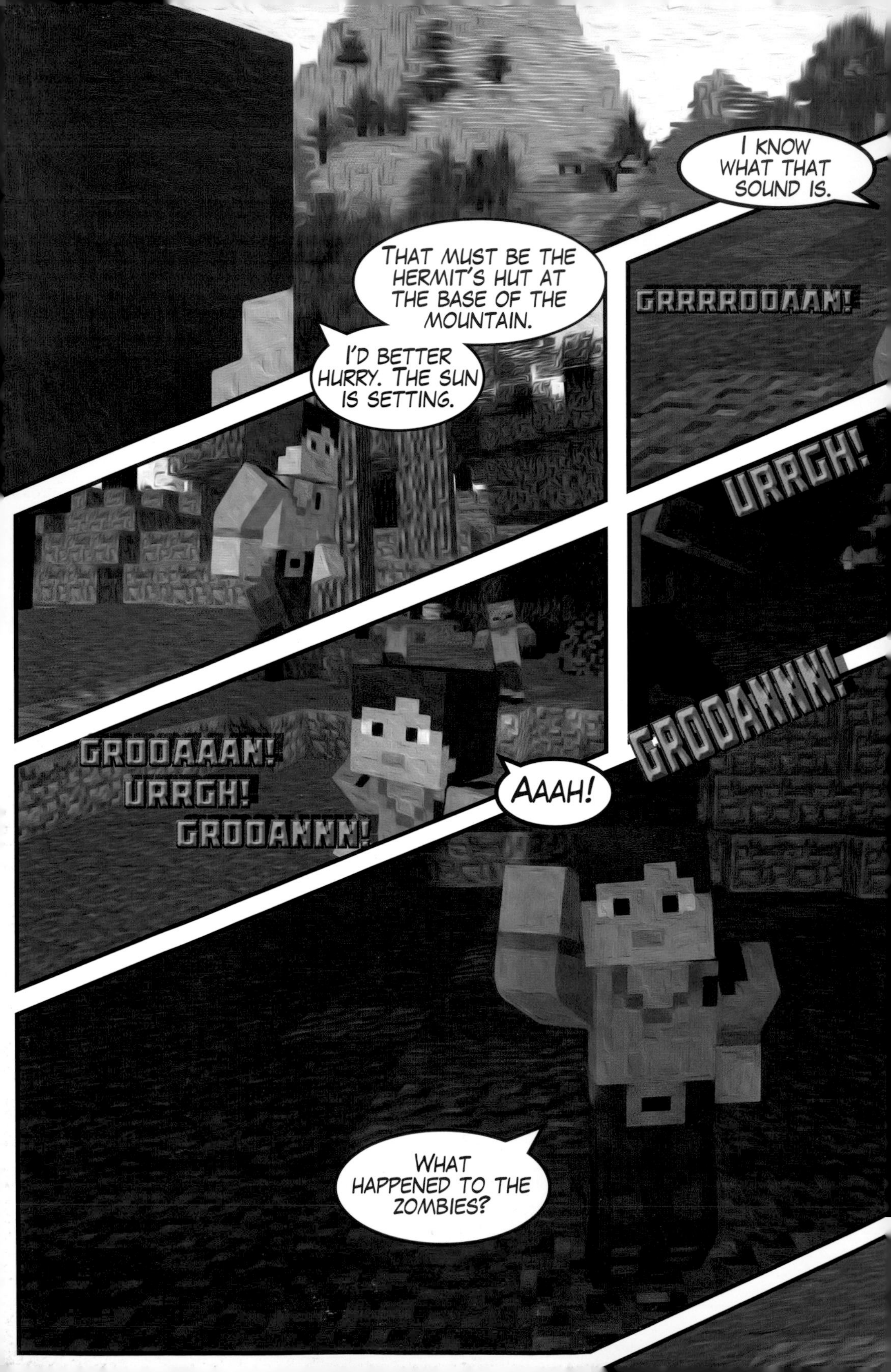
That must be the hermit's hut at the base of the mountain.
I'd better hurry. The sun is setting.
I know what that sound is.
GRRRROOAAN!
URRGH!
GROOAAAN!
URRGH!
GROOANNN!
GROOANNN!
AAAH!
What happened to the zombies?

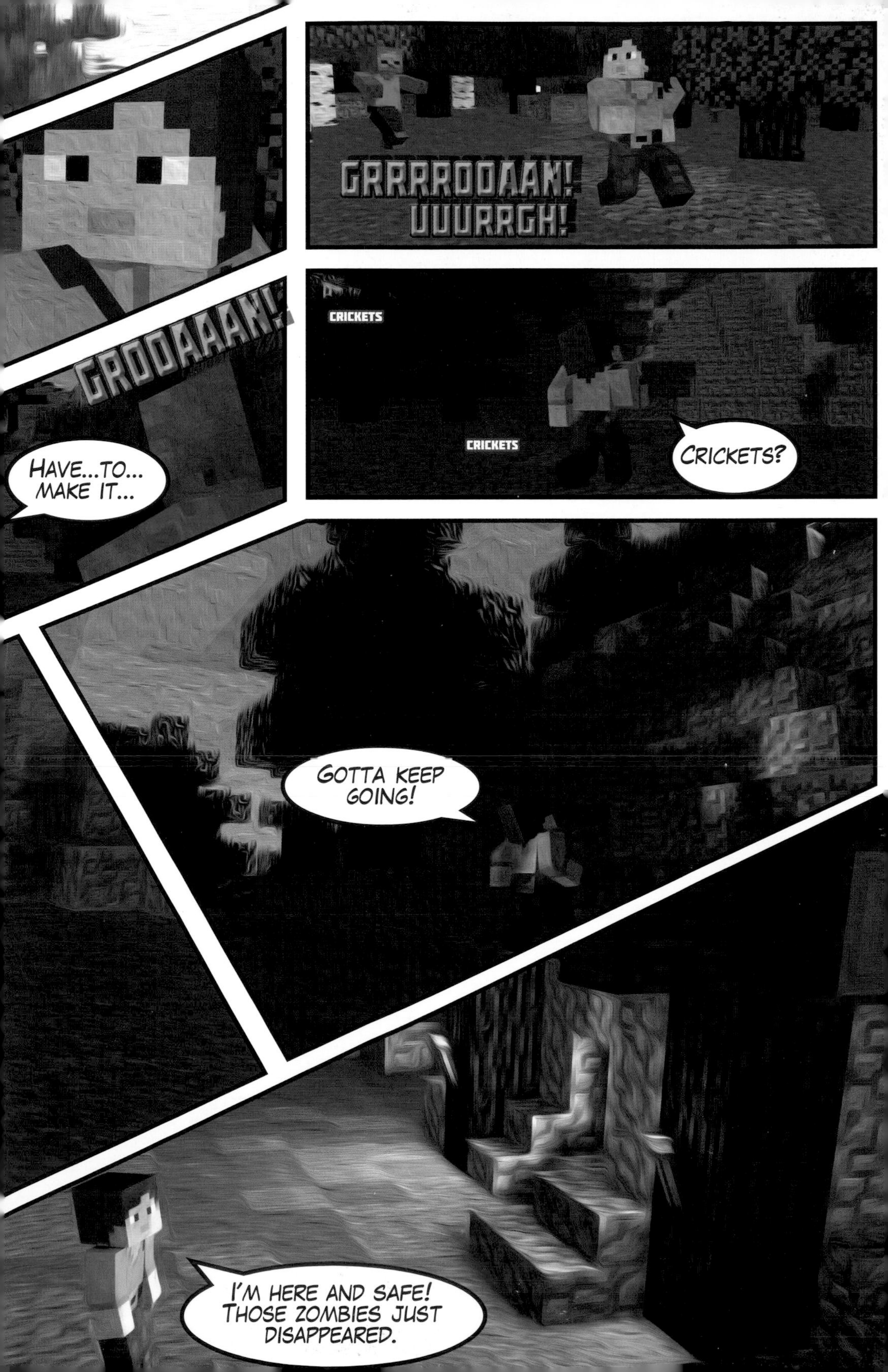
GRRRROOAAN!
UUURRGH!
GROOAAAN!
HAVE...TO... MAKE IT...
CRICKETS
CRICKETS
CRICKETS?
GOTTA KEEP GOING!
I'M HERE AND SAFE! THOSE ZOMBIES JUST DISAPPEARED.

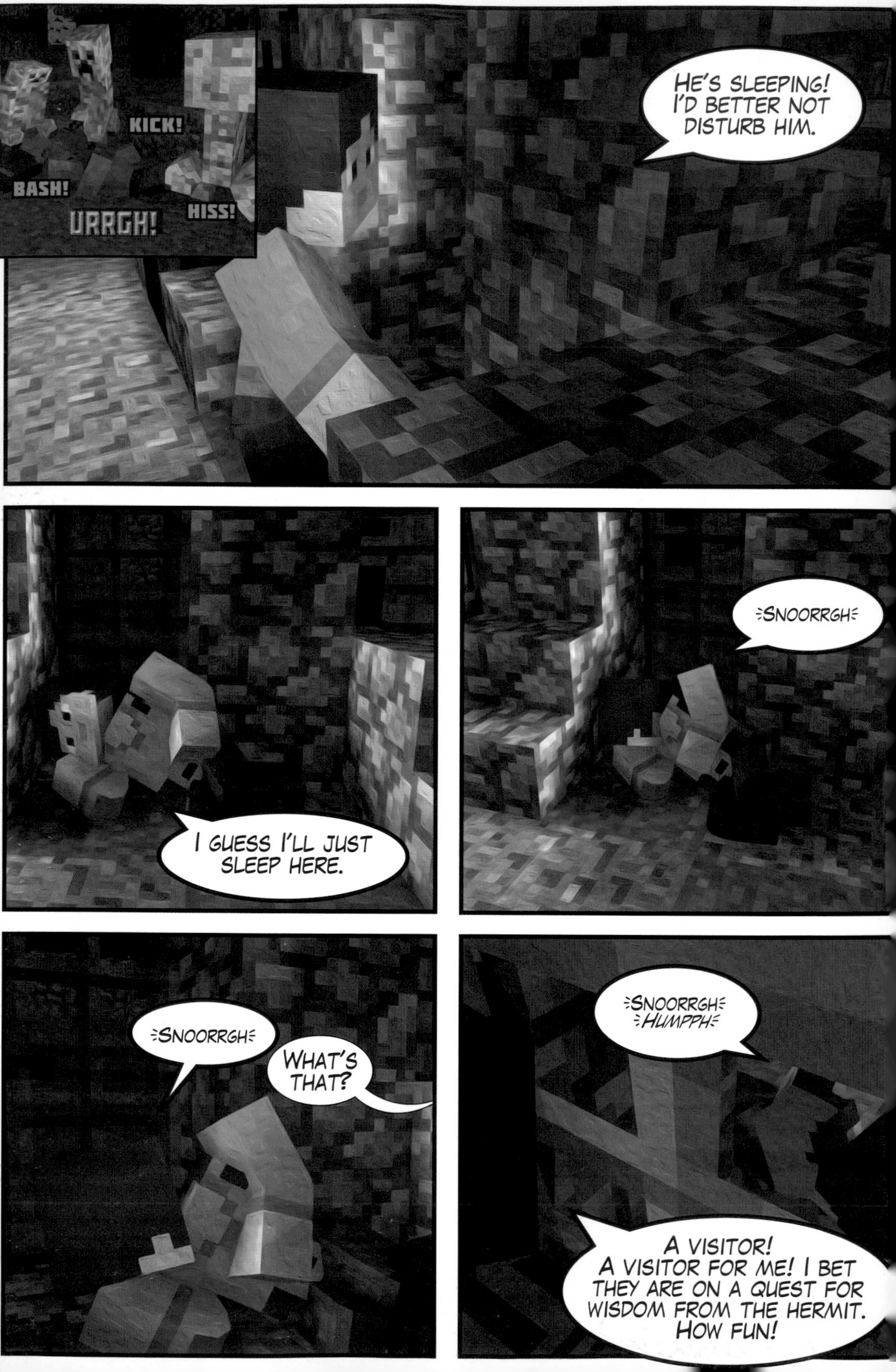
KICK!
BASH!
URRGH!
HISS!
HE'S SLEEPING! I'D BETTER NOT DISTURB HIM.
I GUESS I'LL JUST SLEEP HERE.
SNOORRGH
SNOORRGH
WHAT'S THAT?
SNOORRGH HUMPPH
A VISITOR! A VISITOR FOR ME! I BET THEY ARE ON A QUEST FOR WISDOM FROM THE HERMIT. HOW FUN!

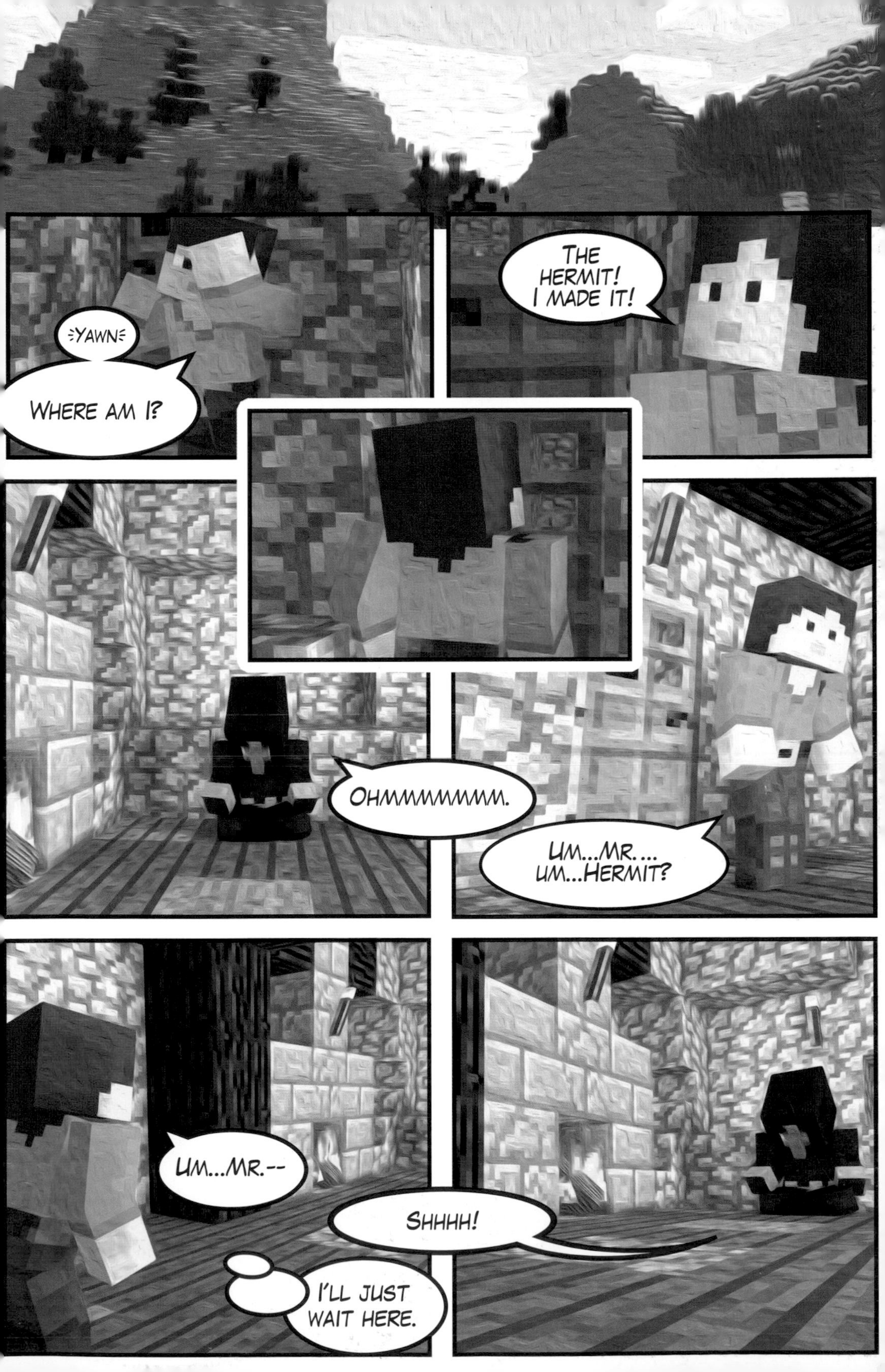

YAWN
WHERE AM I?
THE HERMIT! I MADE IT!
OHMMMMMMM.
UM...MR.... UM...HERMIT?
UM...MR.--
SHHHH!
I'LL JUST WAIT HERE.

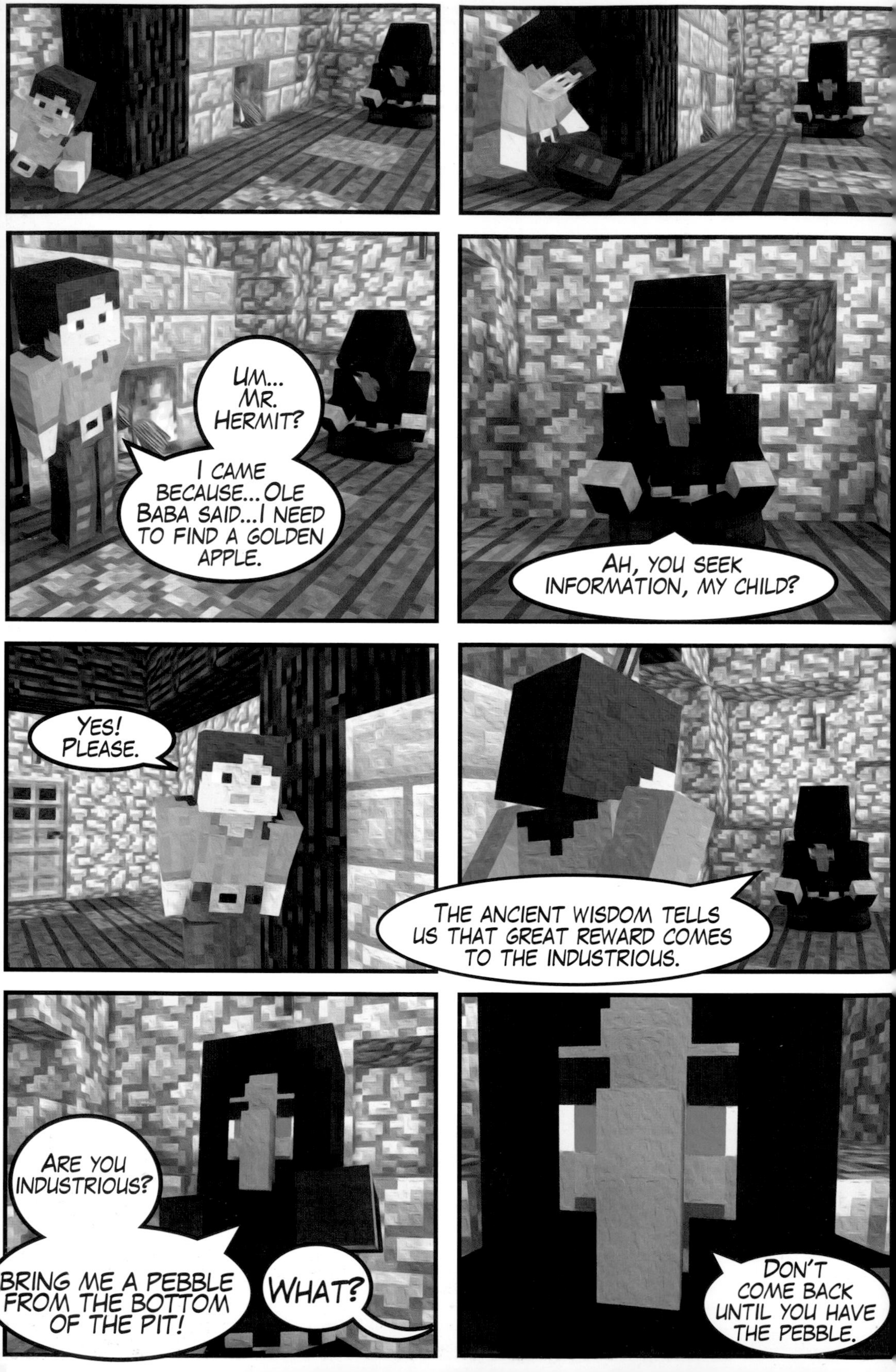
UM... MR. HERMIT?
I CAME BECAUSE...OLE BABA SAID...I NEED TO FIND A GOLDEN APPLE.
AH, YOU SEEK INFORMATION, MY CHILD?
YES! PLEASE.
THE ANCIENT WISDOM TELLS US THAT GREAT REWARD COMES TO THE INDUSTRIOUS.
ARE YOU INDUSTRIOUS?
BRING ME A PEBBLE FROM THE BOTTOM OF THE PIT!
WHAT?
DON'T COME BACK UNTIL YOU HAVE THE PEBBLE.

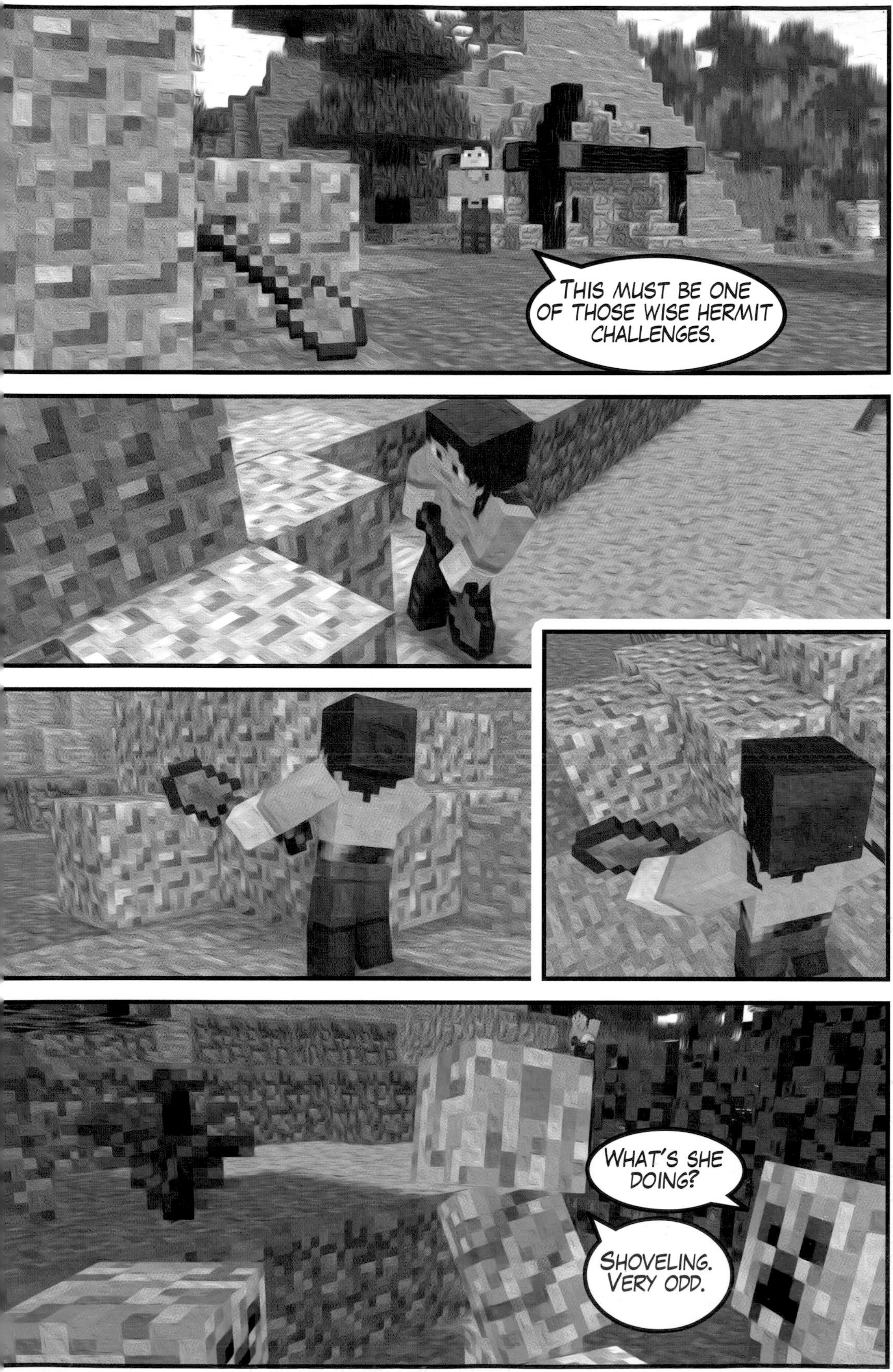
THIS MUST BE ONE OF THOSE WISE HERMIT CHALLENGES.
WHAT'S SHE DOING?
SHOVELING. VERY ODD.

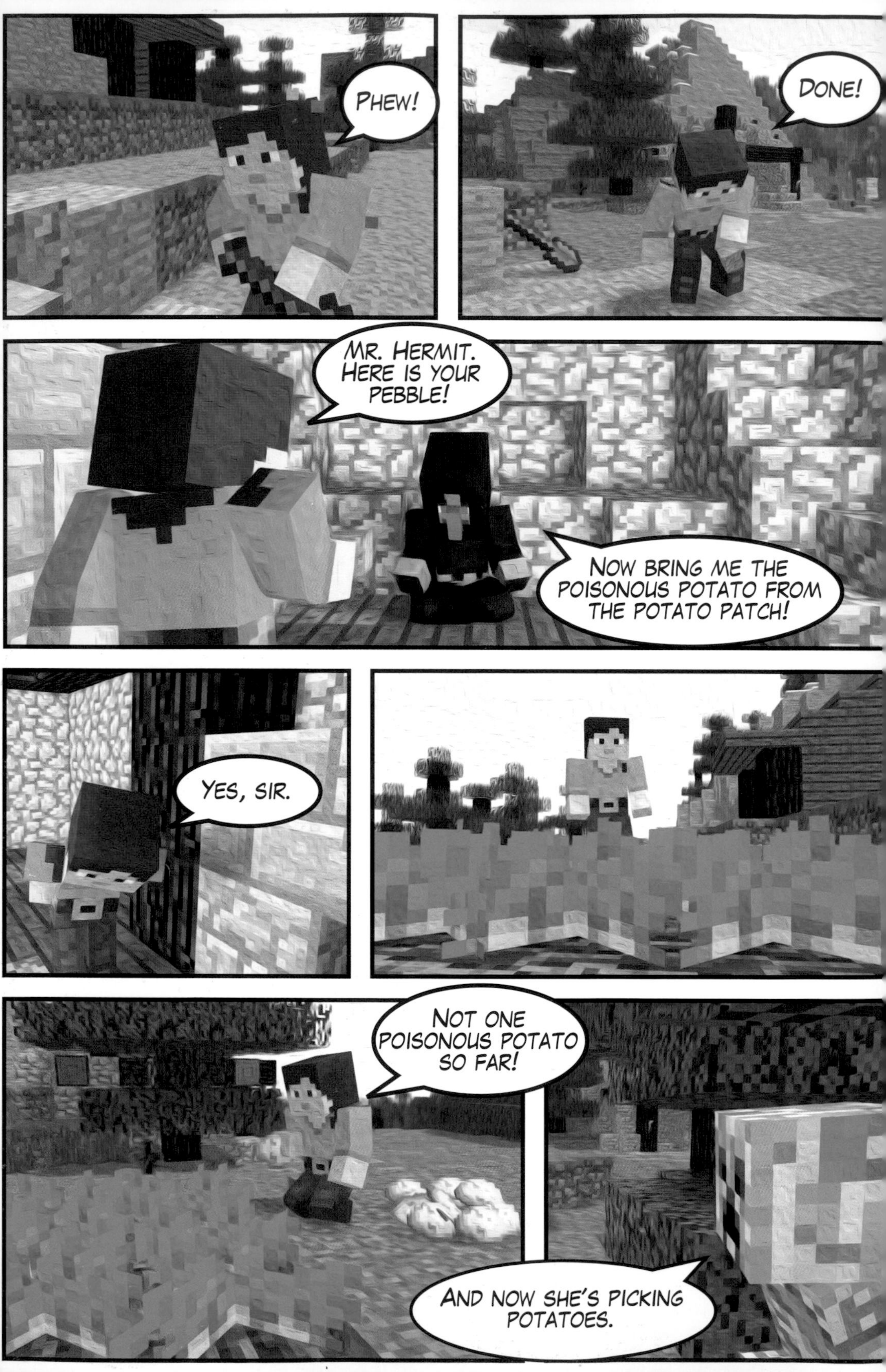
PHEW!
DONE!
MR. HERMIT. HERE IS YOUR PEBBLE!
NOW BRING ME THE POISONOUS POTATO FROM THE POTATO PATCH!
YES, SIR.
NOT ONE POISONOUS POTATO SO FAR!
AND NOW SHE'S PICKING POTATOES.

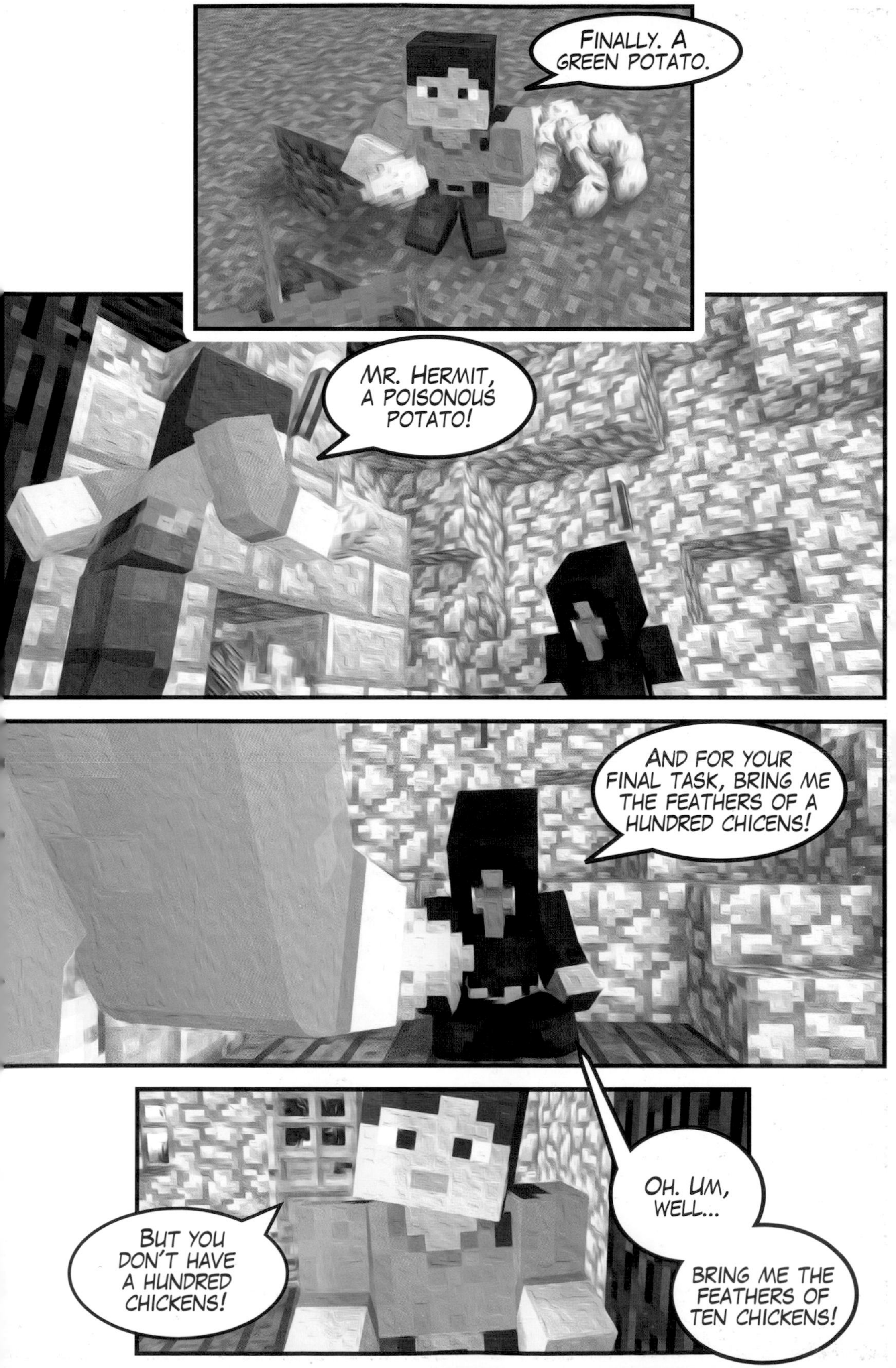
FINALLY. A GREEN POTATO.
MR. HERMIT, A POISONOUS POTATO!
AND FOR YOUR FINAL TASK, BRING ME THE FEATHERS OF A HUNDRED CHICENS!
BUT YOU DON'T HAVE A HUNDRED CHICKENS!
OH. UM, WELL...
BRING ME THE FEATHERS OF TEN CHICKENS!

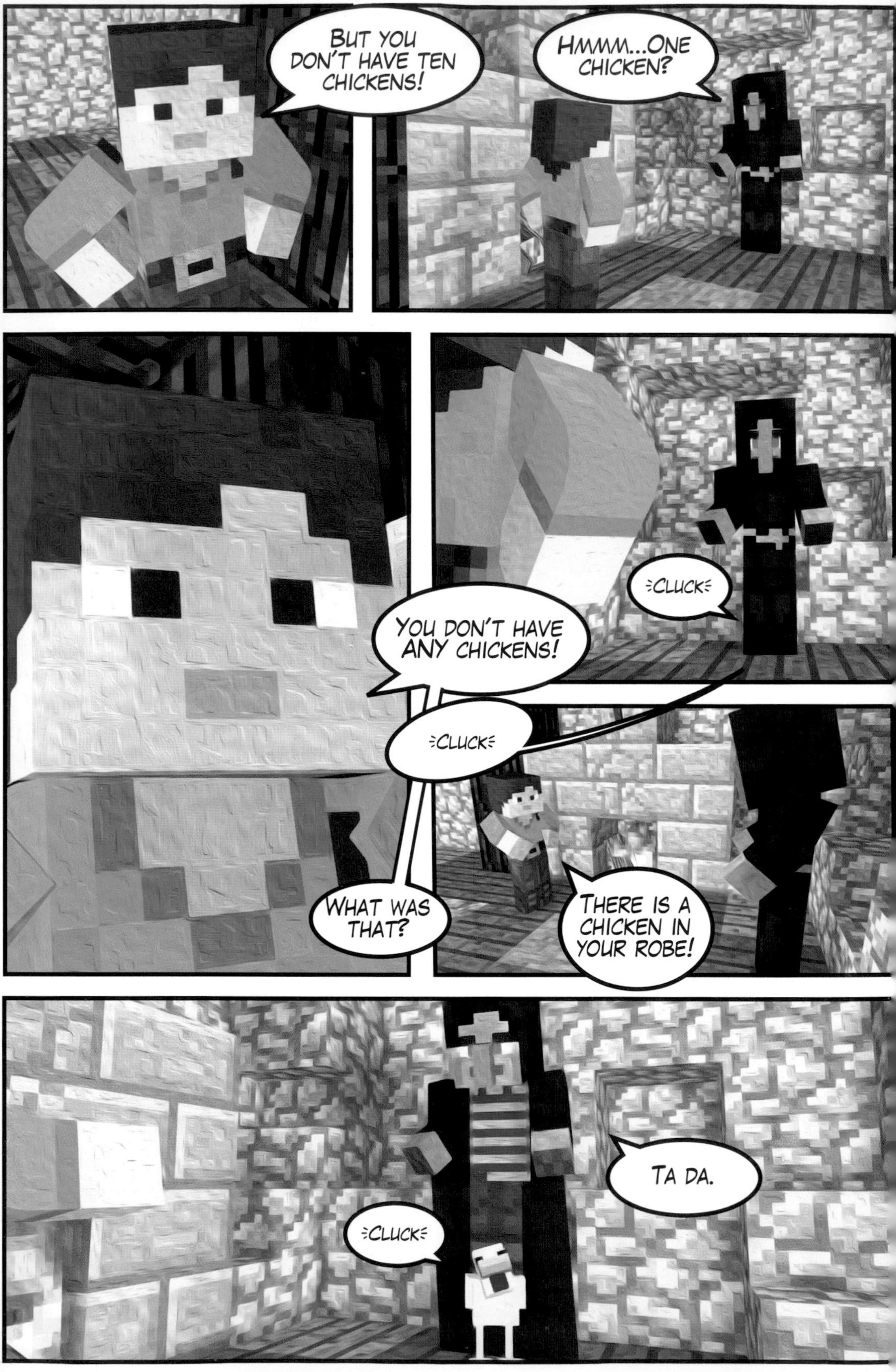
BUT YOU DON'T HAVE TEN CHICKENS!
HMMM...ONE CHICKEN?
CLUCK
YOU DON'T HAVE ANY CHICKENS!
CLUCK
WHAT WAS THAT?
THERE IS A CHICKEN IN YOUR ROBE!
TA DA.
CLUCK

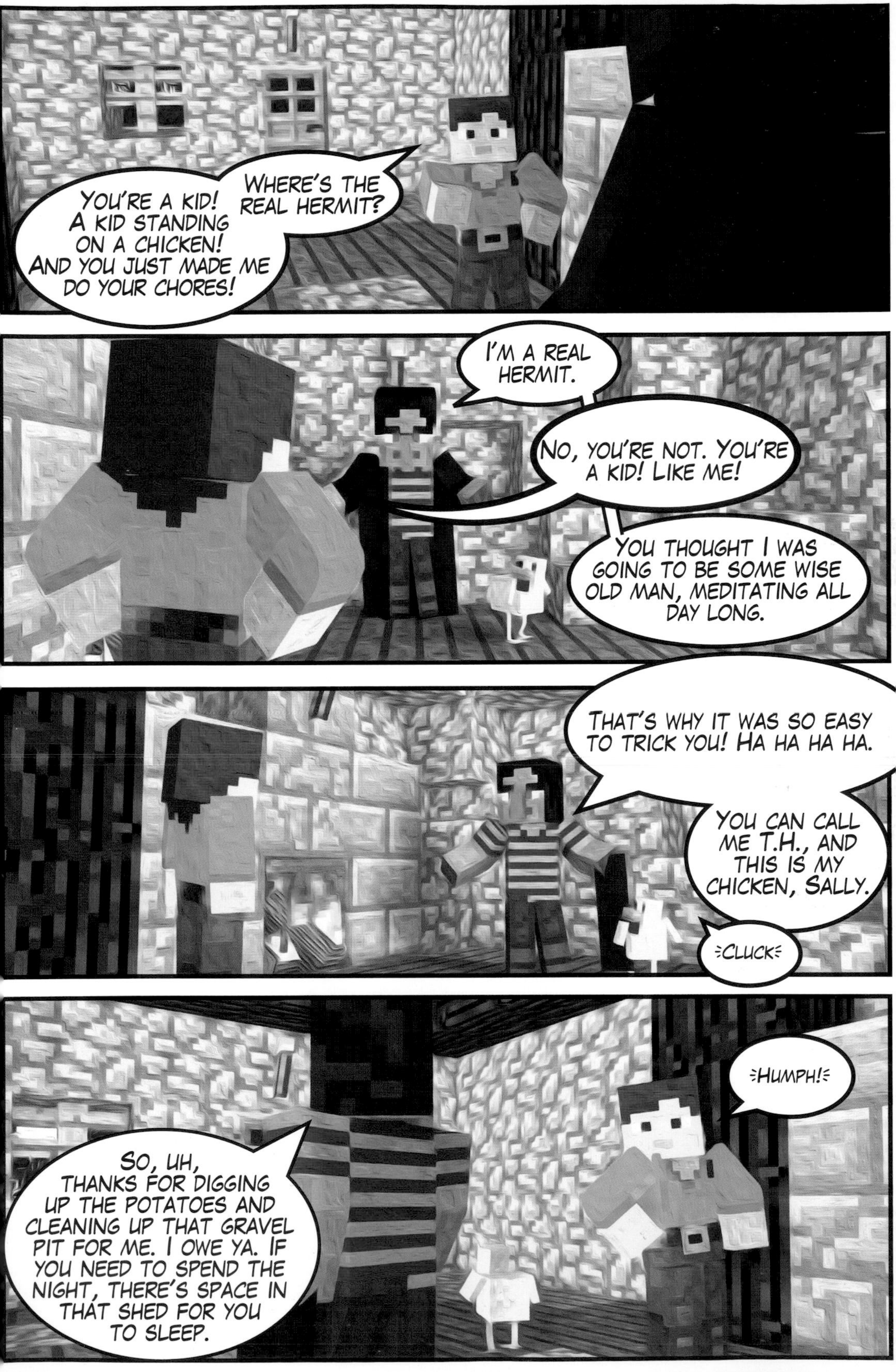

Where's the real hermit?
You're a kid! A kid standing on a chicken! And you just made me do your chores!
I'm a real hermit.
No, you're not. You're a kid! Like me!
You thought I was going to be some wise old man, meditating all day long.
That's why it was so easy to trick you! Ha ha ha ha.
You can call me T.H., and this is my chicken, Sally.
Cluck
Humph!
So, uh, thanks for digging up the potatoes and cleaning up that gravel pit for me. I owe ya. If you need to spend the night, there's space in that shed for you to sleep.

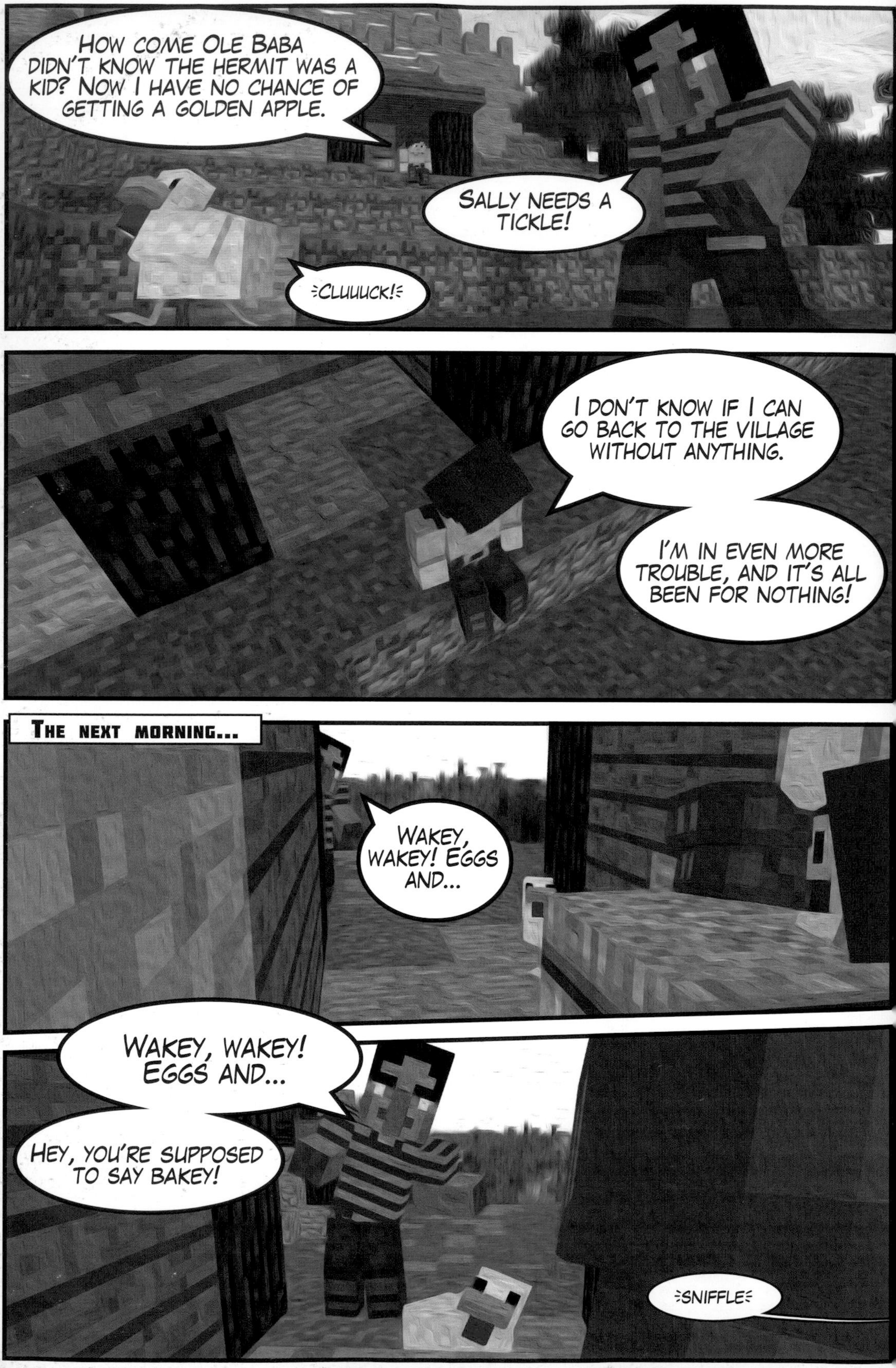
HOW COME OLE BABA DIDN'T KNOW THE HERMIT WAS A KID? NOW I HAVE NO CHANCE OF GETTING A GOLDEN APPLE.
SALLY NEEDS A TICKLE!
CLUUUCK!
I DON'T KNOW IF I CAN GO BACK TO THE VILLAGE WITHOUT ANYTHING.
I'M IN EVEN MORE TROUBLE, AND IT'S ALL BEEN FOR NOTHING!
THE NEXT MORNING...
WAKEY, WAKEY! EGGS AND...
WAKEY, WAKEY! EGGS AND...
HEY, YOU'RE SUPPOSED TO SAY BAKEY!
SNIFFLE

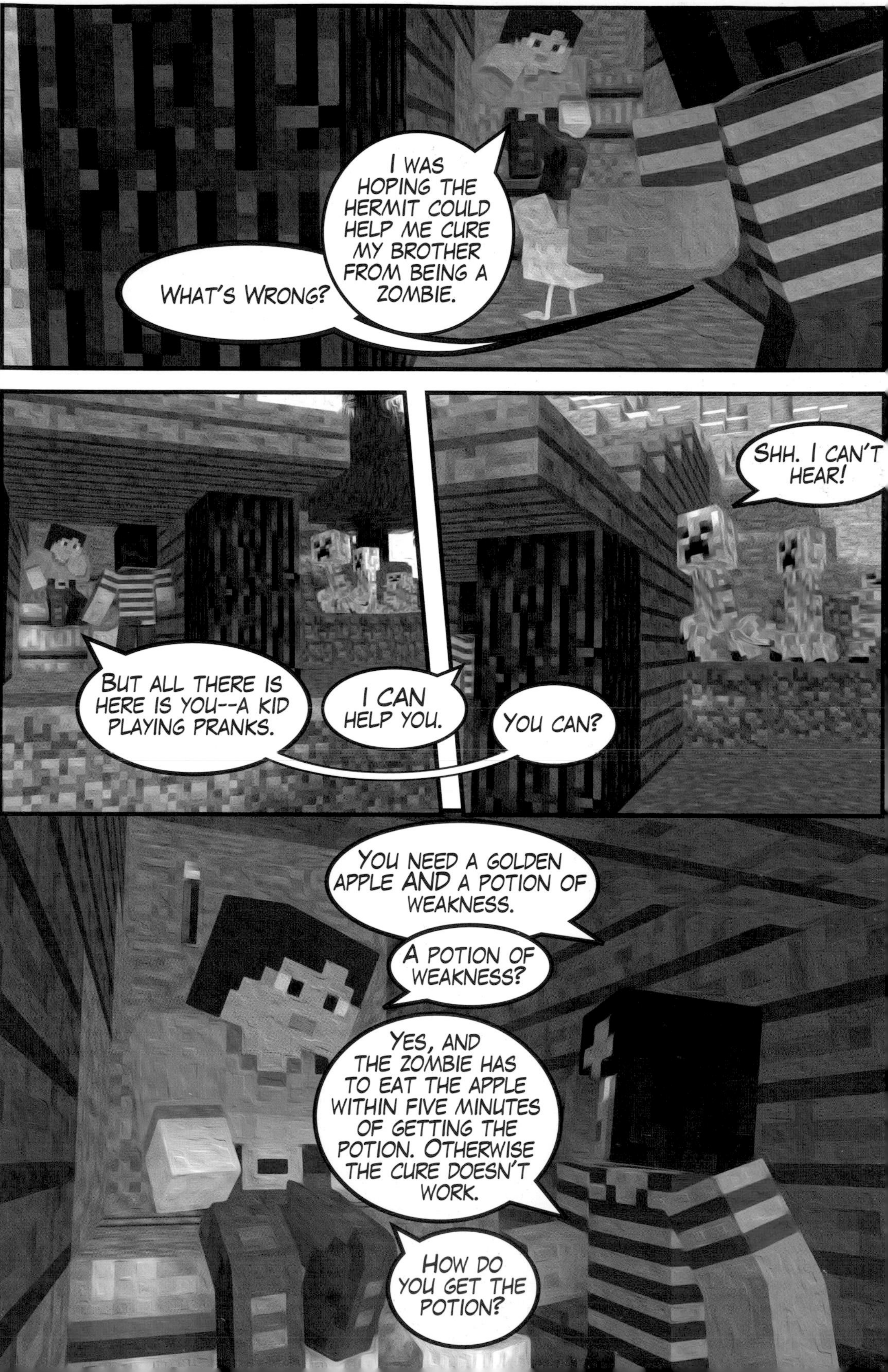
WHAT'S WRONG?
I WAS HOPING THE HERMIT COULD HELP ME CURE MY BROTHER FROM BEING A ZOMBIE.
SHH. I CAN'T HEAR!
BUT ALL THERE IS HERE IS YOU--A KID PLAYING PRANKS.
I CAN HELP YOU.
YOU CAN?
YOU NEED A GOLDEN APPLE AND A POTION OF WEAKNESS.
A POTION OF WEAKNESS?
YES, AND THE ZOMBIE HAS TO EAT THE APPLE WITHIN FIVE MINUTES OF GETTING THE POTION. OTHERWISE THE CURE DOESN'T WORK.
HOW DO YOU GET THE POTION?

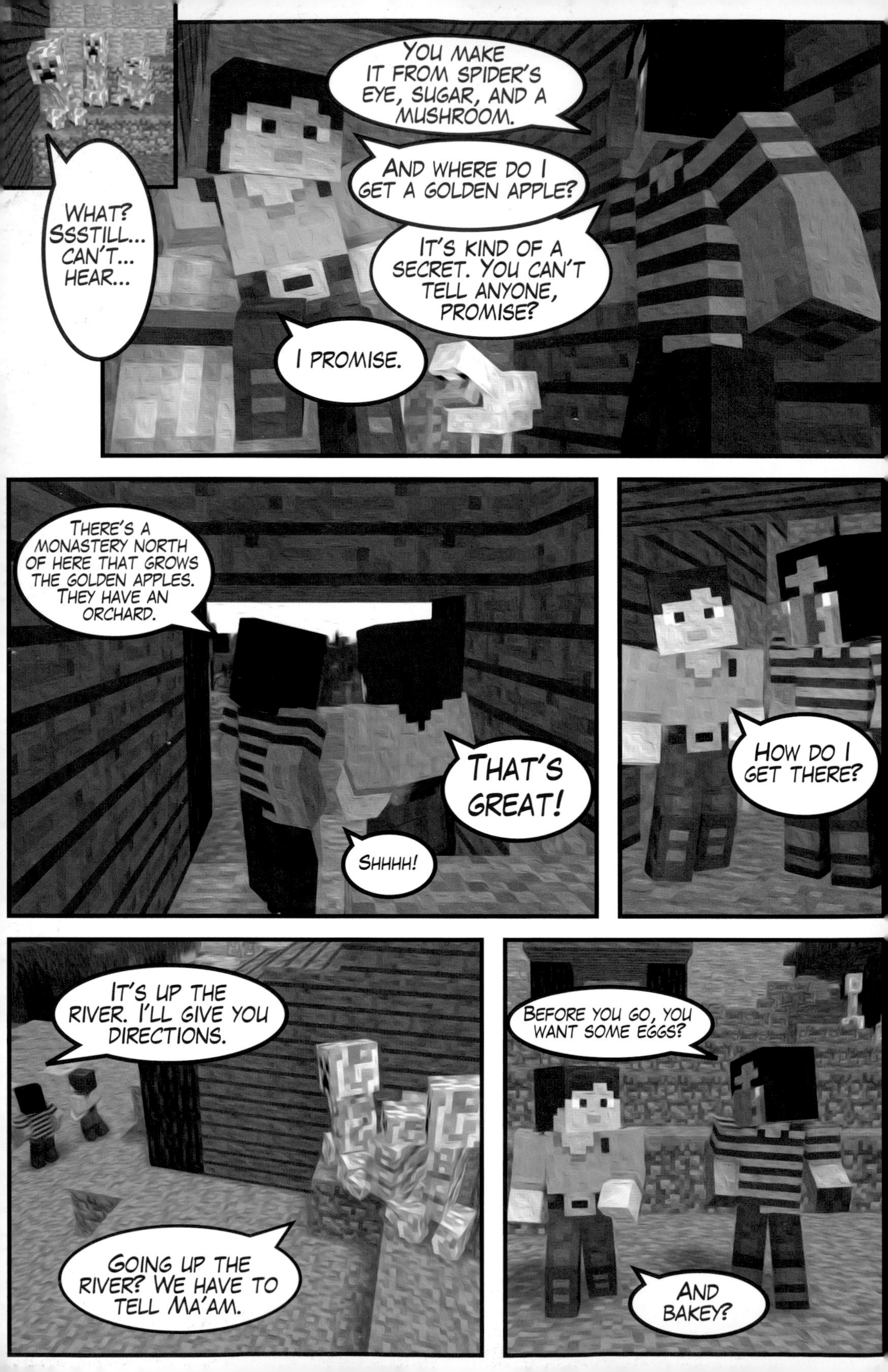
YOU MAKE IT FROM SPIDER'S EYE, SUGAR, AND A MUSHROOM.
AND WHERE DO I GET A GOLDEN APPLE?
IT'S KIND OF A SECRET. YOU CAN'T TELL ANYONE, PROMISE?
I PROMISE.
WHAT? SSSTILL... CAN'T... HEAR...
THERE'S A MONASTERY NORTH OF HERE THAT GROWS THE GOLDEN APPLES. THEY HAVE AN ORCHARD.
THAT'S GREAT!
SHHHH!
HOW DO I GET THERE?
IT'S UP THE RIVER. I'LL GIVE YOU DIRECTIONS.
GOING UP THE RIVER? WE HAVE TO TELL MA'AM.
BEFORE YOU GO, YOU WANT SOME EGGS?
AND BAKEY?

CHAPTER 5
A WOLF

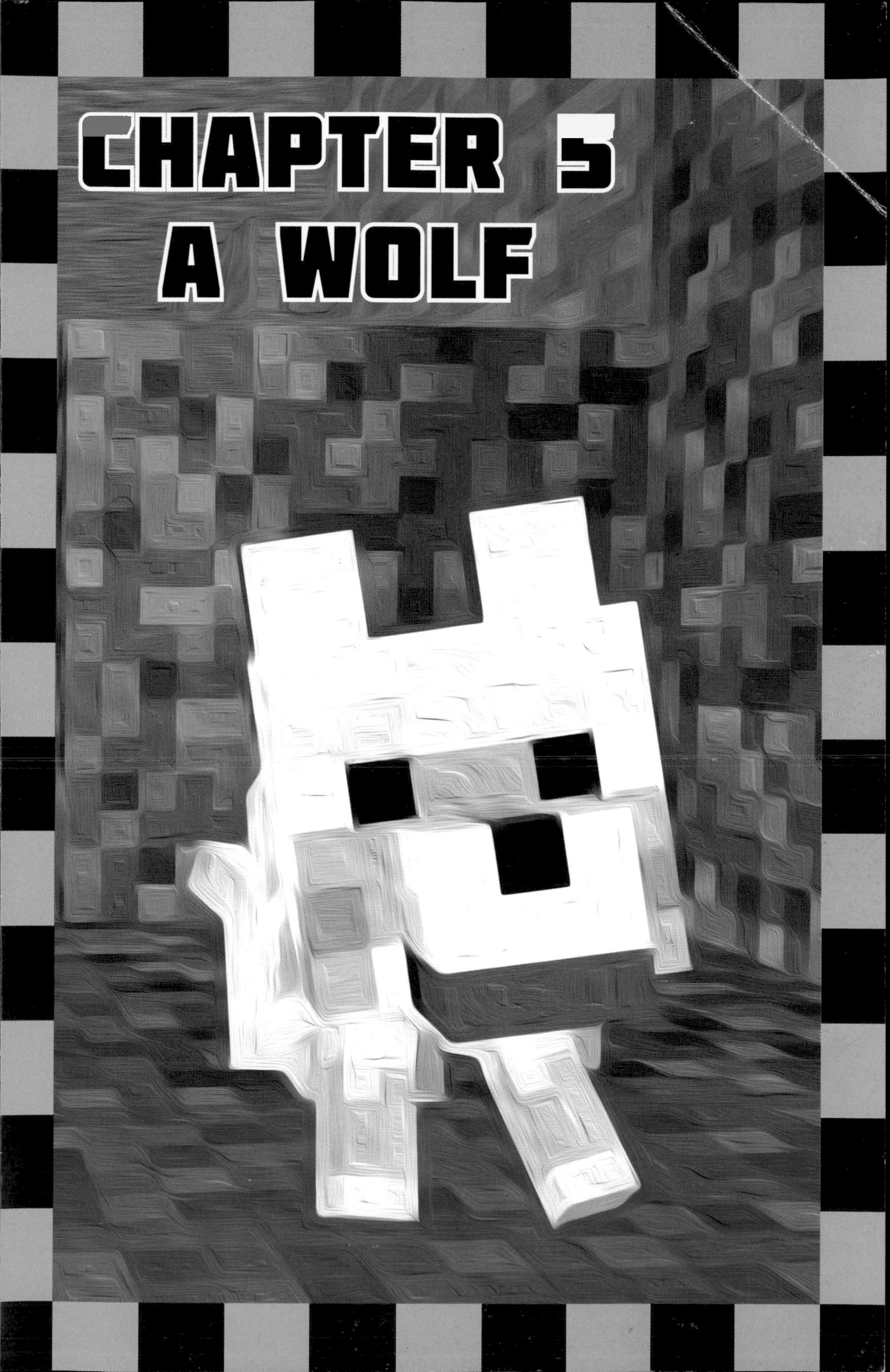

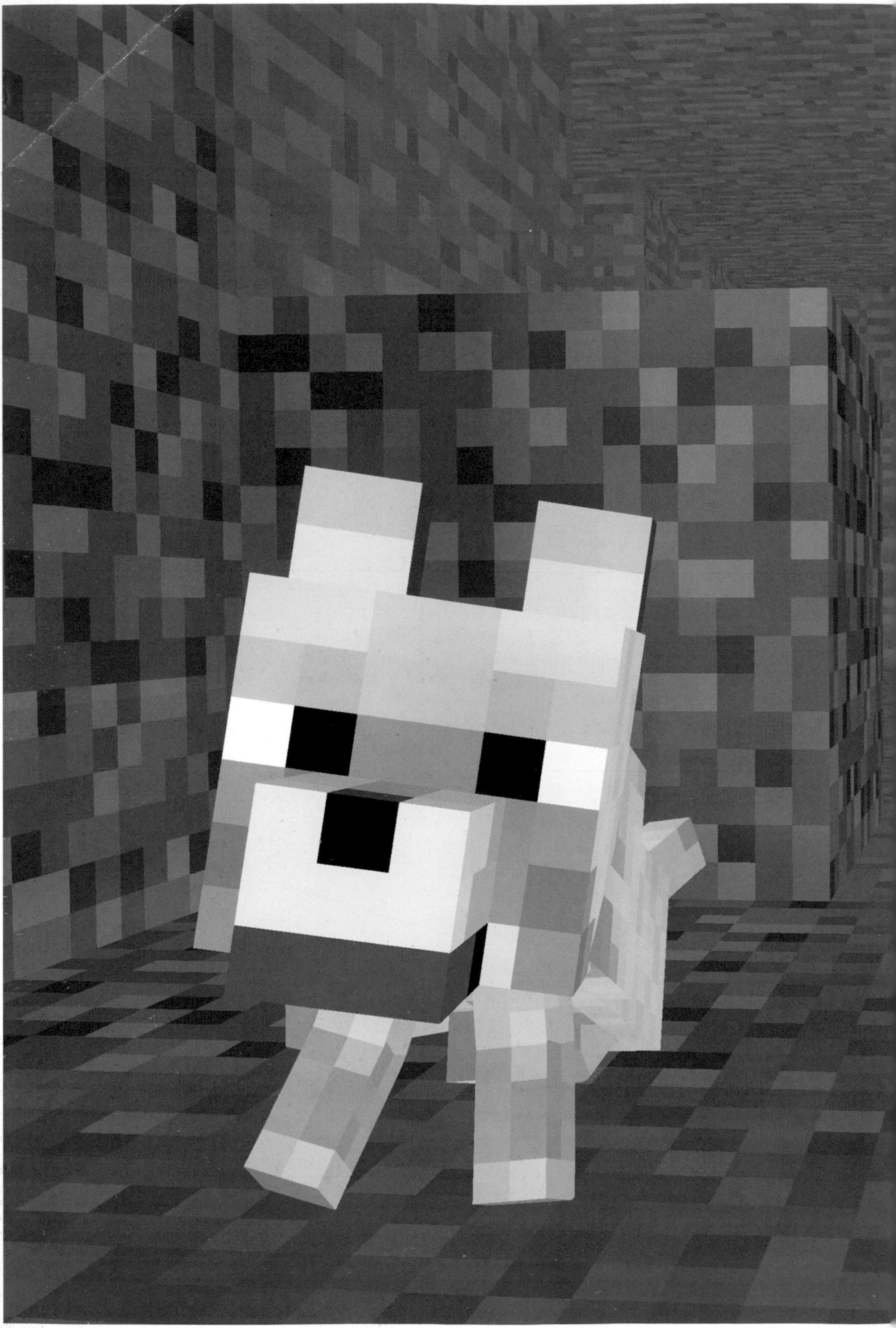

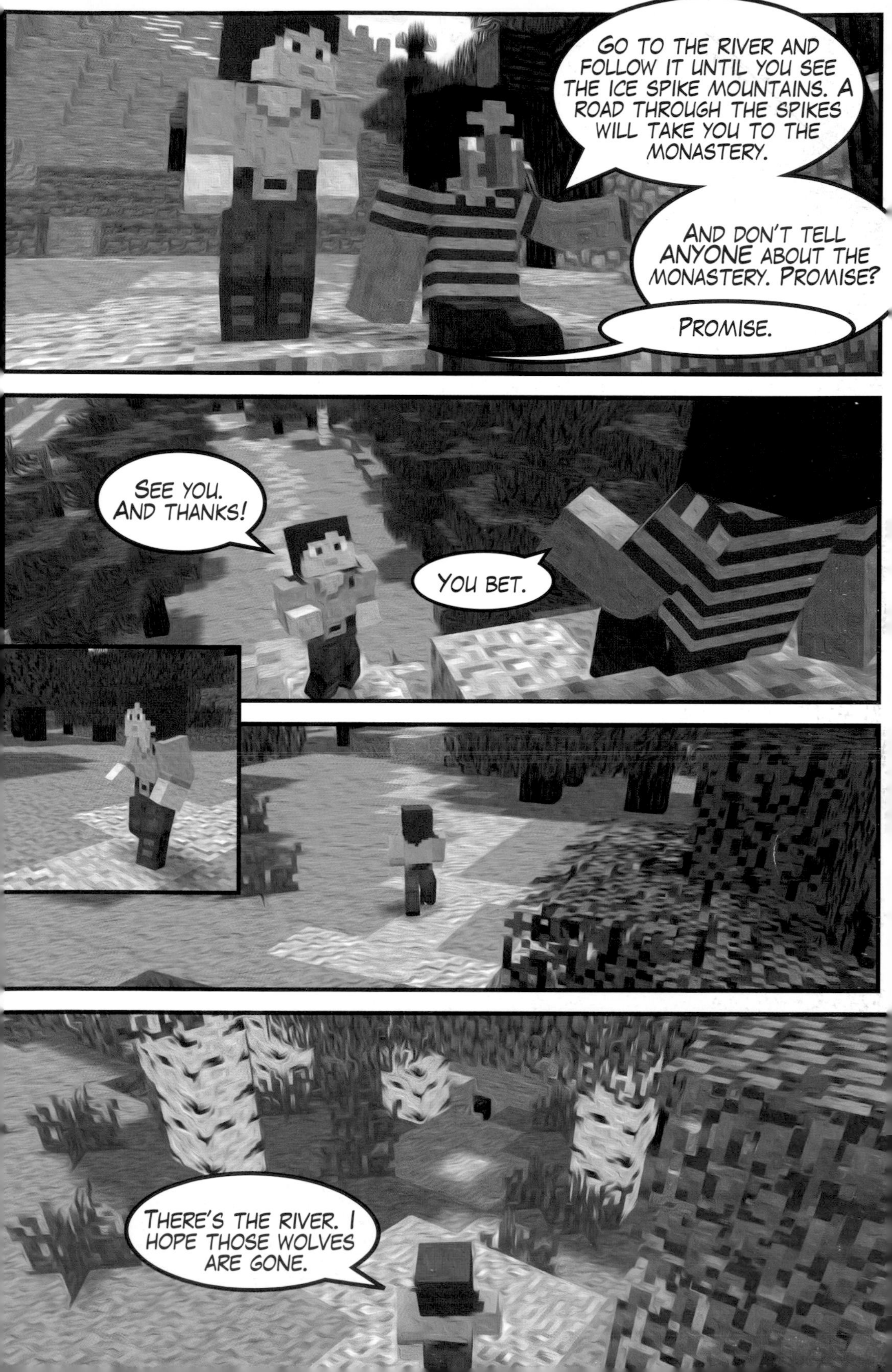
GO TO THE RIVER AND FOLLOW IT UNTIL YOU SEE THE ICE SPIKE MOUNTAINS. A ROAD THROUGH THE SPIKES WILL TAKE YOU TO THE MONASTERY.
AND DON'T TELL ANYONE ABOUT THE MONASTERY. PROMISE?
PROMISE.
SEE YOU. AND THANKS!
YOU BET.
THERE'S THE RIVER. I HOPE THOSE WOLVES ARE GONE.

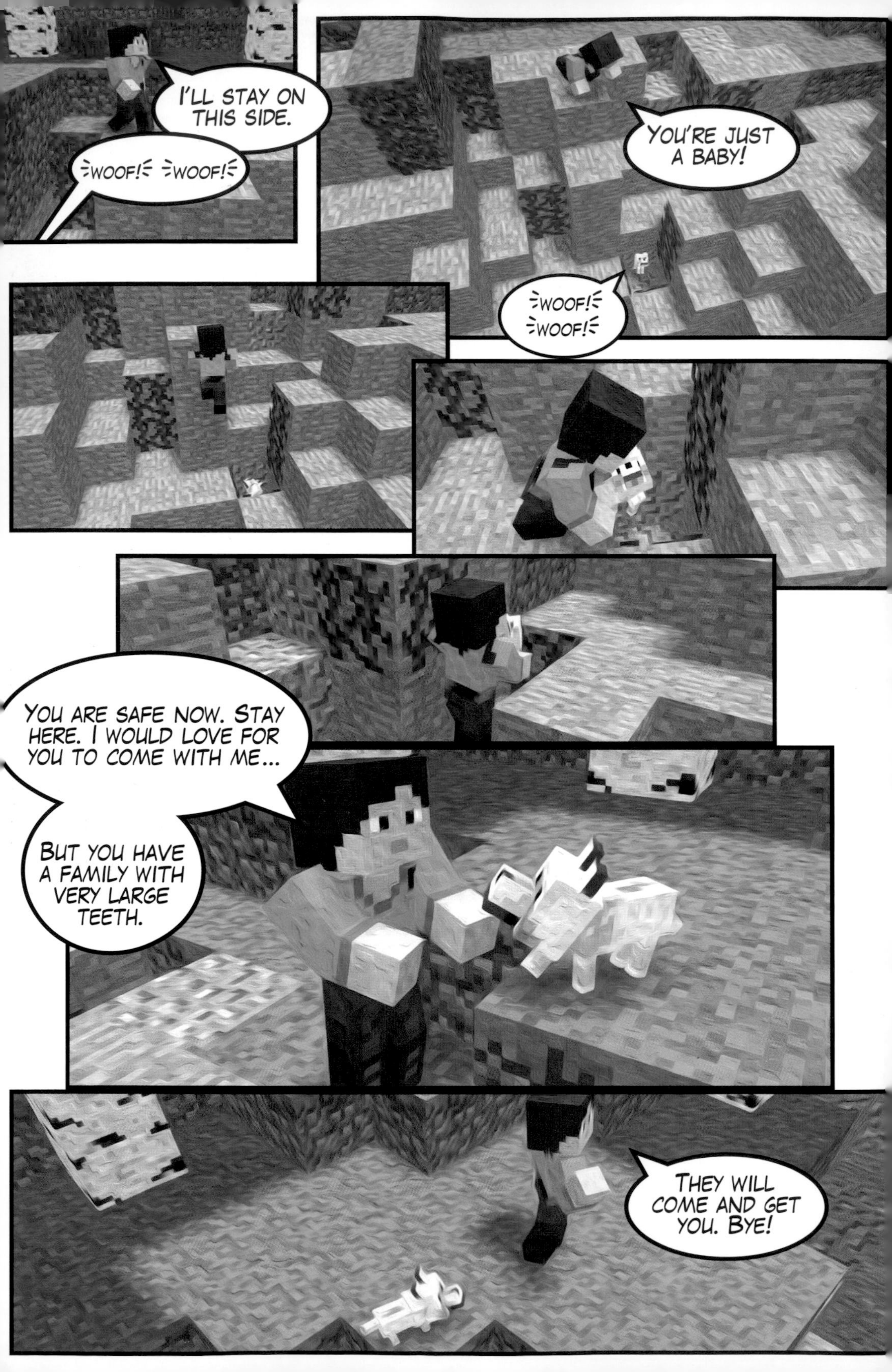
I'LL STAY ON THIS SIDE.
WOOF! WOOF!
YOU'RE JUST A BABY!
WOOF! WOOF!
YOU ARE SAFE NOW. STAY HERE. I WOULD LOVE FOR YOU TO COME WITH ME...
BUT YOU HAVE A FAMILY WITH VERY LARGE TEETH.
THEY WILL COME AND GET YOU. BYE!

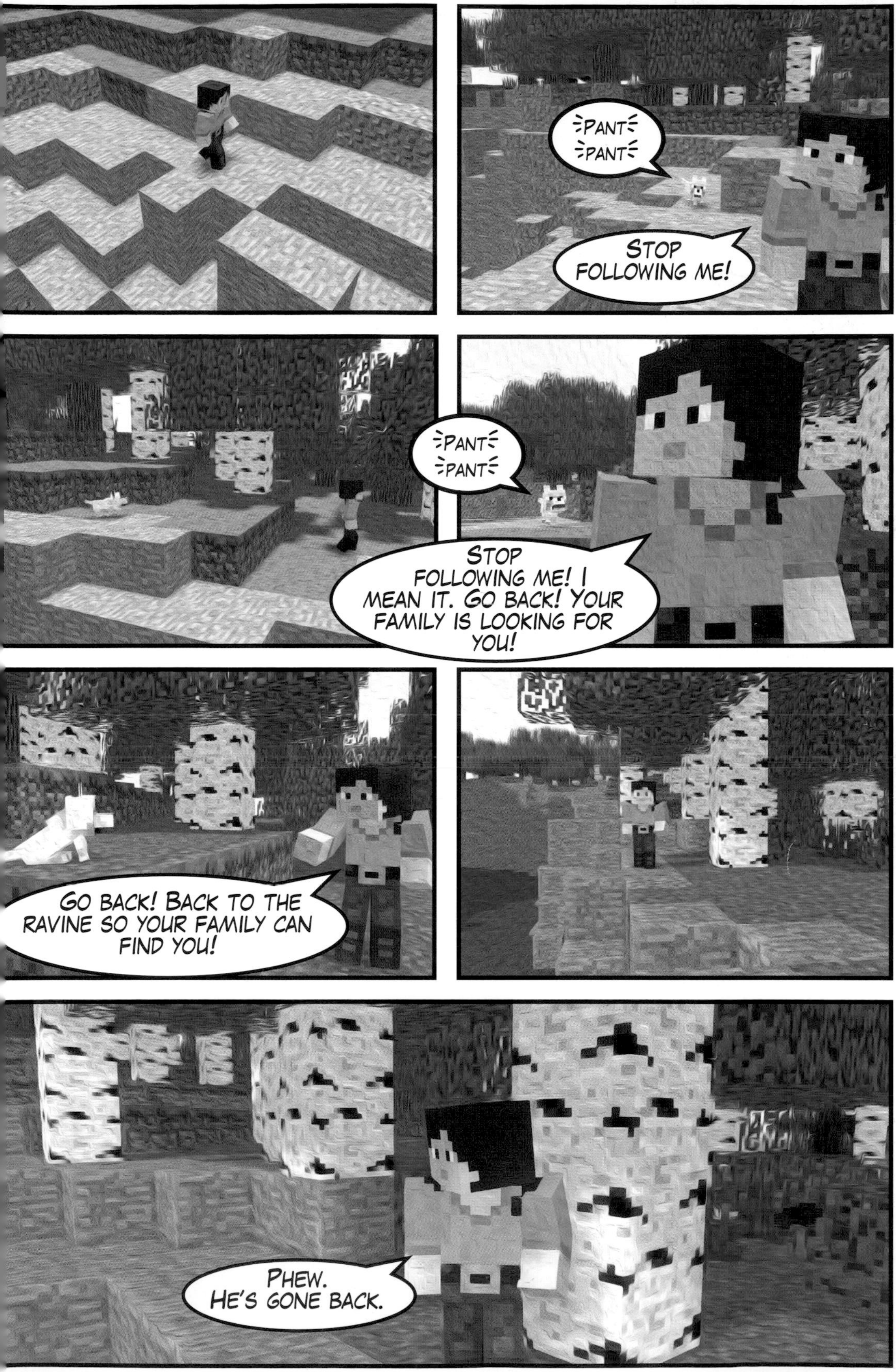
PANT
PANT
STOP FOLLOWING ME!
PANT
PANT
STOP FOLLOWING ME! I MEAN IT. GO BACK! YOUR FAMILY IS LOOKING FOR YOU!
GO BACK! BACK TO THE RAVINE SO YOUR FAMILY CAN FIND YOU!
PHEW. HE'S GONE BACK.

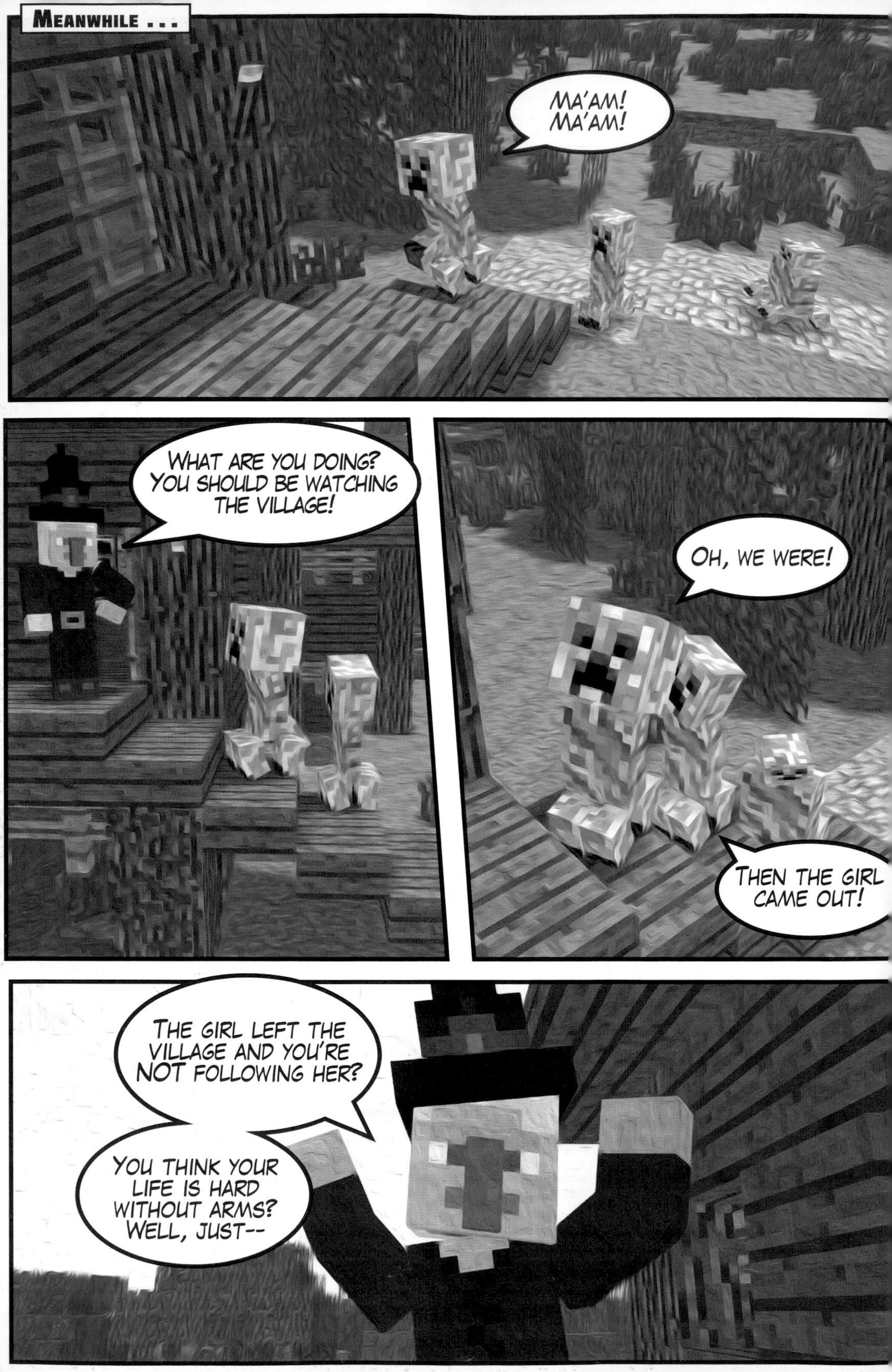
MEANWHILE . . .
MA'AM! MA'AM!
WHAT ARE YOU DOING? YOU SHOULD BE WATCHING THE VILLAGE!
OH, WE WERE!
THEN THE GIRL CAME OUT!
THE GIRL LEFT THE VILLAGE AND YOU'RE NOT FOLLOWING HER?
YOU THINK YOUR LIFE IS HARD WITHOUT ARMS? WELL, JUST--

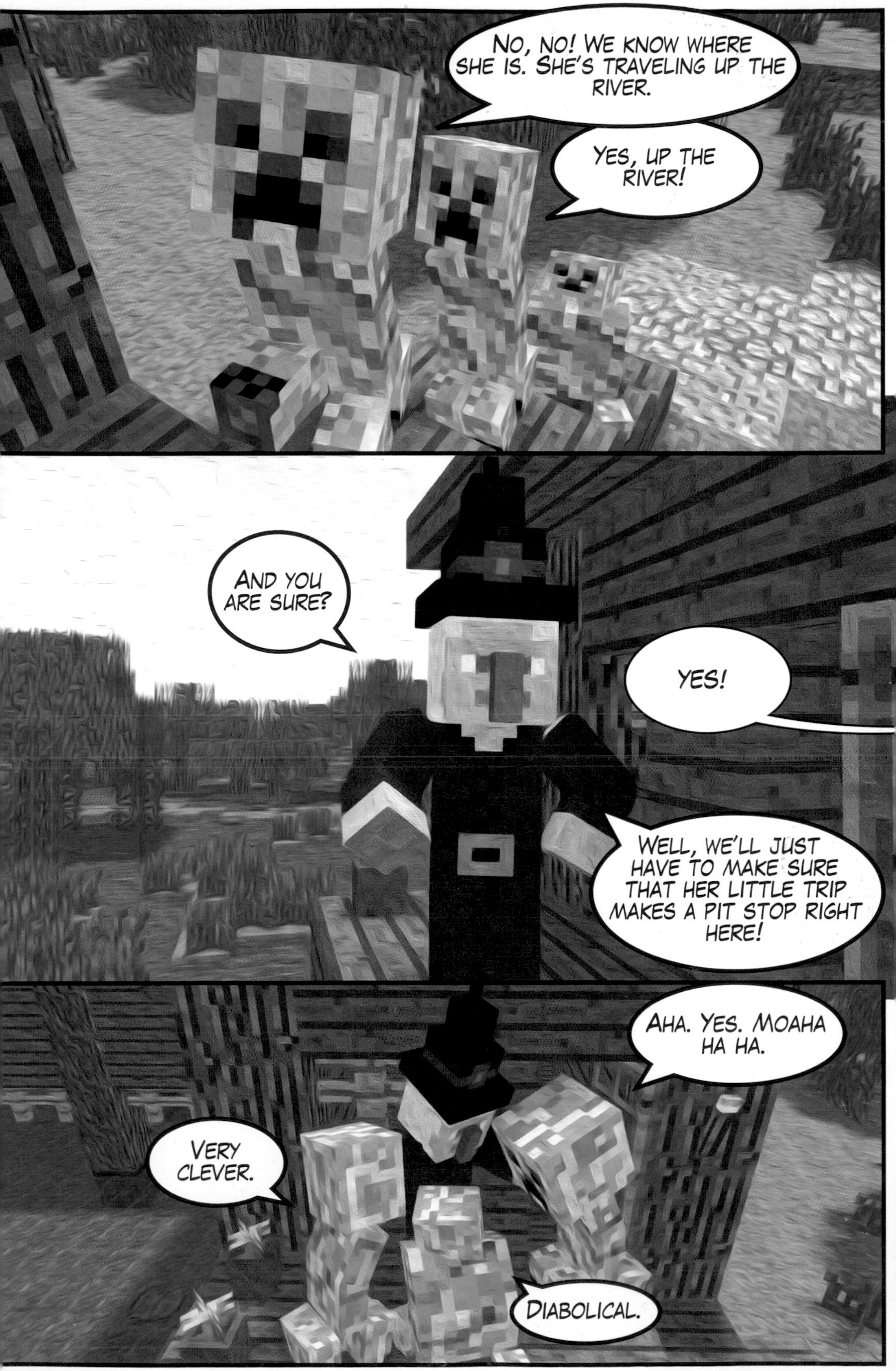
No, no! We know where she is. She's traveling up the river.
Yes, up the river!
And you are sure?
Yes!
Well, we'll just have to make sure that her little trip makes a pit stop right here!
Aha. Yes. Moaha ha ha.
Very clever.
Diabolical.

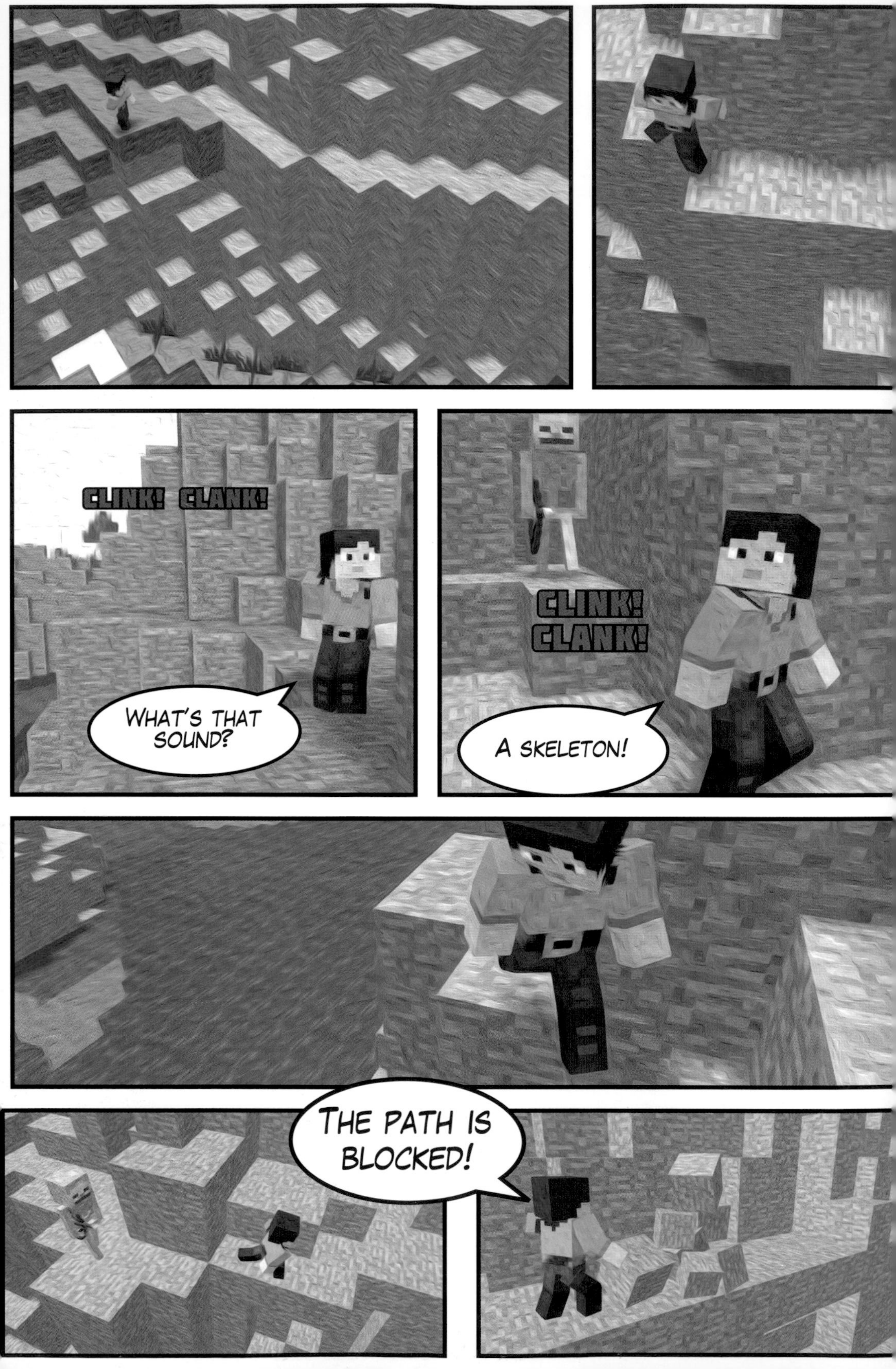
CLINK! CLANK!
WHAT'S THAT SOUND?
CLINK! CLANK!
A SKELETON!
THE PATH IS BLOCKED!

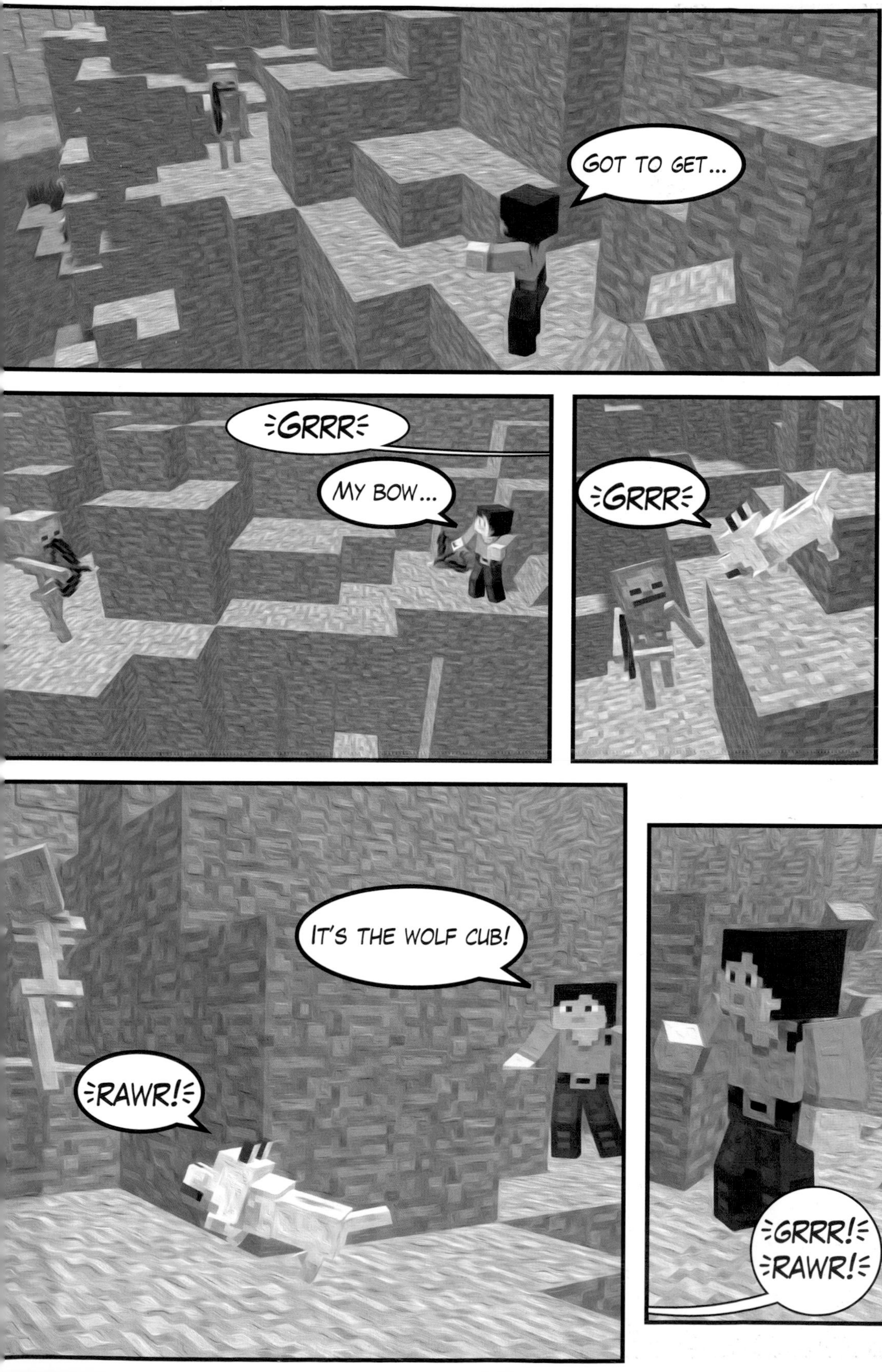
GOT TO GET...
GRRR
MY BOW...
GRRR
IT'S THE WOLF CUB!
RAWR!
GRRR!
RAWR!

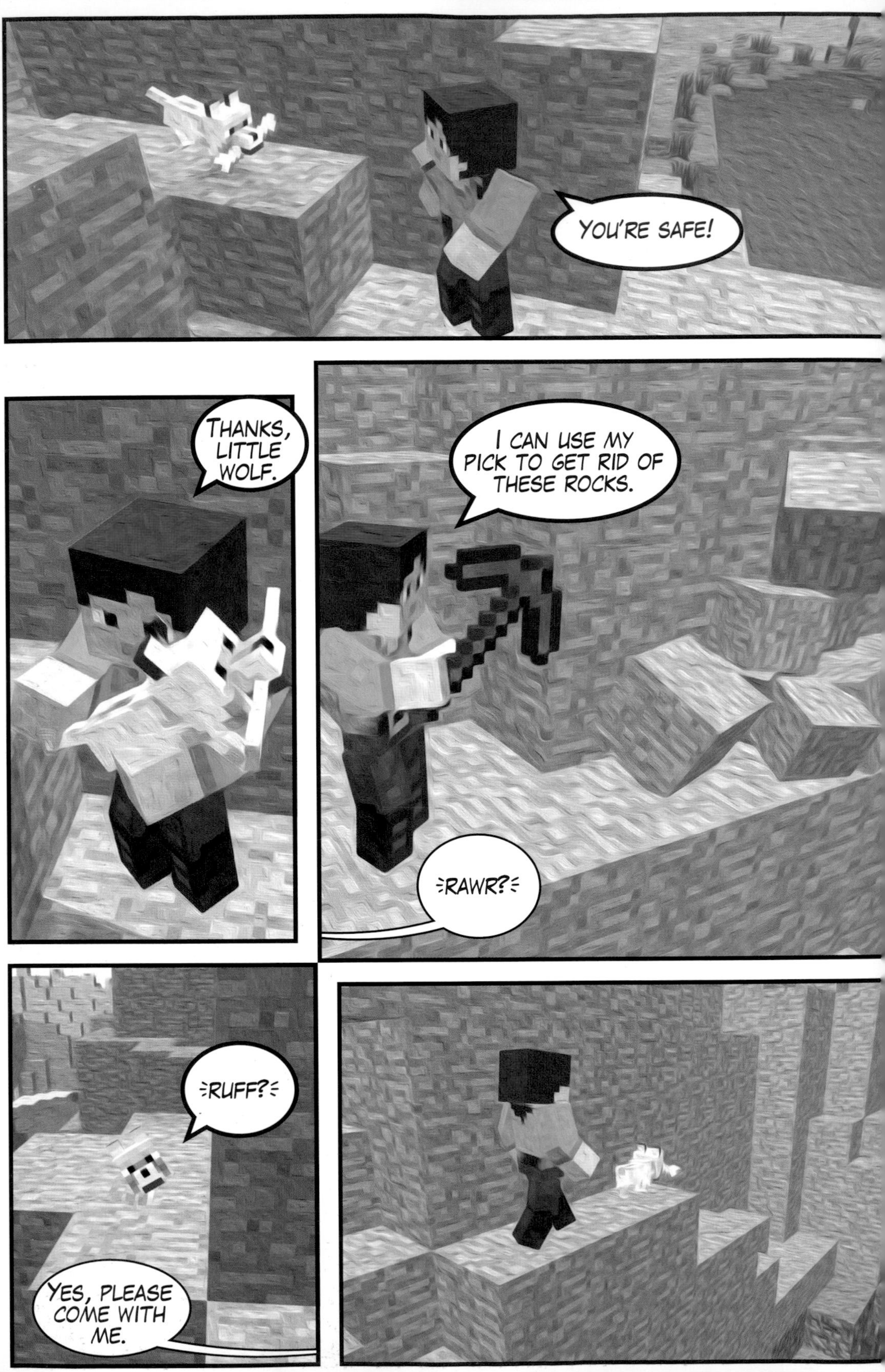
YOU'RE SAFE!
THANKS, LITTLE WOLF.
I CAN USE MY PICK TO GET RID OF THESE ROCKS.
RAWR?
RUFF?
YES, PLEASE COME WITH ME.

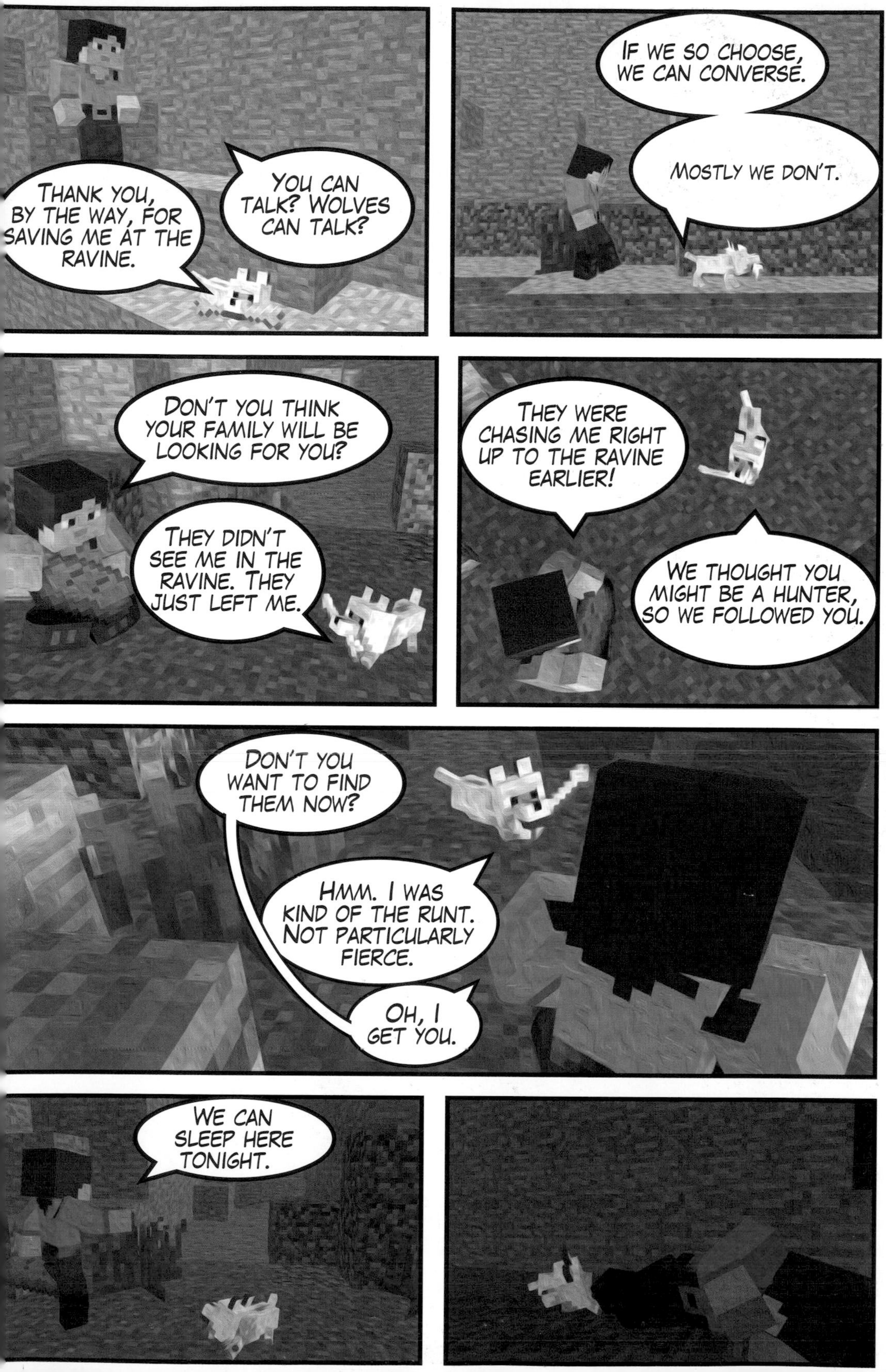

THANK YOU, BY THE WAY, FOR SAVING ME AT THE RAVINE.
YOU CAN TALK? WOLVES CAN TALK?
IF WE SO CHOOSE, WE CAN CONVERSE.
MOSTLY WE DON'T.
DON'T YOU THINK YOUR FAMILY WILL BE LOOKING FOR YOU?
THEY DIDN'T SEE ME IN THE RAVINE. THEY JUST LEFT ME.
THEY WERE CHASING ME RIGHT UP TO THE RAVINE EARLIER!
WE THOUGHT YOU MIGHT BE A HUNTER, SO WE FOLLOWED YOU.
DON'T YOU WANT TO FIND THEM NOW?
HMM. I WAS KIND OF THE RUNT. NOT PARTICULARLY FIERCE.
OH, I GET YOU.
WE CAN SLEEP HERE TONIGHT.

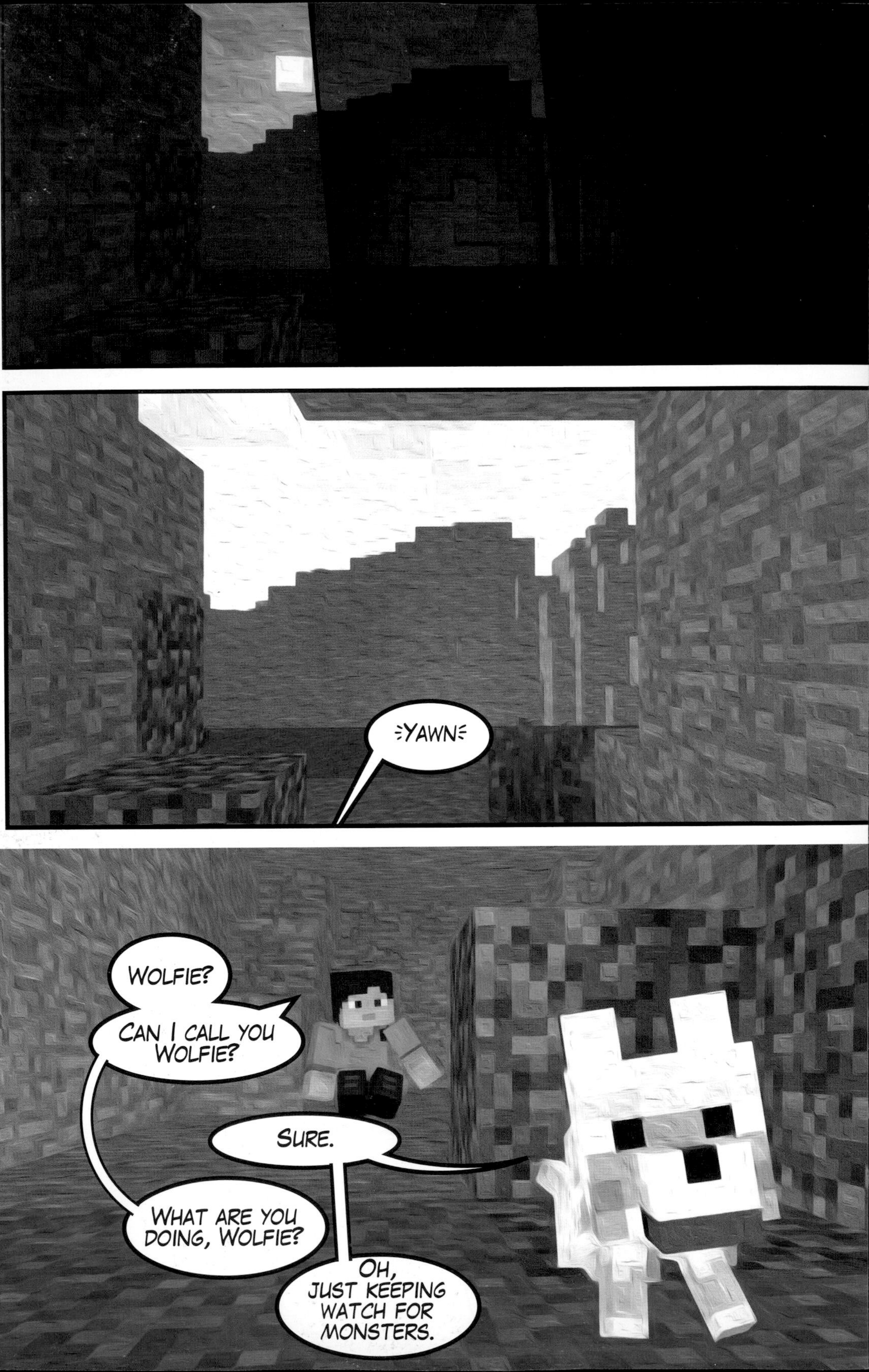
YAWN
WOLFIE?
CAN I CALL YOU WOLFIE?
SURE.
WHAT ARE YOU DOING, WOLFIE?
OH, JUST KEEPING WATCH FOR MONSTERS.

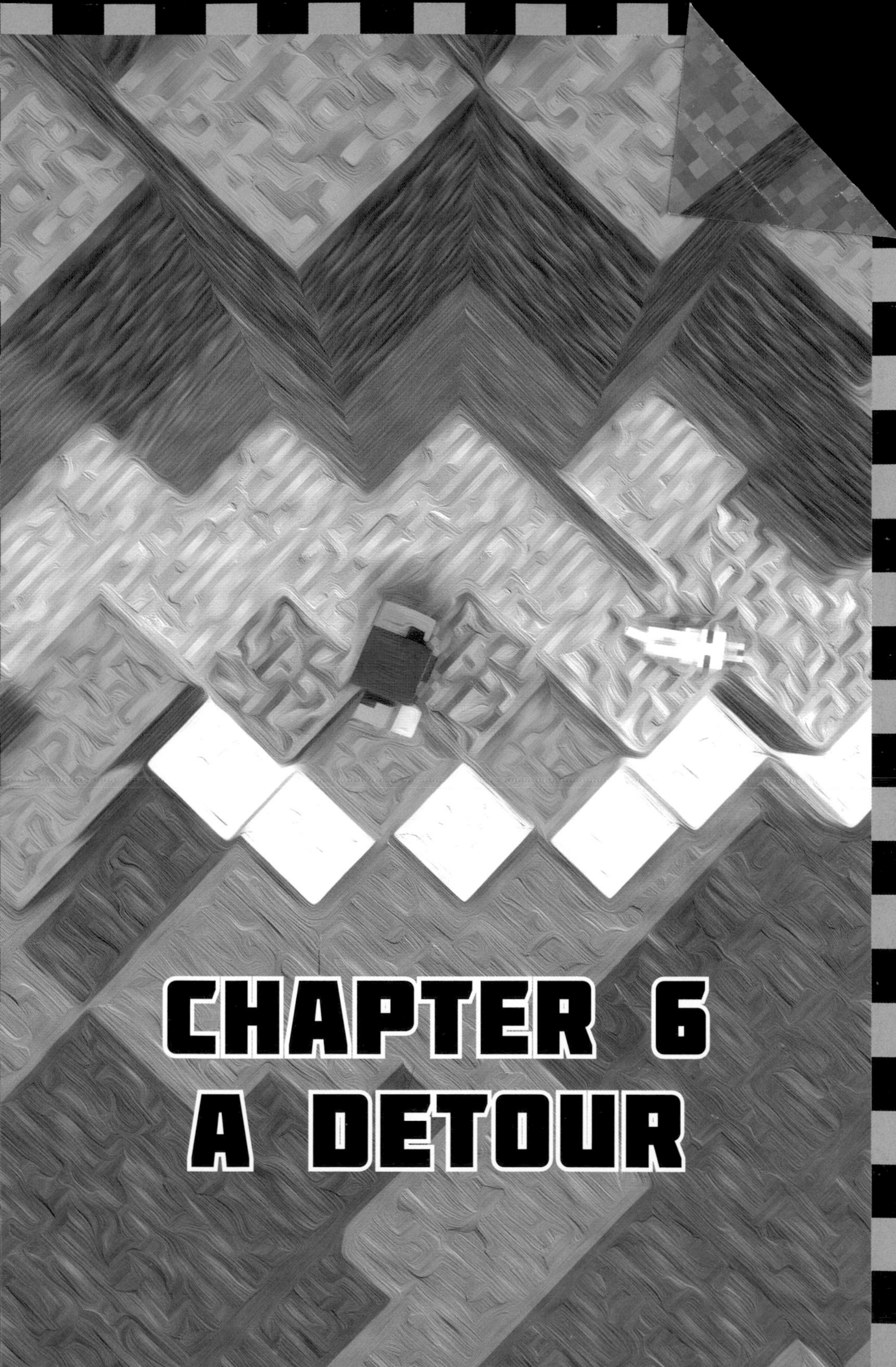

CHAPTER 6
A DETOUR

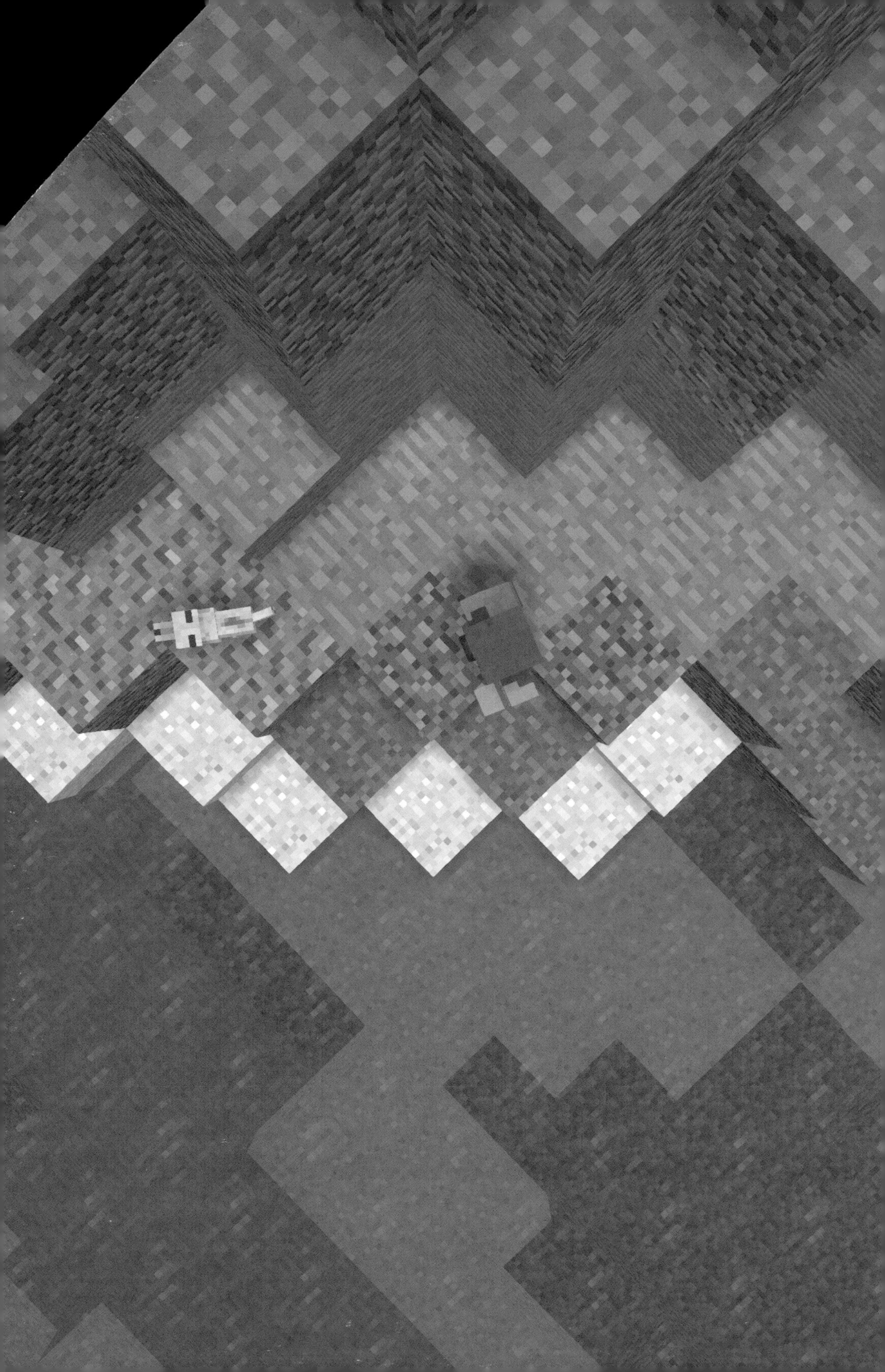

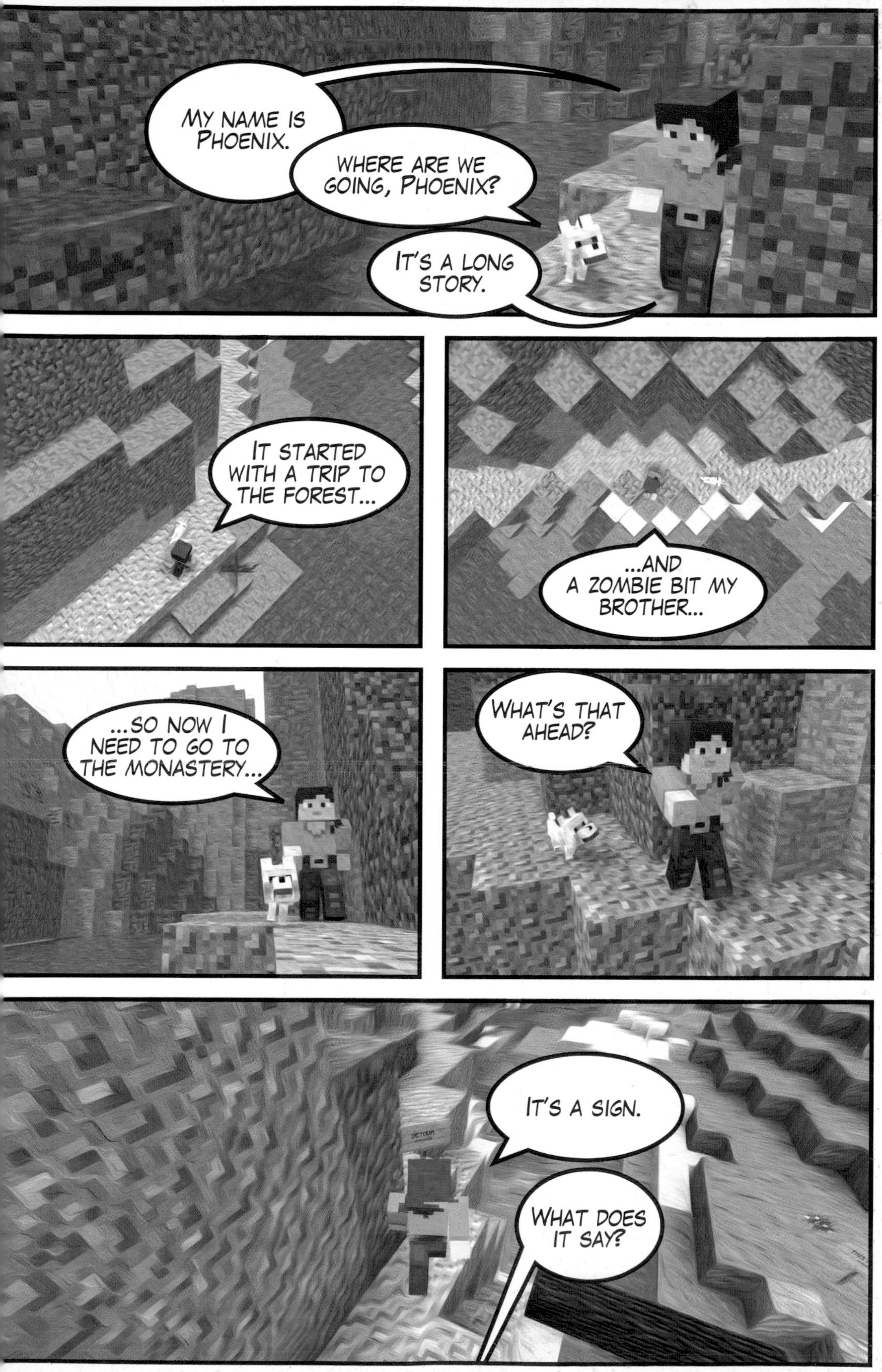
MY NAME IS PHOENIX.
WHERE ARE WE GOING, PHOENIX?
IT'S A LONG STORY.
IT STARTED WITH A TRIP TO THE FOREST...
...AND A ZOMBIE BIT MY BROTHER...
...SO NOW I NEED TO GO TO THE MONASTERY...
WHAT'S THAT AHEAD?
IT'S A SIGN.
WHAT DOES IT SAY?

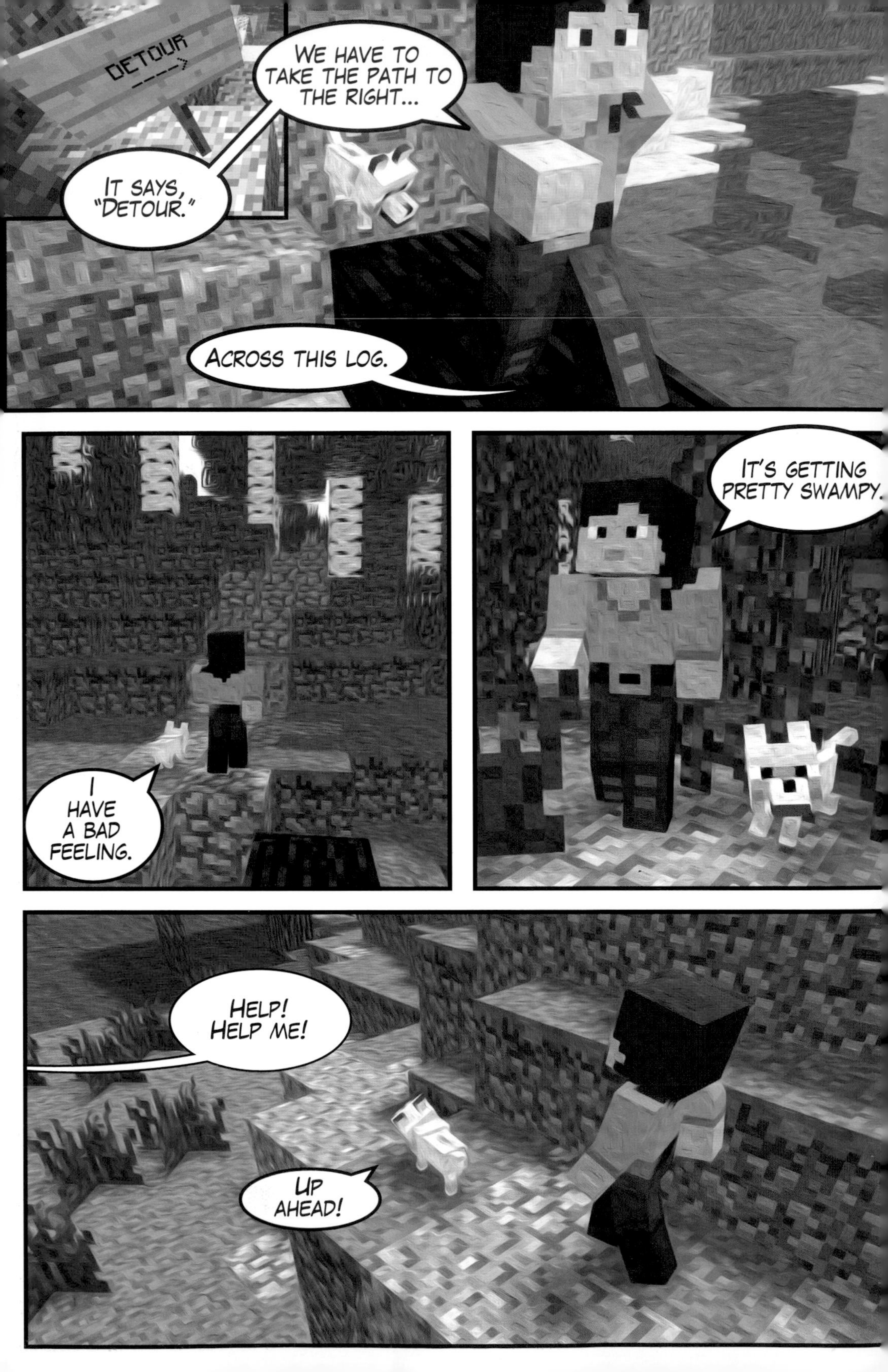
DETOUR ---->
WE HAVE TO TAKE THE PATH TO THE RIGHT...
IT SAYS, "DETOUR."
ACROSS THIS LOG.
I HAVE A BAD FEELING.
IT'S GETTING PRETTY SWAMPY.
HELP! HELP ME!
UP AHEAD!

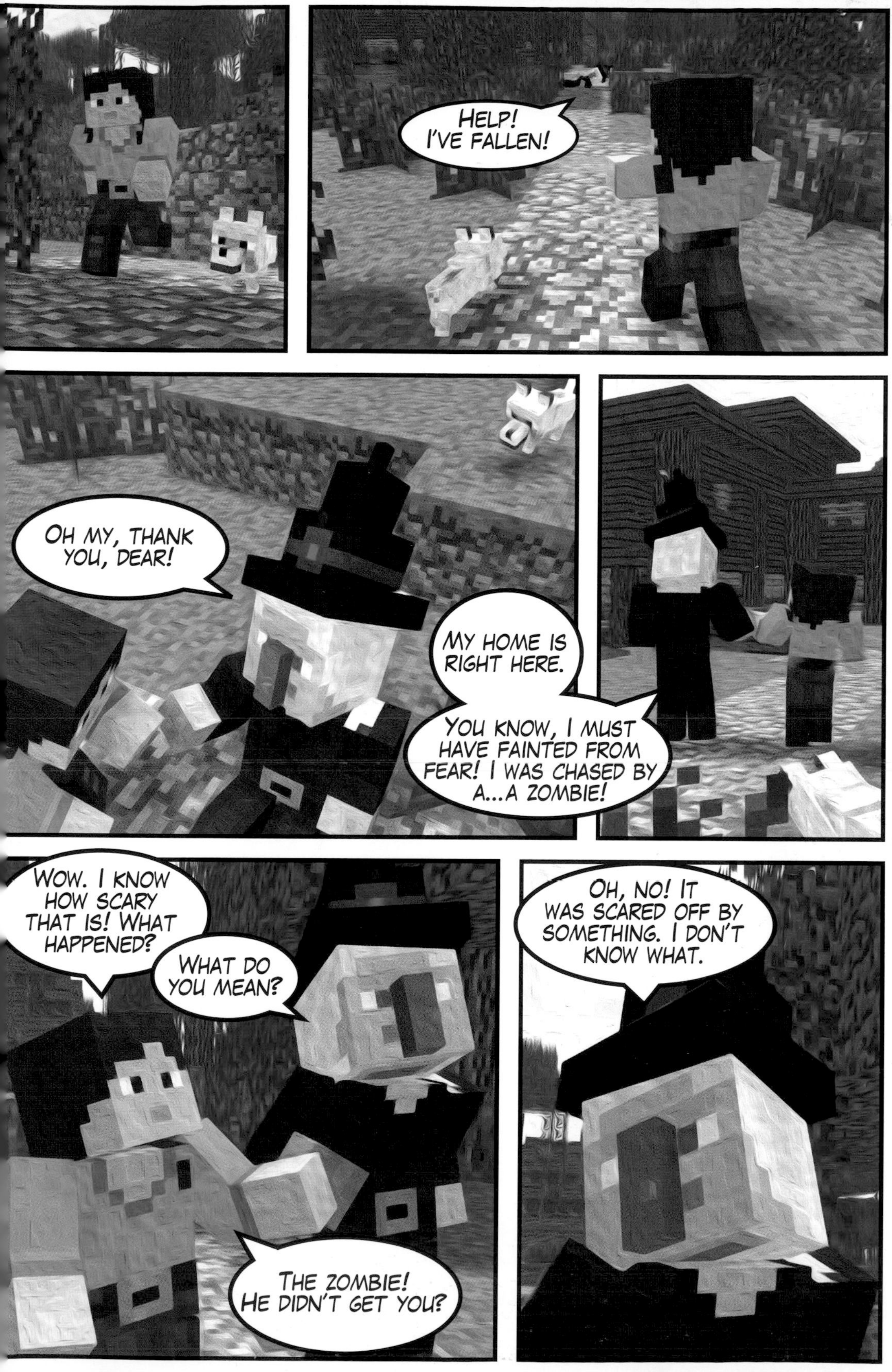
HELP! I'VE FALLEN!
OH MY, THANK YOU, DEAR!
MY HOME IS RIGHT HERE.
YOU KNOW, I MUST HAVE FAINTED FROM FEAR! I WAS CHASED BY A...A ZOMBIE!
WOW. I KNOW HOW SCARY THAT IS! WHAT HAPPENED?
WHAT DO YOU MEAN?
THE ZOMBIE! HE DIDN'T GET YOU?
OH, NO! IT WAS SCARED OFF BY SOMETHING. I DON'T KNOW WHAT.

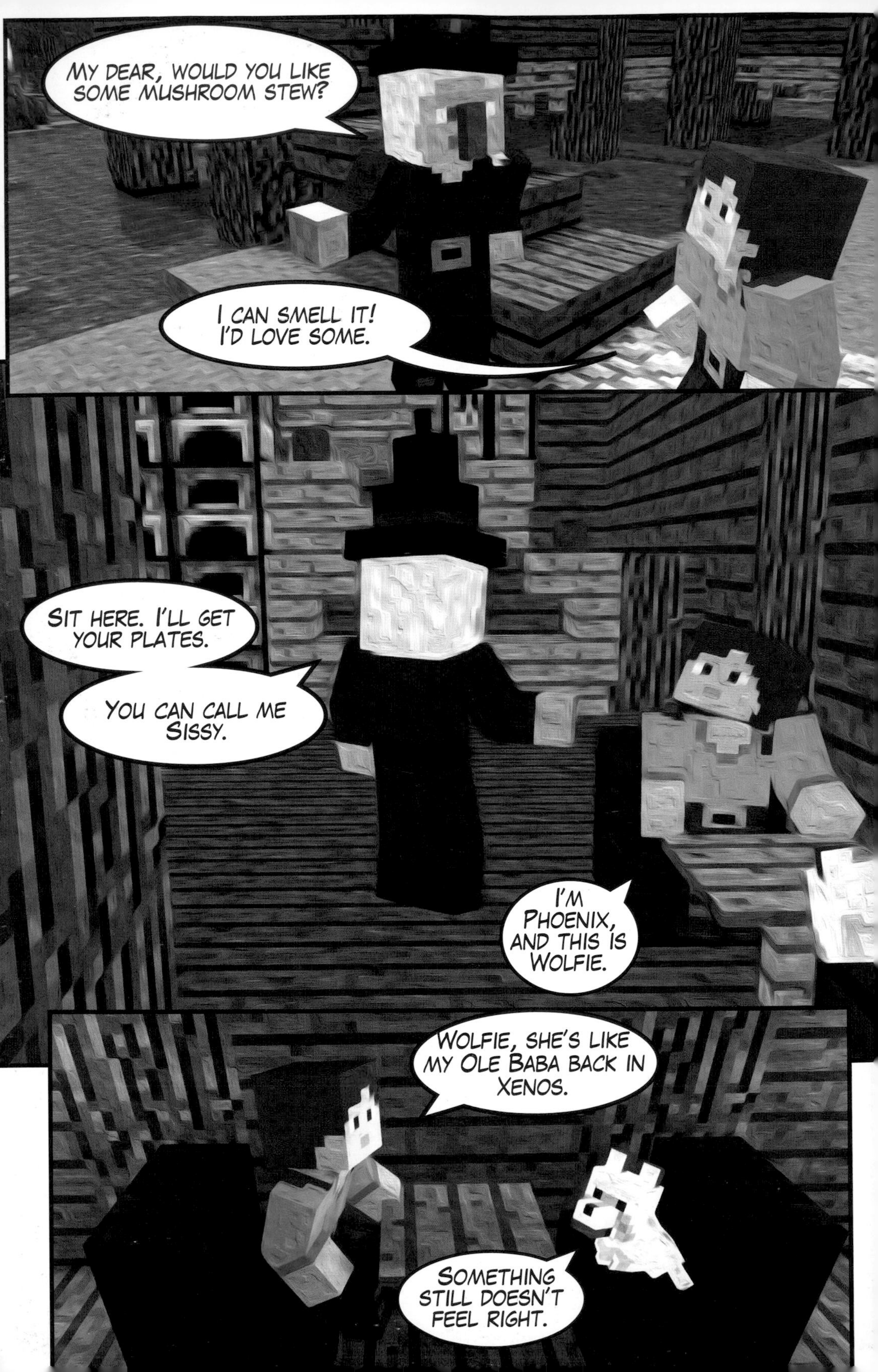
MY DEAR, WOULD YOU LIKE SOME MUSHROOM STEW?
I CAN SMELL IT! I'D LOVE SOME.
SIT HERE. I'LL GET YOUR PLATES.
YOU CAN CALL ME SISSY.
I'M PHOENIX, AND THIS IS WOLFIE.
WOLFIE, SHE'S LIKE MY OLE BABA BACK IN XENOS.
SOMETHING STILL DOESN'T FEEL RIGHT.

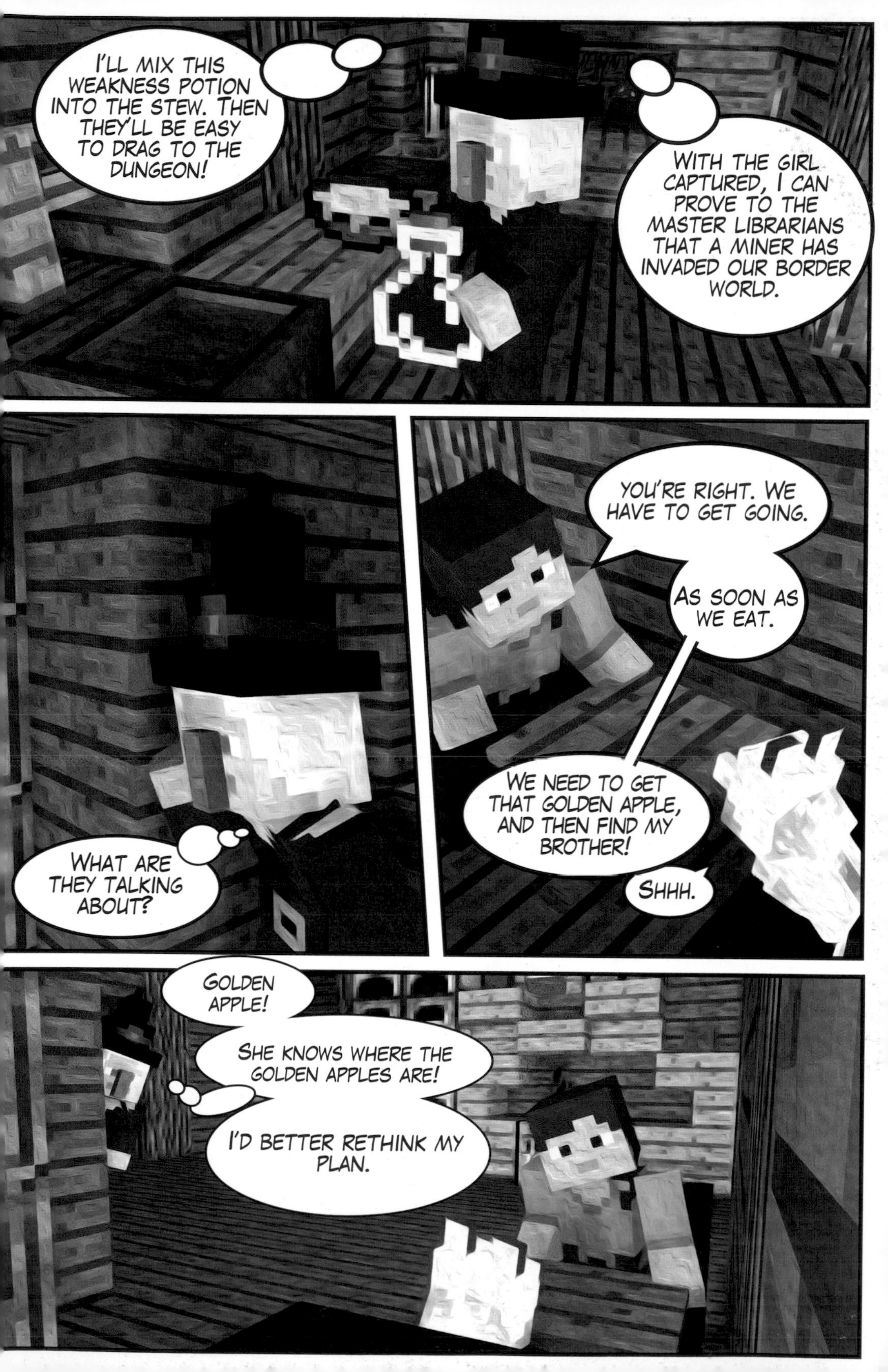
I'LL MIX THIS WEAKNESS POTION INTO THE STEW. THEN THEY'LL BE EASY TO DRAG TO THE DUNGEON!
WITH THE GIRL CAPTURED, I CAN PROVE TO THE MASTER LIBRARIANS THAT A MINER HAS INVADED OUR BORDER WORLD.
YOU'RE RIGHT. WE HAVE TO GET GOING.
AS SOON AS WE EAT.
WE NEED TO GET THAT GOLDEN APPLE, AND THEN FIND MY BROTHER!
SHHH.
WHAT ARE THEY TALKING ABOUT?
GOLDEN APPLE!
SHE KNOWS WHERE THE GOLDEN APPLES ARE!
I'D BETTER RETHINK MY PLAN.

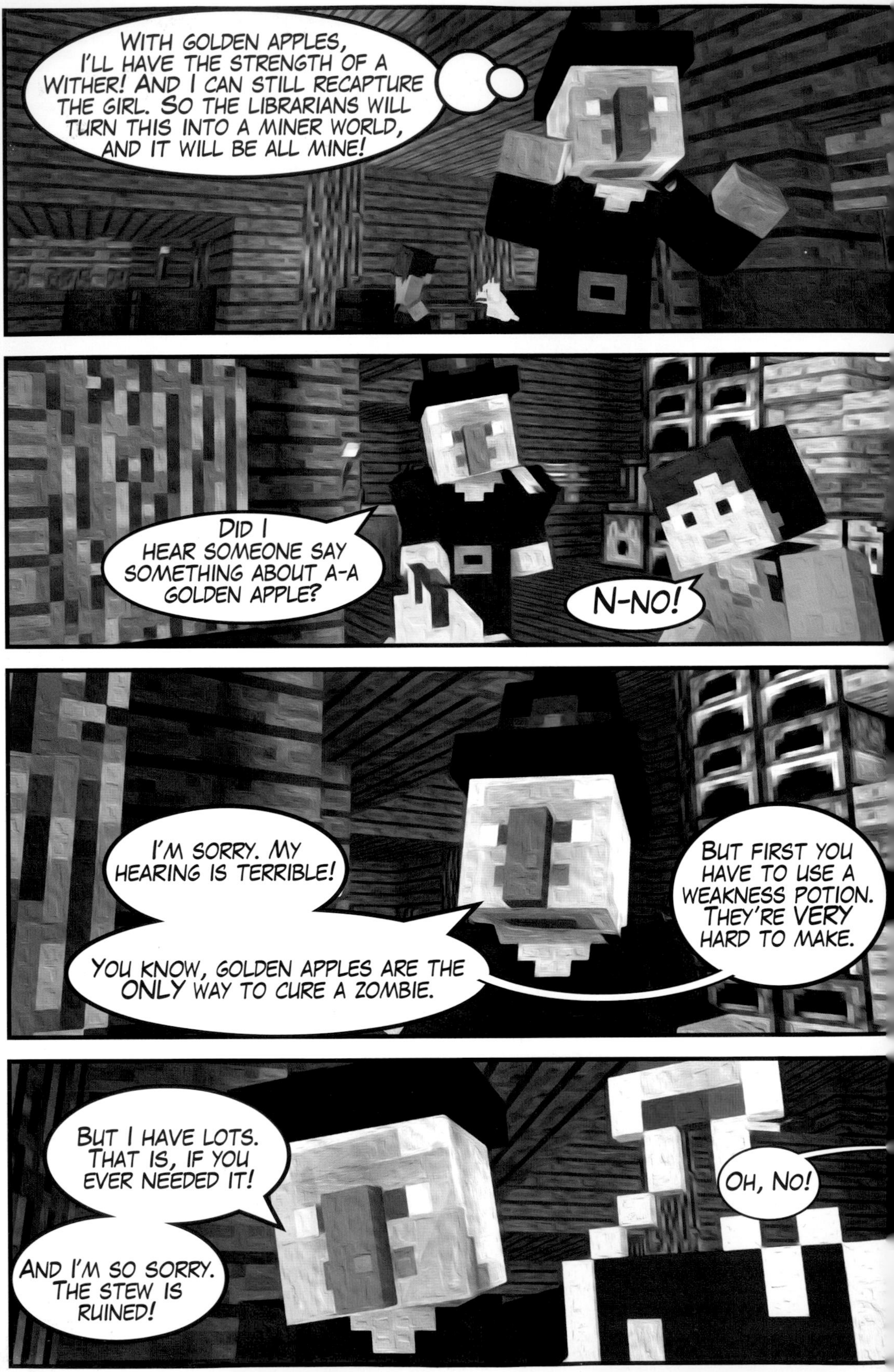
WITH GOLDEN APPLES, I'LL HAVE THE STRENGTH OF A WITHER! AND I CAN STILL RECAPTURE THE GIRL. SO THE LIBRARIANS WILL TURN THIS INTO A MINER WORLD, AND IT WILL BE ALL MINE!
DID I HEAR SOMEONE SAY SOMETHING ABOUT A-A GOLDEN APPLE?
N-NO!
I'M SORRY. MY HEARING IS TERRIBLE!
YOU KNOW, GOLDEN APPLES ARE THE ONLY WAY TO CURE A ZOMBIE.
BUT FIRST YOU HAVE TO USE A WEAKNESS POTION. THEY'RE VERY HARD TO MAKE.
BUT I HAVE LOTS. THAT IS, IF YOU EVER NEEDED IT!
AND I'M SO SORRY. THE STEW IS RUINED!
OH, NO!

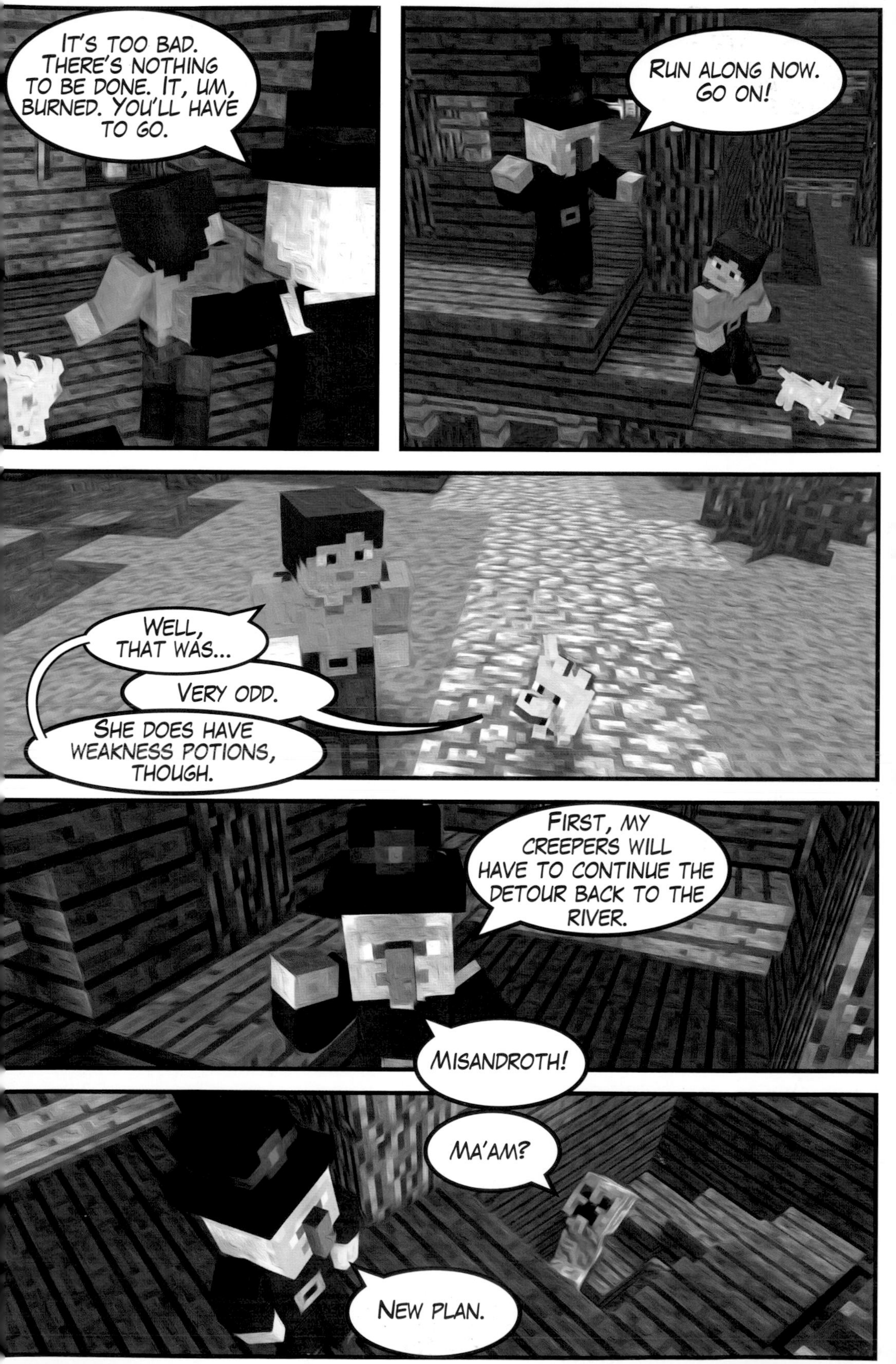
IT'S TOO BAD. THERE'S NOTHING TO BE DONE. IT, UM, BURNED. YOU'LL HAVE TO GO.
RUN ALONG NOW. GO ON!
WELL, THAT WAS...
VERY ODD.
SHE DOES HAVE WEAKNESS POTIONS, THOUGH.
FIRST, MY CREEPERS WILL HAVE TO CONTINUE THE DETOUR BACK TO THE RIVER.
MISANDROTH!
MA'AM?
NEW PLAN.

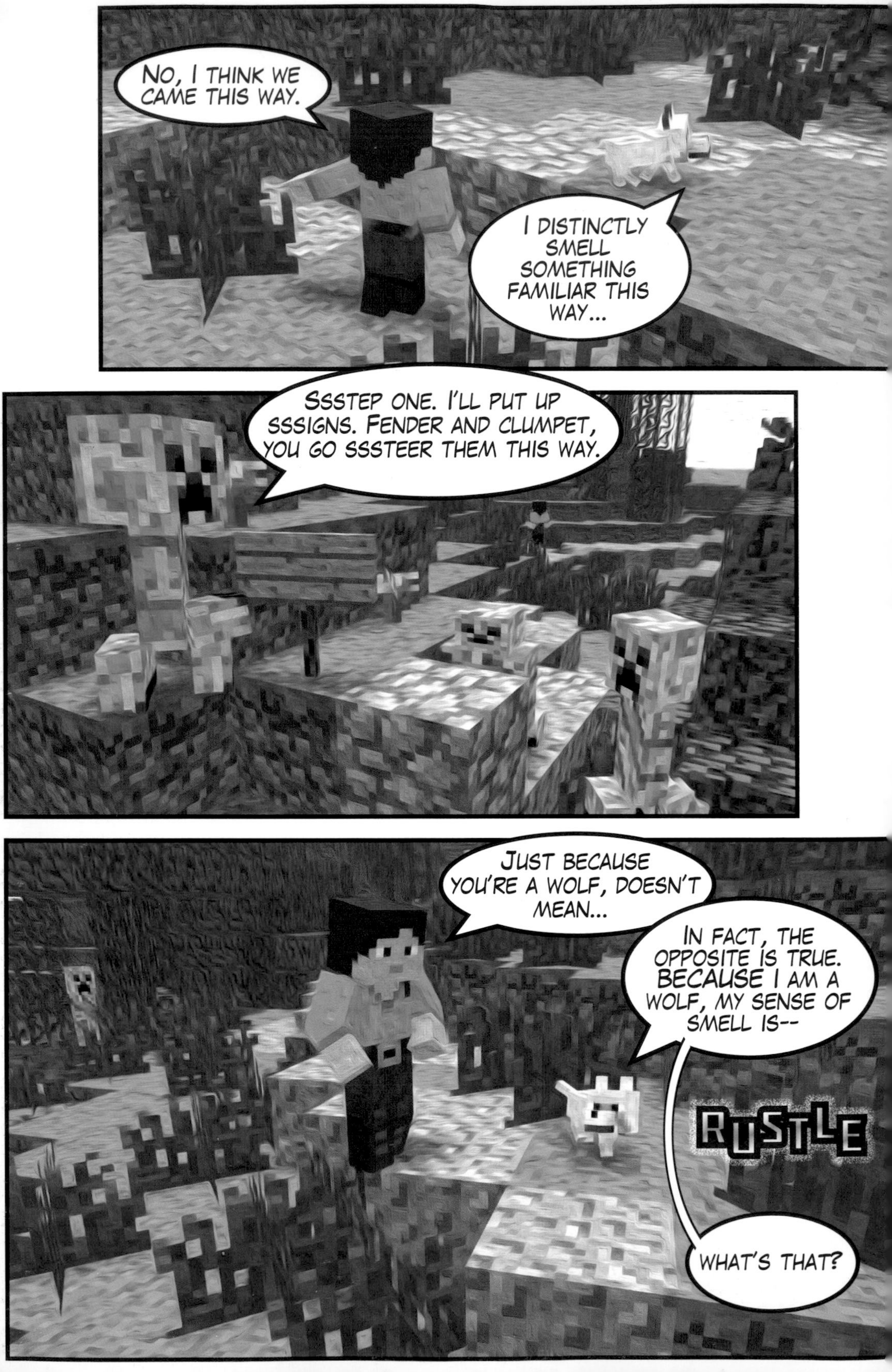
No, I think we came this way.
I distinctly smell something familiar this way...
Ssstep one. I'll put up sssigns. Fender and Clumpet, you go sssteer them this way.
Just because you're a wolf, doesn't mean...
In fact, the opposite is true. BECAUSE I am a wolf, my sense of smell is--
RUSTLE
What's that?

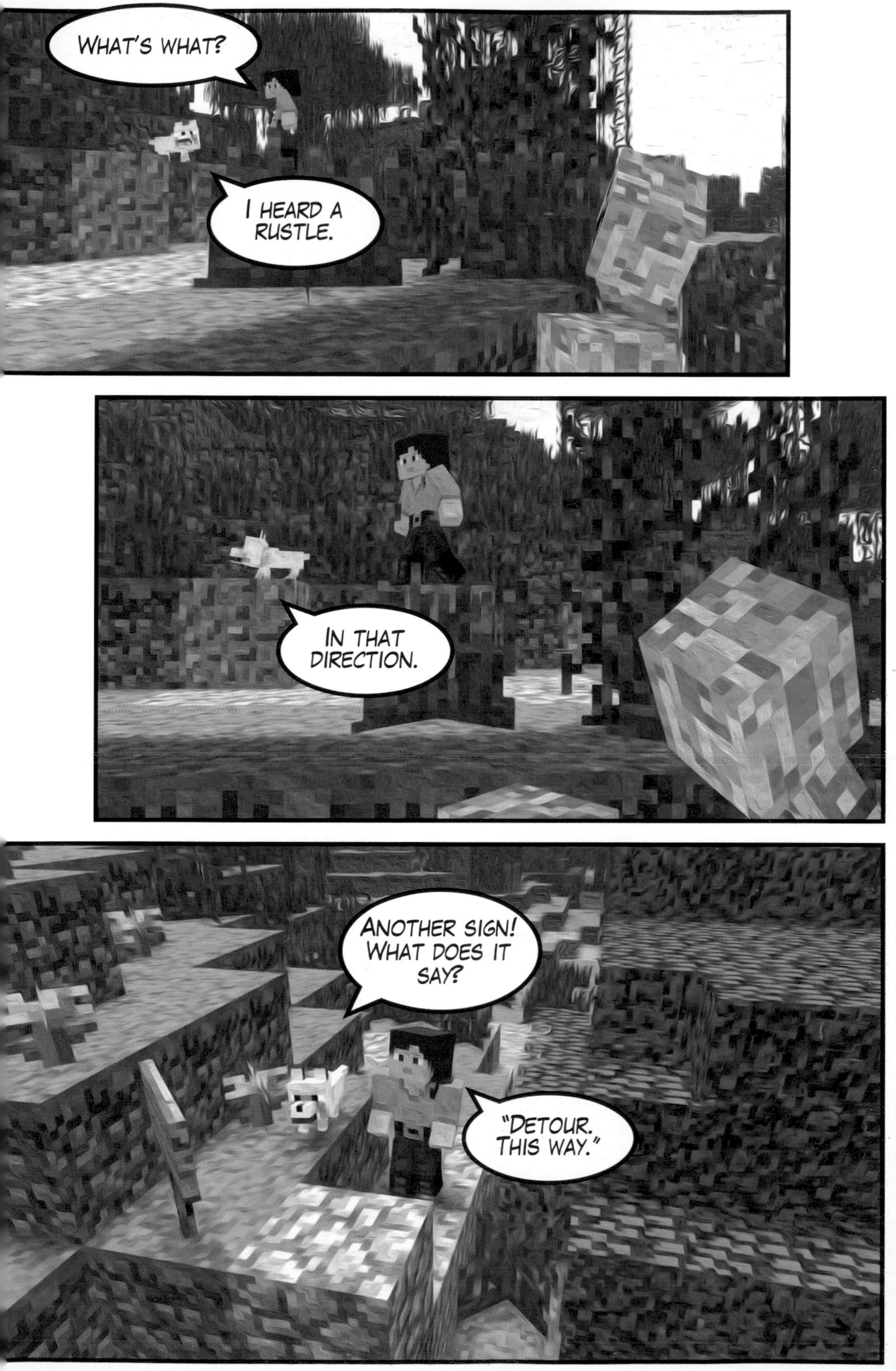
WHAT'S WHAT?
I HEARD A RUSTLE.
IN THAT DIRECTION.
ANOTHER SIGN! WHAT DOES IT SAY?
"DETOUR. THIS WAY."

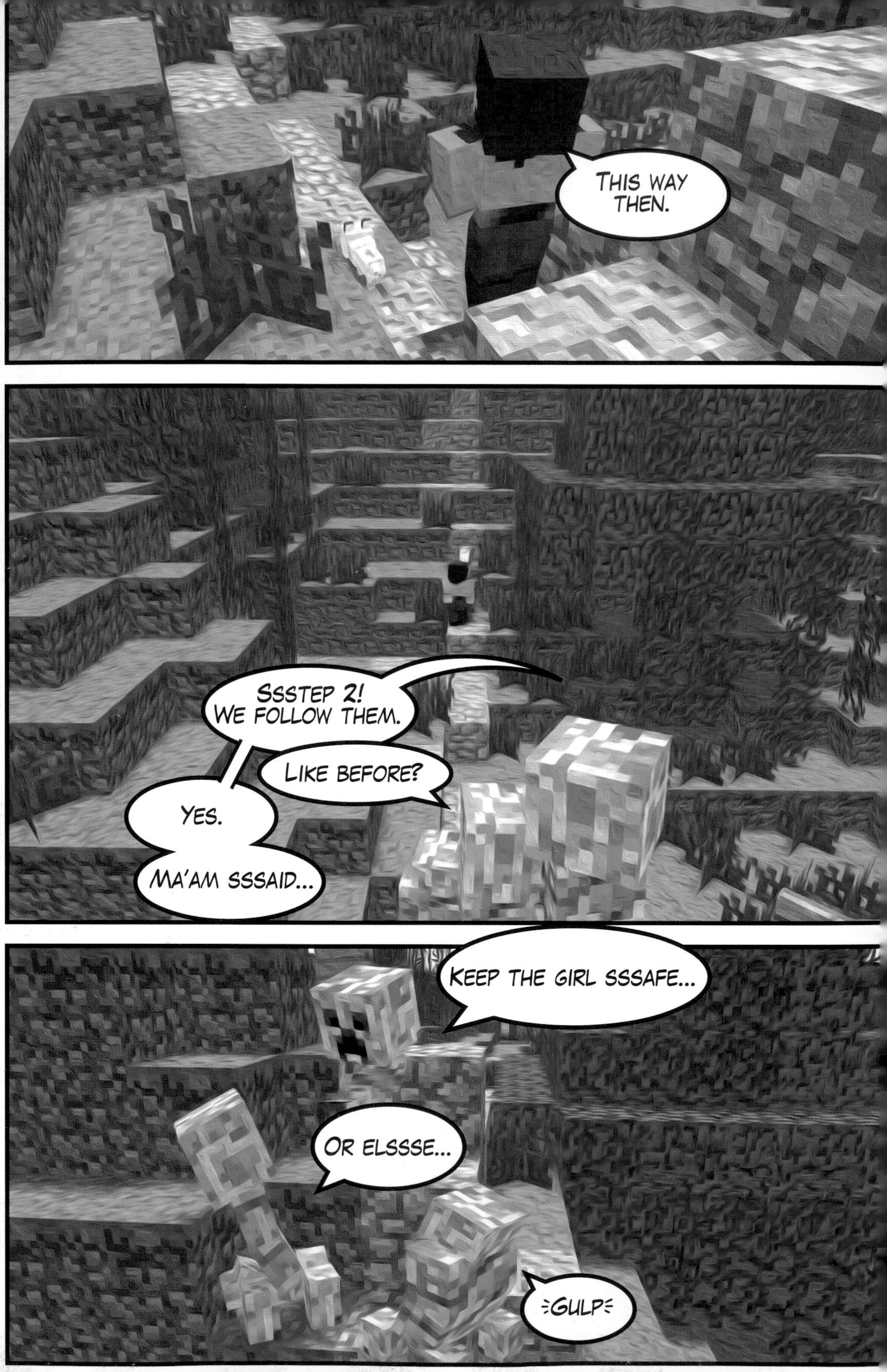
THIS WAY THEN.
SSSTEP 2! WE FOLLOW THEM.
LIKE BEFORE?
YES.
MA'AM SSSAID...
KEEP THE GIRL SSSAFE...
OR ELSSSE...
GULP

CHAPTER 7
THE JOURNEY

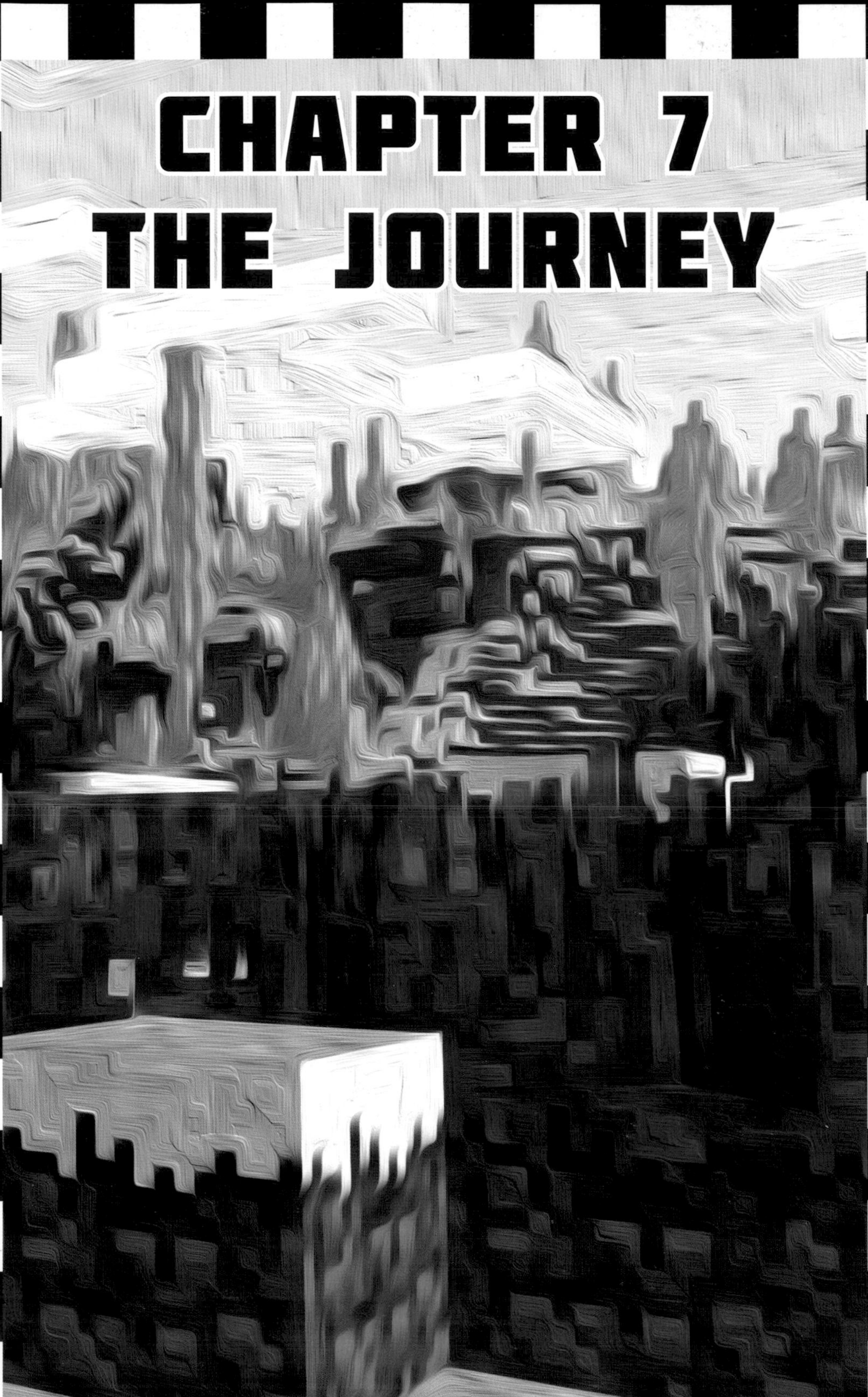

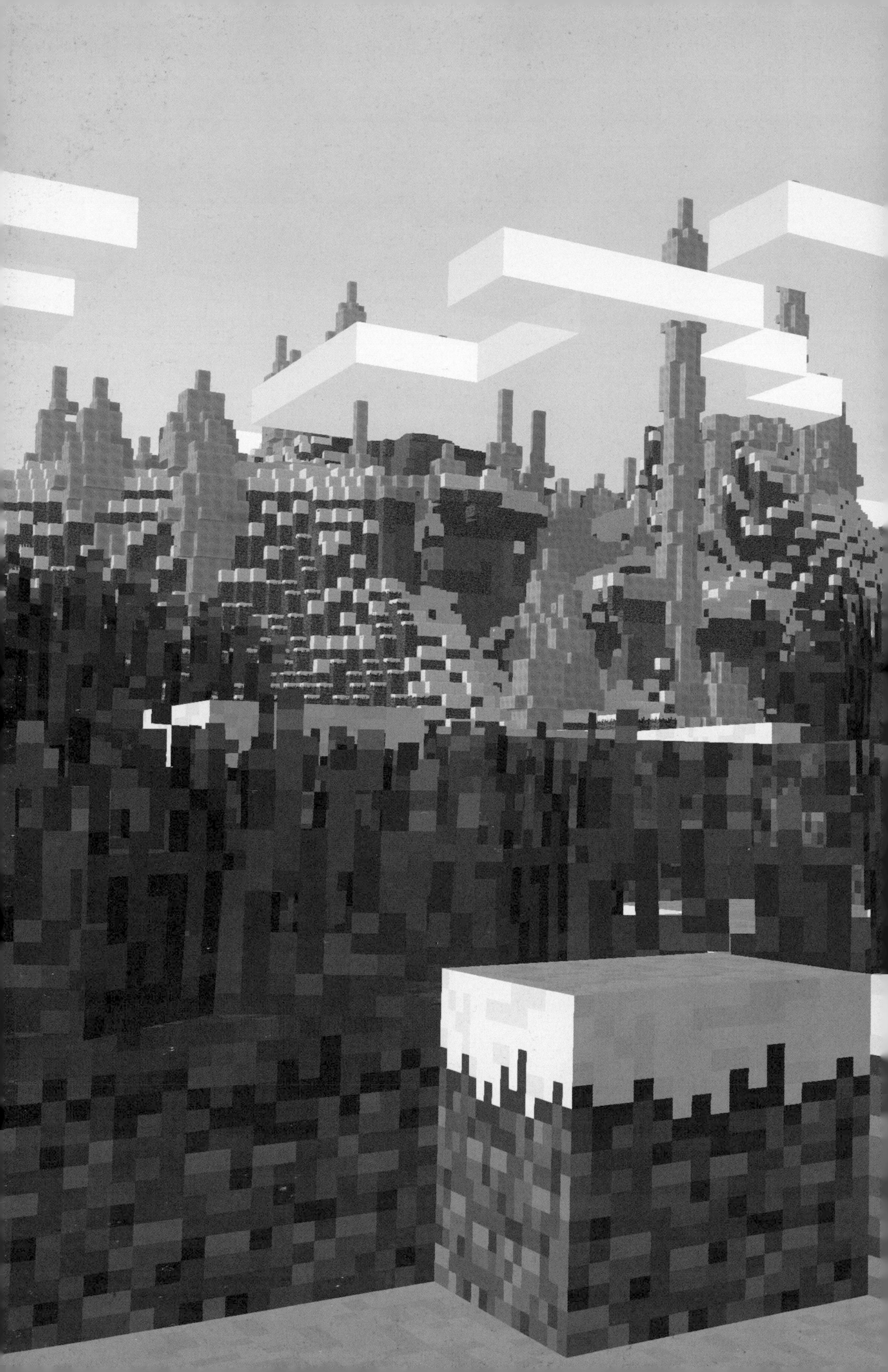

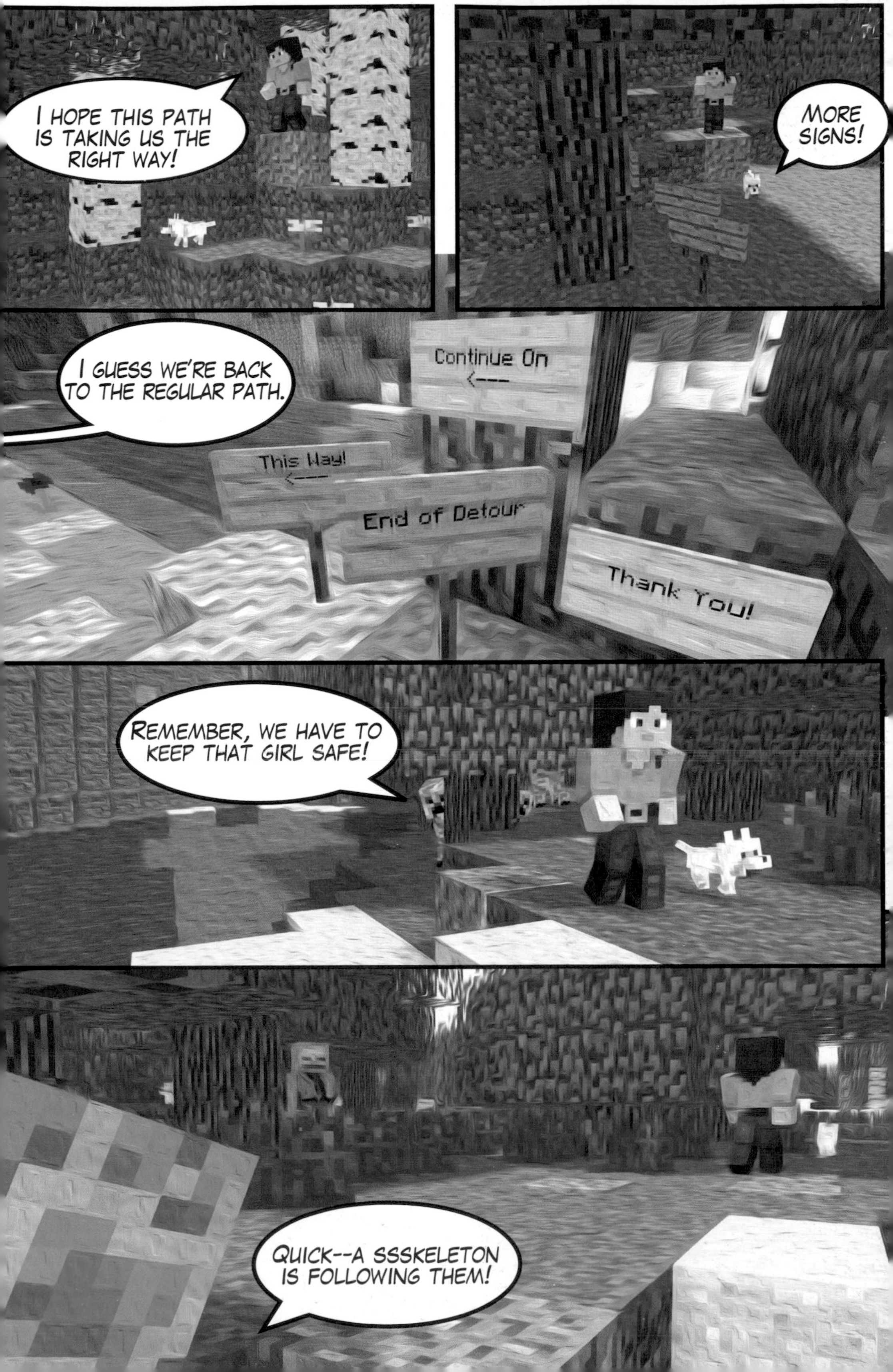
I HOPE THIS PATH IS TAKING US THE RIGHT WAY!
MORE SIGNS!
I GUESS WE'RE BACK TO THE REGULAR PATH.
Continue On
This Way!
End of Detour
Thank You!
REMEMBER, WE HAVE TO KEEP THAT GIRL SAFE!
QUICK--A SSSKELETON IS FOLLOWING THEM!

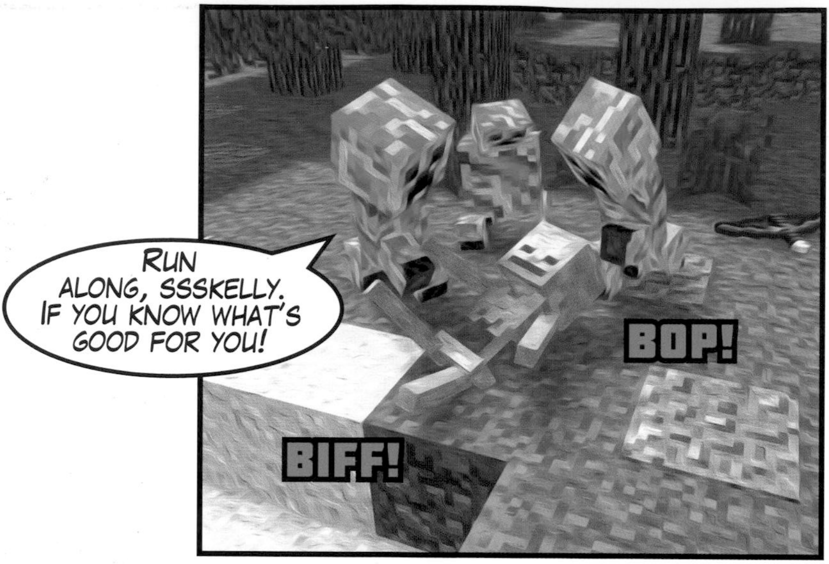
RUN ALONG, SSSKELLY. IF YOU KNOW WHAT'S GOOD FOR YOU!
BOP!
BIFF!

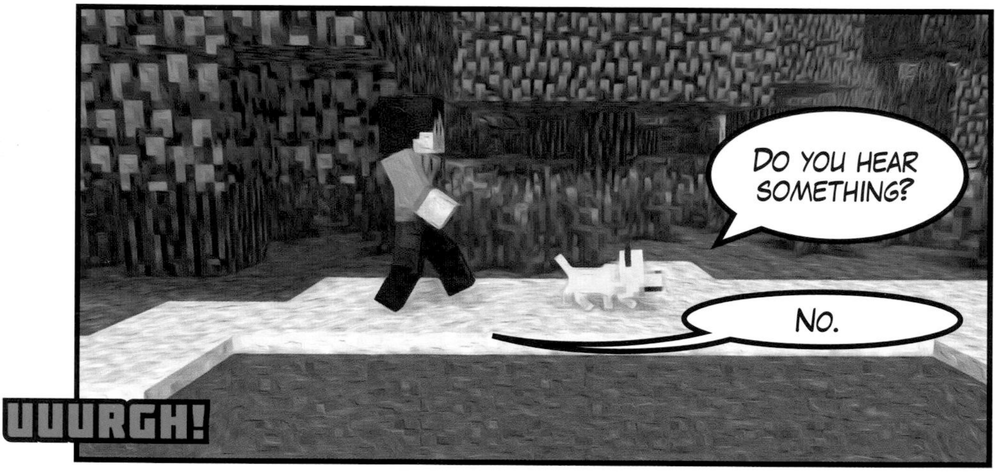
DO YOU HEAR SOMETHING?
NO.
UUURGH!

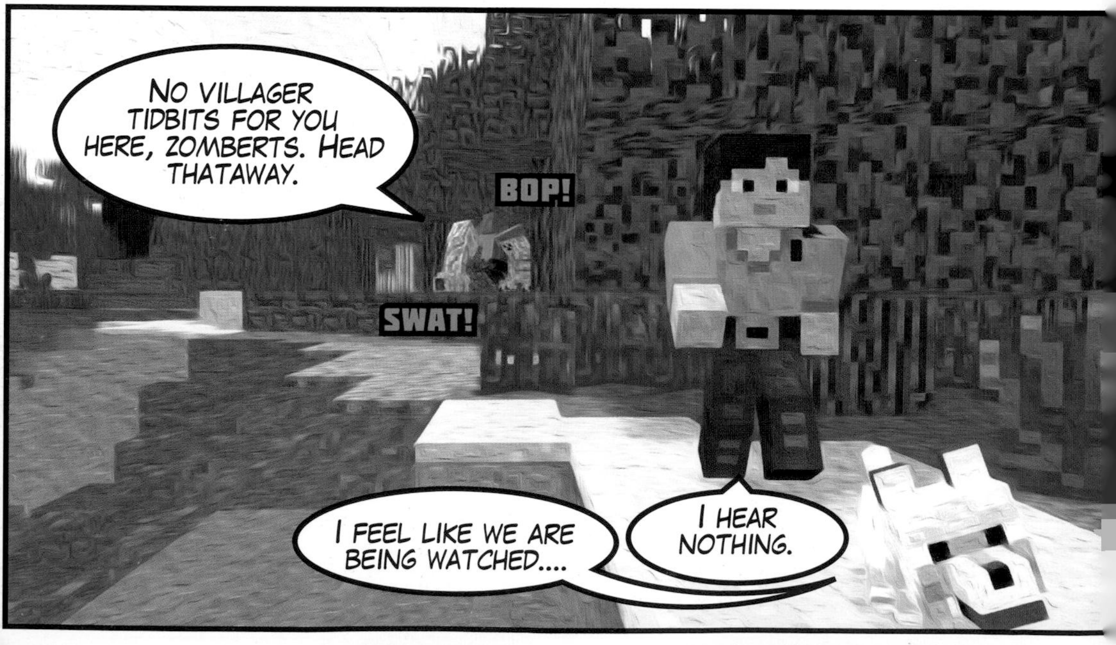
NO VILLAGER TIDBITS FOR YOU HERE, ZOMBERTS. HEAD THATAWAY.
BOP!
SWAT!
I FEEL LIKE WE ARE BEING WATCHED....
I HEAR NOTHING.

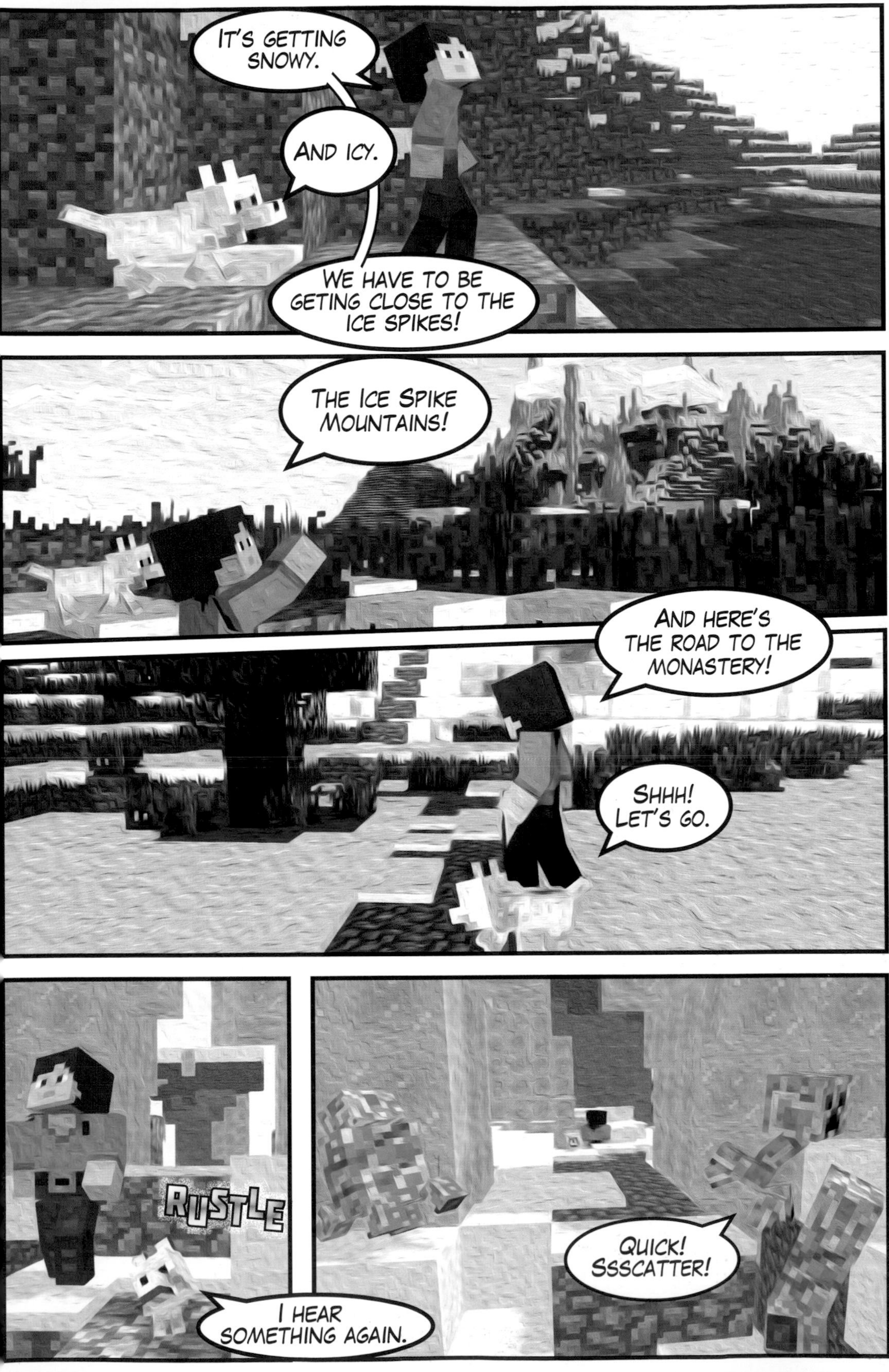
IT'S GETTING SNOWY.
AND ICY.
WE HAVE TO BE GETING CLOSE TO THE ICE SPIKES!
THE ICE SPIKE MOUNTAINS!
AND HERE'S THE ROAD TO THE MONASTERY!
SHHH! LET'S GO.
RUSTLE
I HEAR SOMETHING AGAIN.
QUICK! SSSCATTER!

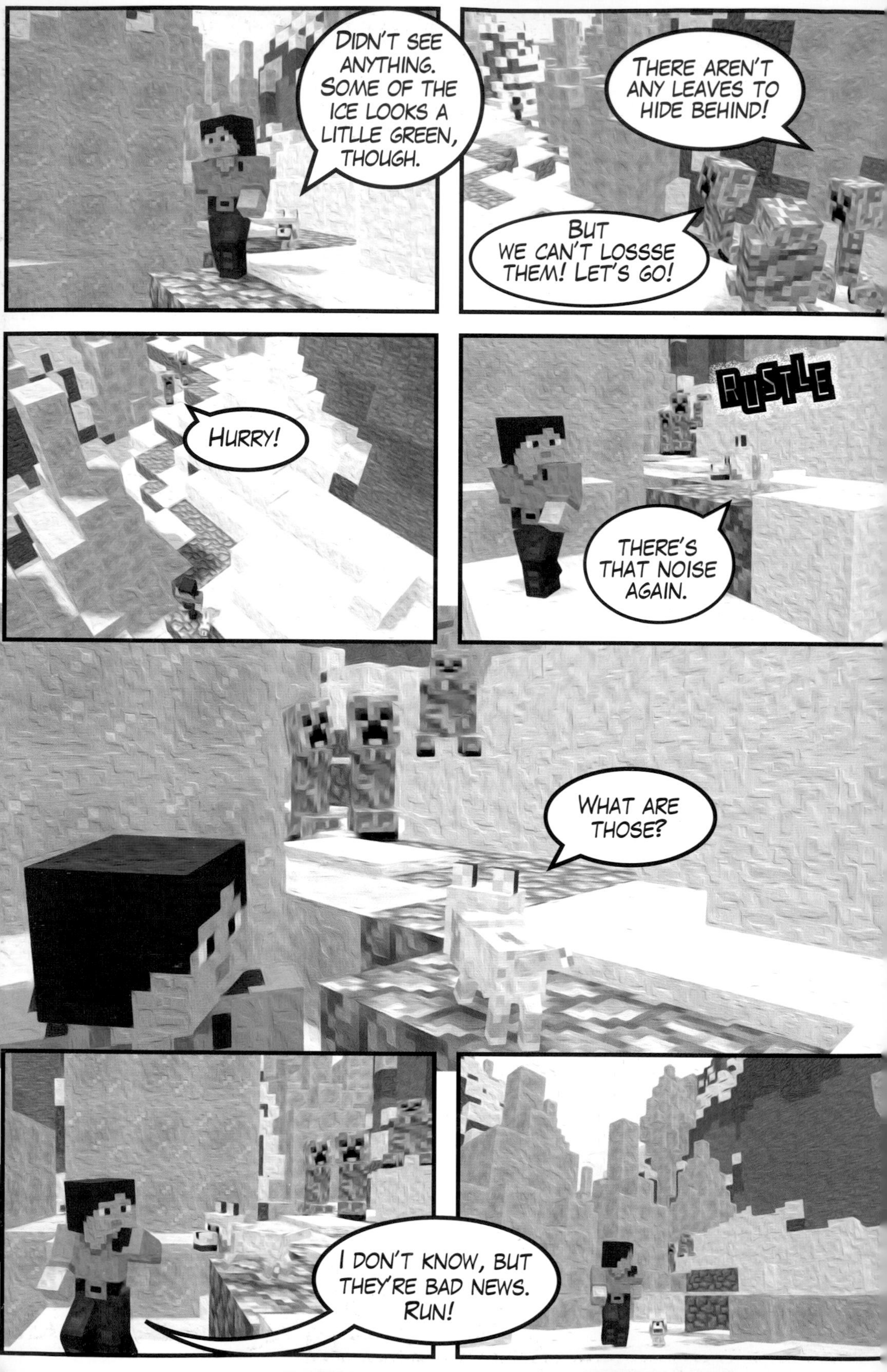
DIDN'T SEE ANYTHING. SOME OF THE ICE LOOKS A LITLLE GREEN, THOUGH.
THERE AREN'T ANY LEAVES TO HIDE BEHIND!
BUT WE CAN'T LOSSSE THEM! LET'S GO!
HURRY!
RUSTLE
THERE'S THAT NOISE AGAIN.
WHAT ARE THOSE?
I DON'T KNOW, BUT THEY'RE BAD NEWS. RUN!

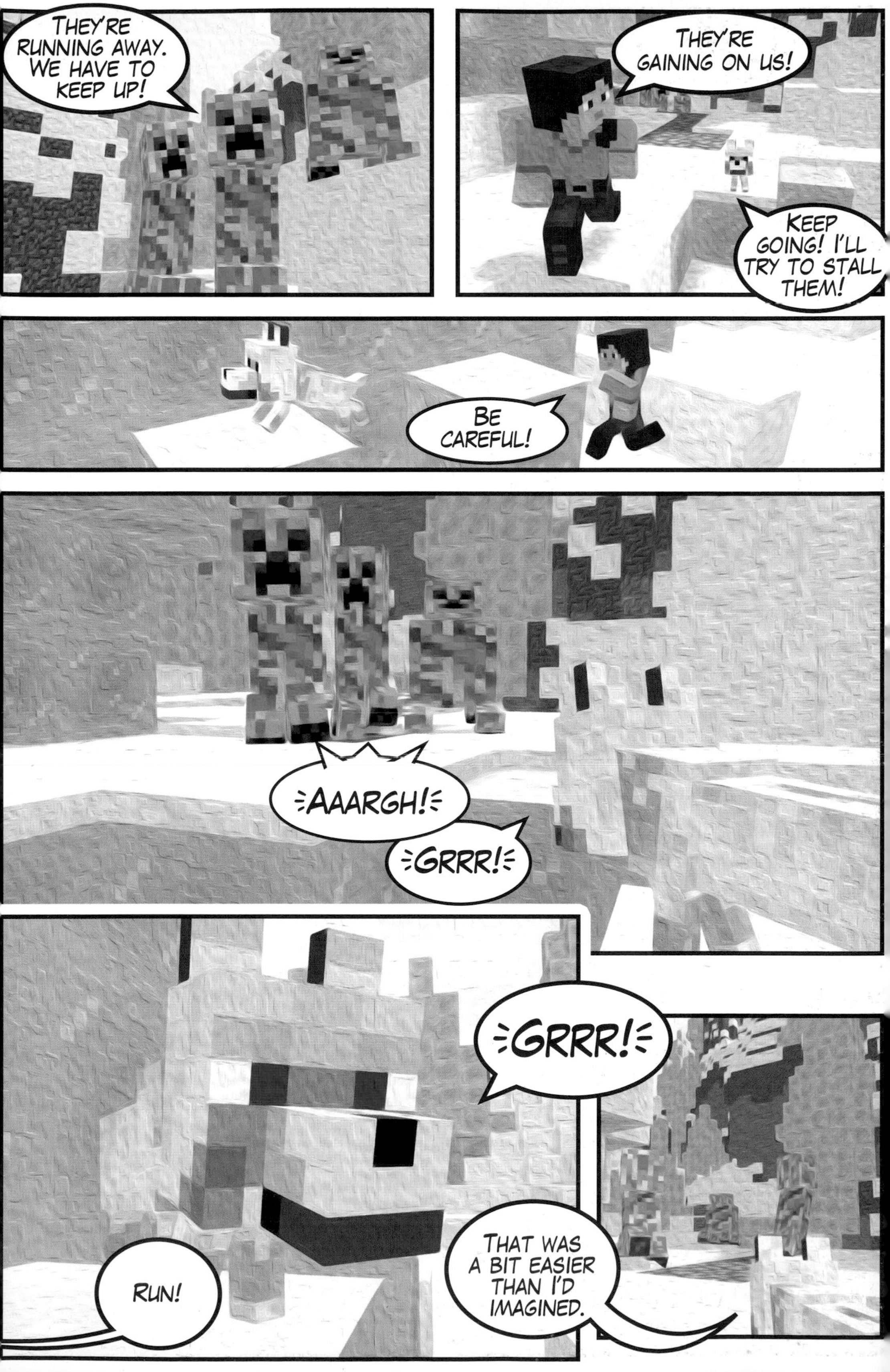
THEY'RE RUNNING AWAY. WE HAVE TO KEEP UP!
THEY'RE GAINING ON US!
KEEP GOING! I'LL TRY TO STALL THEM!
BE CAREFUL!
AAARGH!
GRRR!
GRRR!
RUN!
THAT WAS A BIT EASIER THAN I'D IMAGINED.

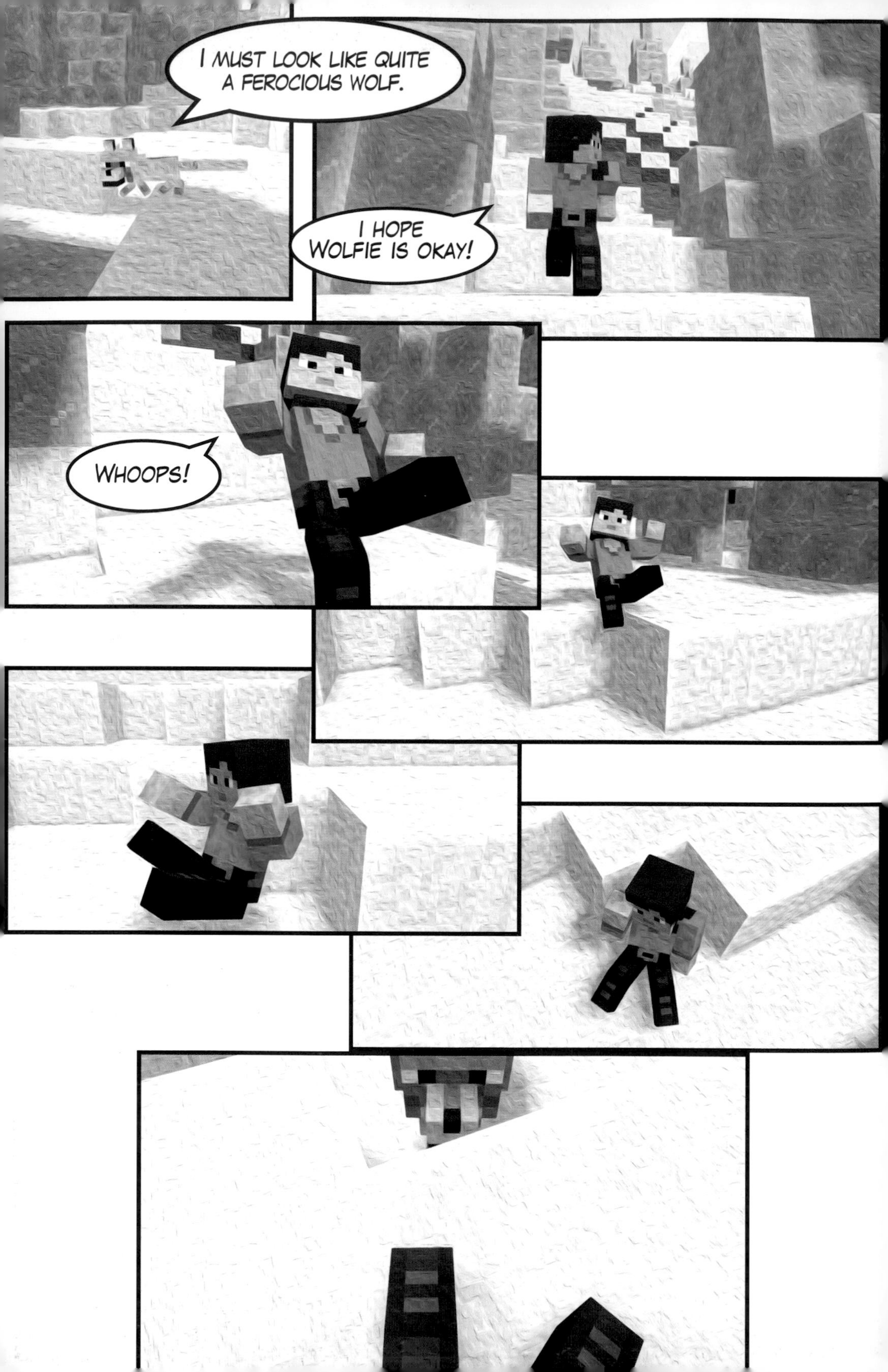
I MUST LOOK LIKE QUITE A FEROCIOUS WOLF.
I HOPE WOLFIE IS OKAY!
WHOOPS!

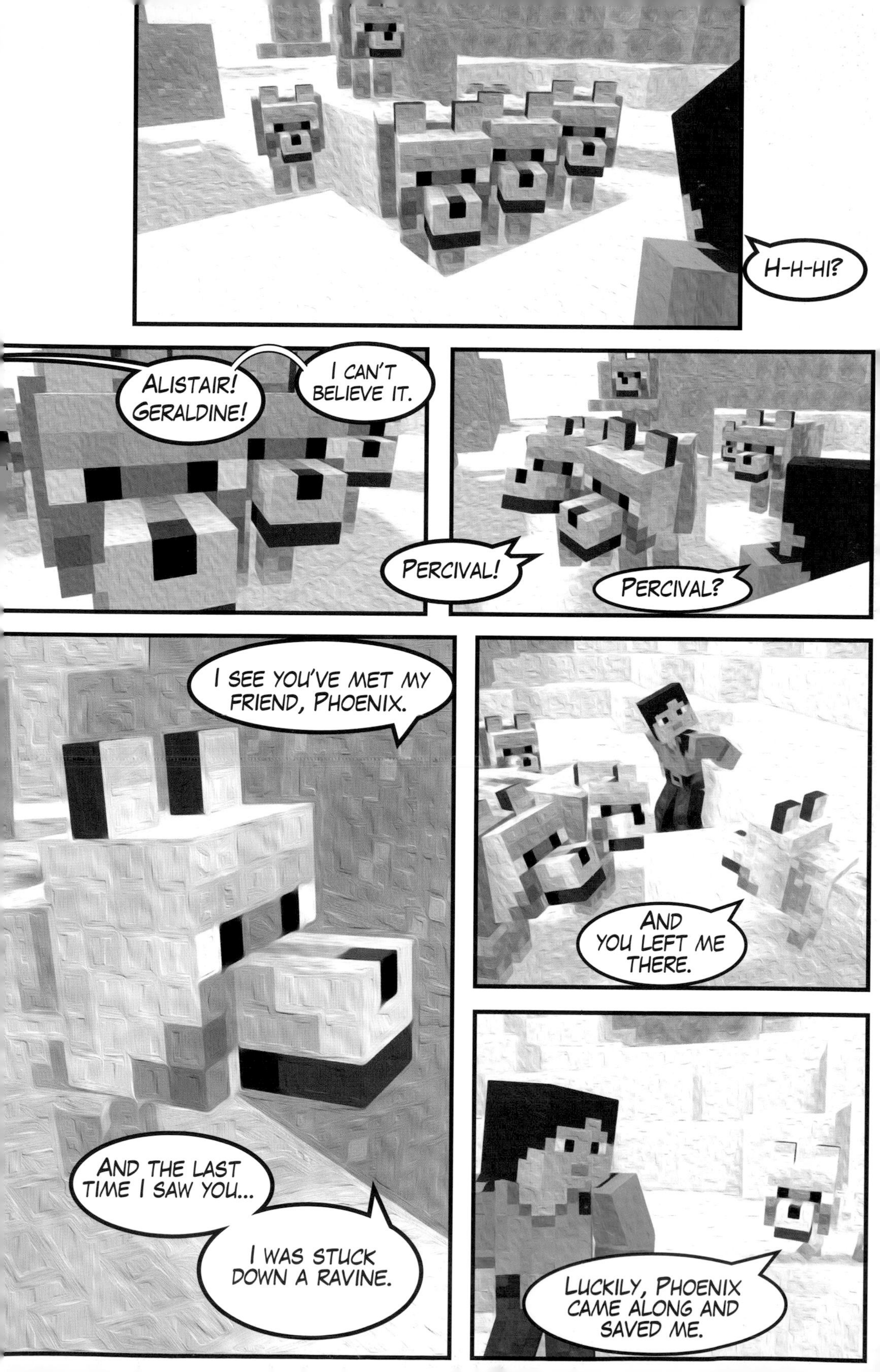
H-H-HI?
ALISTAIR! GERALDINE!
I CAN'T BELIEVE IT.
PERCIVAL!
PERCIVAL?
I SEE YOU'VE MET MY FRIEND, PHOENIX.
AND THE LAST TIME I SAW YOU...
I WAS STUCK DOWN A RAVINE.
AND YOU LEFT ME THERE.
LUCKILY, PHOENIX CAME ALONG AND SAVED ME.

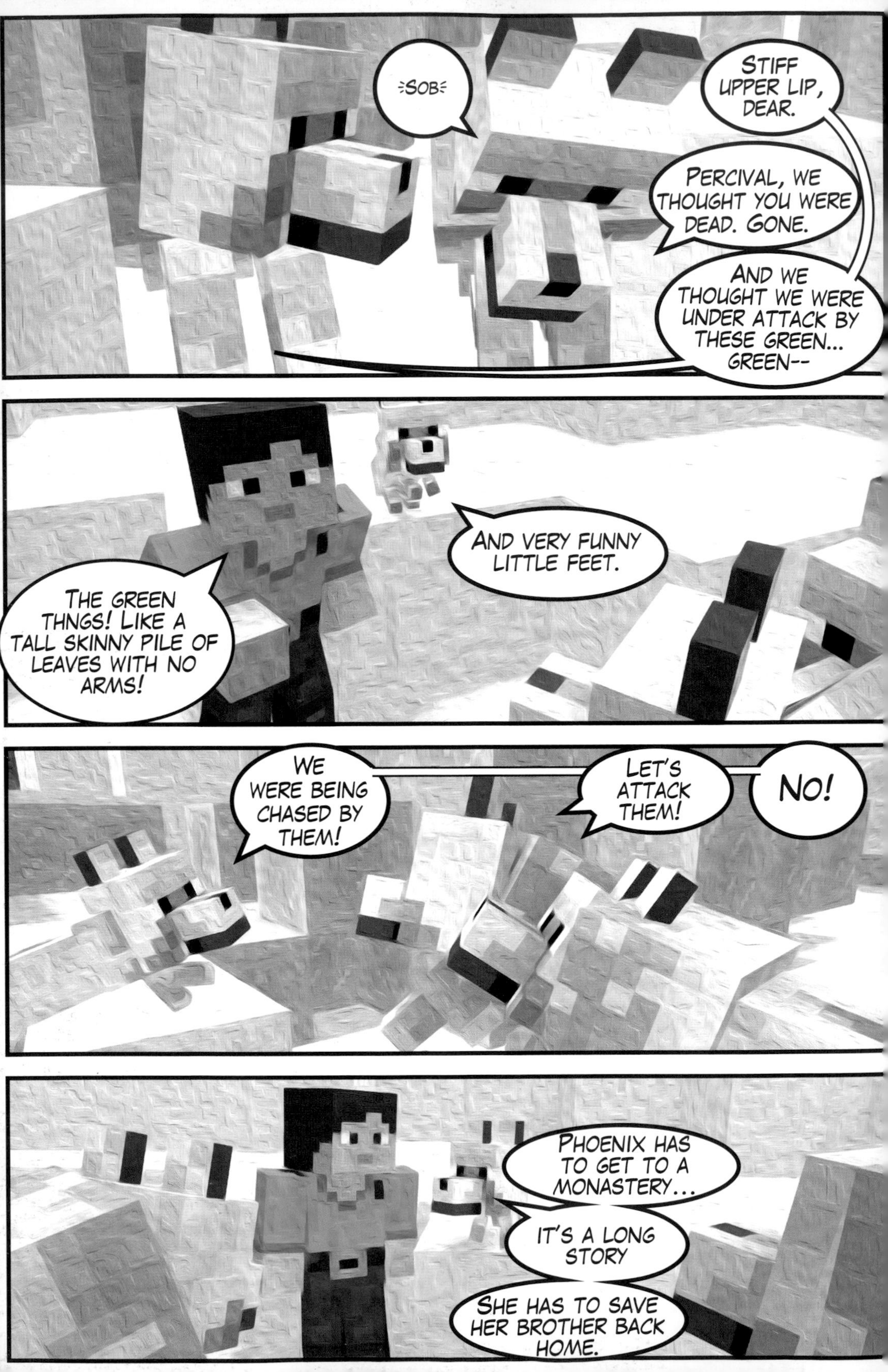

STIFF UPPER LIP, DEAR.
SOB
PERCIVAL, WE THOUGHT YOU WERE DEAD. GONE.
AND WE THOUGHT WE WERE UNDER ATTACK BY THESE GREEN... GREEN--
THE GREEN THNGS! LIKE A TALL SKINNY PILE OF LEAVES WITH NO ARMS!
AND VERY FUNNY LITTLE FEET.
WE WERE BEING CHASED BY THEM!
LET'S ATTACK THEM!
NO!
PHOENIX HAS TO GET TO A MONASTERY...
IT'S A LONG STORY
SHE HAS TO SAVE HER BROTHER BACK HOME.

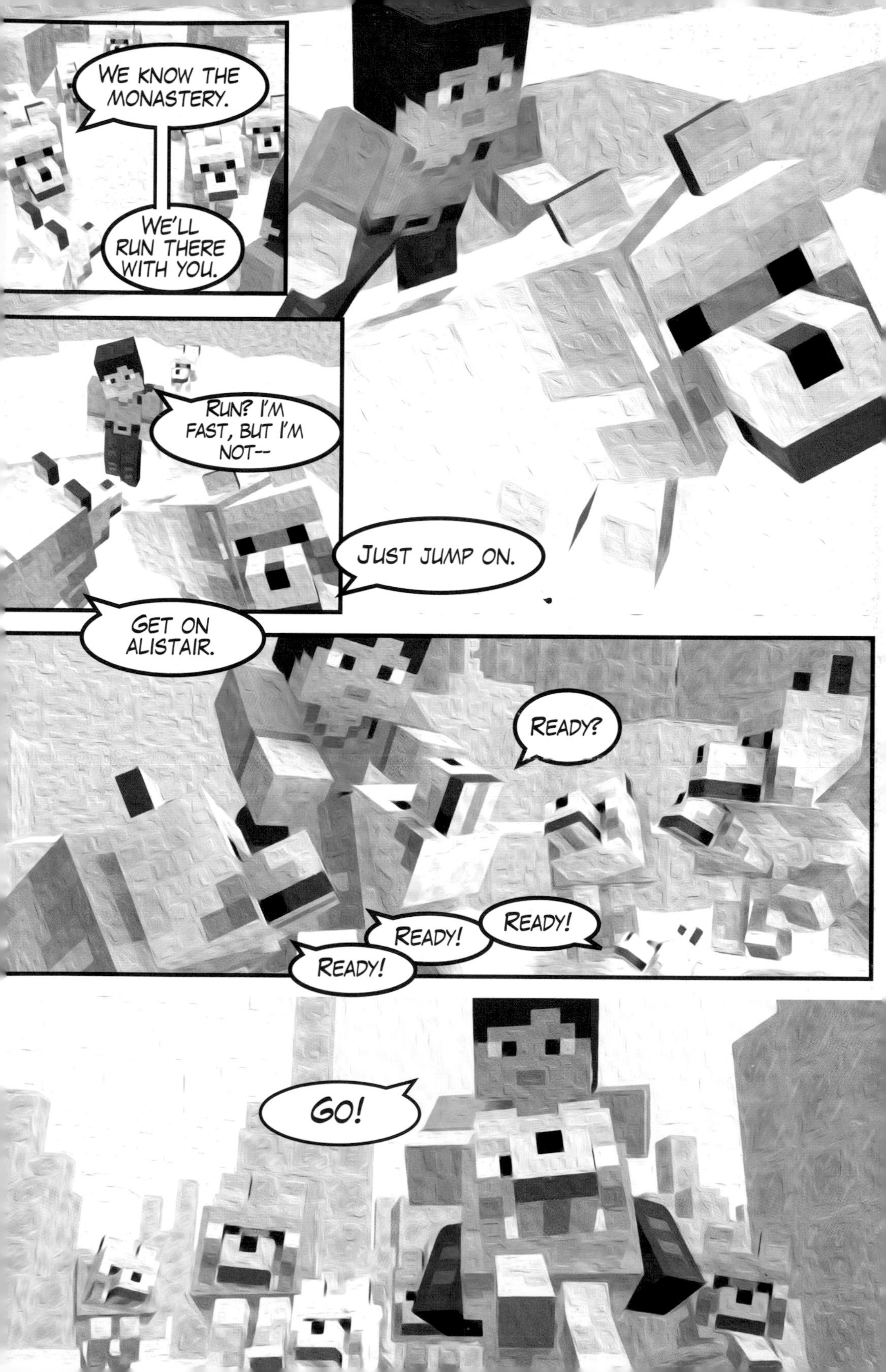
WE KNOW THE MONASTERY.
WE'LL RUN THERE WITH YOU.
RUN? I'M FAST, BUT I'M NOT--
JUST JUMP ON.
GET ON ALISTAIR.
READY?
READY!
READY!
READY!
GO!

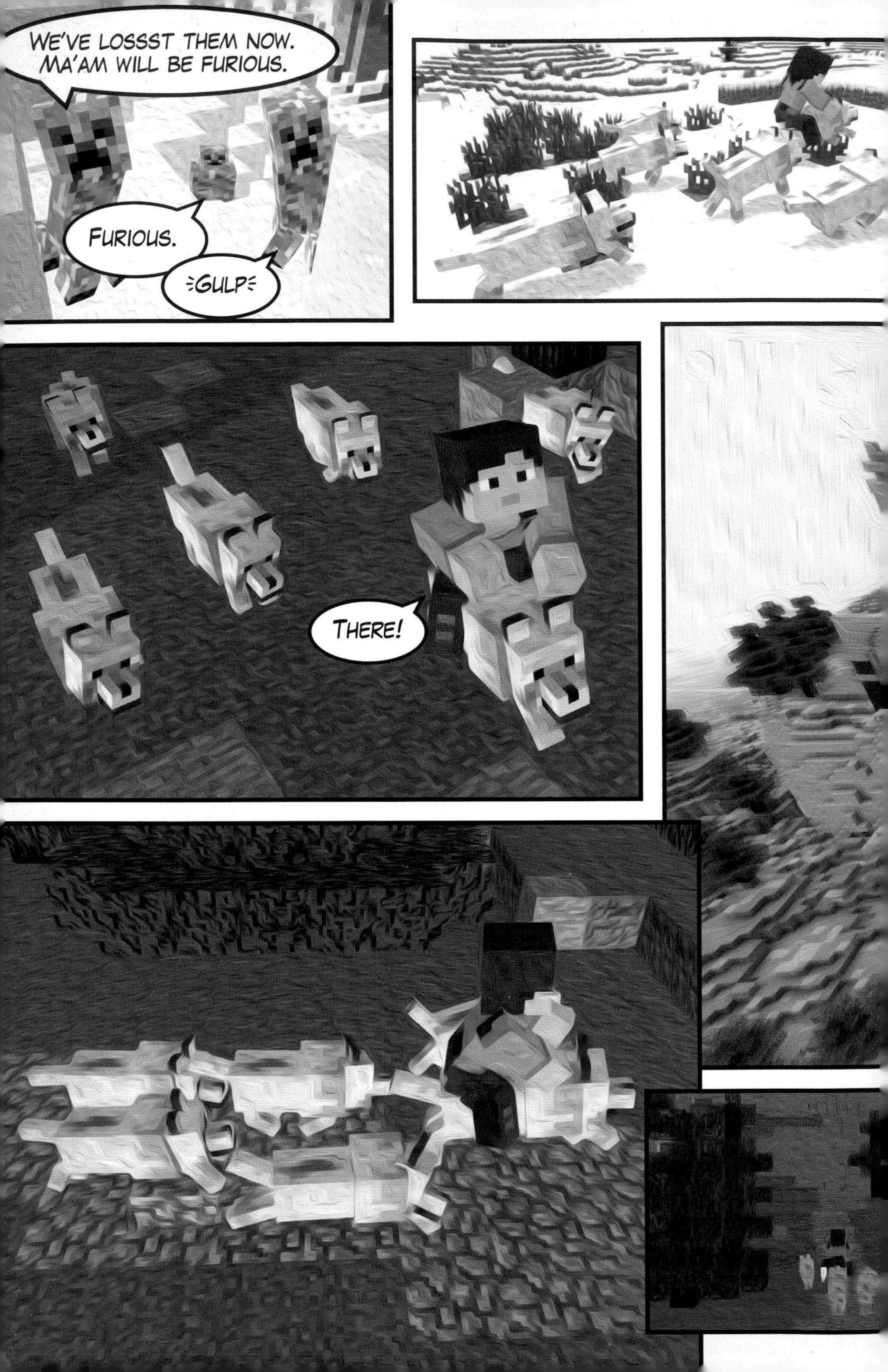
WE'VE LOSSST THEM NOW. MA'AM WILL BE FURIOUS.
FURIOUS.
GULP
THERE!

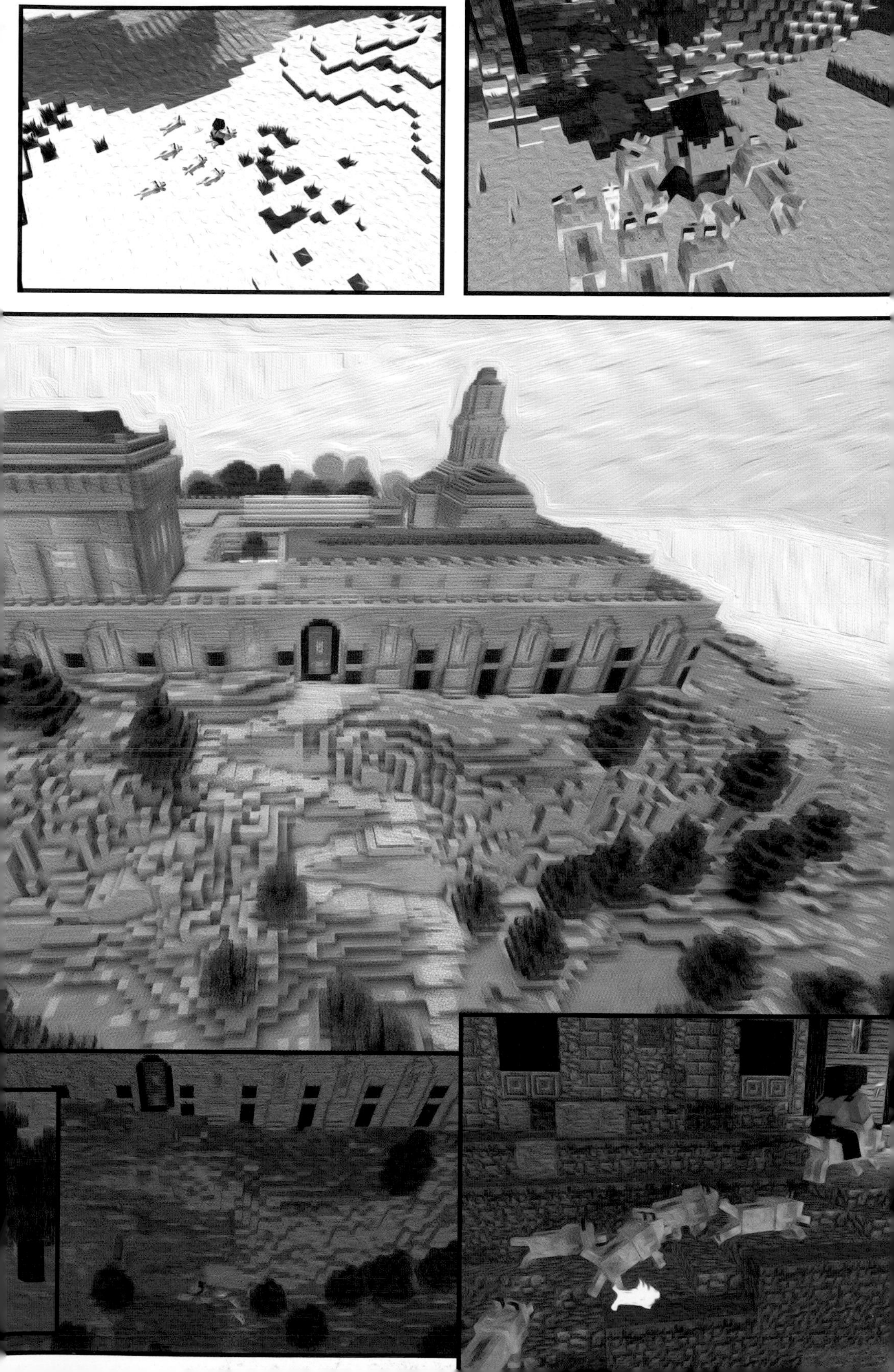

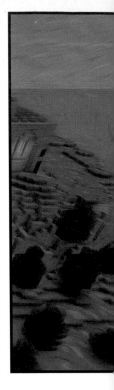

WE MADE IT! NOW, TIME TO FIND THAT GOLDEN APPLE!

CHAPTER 8
THE MONASTERY

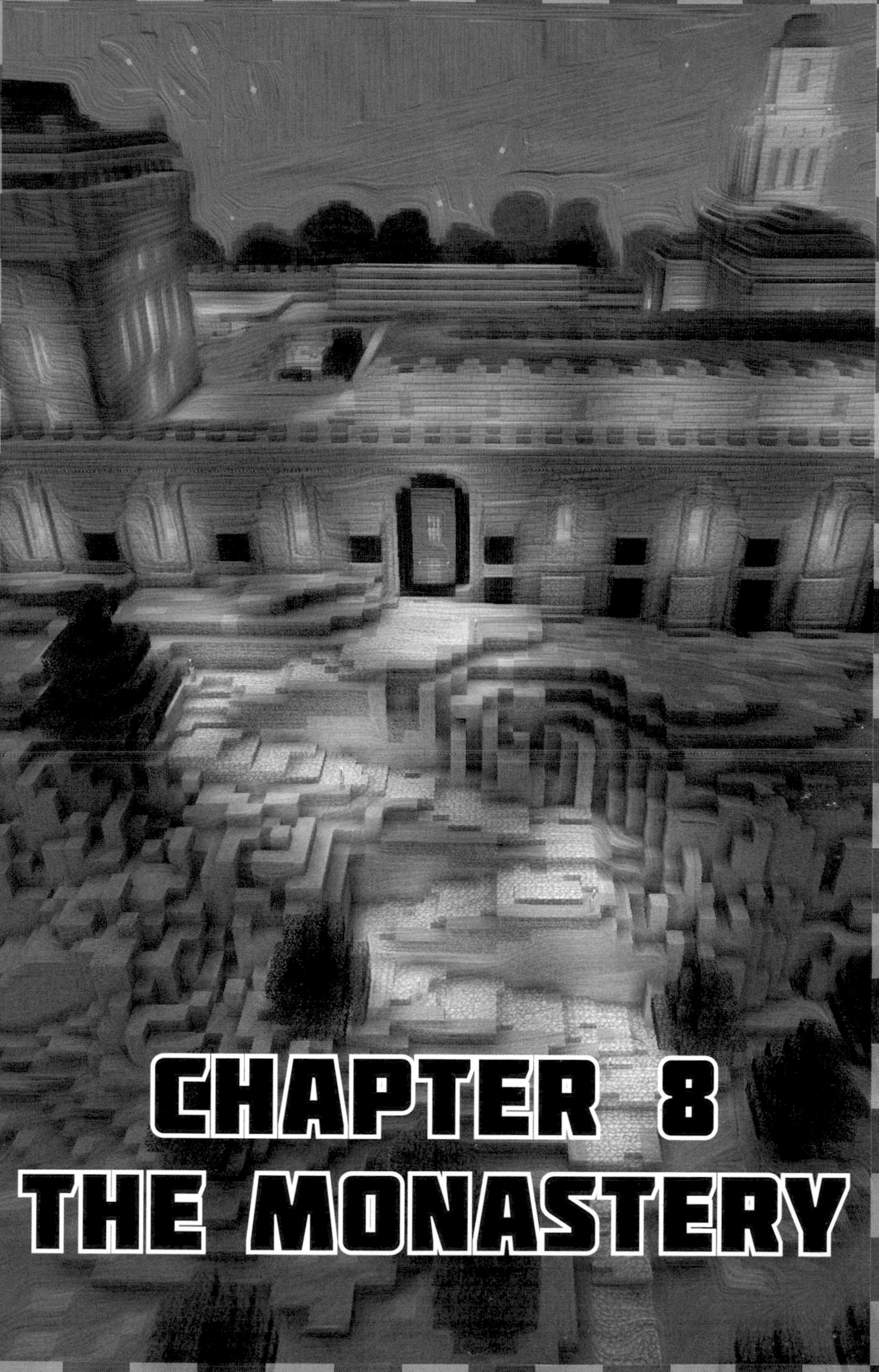

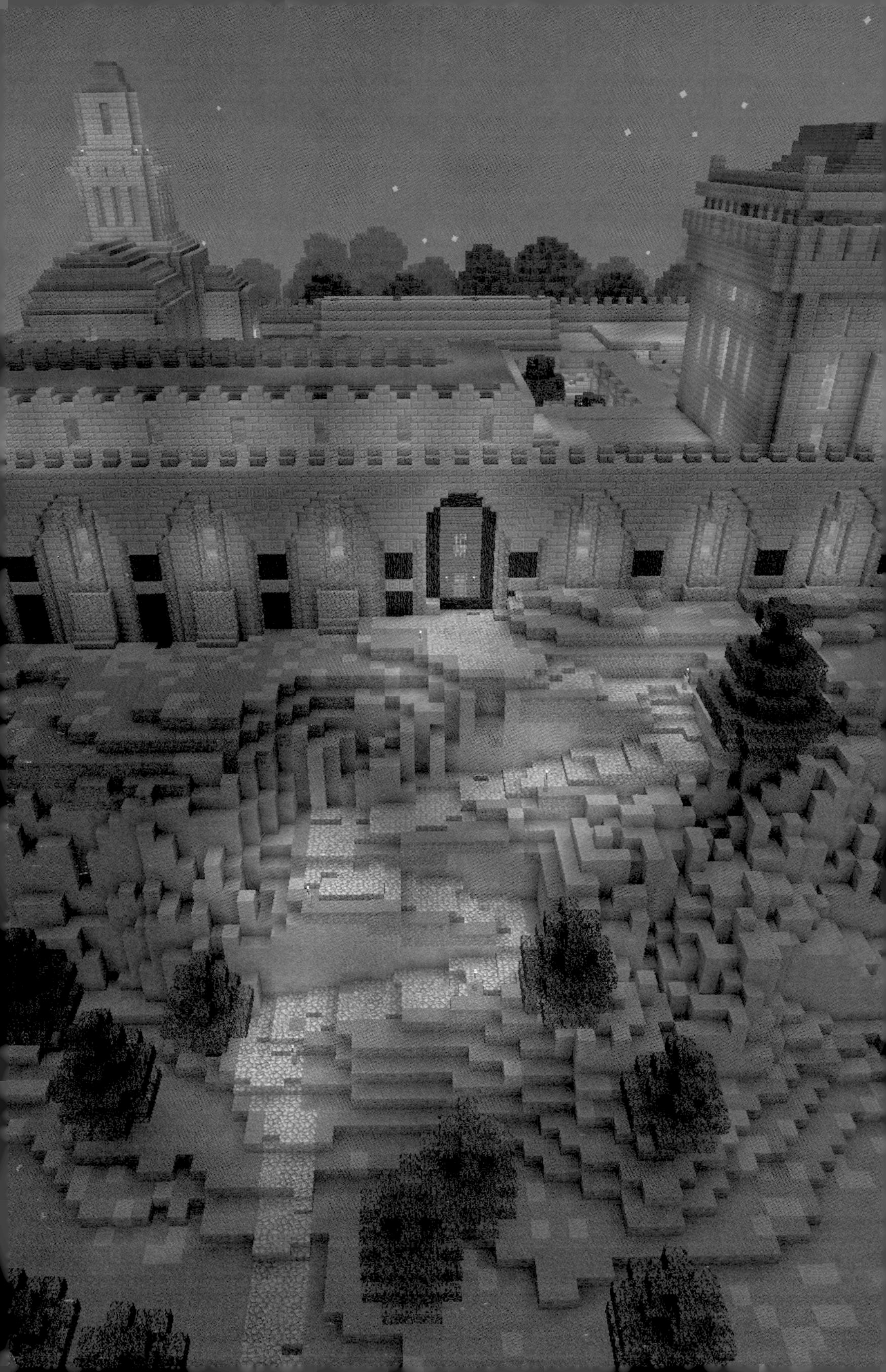

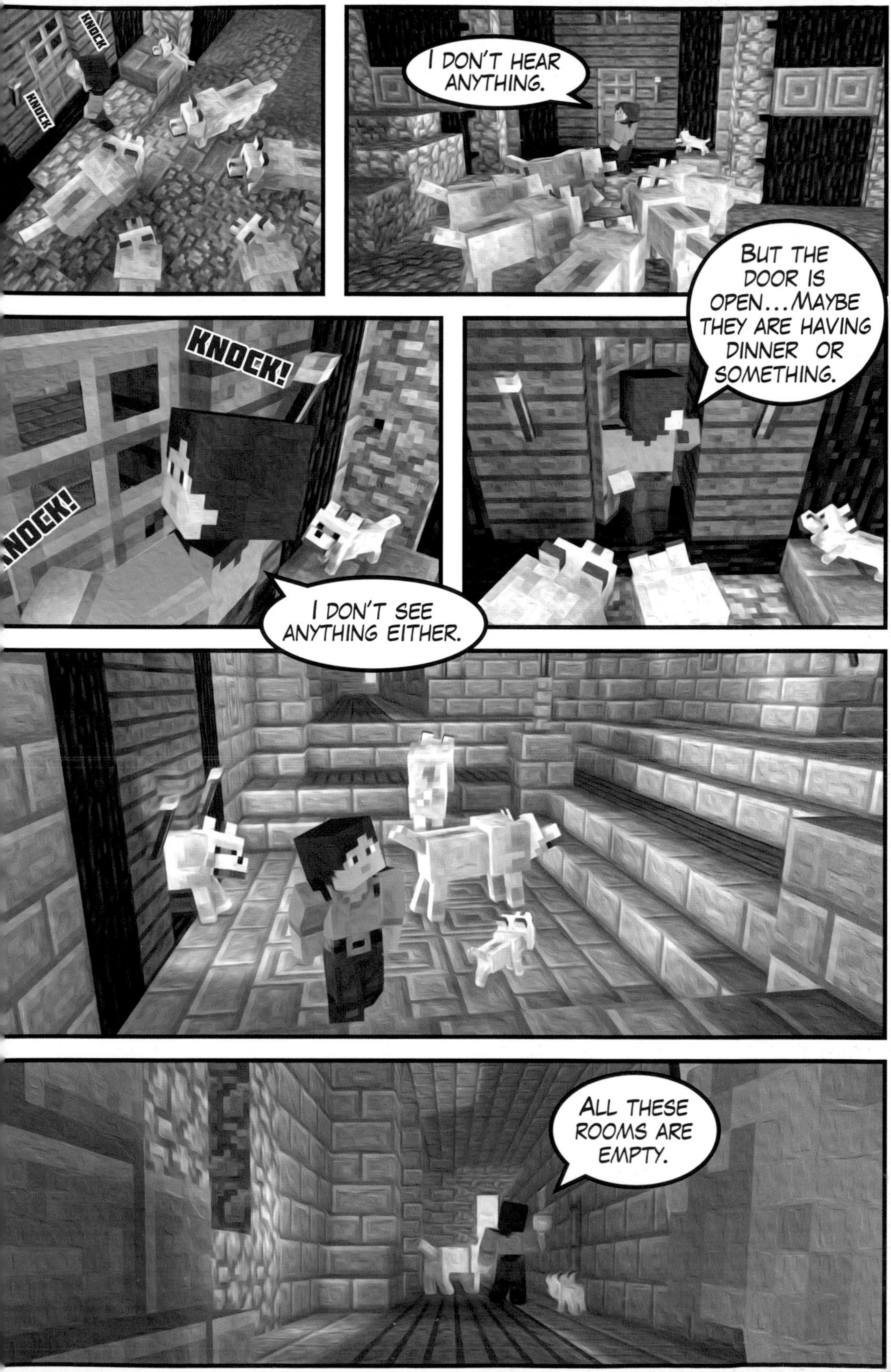
KNOCK
KNOCK
I DON'T HEAR ANYTHING.
BUT THE DOOR IS OPEN…MAYBE THEY ARE HAVING DINNER OR SOMETHING.
KNOCK!
KNOCK!
I DON'T SEE ANYTHING EITHER.
ALL THESE ROOMS ARE EMPTY.

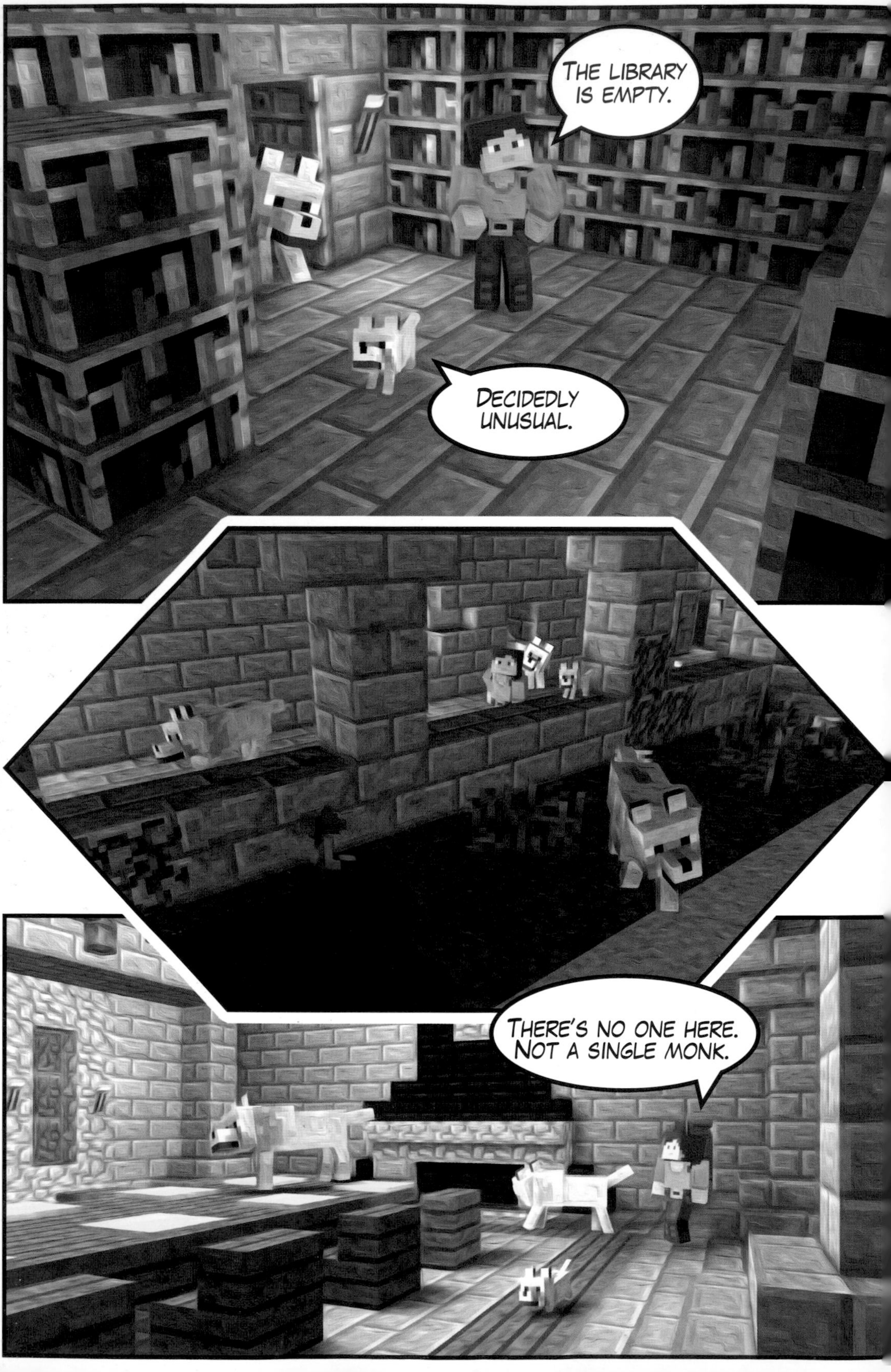
THE LIBRARY IS EMPTY.
DECIDEDLY UNUSUAL.
THERE'S NO ONE HERE. NOT A SINGLE MONK.

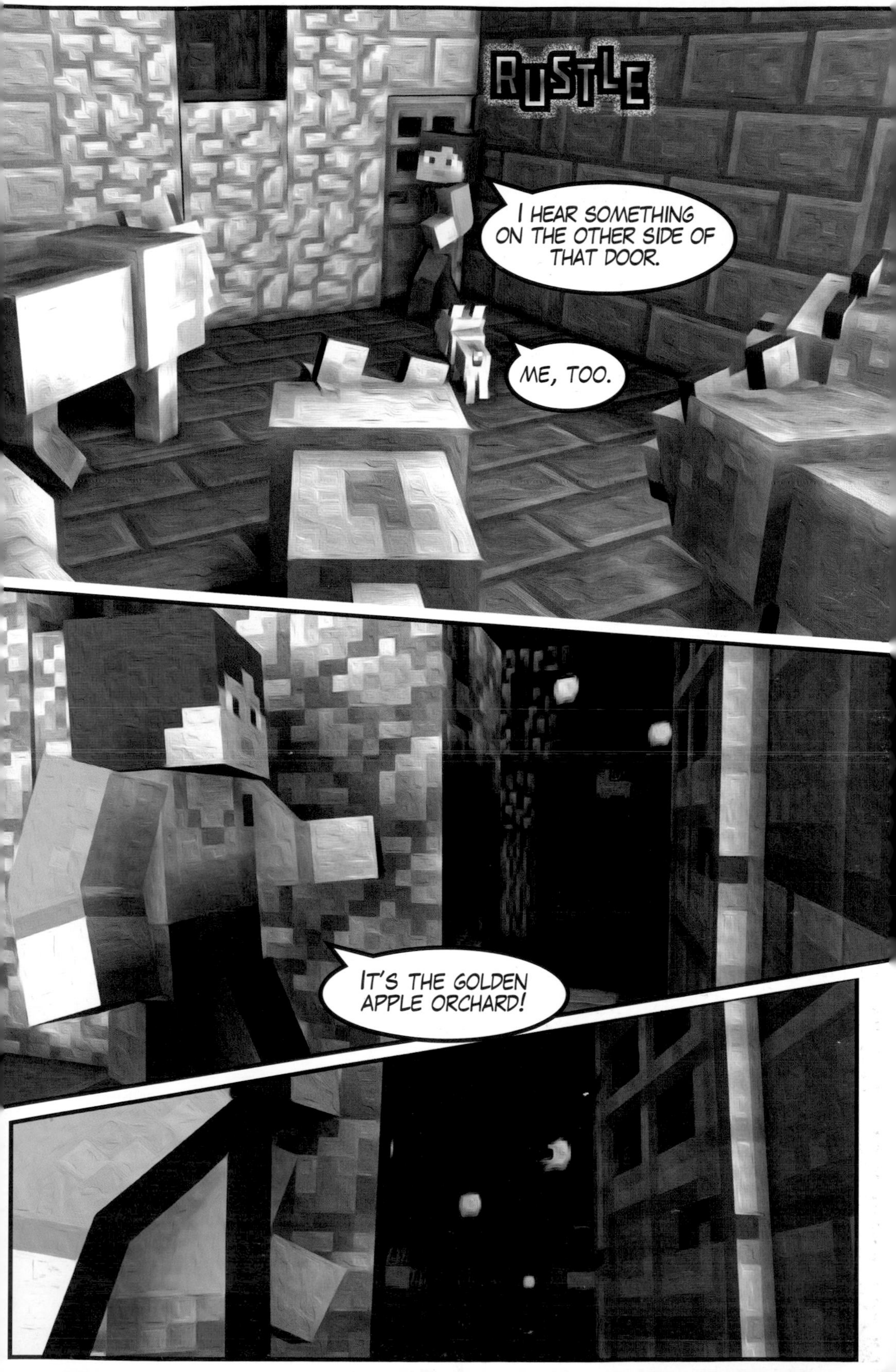
RUSTLE
I HEAR SOMETHING ON THE OTHER SIDE OF THAT DOOR.
ME, TOO.
IT'S THE GOLDEN APPLE ORCHARD!

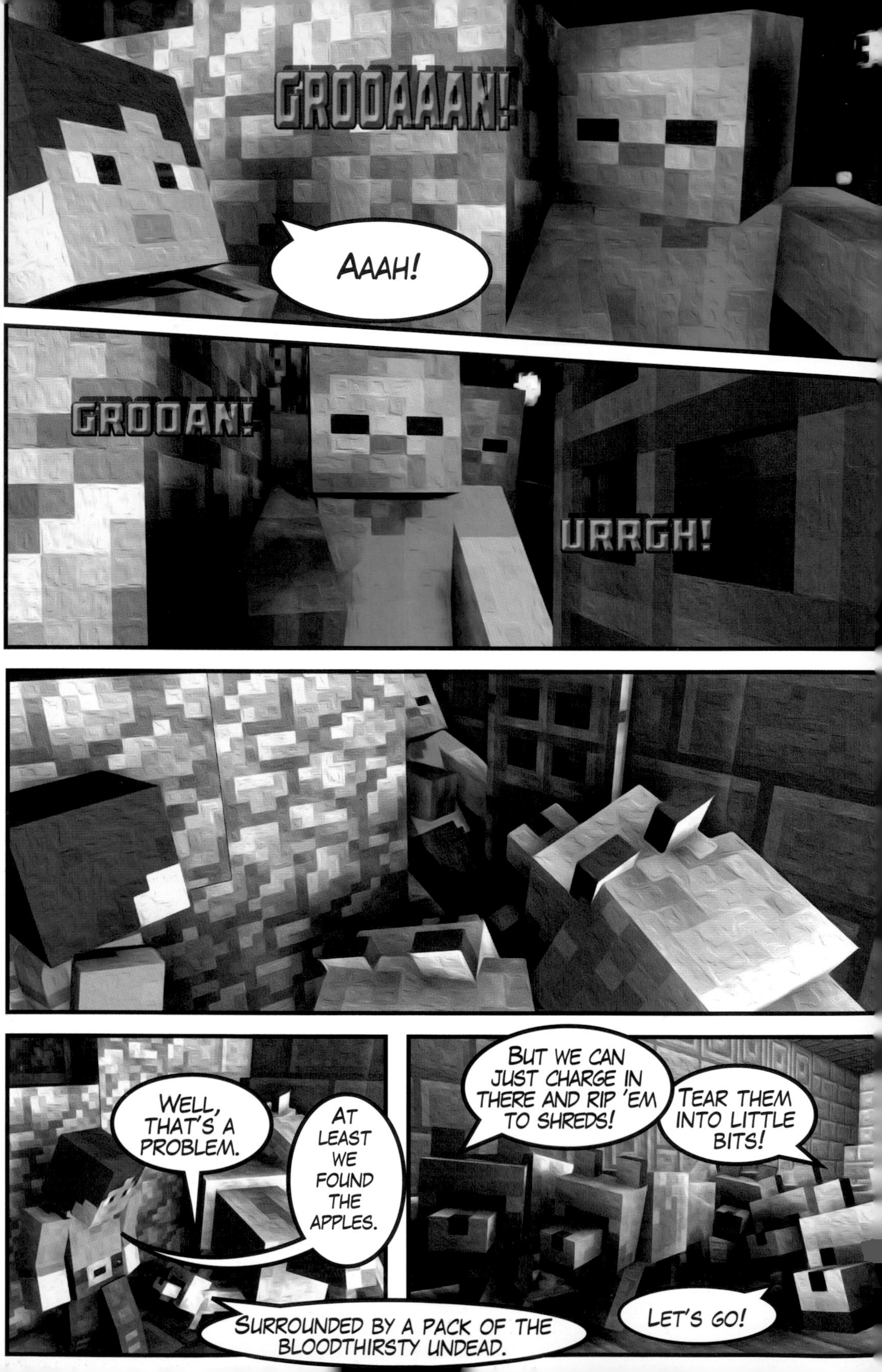
GROOAAAN!
AAAH!
GROOAN!
URRGH!
WELL, THAT'S A PROBLEM.
AT LEAST WE FOUND THE APPLES.
SURROUNDED BY A PACK OF THE BLOODTHIRSTY UNDEAD.
BUT WE CAN JUST CHARGE IN THERE AND RIP 'EM TO SHREDS!
TEAR THEM INTO LITTLE BITS!
LET'S GO!

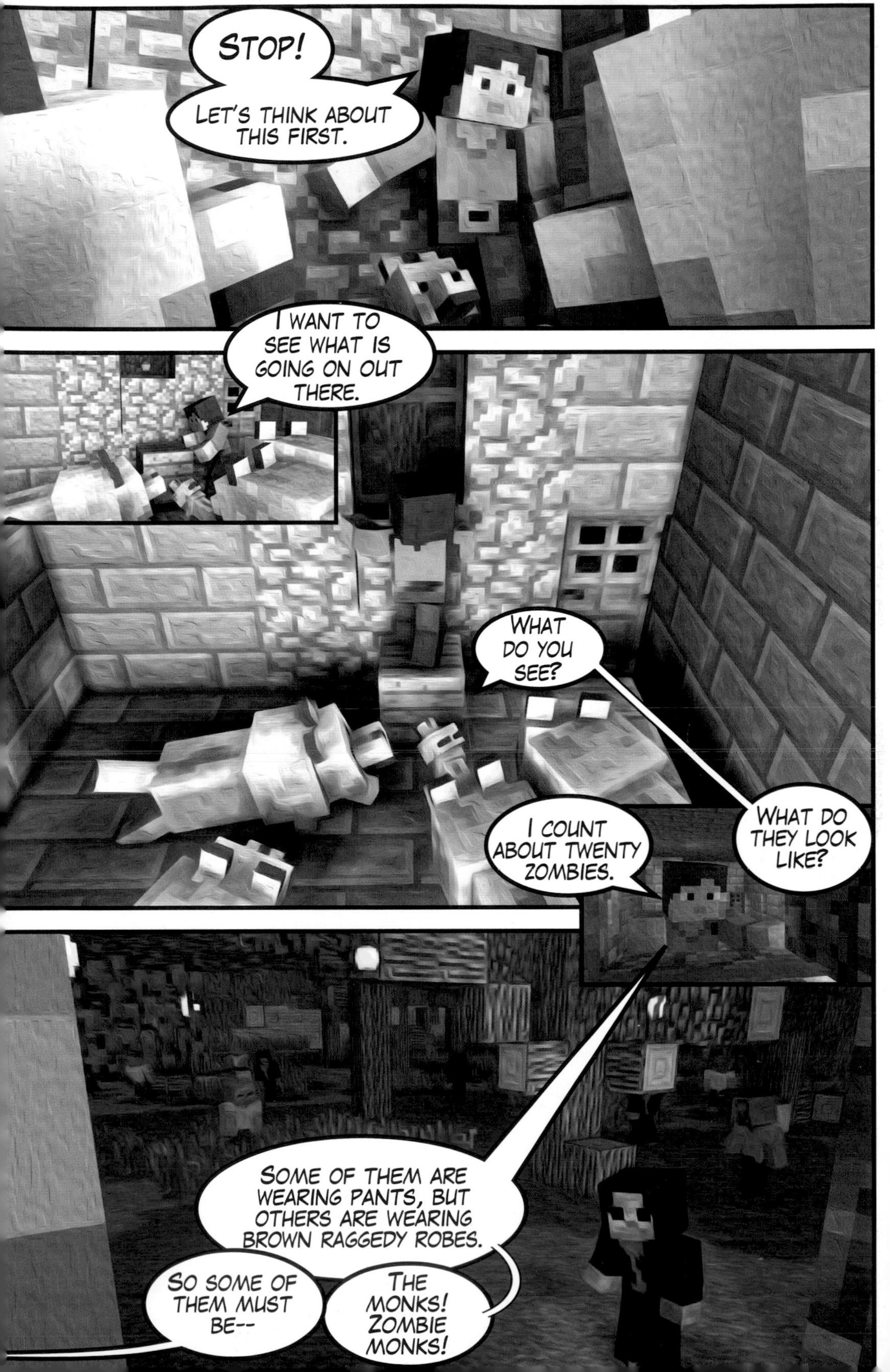
STOP!
LET'S THINK ABOUT THIS FIRST.
I WANT TO SEE WHAT IS GOING ON OUT THERE.
WHAT DO YOU SEE?
I COUNT ABOUT TWENTY ZOMBIES.
WHAT DO THEY LOOK LIKE?
SOME OF THEM ARE WEARING PANTS, BUT OTHERS ARE WEARING BROWN RAGGEDY ROBES.
SO SOME OF THEM MUST BE--
THE MONKS! ZOMBIE MONKS!

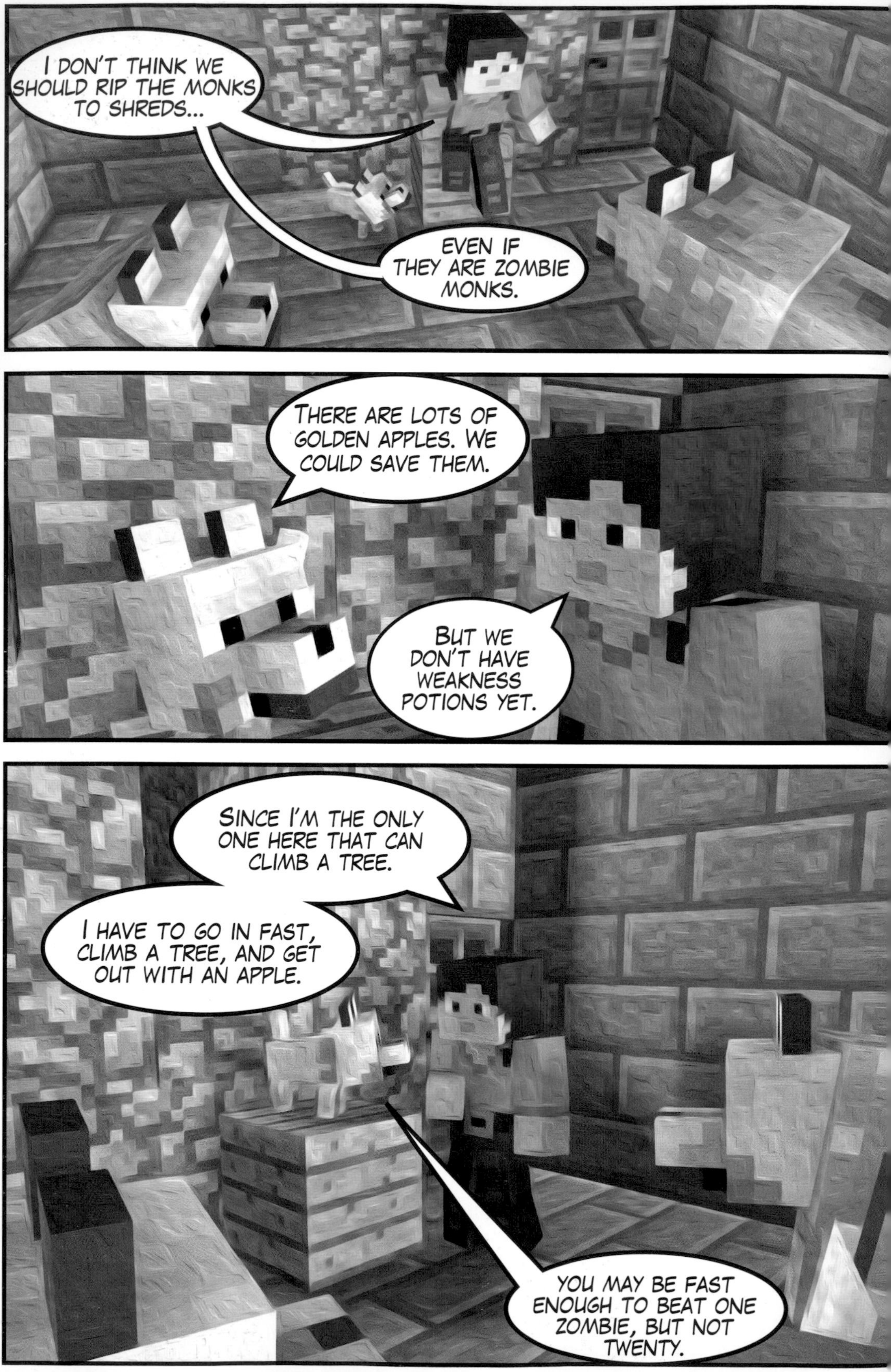

I DON'T THINK WE SHOULD RIP THE MONKS TO SHREDS...
EVEN IF THEY ARE ZOMBIE MONKS.
THERE ARE LOTS OF GOLDEN APPLES. WE COULD SAVE THEM.
BUT WE DON'T HAVE WEAKNESS POTIONS YET.
SINCE I'M THE ONLY ONE HERE THAT CAN CLIMB A TREE.
I HAVE TO GO IN FAST, CLIMB A TREE, AND GET OUT WITH AN APPLE.
YOU MAY BE FAST ENOUGH TO BEAT ONE ZOMBIE, BUT NOT TWENTY.

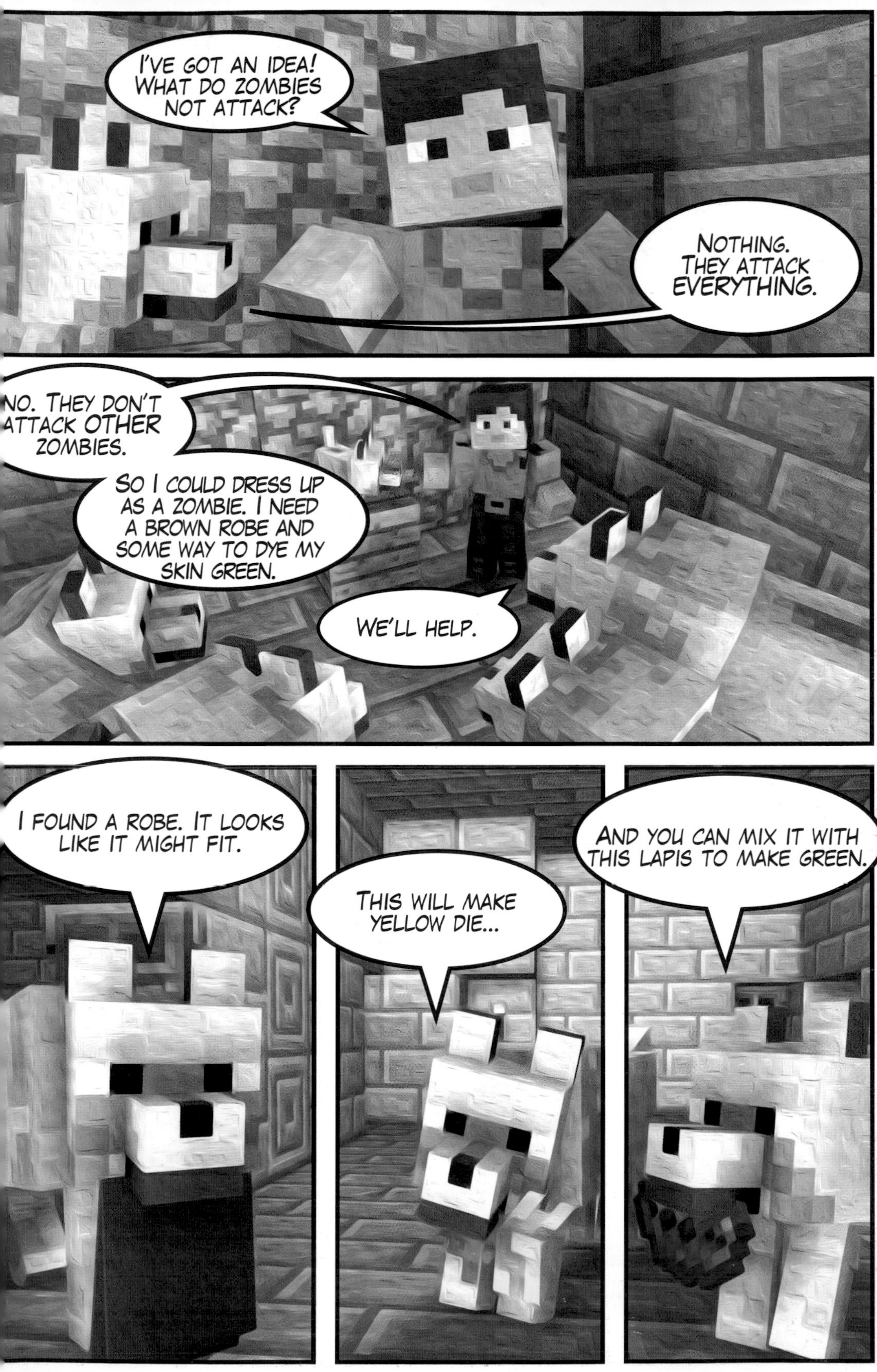
I'VE GOT AN IDEA! WHAT DO ZOMBIES NOT ATTACK?
NOTHING. THEY ATTACK EVERYTHING.
NO. THEY DON'T ATTACK OTHER ZOMBIES.
SO I COULD DRESS UP AS A ZOMBIE. I NEED A BROWN ROBE AND SOME WAY TO DYE MY SKIN GREEN.
WE'LL HELP.
I FOUND A ROBE. IT LOOKS LIKE IT MIGHT FIT.
THIS WILL MAKE YELLOW DIE...
AND YOU CAN MIX IT WITH THIS LAPIS TO MAKE GREEN.

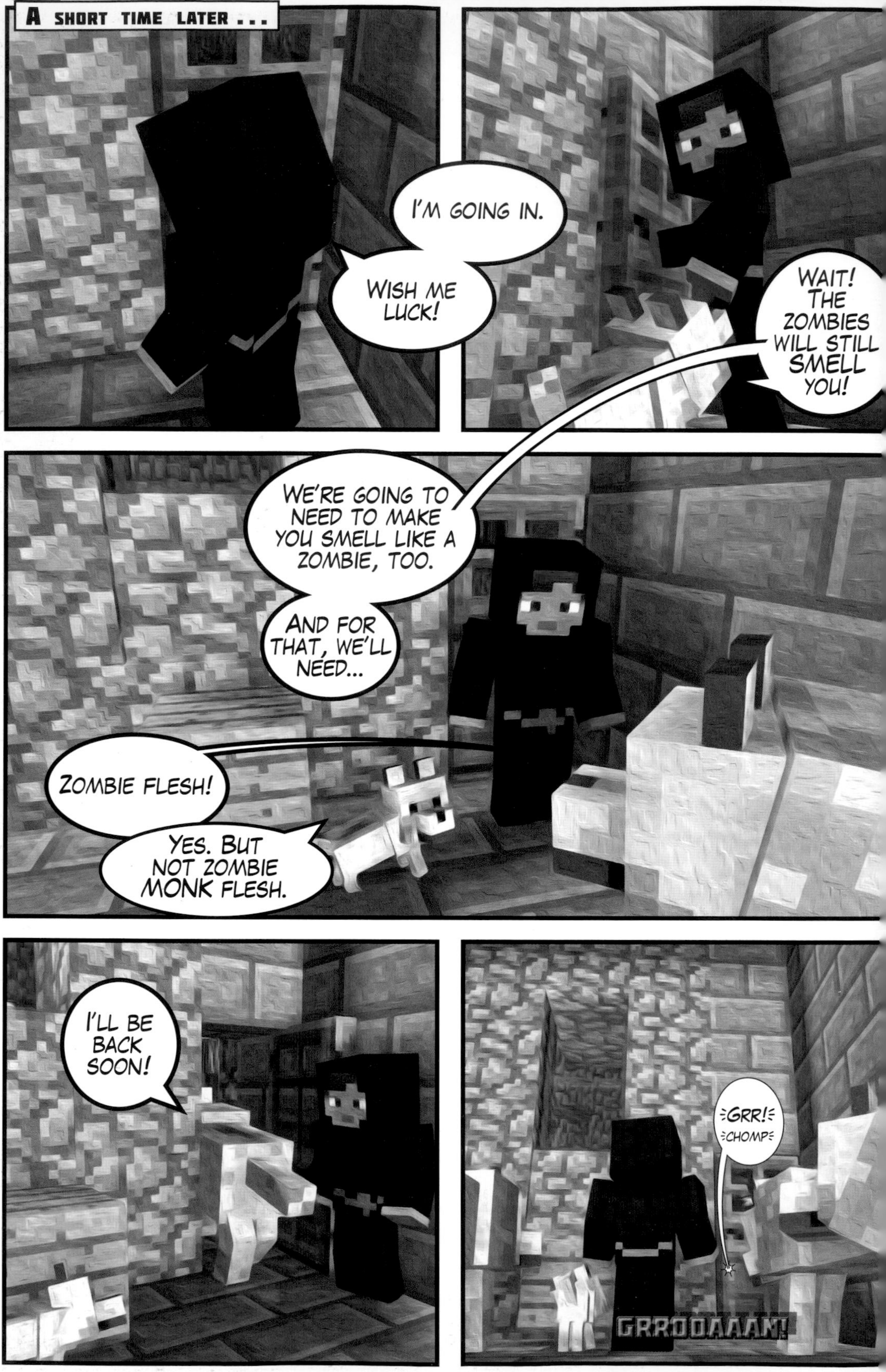
A SHORT TIME LATER . . .
I'M GOING IN.
WISH ME LUCK!
WAIT! THE ZOMBIES WILL STILL SMELL YOU!
WE'RE GOING TO NEED TO MAKE YOU SMELL LIKE A ZOMBIE, TOO.
AND FOR THAT, WE'LL NEED...
ZOMBIE FLESH!
YES. BUT NOT ZOMBIE MONK FLESH.
I'LL BE BACK SOON!
GRR!
CHOMP
GRROOAAAN!

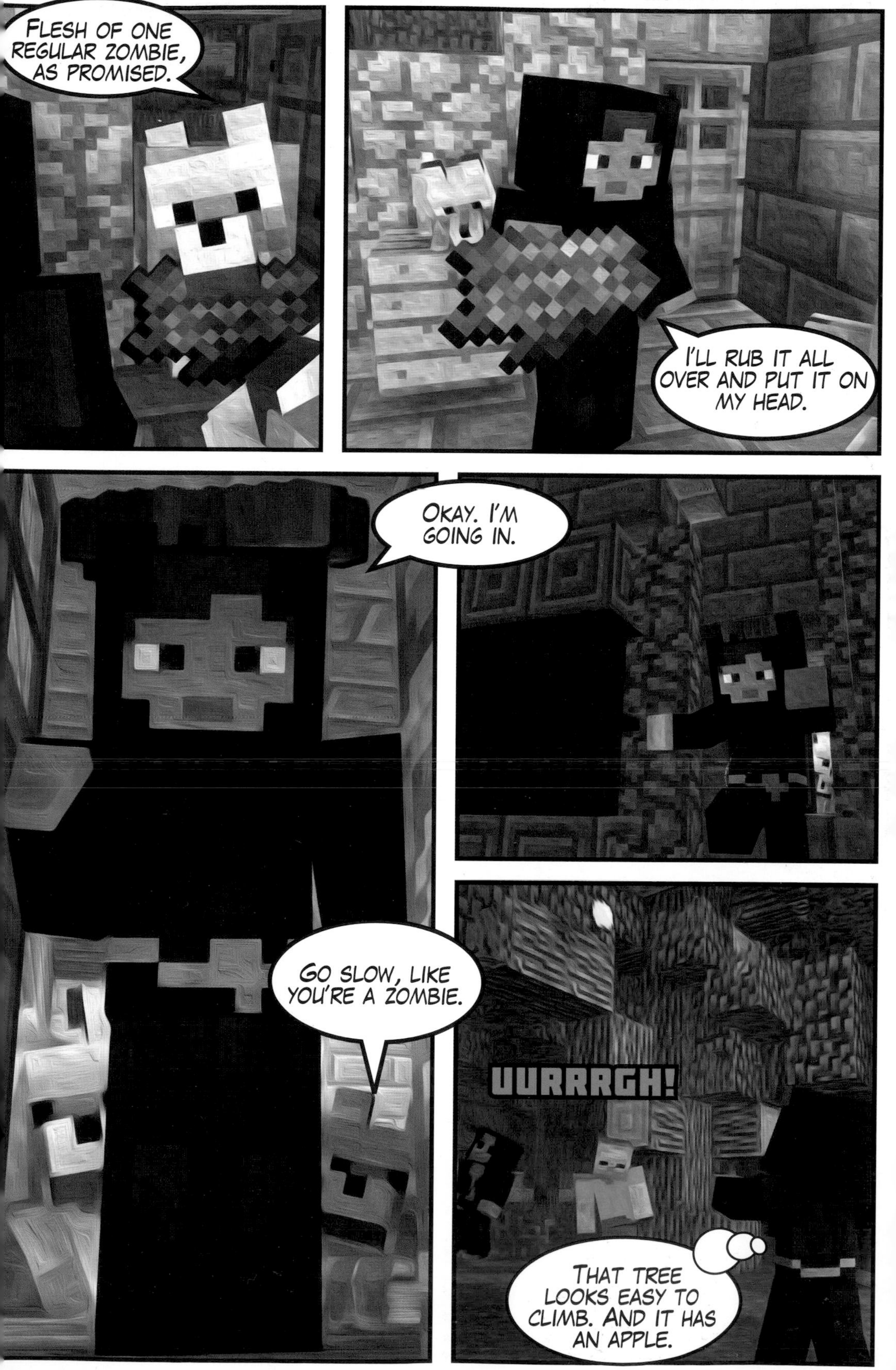
FLESH OF ONE REGULAR ZOMBIE, AS PROMISED.
I'LL RUB IT ALL OVER AND PUT IT ON MY HEAD.
OKAY. I'M GOING IN.
GO SLOW, LIKE YOU'RE A ZOMBIE.
UURRRGH!
THAT TREE LOOKS EASY TO CLIMB. AND IT HAS AN APPLE.

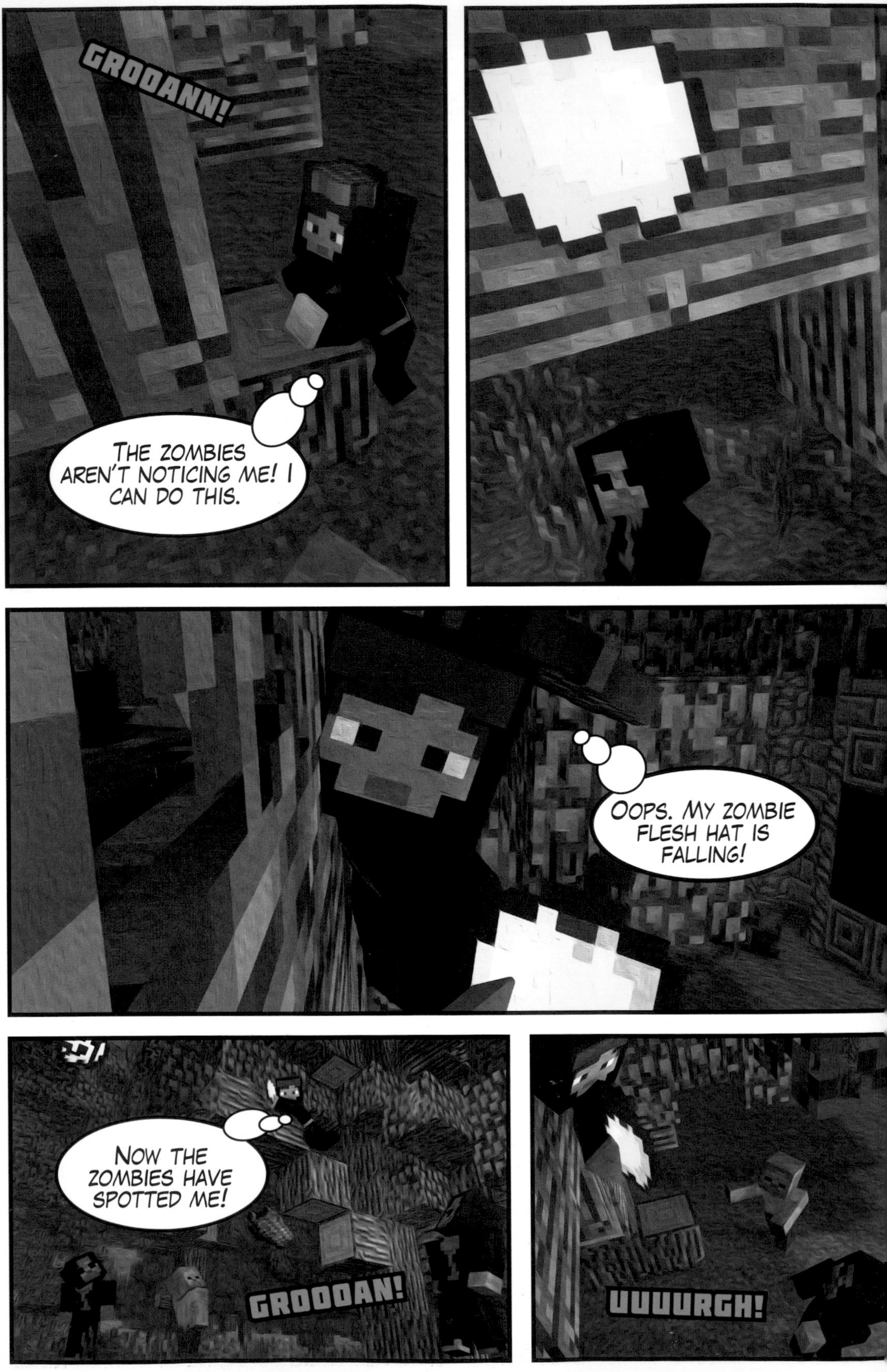
GROOANN!
THE ZOMBIES AREN'T NOTICING ME! I CAN DO THIS.
OOPS. MY ZOMBIE FLESH HAT IS FALLING!
NOW THE ZOMBIES HAVE SPOTTED ME!
GROOOAN!
UUUURGH!

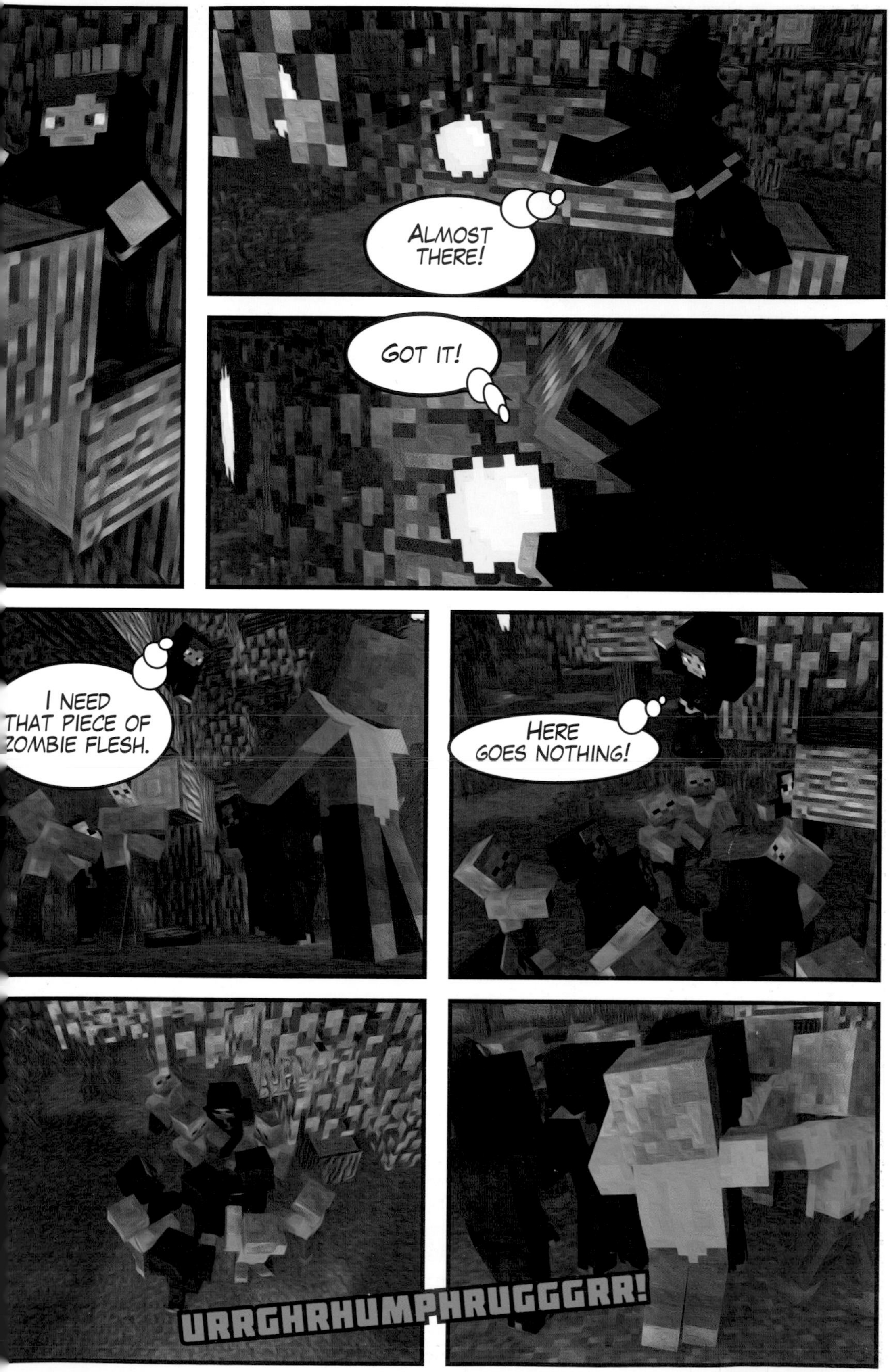
ALMOST THERE!
GOT IT!
I NEED THAT PIECE OF ZOMBIE FLESH.
HERE GOES NOTHING!
URRGHRHUMPHRUGGGRR!

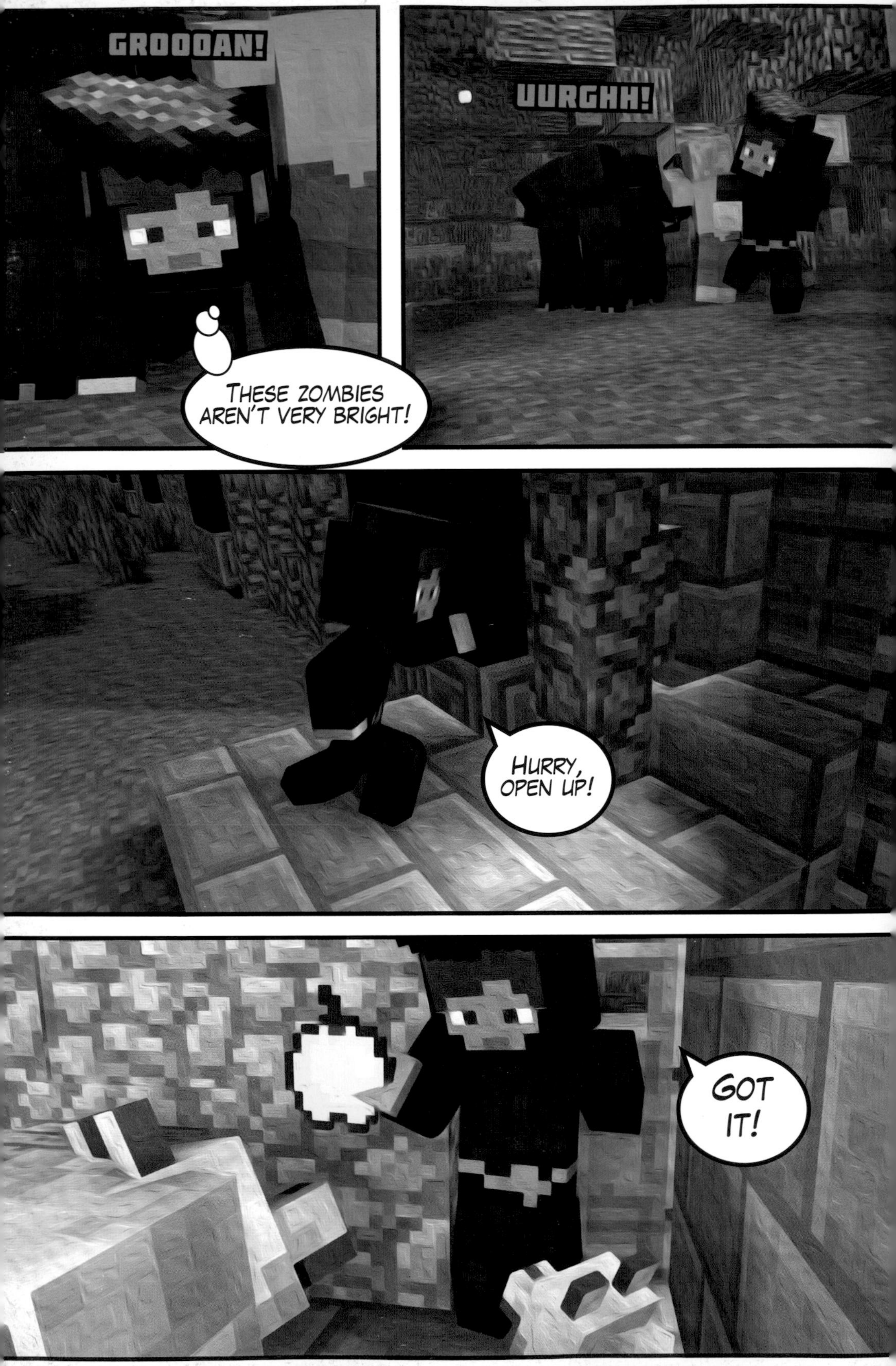
GROOOAN!
UURGHH!
THESE ZOMBIES AREN'T VERY BRIGHT!
HURRY, OPEN UP!
GOT IT!

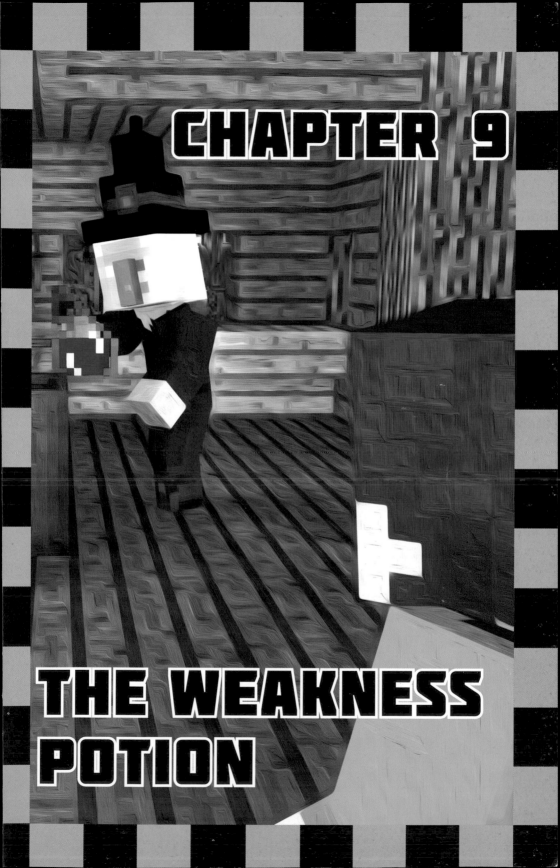

CHAPTER 9

THE WEAKNESS POTION

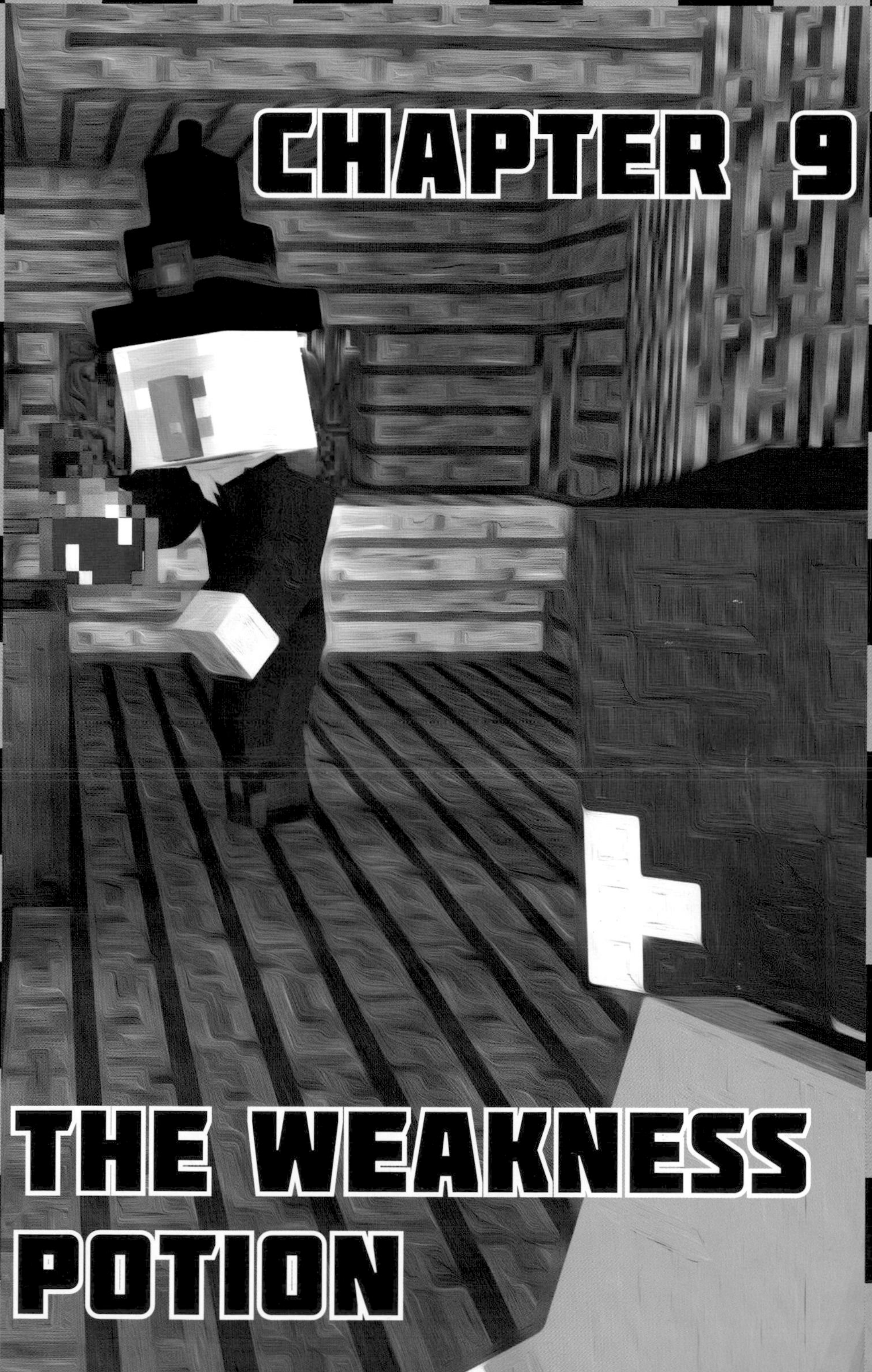

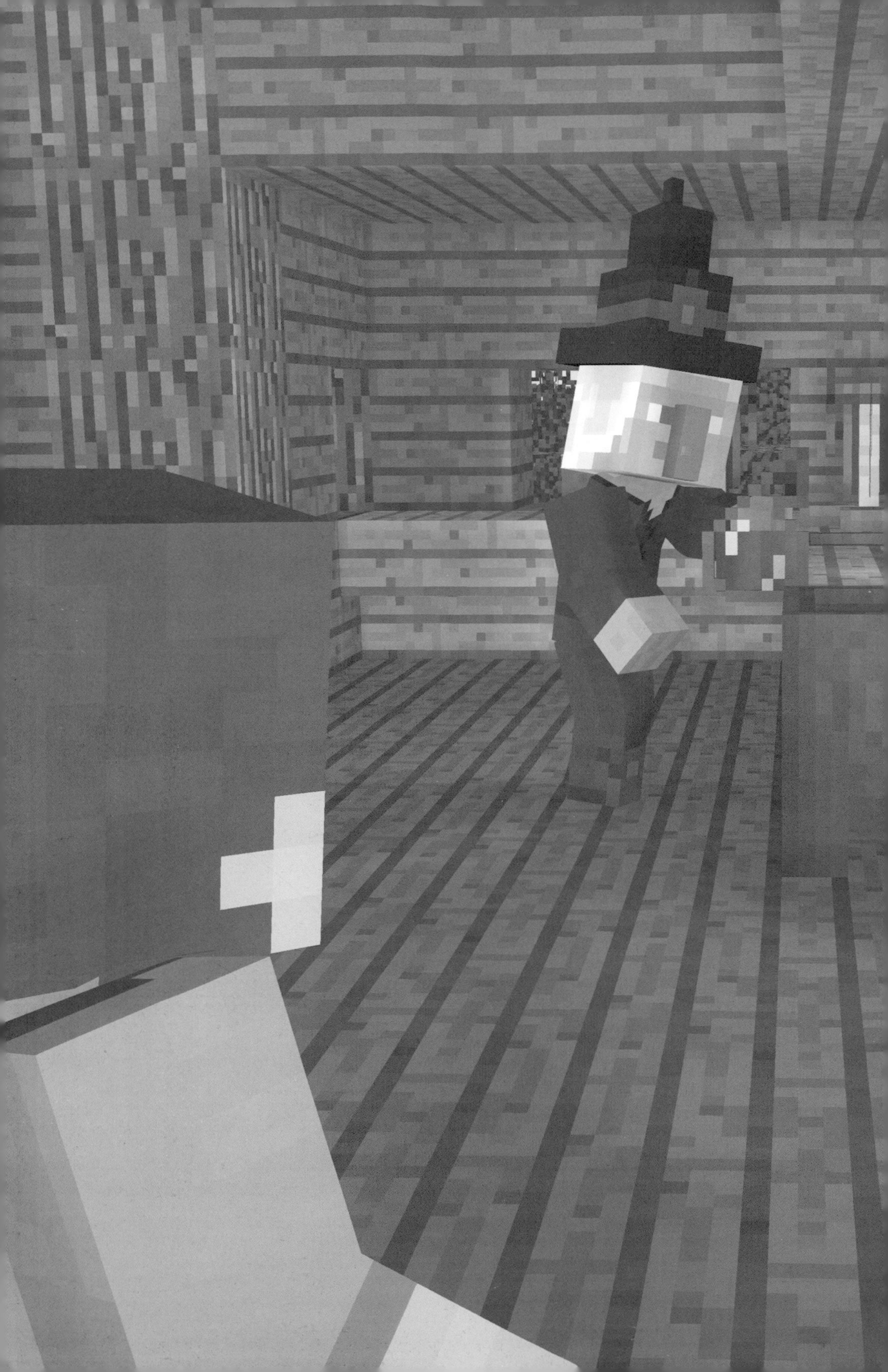

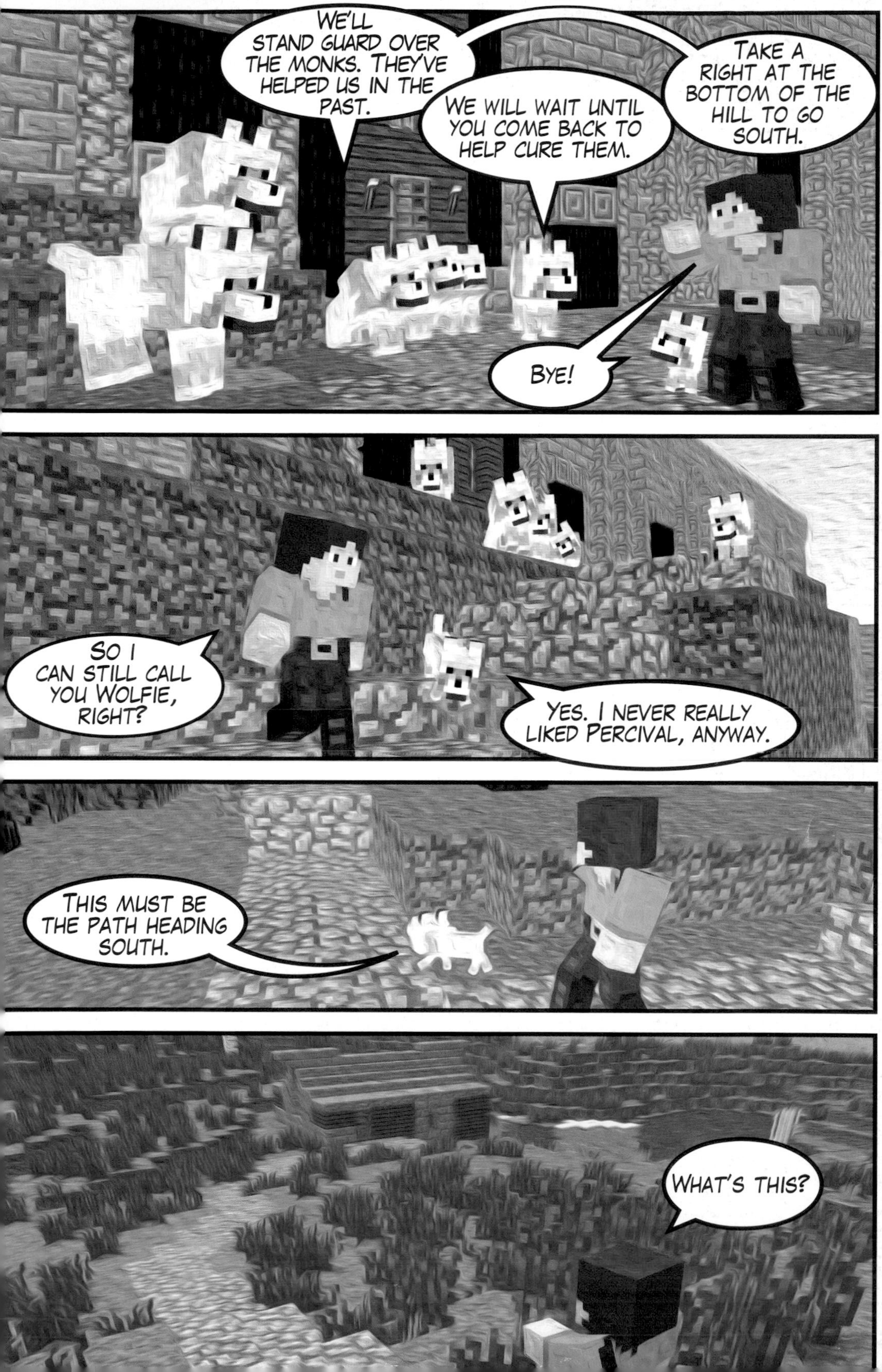
WE'LL STAND GUARD OVER THE MONKS. THEY'VE HELPED US IN THE PAST.
WE WILL WAIT UNTIL YOU COME BACK TO HELP CURE THEM.
TAKE A RIGHT AT THE BOTTOM OF THE HILL TO GO SOUTH.
BYE!
SO I CAN STILL CALL YOU WOLFIE, RIGHT?
YES. I NEVER REALLY LIKED PERCIVAL, ANYWAY.
THIS MUST BE THE PATH HEADING SOUTH.
WHAT'S THIS?

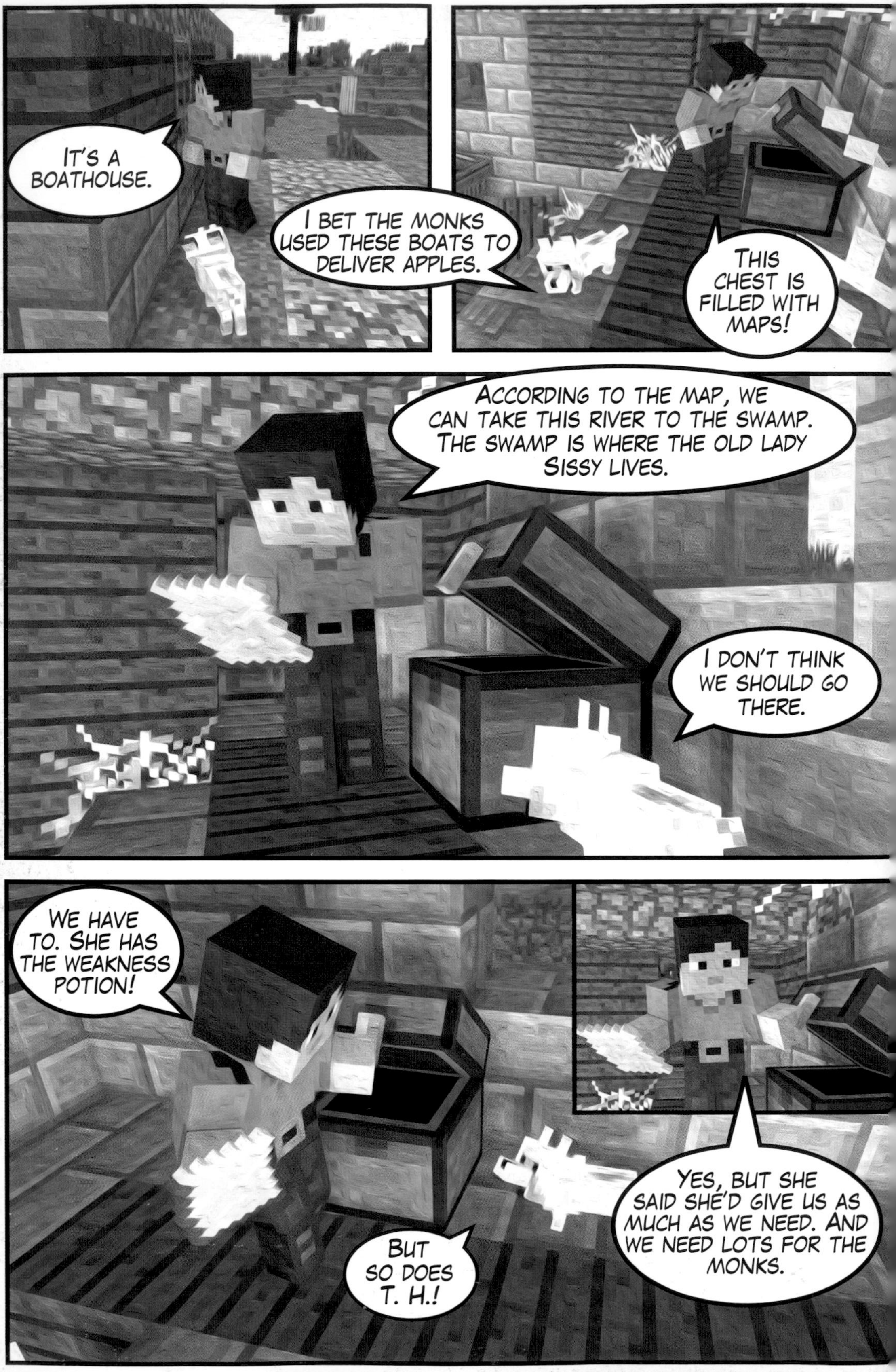
It's a boathouse.
I bet the monks used these boats to deliver apples.
This chest is filled with maps!
According to the map, we can take this river to the swamp. The swamp is where the old lady Sissy lives.
I don't think we should go there.
We have to. She has the weakness potion!
But so does T. H.!
Yes, but she said she'd give us as much as we need. And we need lots for the monks.

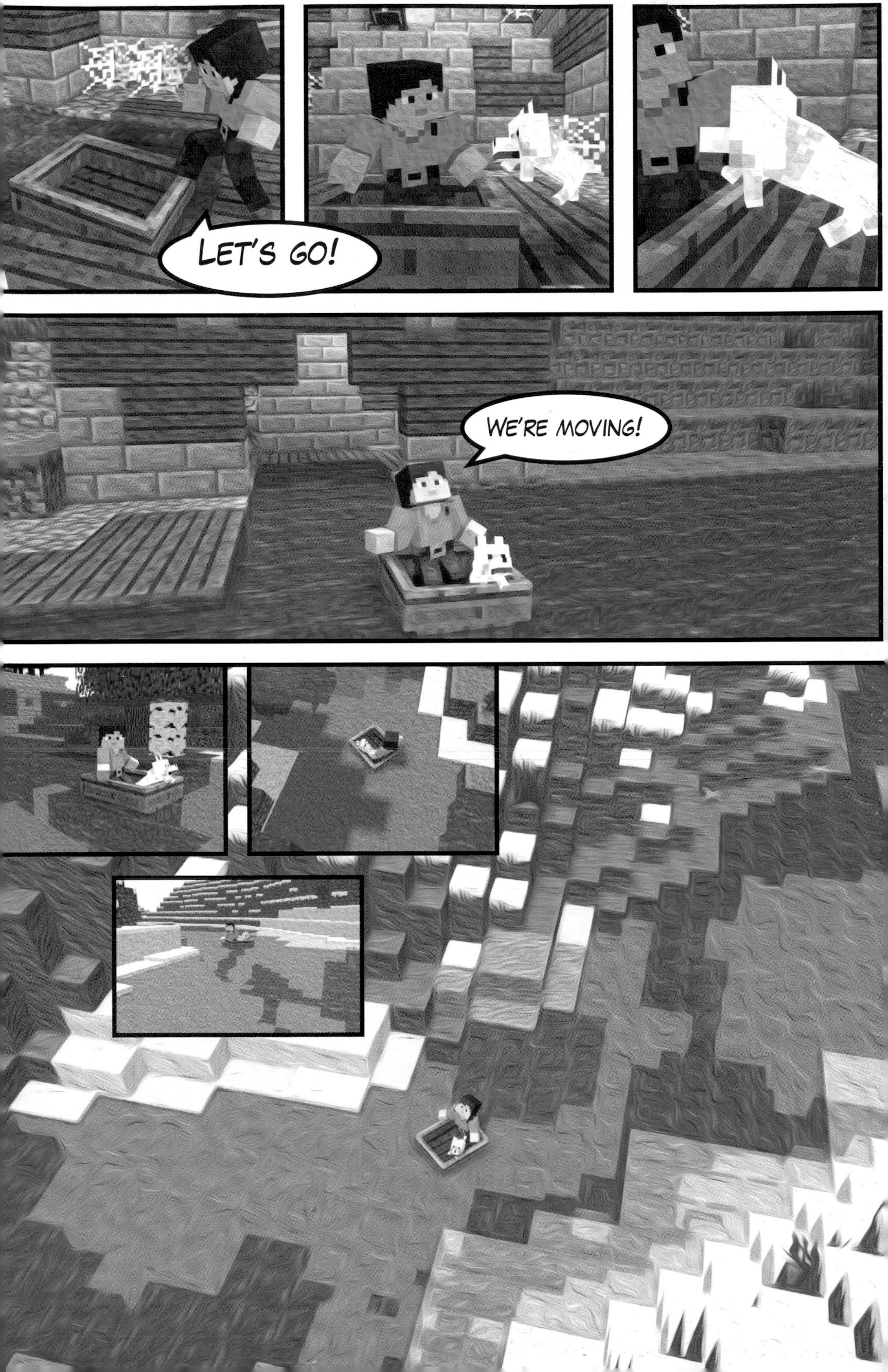
LET'S GO!
WE'RE MOVING!

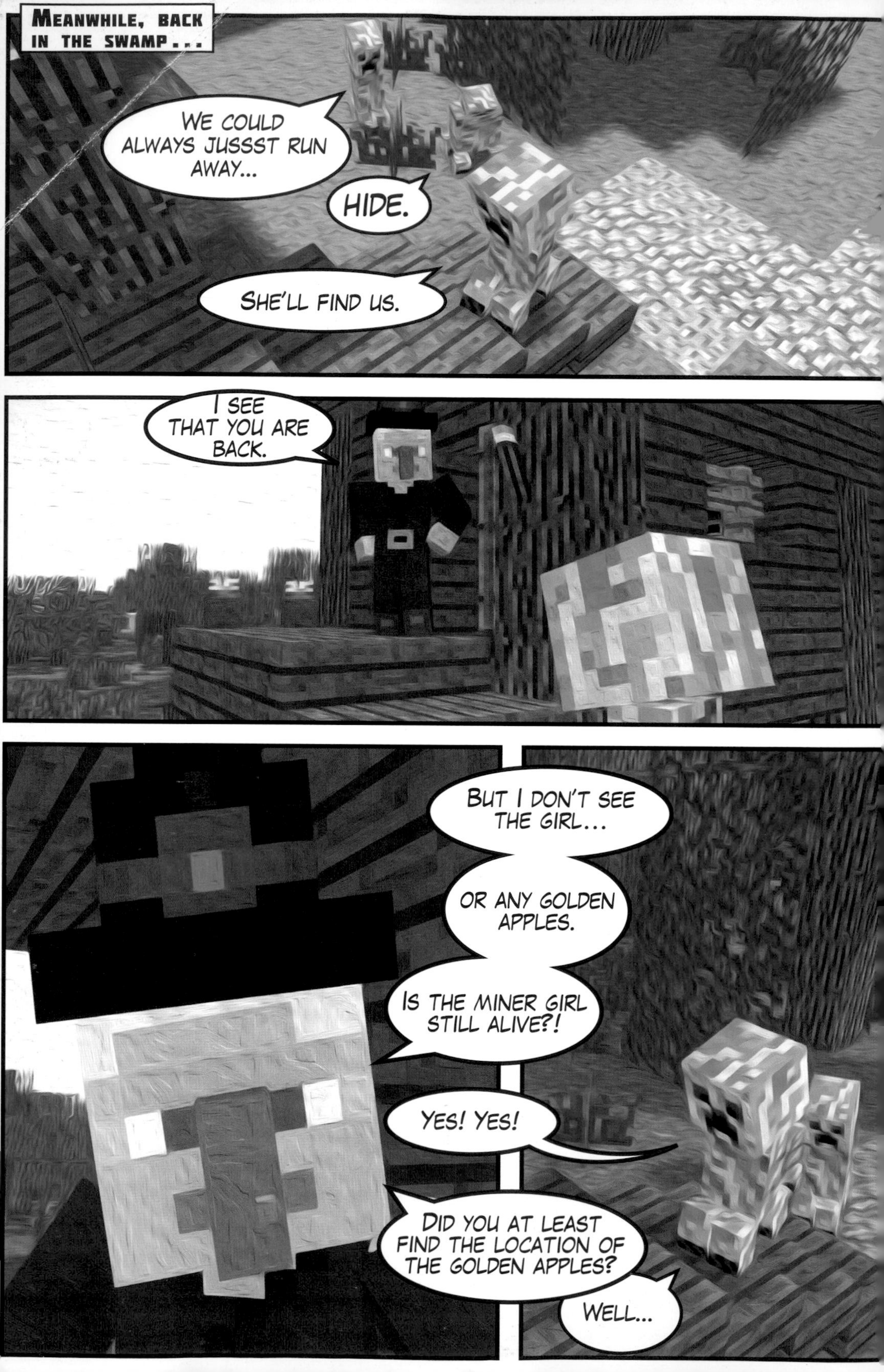
MEANWHILE, BACK IN THE SWAMP . . .
WE COULD ALWAYS JUSSST RUN AWAY...
HIDE.
SHE'LL FIND US.
I SEE THAT YOU ARE BACK.
BUT I DON'T SEE THE GIRL...
OR ANY GOLDEN APPLES.
IS THE MINER GIRL STILL ALIVE?!
YES! YES!
DID YOU AT LEAST FIND THE LOCATION OF THE GOLDEN APPLES?
WELL...

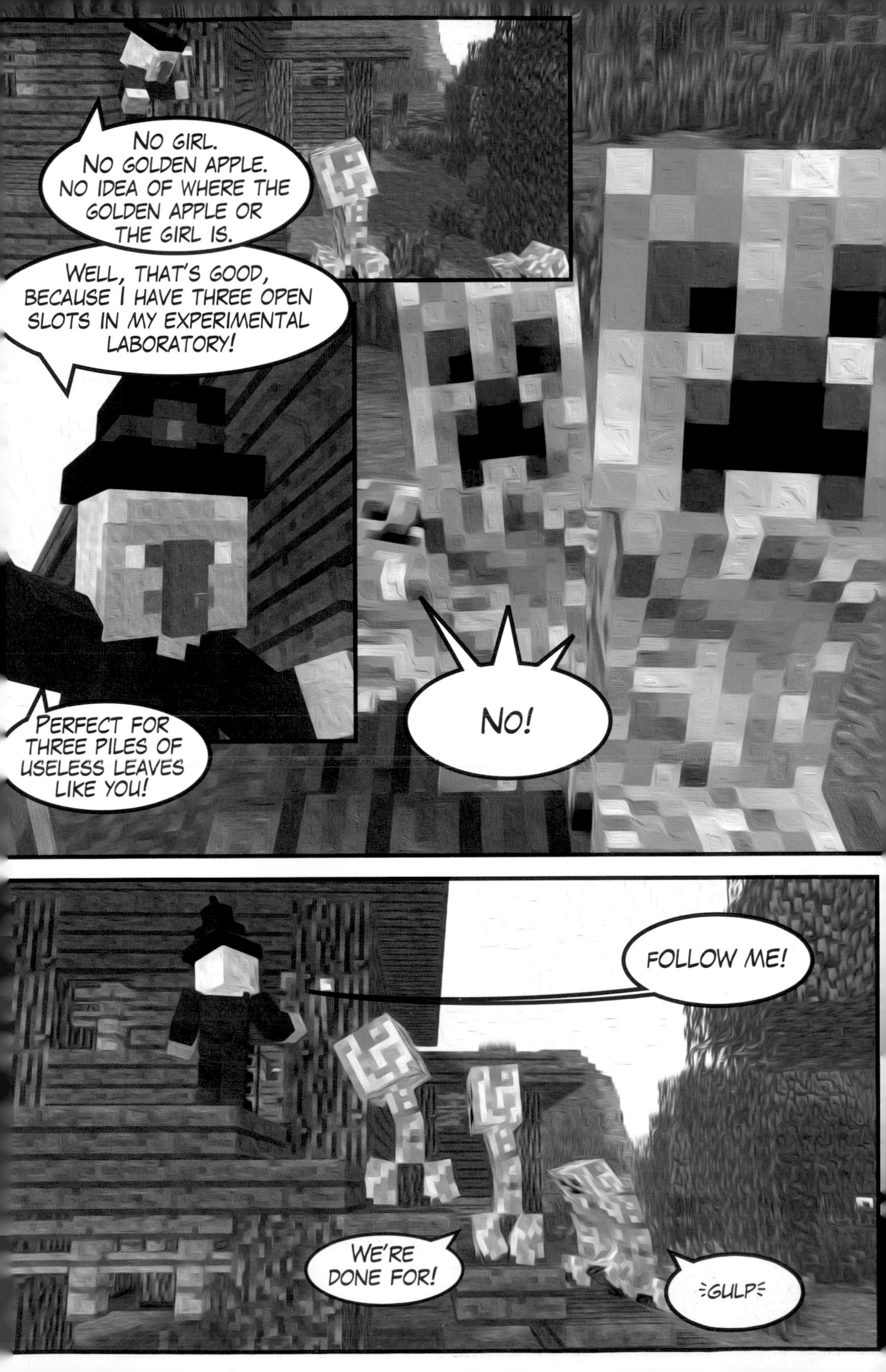
NO GIRL. NO GOLDEN APPLE. NO IDEA OF WHERE THE GOLDEN APPLE OR THE GIRL IS.
WELL, THAT'S GOOD, BECAUSE I HAVE THREE OPEN SLOTS IN MY EXPERIMENTAL LABORATORY!
PERFECT FOR THREE PILES OF USELESS LEAVES LIKE YOU!
NO!
FOLLOW ME!
WE'RE DONE FOR!
GULP

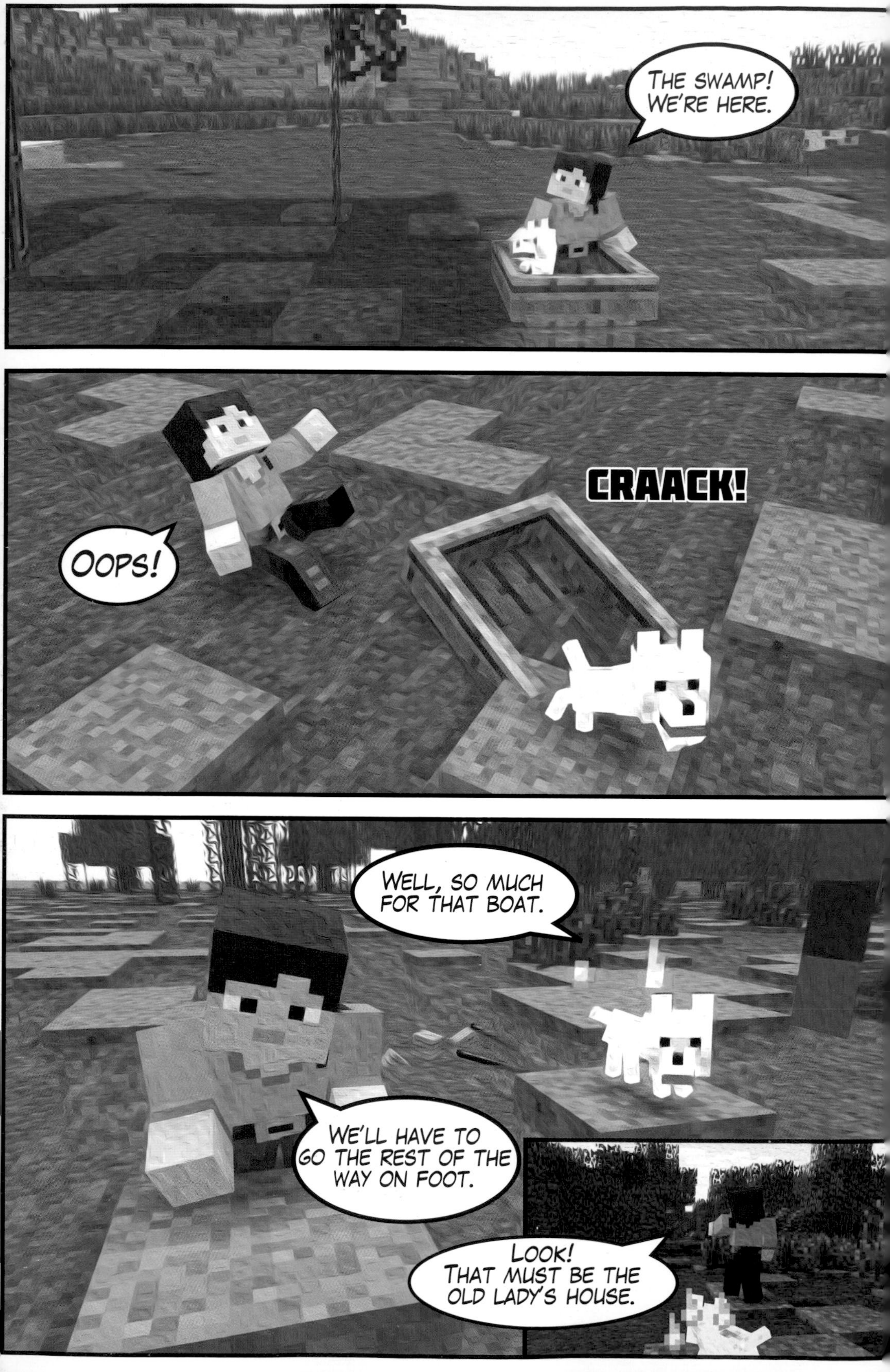
THE SWAMP! WE'RE HERE.
CRAACK!
OOPS!
WELL, SO MUCH FOR THAT BOAT.
WE'LL HAVE TO GO THE REST OF THE WAY ON FOOT.
LOOK! THAT MUST BE THE OLD LADY'S HOUSE.

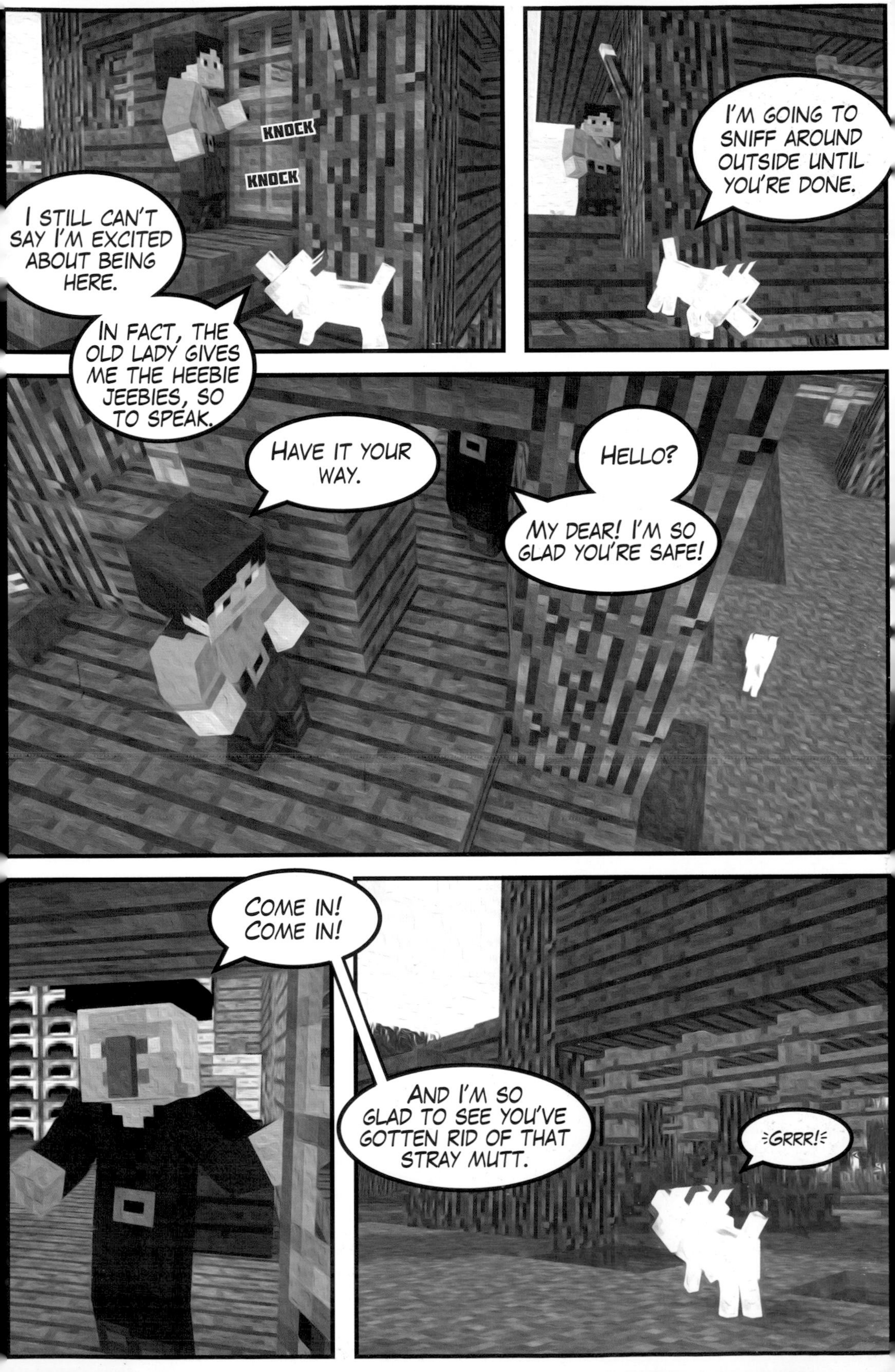
KNOCK
KNOCK
I STILL CAN'T SAY I'M EXCITED ABOUT BEING HERE.
IN FACT, THE OLD LADY GIVES ME THE HEEBIE JEEBIES, SO TO SPEAK.
I'M GOING TO SNIFF AROUND OUTSIDE UNTIL YOU'RE DONE.
HAVE IT YOUR WAY.
HELLO?
MY DEAR! I'M SO GLAD YOU'RE SAFE!
COME IN! COME IN!
AND I'M SO GLAD TO SEE YOU'VE GOTTEN RID OF THAT STRAY MUTT.
GRRR!

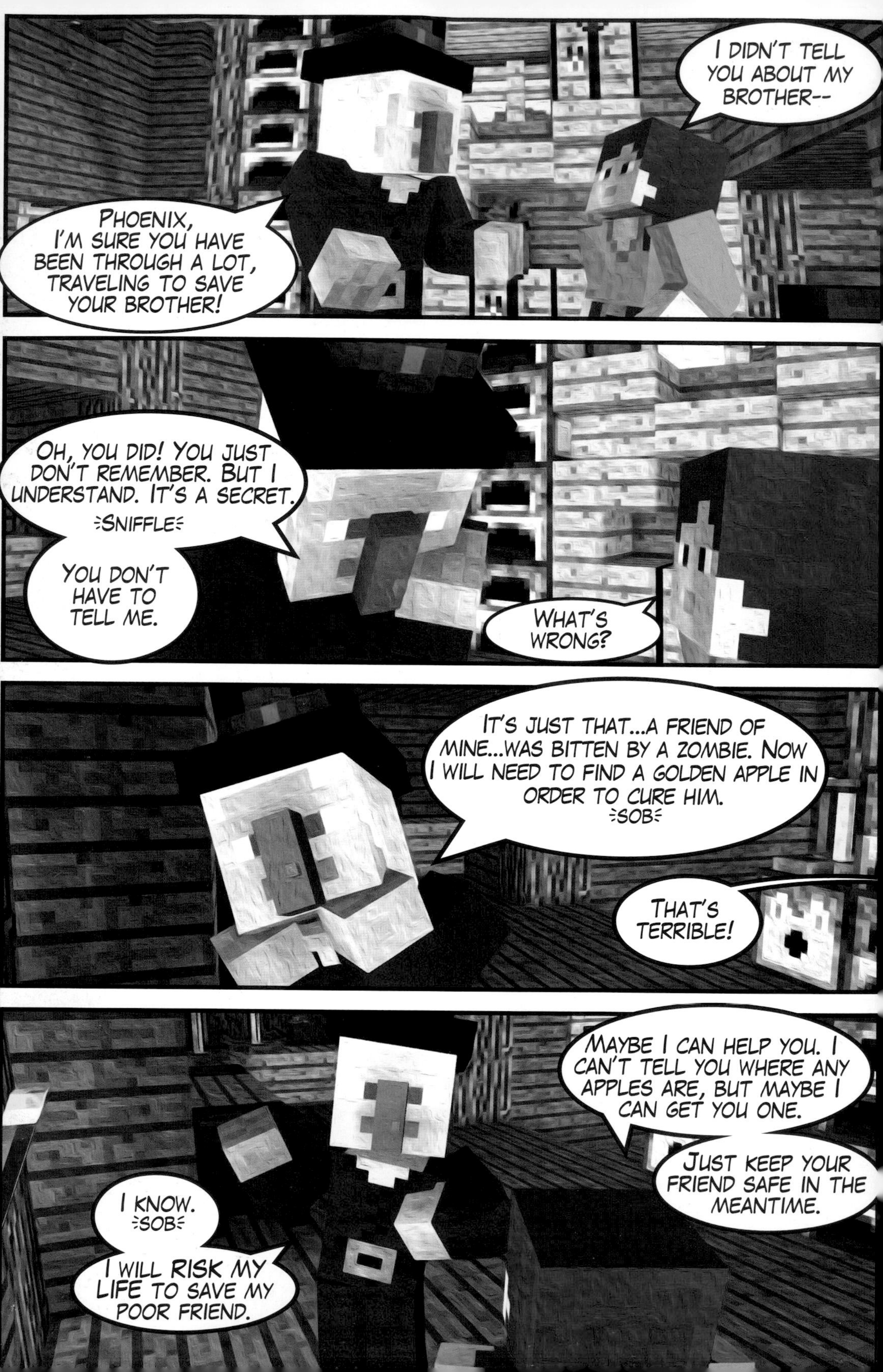
I DIDN'T TELL YOU ABOUT MY BROTHER--
PHOENIX, I'M SURE YOU HAVE BEEN THROUGH A LOT, TRAVELING TO SAVE YOUR BROTHER!
OH, YOU DID! YOU JUST DON'T REMEMBER. BUT I UNDERSTAND. IT'S A SECRET.
SNIFFLE
YOU DON'T HAVE TO TELL ME.
WHAT'S WRONG?
IT'S JUST THAT...A FRIEND OF MINE...WAS BITTEN BY A ZOMBIE. NOW I WILL NEED TO FIND A GOLDEN APPLE IN ORDER TO CURE HIM.
SOB
THAT'S TERRIBLE!
MAYBE I CAN HELP YOU. I CAN'T TELL YOU WHERE ANY APPLES ARE, BUT MAYBE I CAN GET YOU ONE.
JUST KEEP YOUR FRIEND SAFE IN THE MEANTIME.
I KNOW.
SOB
I WILL RISK MY LIFE TO SAVE MY POOR FRIEND.

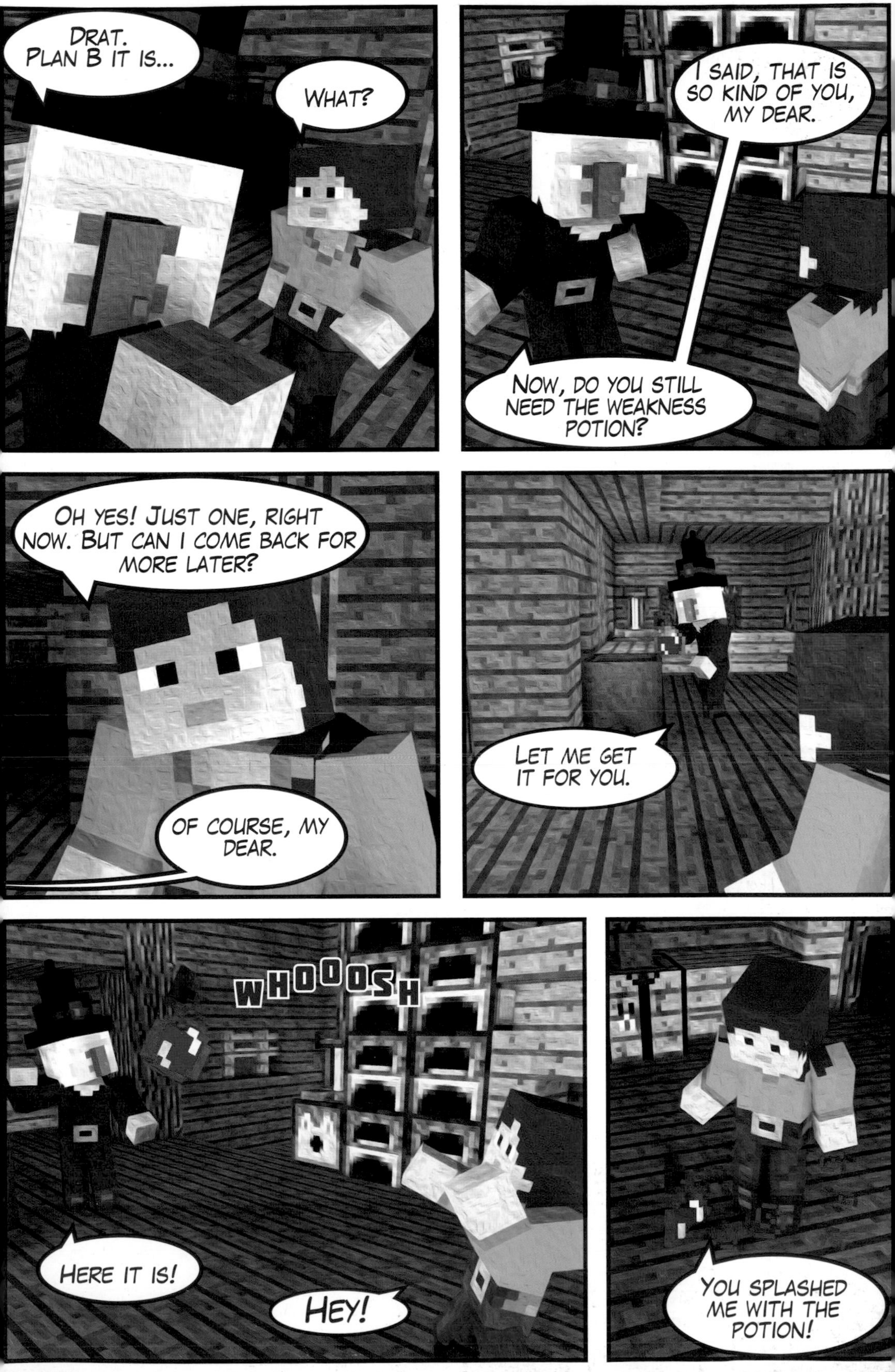
DRAT. PLAN B IT IS...
WHAT?
I SAID, THAT IS SO KIND OF YOU, MY DEAR.
NOW, DO YOU STILL NEED THE WEAKNESS POTION?
OH YES! JUST ONE, RIGHT NOW. BUT CAN I COME BACK FOR MORE LATER?
OF COURSE, MY DEAR.
LET ME GET IT FOR YOU.
WHOOOSH
HERE IT IS!
HEY!
YOU SPLASHED ME WITH THE POTION!

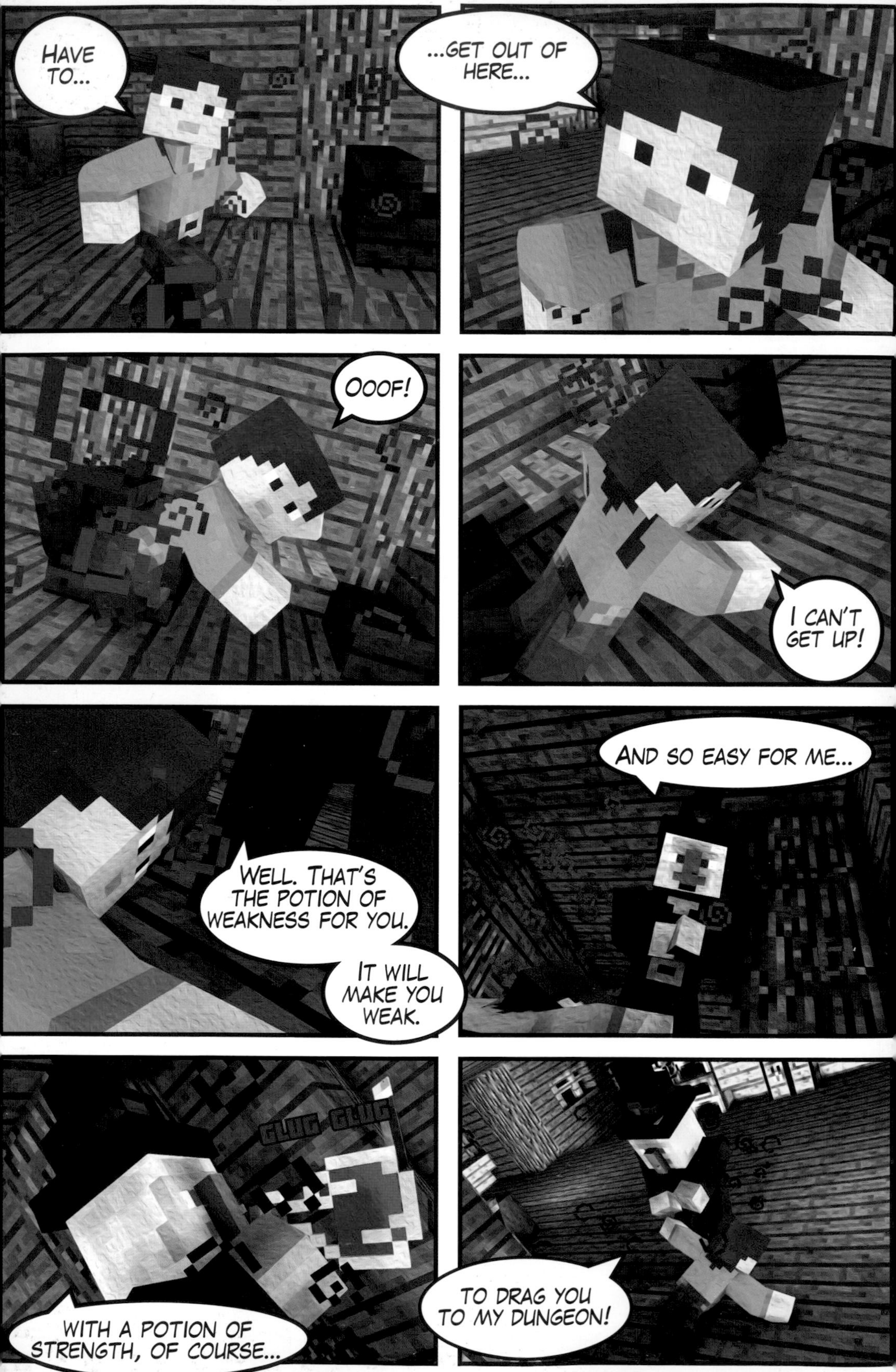
HAVE TO...
...GET OUT OF HERE...
OOOF!
I CAN'T GET UP!
WELL. THAT'S THE POTION OF WEAKNESS FOR YOU.
IT WILL MAKE YOU WEAK.
AND SO EASY FOR ME...
GLUG GLUG
WITH A POTION OF STRENGTH, OF COURSE...
TO DRAG YOU TO MY DUNGEON!

CHAPTER 10
THE DUNGEON

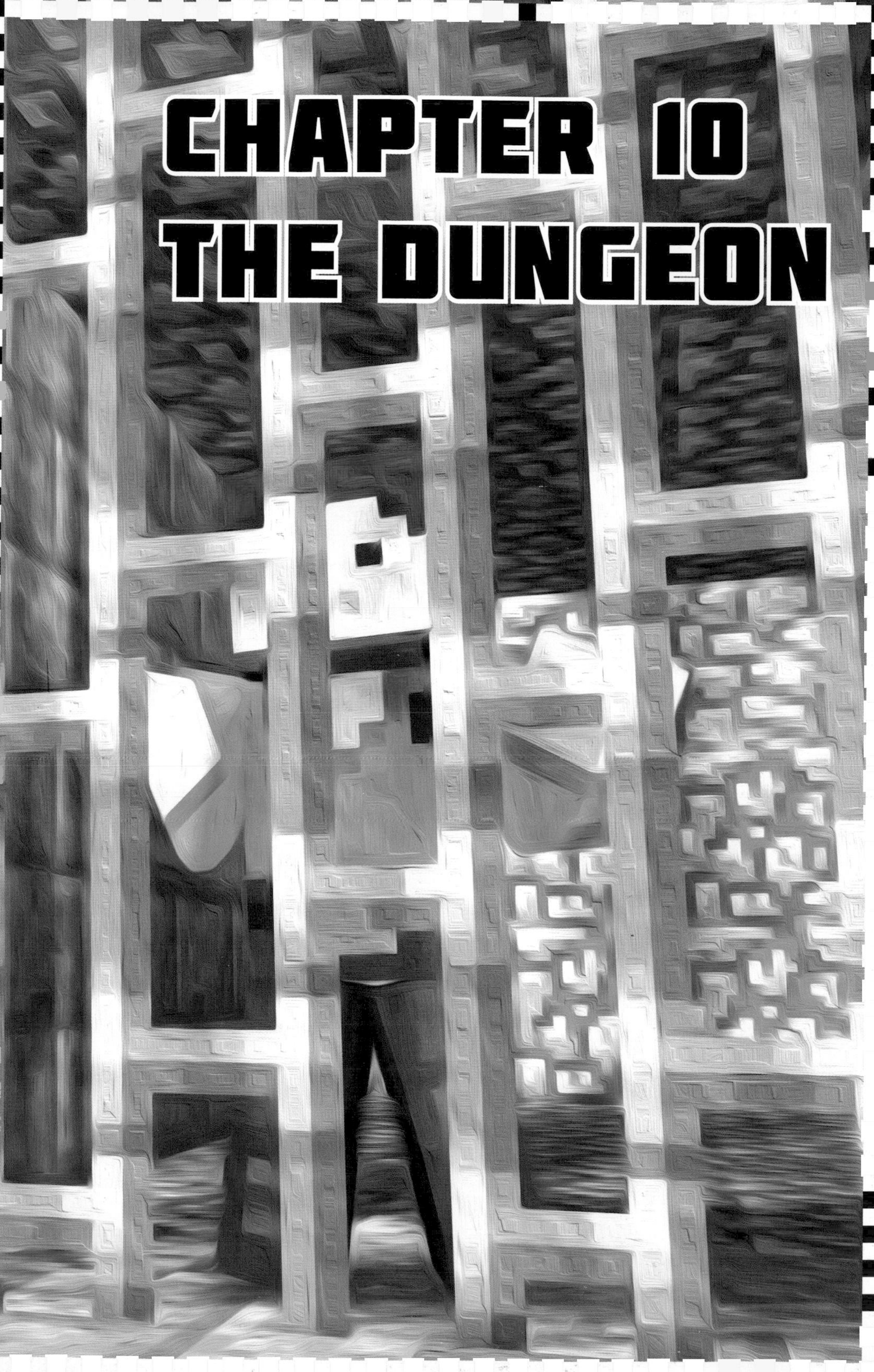

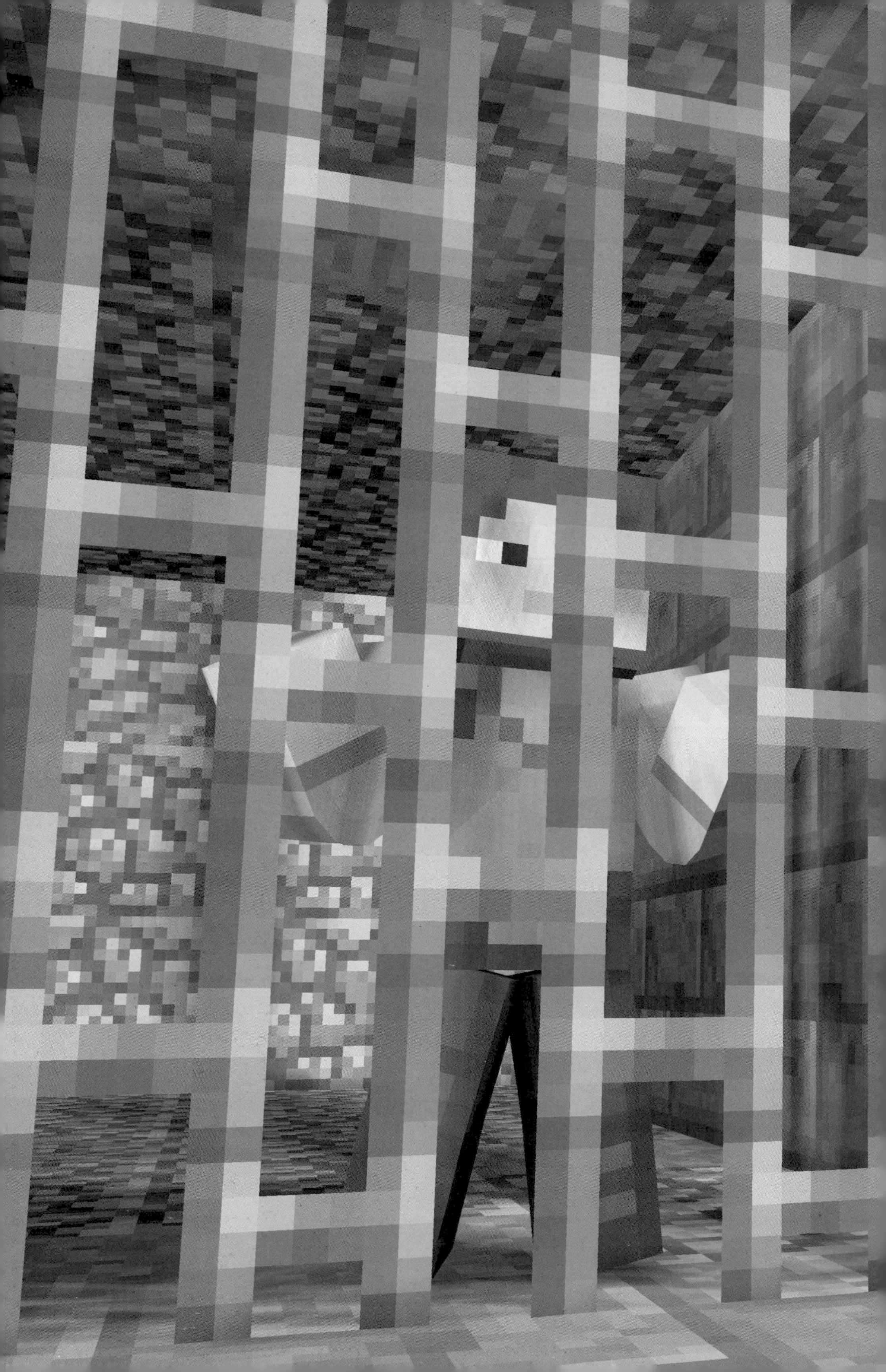

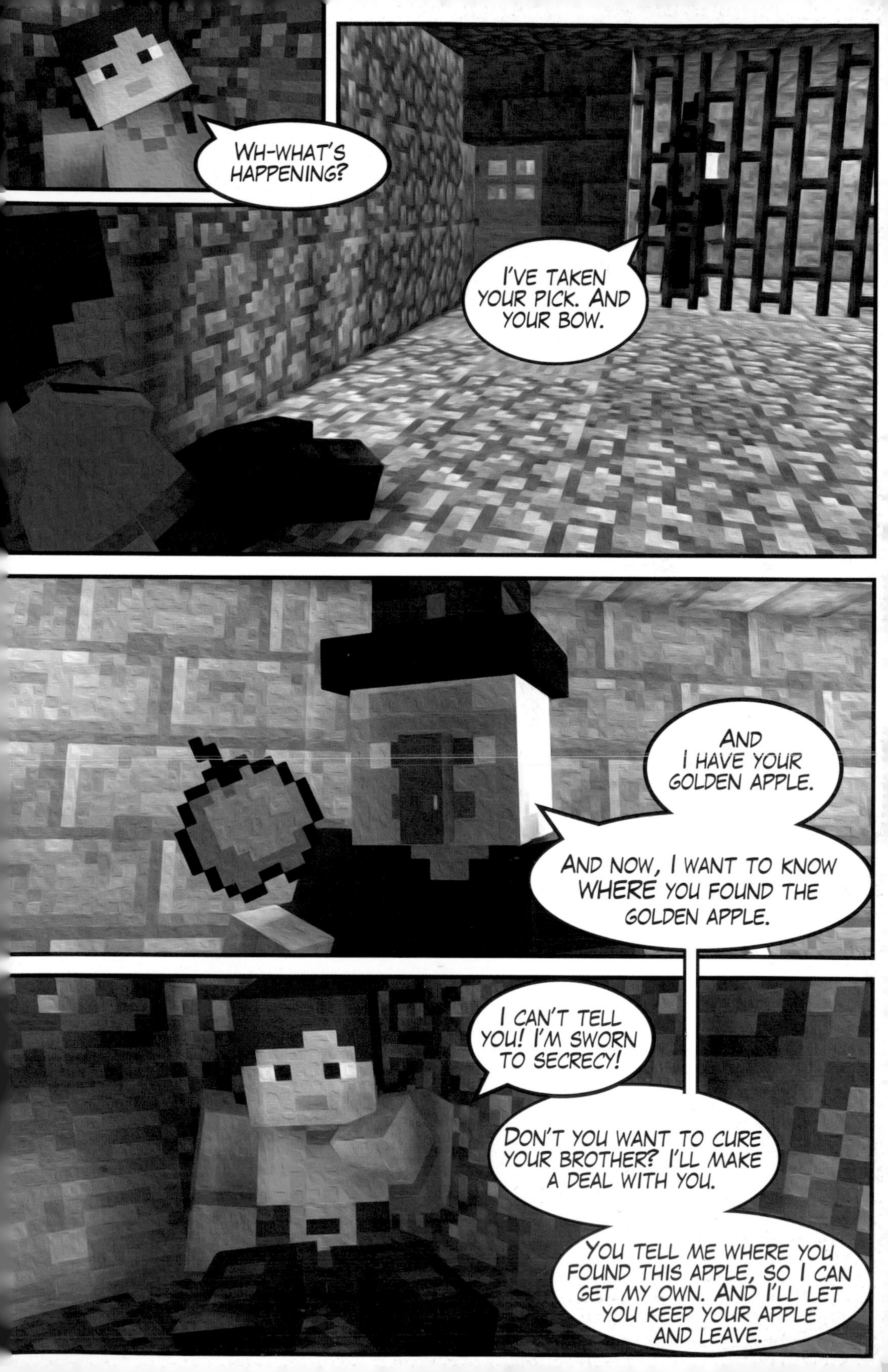
WH-WHAT'S HAPPENING?
I'VE TAKEN YOUR PICK. AND YOUR BOW.
AND I HAVE YOUR GOLDEN APPLE.
AND NOW, I WANT TO KNOW WHERE YOU FOUND THE GOLDEN APPLE.
I CAN'T TELL YOU! I'M SWORN TO SECRECY!
DON'T YOU WANT TO CURE YOUR BROTHER? I'LL MAKE A DEAL WITH YOU.
YOU TELL ME WHERE YOU FOUND THIS APPLE, SO I CAN GET MY OWN. AND I'LL LET YOU KEEP YOUR APPLE AND LEAVE.

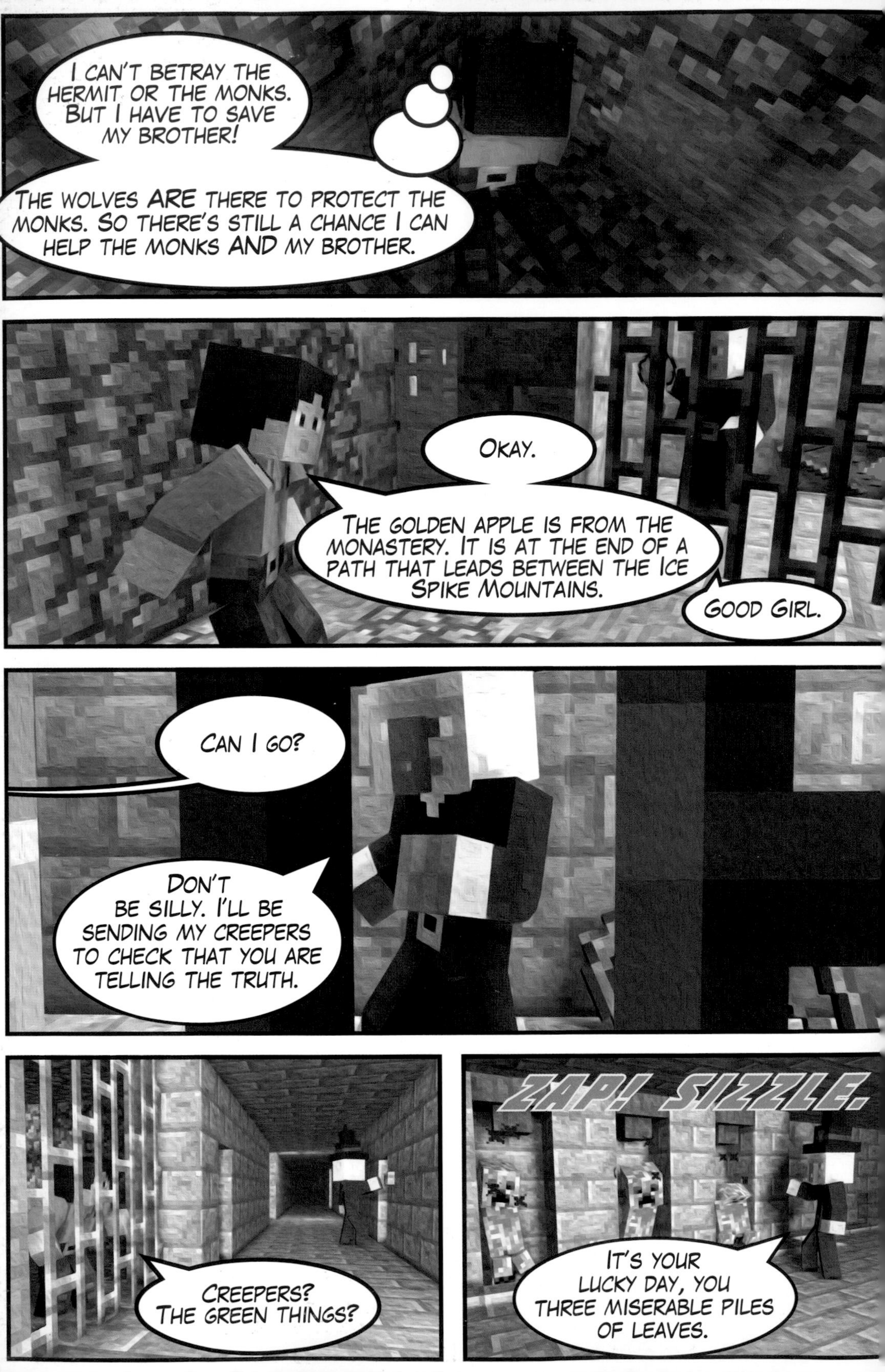
I CAN'T BETRAY THE HERMIT OR THE MONKS. BUT I HAVE TO SAVE MY BROTHER!
THE WOLVES ARE THERE TO PROTECT THE MONKS. SO THERE'S STILL A CHANCE I CAN HELP THE MONKS AND MY BROTHER.
OKAY.
THE GOLDEN APPLE IS FROM THE MONASTERY. IT IS AT THE END OF A PATH THAT LEADS BETWEEN THE ICE SPIKE MOUNTAINS.
GOOD GIRL.
CAN I GO?
DON'T BE SILLY. I'LL BE SENDING MY CREEPERS TO CHECK THAT YOU ARE TELLING THE TRUTH.
CREEPERS? THE GREEN THINGS?
ZAP! SIZZLE.
IT'S YOUR LUCKY DAY, YOU THREE MISERABLE PILES OF LEAVES.

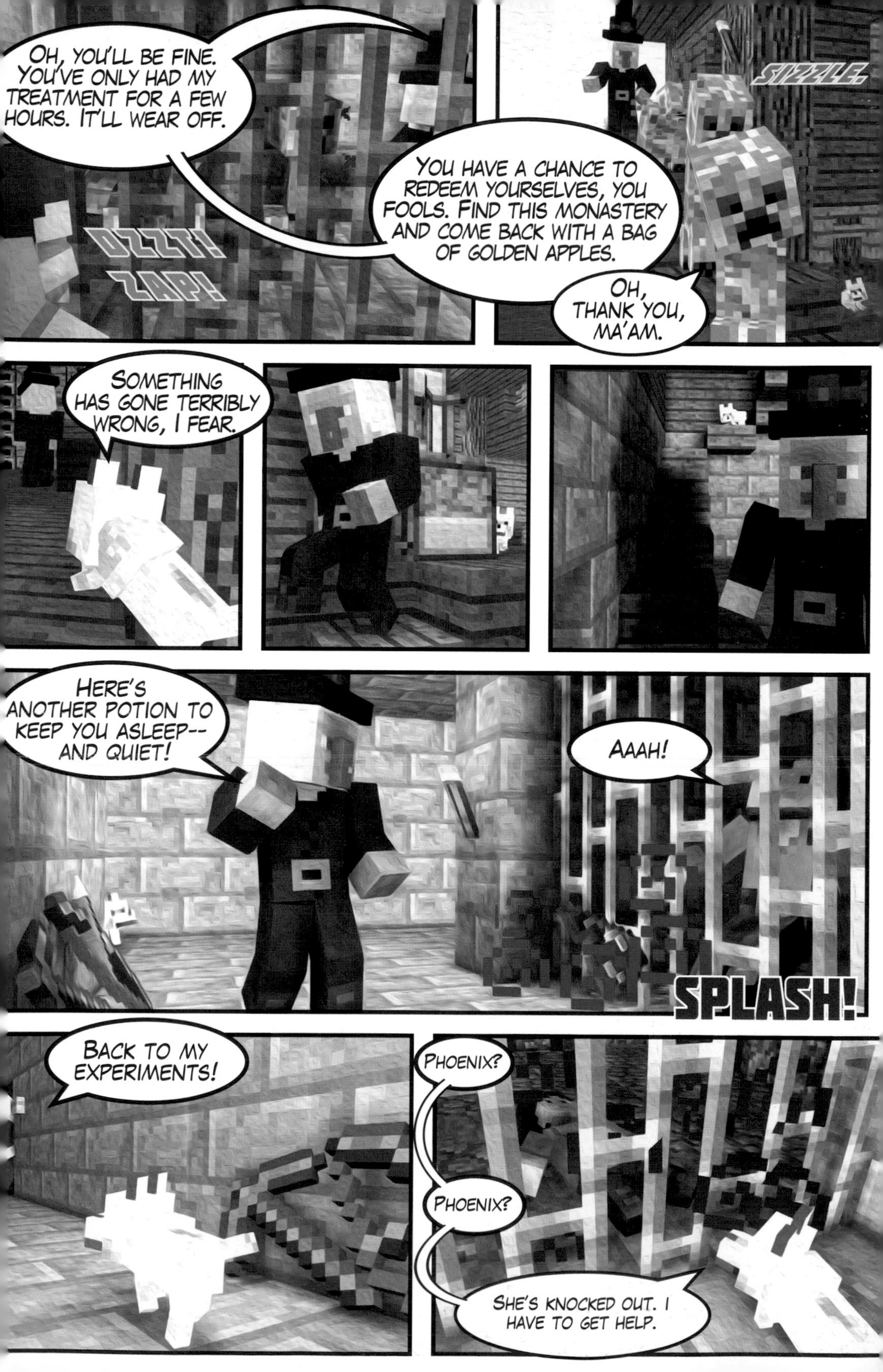
OH, YOU'LL BE FINE. YOU'VE ONLY HAD MY TREATMENT FOR A FEW HOURS. IT'LL WEAR OFF.
DZZZT!
ZAP!
SIZZLE.
YOU HAVE A CHANCE TO REDEEM YOURSELVES, YOU FOOLS. FIND THIS MONASTERY AND COME BACK WITH A BAG OF GOLDEN APPLES.
OH, THANK YOU, MA'AM.
SOMETHING HAS GONE TERRIBLY WRONG, I FEAR.
HERE'S ANOTHER POTION TO KEEP YOU ASLEEP-- AND QUIET!
AAAH!
SPLASH!
BACK TO MY EXPERIMENTS!
PHOENIX?
PHOENIX?
SHE'S KNOCKED OUT. I HAVE TO GET HELP.

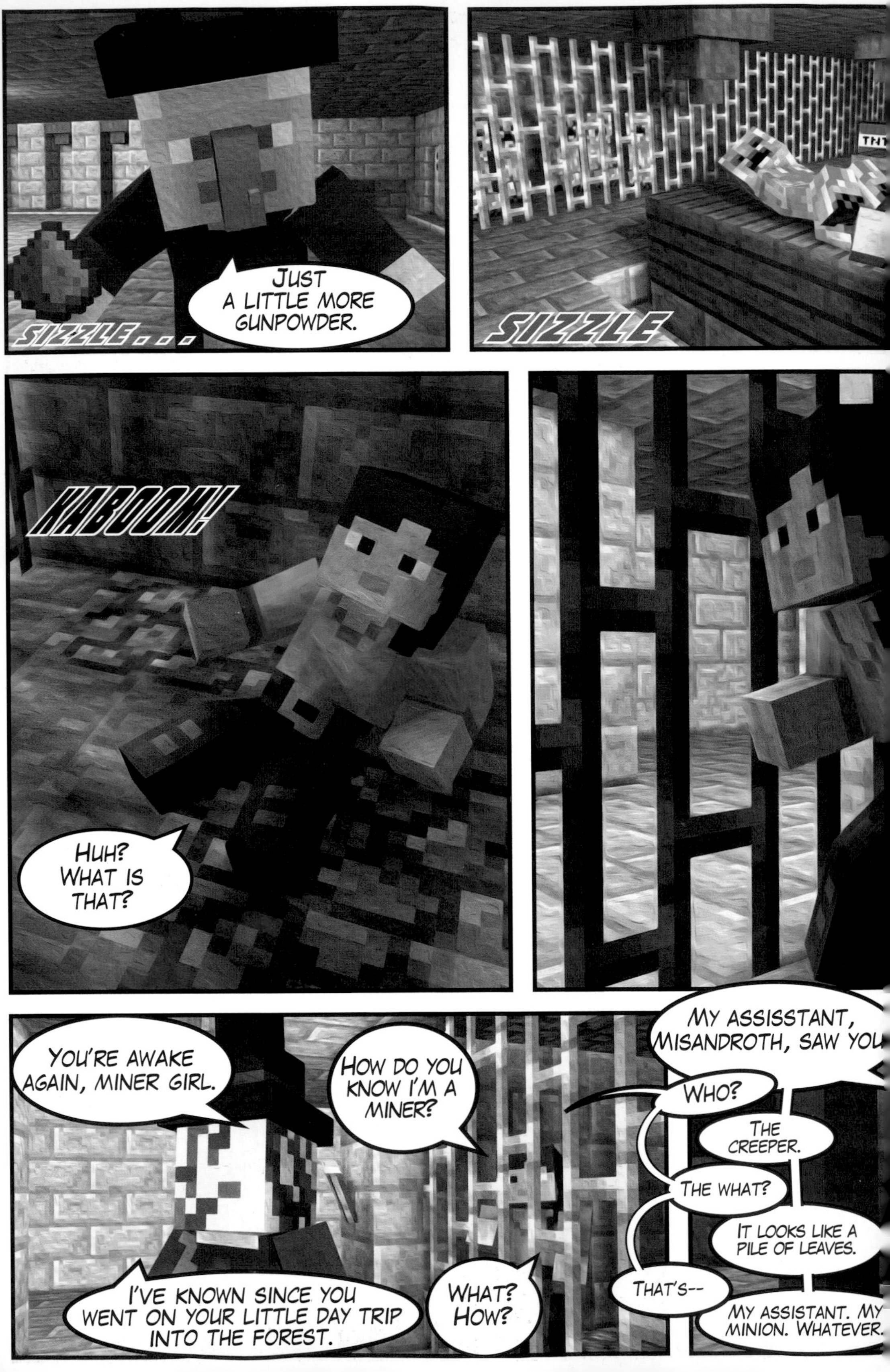
JUST A LITTLE MORE GUNPOWDER.
SIZZLE . . .
TNT
SIZZLE
KABOOM!
HUH? WHAT IS THAT?
YOU'RE AWAKE AGAIN, MINER GIRL.
HOW DO YOU KNOW I'M A MINER?
I'VE KNOWN SINCE YOU WENT ON YOUR LITTLE DAY TRIP INTO THE FOREST.
WHAT? HOW?
MY ASSISSTANT, MISANDROTH, SAW YOU
WHO?
THE CREEPER.
THE WHAT?
IT LOOKS LIKE A PILE OF LEAVES.
THAT'S--
MY ASSISTANT. MY MINION. WHATEVER.

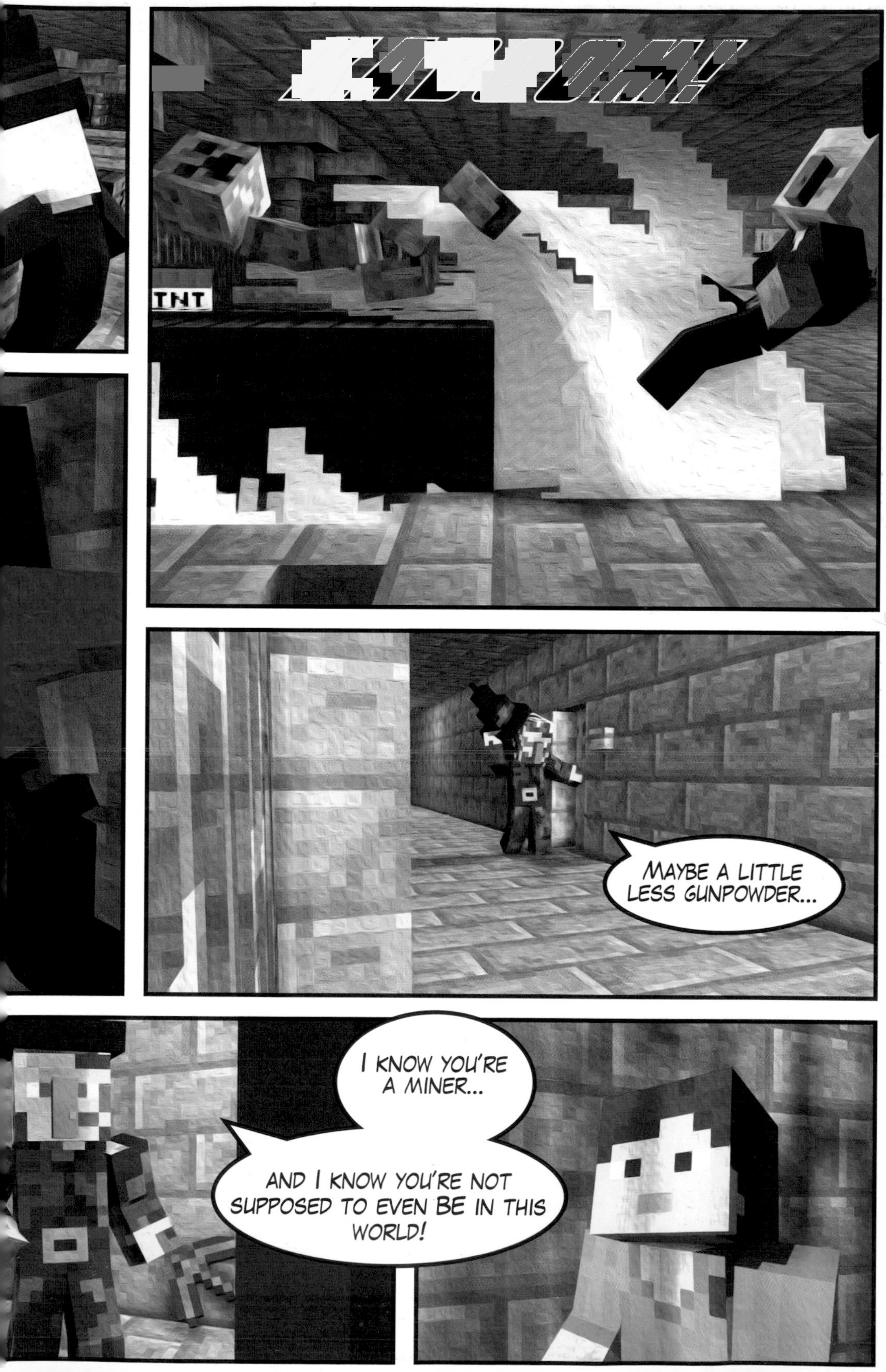

MAYBE A LITTLE LESS GUNPOWDER...
I KNOW YOU'RE A MINER...
AND I KNOW YOU'RE NOT SUPPOSED TO EVEN BE IN THIS WORLD!

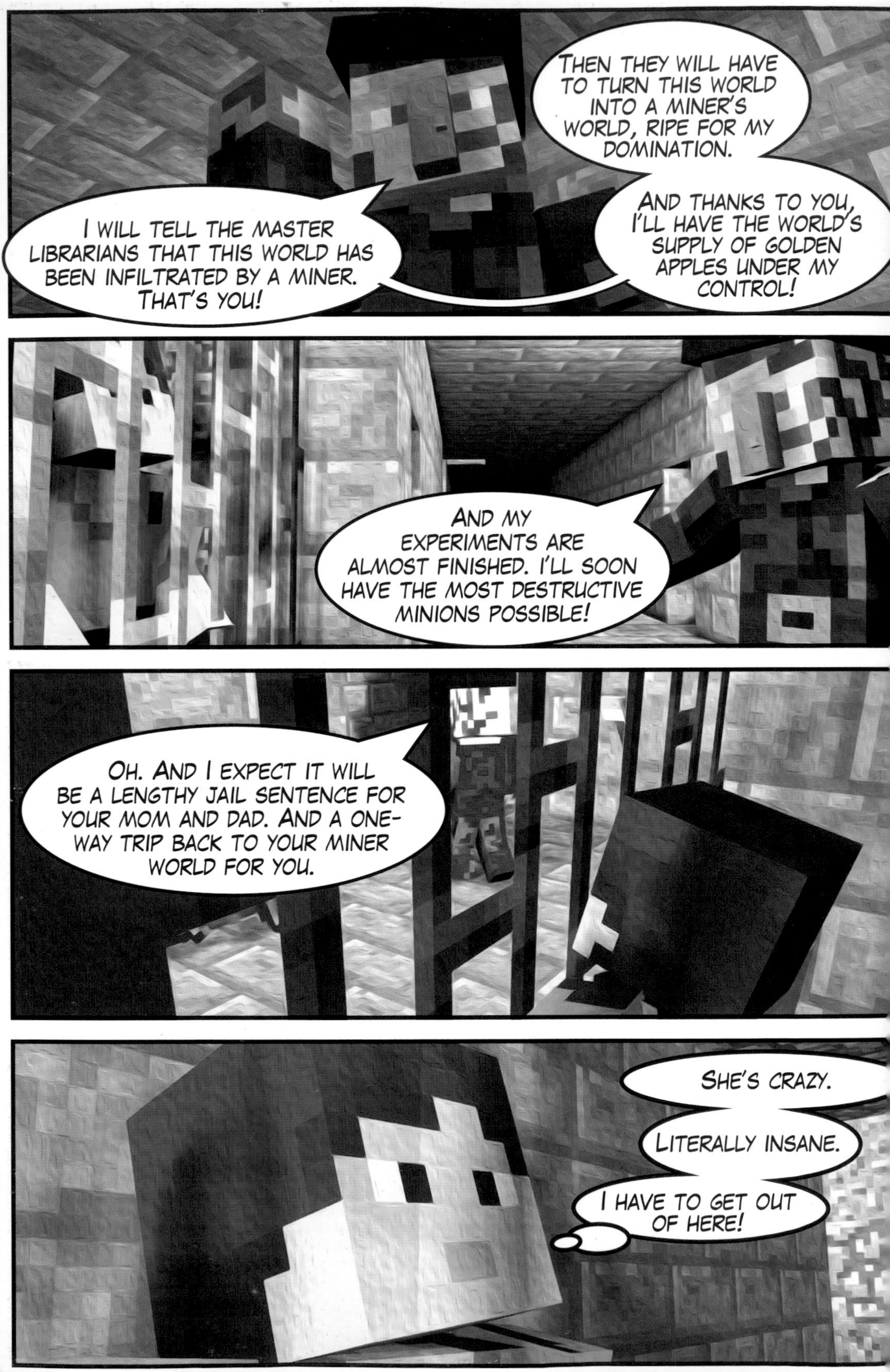
I WILL TELL THE MASTER LIBRARIANS THAT THIS WORLD HAS BEEN INFILTRATED BY A MINER. THAT'S YOU!
THEN THEY WILL HAVE TO TURN THIS WORLD INTO A MINER'S WORLD, RIPE FOR MY DOMINATION.
AND THANKS TO YOU, I'LL HAVE THE WORLD'S SUPPLY OF GOLDEN APPLES UNDER MY CONTROL!
AND MY EXPERIMENTS ARE ALMOST FINISHED. I'LL SOON HAVE THE MOST DESTRUCTIVE MINIONS POSSIBLE!
OH. AND I EXPECT IT WILL BE A LENGTHY JAIL SENTENCE FOR YOUR MOM AND DAD. AND A ONE-WAY TRIP BACK TO YOUR MINER WORLD FOR YOU.
SHE'S CRAZY.
LITERALLY INSANE.
I HAVE TO GET OUT OF HERE!

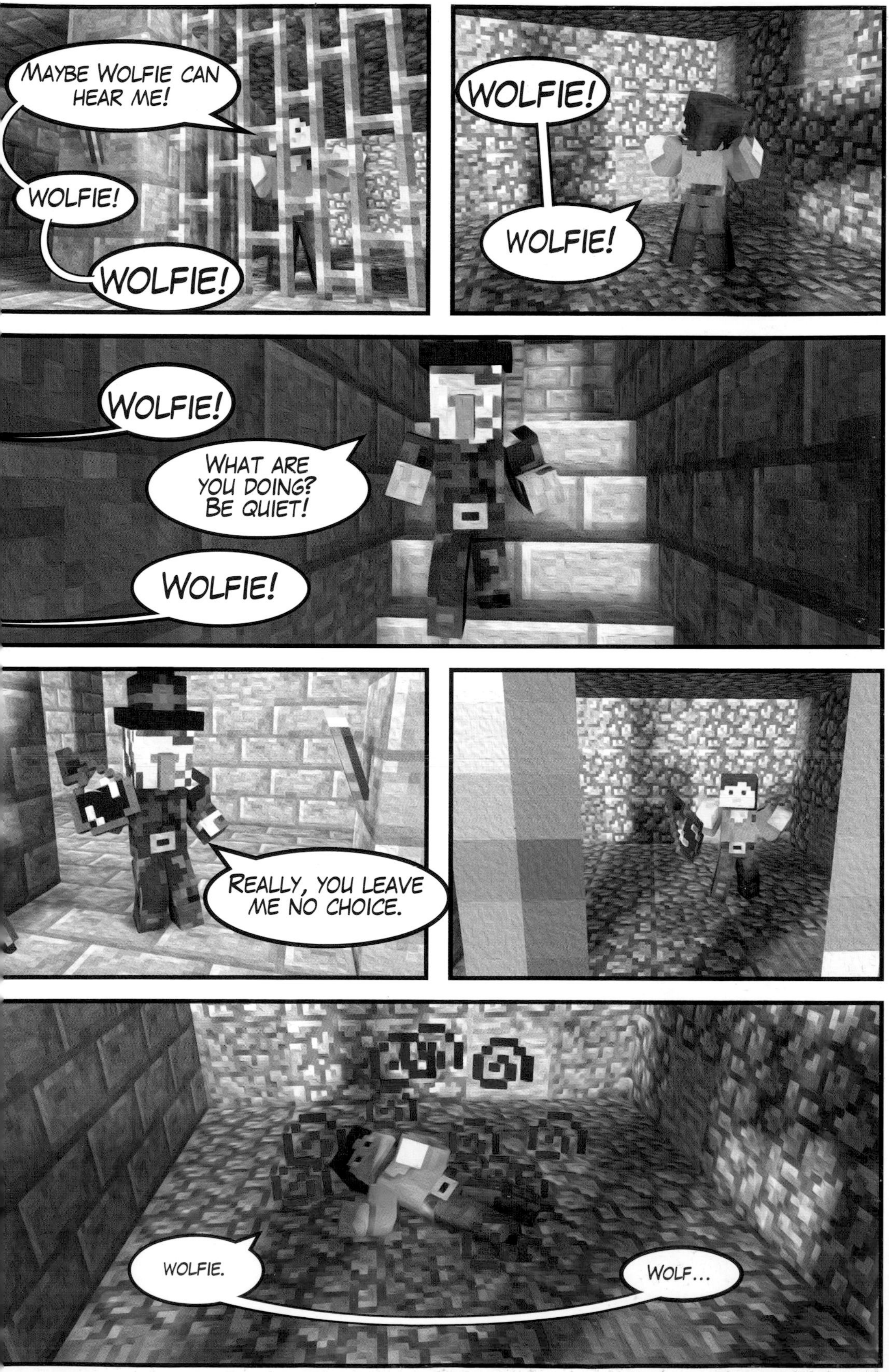
MAYBE WOLFIE CAN HEAR ME!
WOLFIE!
WOLFIE!
WOLFIE!
WOLFIE!
WOLFIE!
WHAT ARE YOU DOING? BE QUIET!
WOLFIE!
REALLY, YOU LEAVE ME NO CHOICE.
WOLFIE.
WOLF...

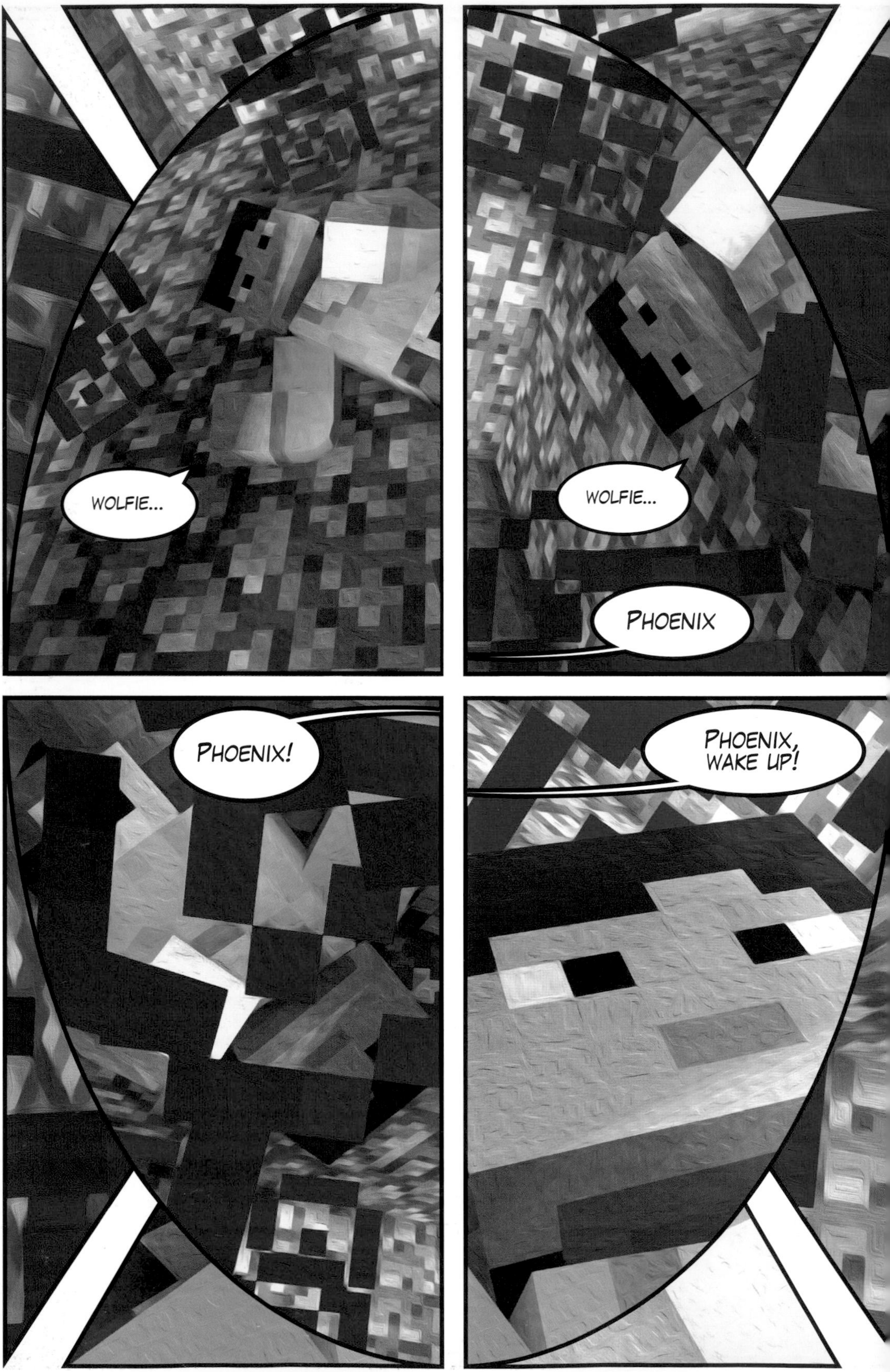
WOLFIE...
WOLFIE...
PHOENIX
PHOENIX!
PHOENIX, WAKE UP!

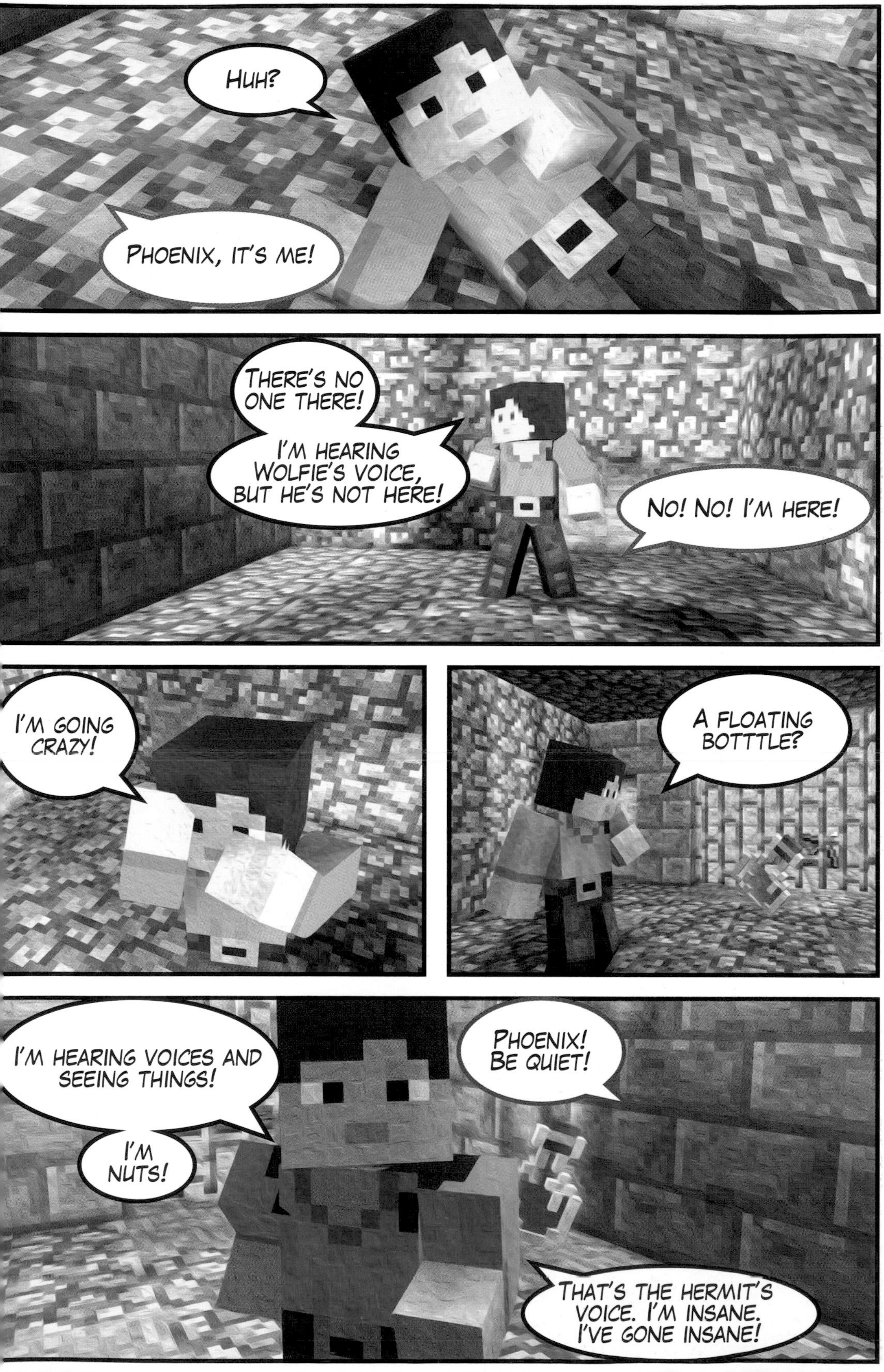
HUH?
PHOENIX, IT'S ME!
THERE'S NO ONE THERE!
I'M HEARING WOLFIE'S VOICE, BUT HE'S NOT HERE!
NO! NO! I'M HERE!
I'M GOING CRAZY!
A FLOATING BOTTTLE?
I'M HEARING VOICES AND SEEING THINGS!
I'M NUTS!
PHOENIX! BE QUIET!
THAT'S THE HERMIT'S VOICE. I'M INSANE. I'VE GONE INSANE!

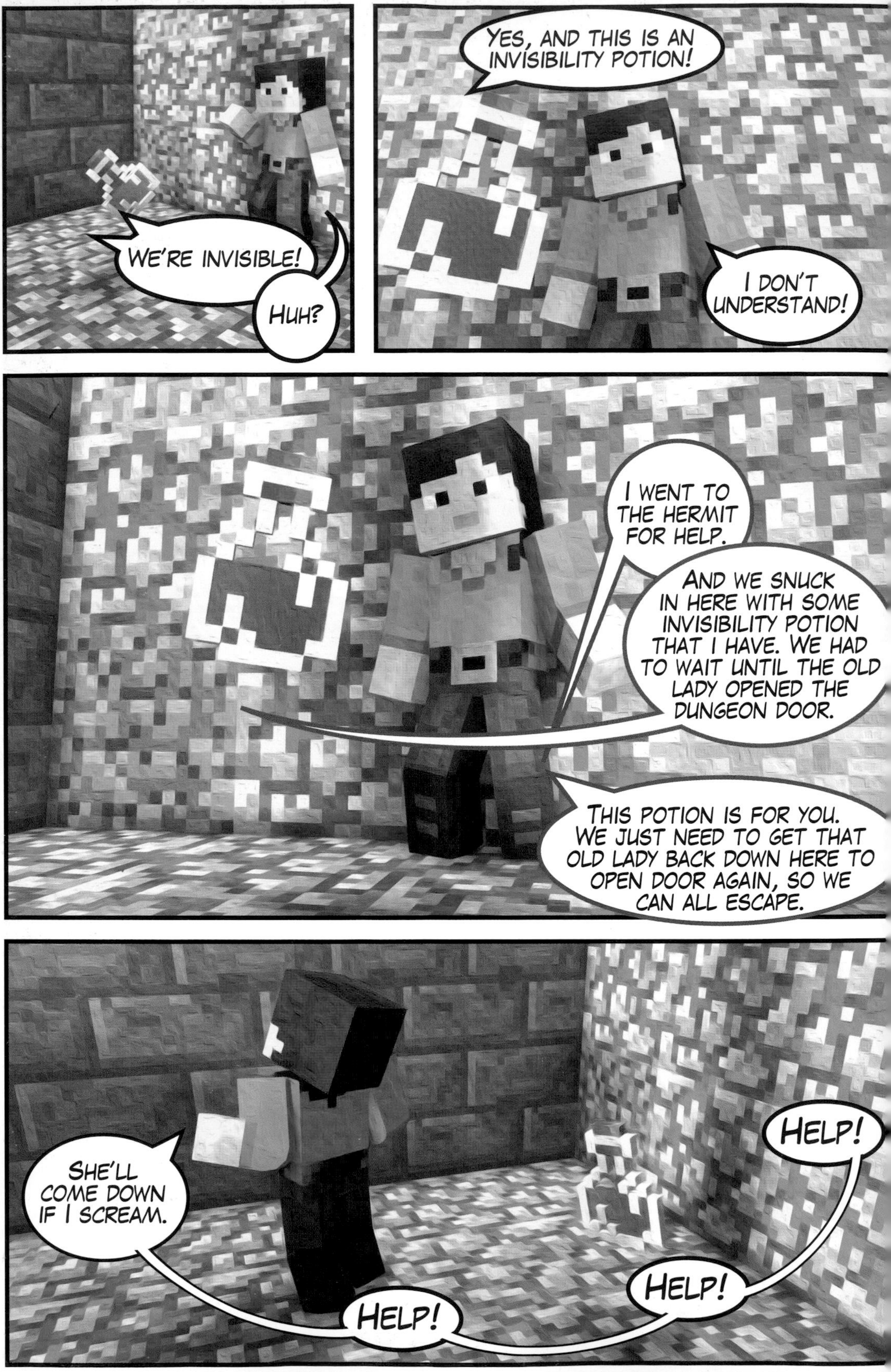
WE'RE INVISIBLE!
HUH?
YES, AND THIS IS AN INVISIBILITY POTION!
I DON'T UNDERSTAND!
I WENT TO THE HERMIT FOR HELP.
AND WE SNUCK IN HERE WITH SOME INVISIBILITY POTION THAT I HAVE. WE HAD TO WAIT UNTIL THE OLD LADY OPENED THE DUNGEON DOOR.
THIS POTION IS FOR YOU. WE JUST NEED TO GET THAT OLD LADY BACK DOWN HERE TO OPEN DOOR AGAIN, SO WE CAN ALL ESCAPE.
SHE'LL COME DOWN IF I SCREAM.
HELP!
HELP!
HELP!

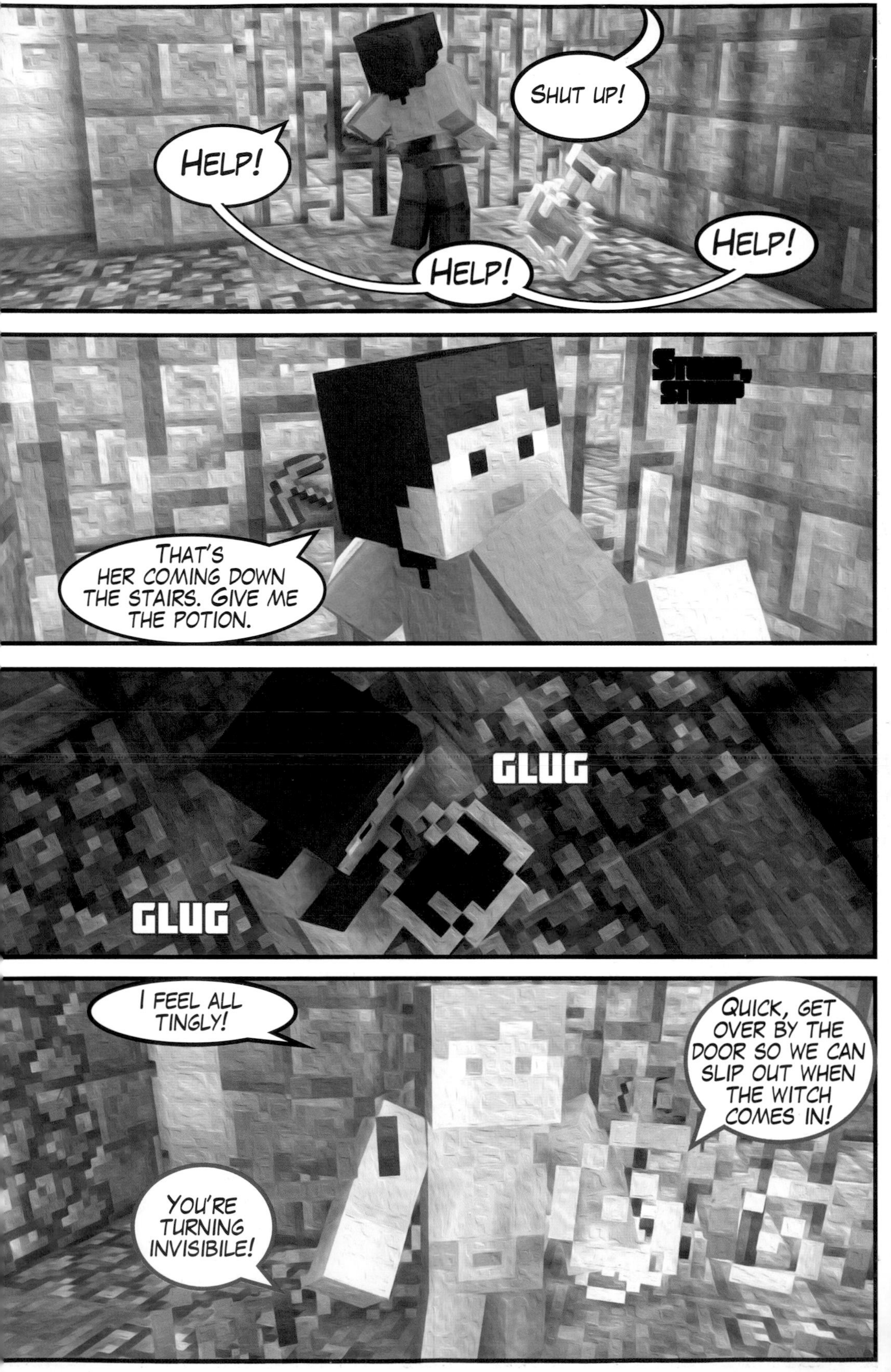
HELP!
SHUT UP!
HELP!
HELP!
THAT'S HER COMING DOWN THE STAIRS. GIVE ME THE POTION.
GLUG
GLUG
I FEEL ALL TINGLY!
QUICK, GET OVER BY THE DOOR SO WE CAN SLIP OUT WHEN THE WITCH COMES IN!
YOU'RE TURNING INVISIBILE!

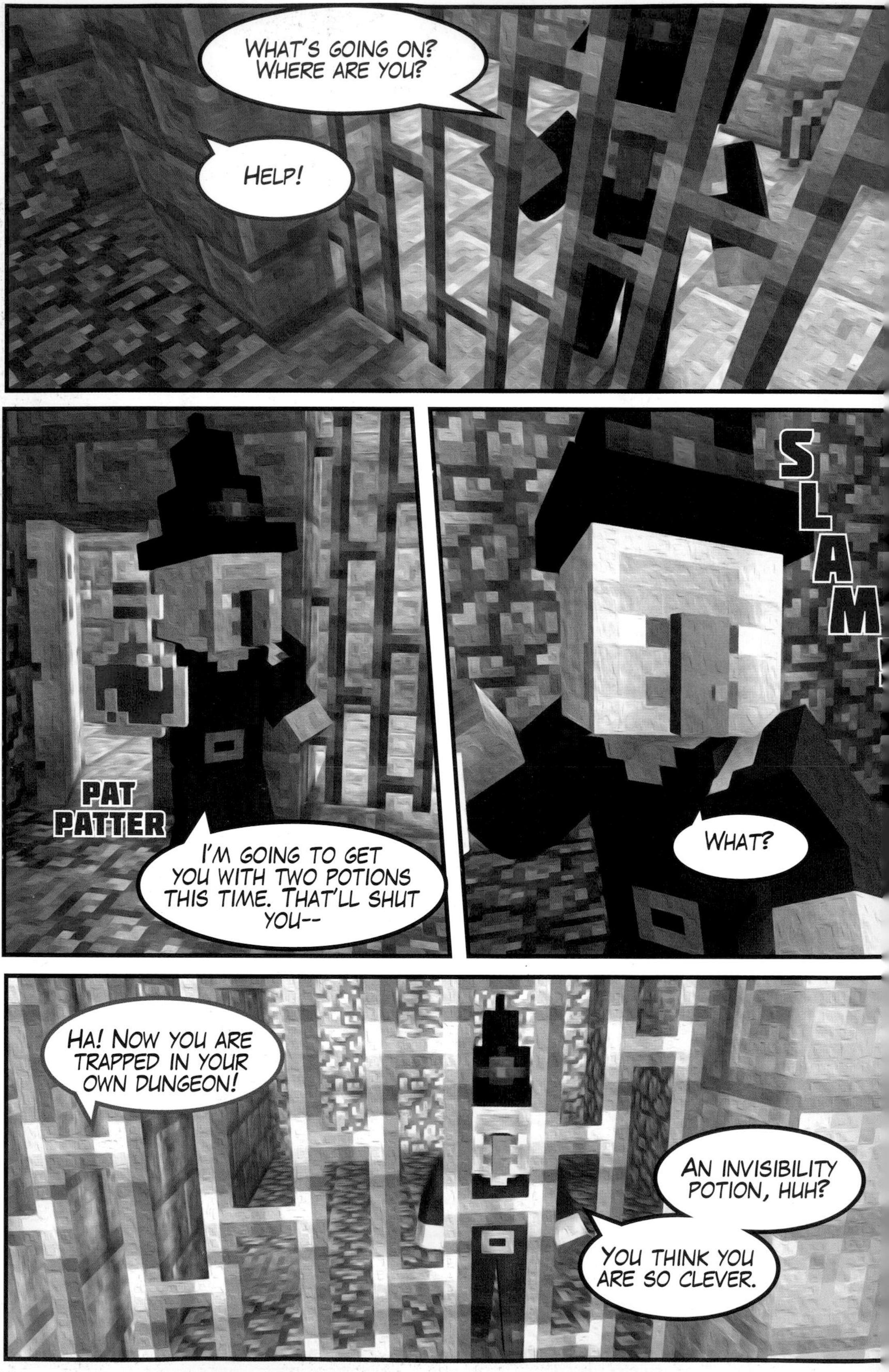
WHAT'S GOING ON? WHERE ARE YOU?
HELP!
PAT PATTER
I'M GOING TO GET YOU WITH TWO POTIONS THIS TIME. THAT'LL SHUT YOU--
SLAM!
WHAT?
HA! NOW YOU ARE TRAPPED IN YOUR OWN DUNGEON!
AN INVISIBILITY POTION, HUH?
YOU THINK YOU ARE SO CLEVER.

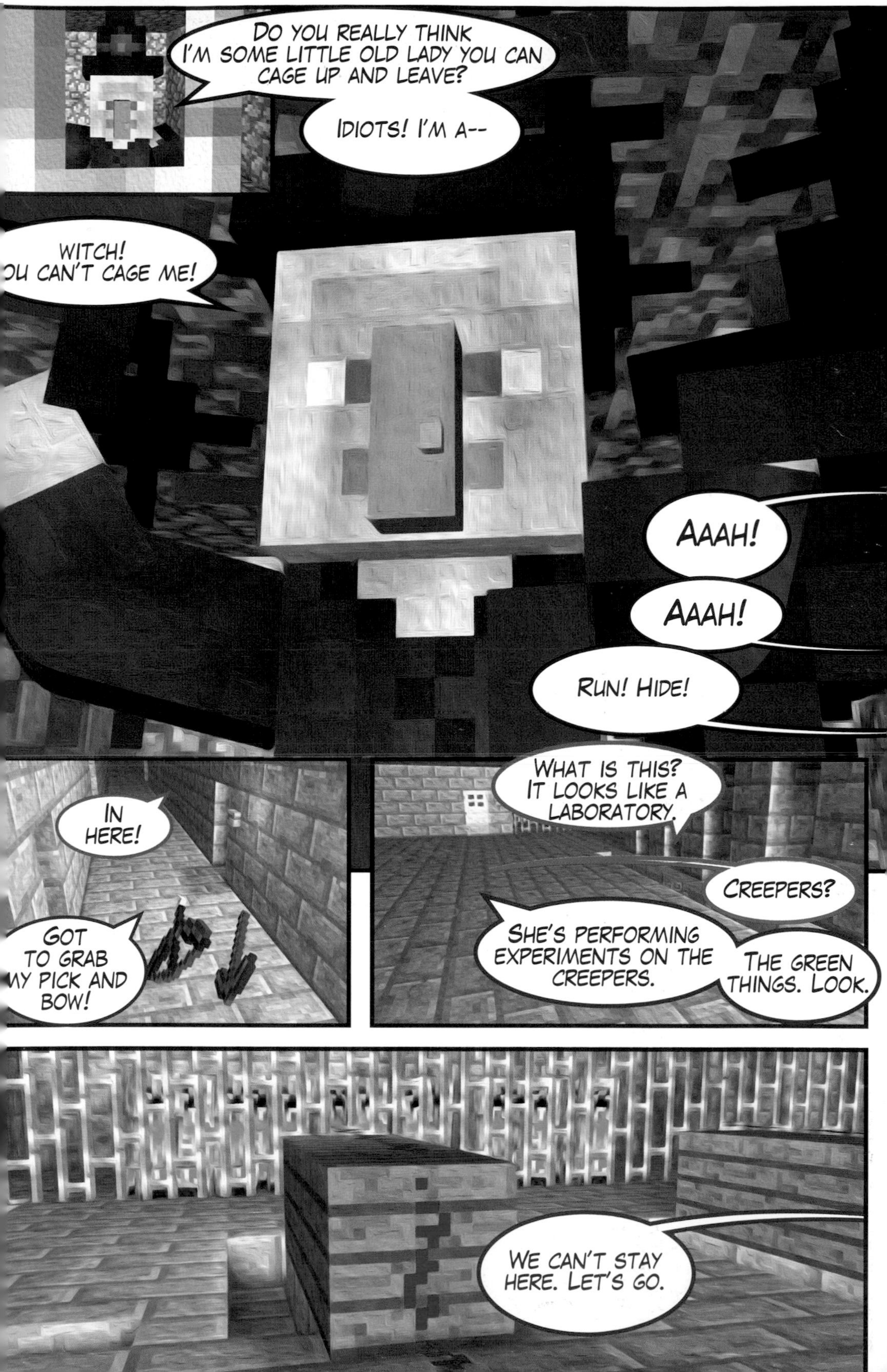
DO YOU REALLY THINK I'M SOME LITTLE OLD LADY YOU CAN CAGE UP AND LEAVE?
IDIOTS! I'M A--
WITCH! OU CAN'T CAGE ME!
AAAH!
AAAH!
RUN! HIDE!
IN HERE!
GOT TO GRAB MY PICK AND BOW!
WHAT IS THIS? IT LOOKS LIKE A LABORATORY.
CREEPERS?
SHE'S PERFORMING EXPERIMENTS ON THE CREEPERS.
THE GREEN THINGS. LOOK.
WE CAN'T STAY HERE. LET'S GO.

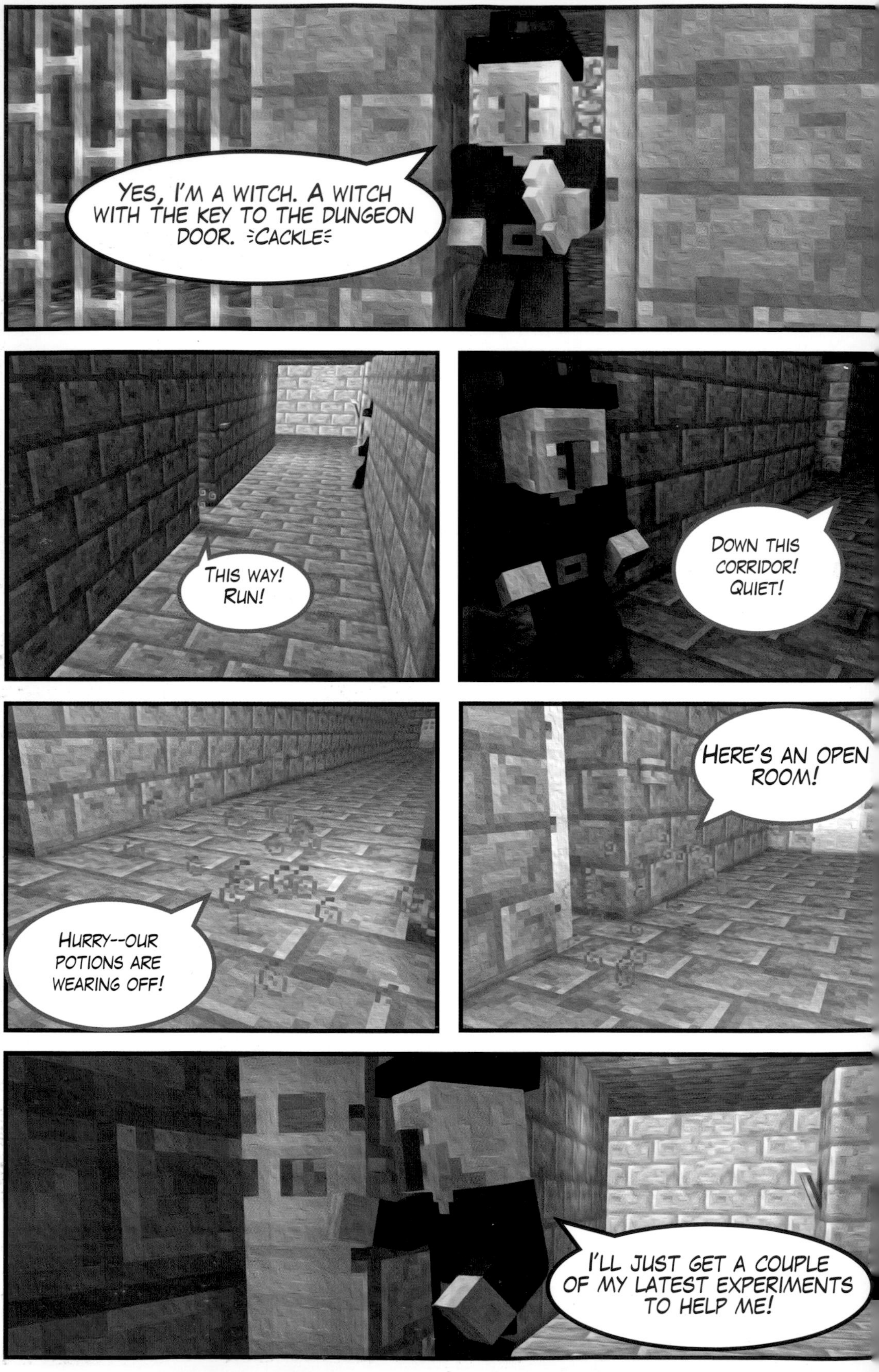
YES, I'M A WITCH. A WITCH WITH THE KEY TO THE DUNGEON DOOR. CACKLE
THIS WAY! RUN!
DOWN THIS CORRIDOR! QUIET!
HURRY--OUR POTIONS ARE WEARING OFF!
HERE'S AN OPEN ROOM!
I'LL JUST GET A COUPLE OF MY LATEST EXPERIMENTS TO HELP ME!

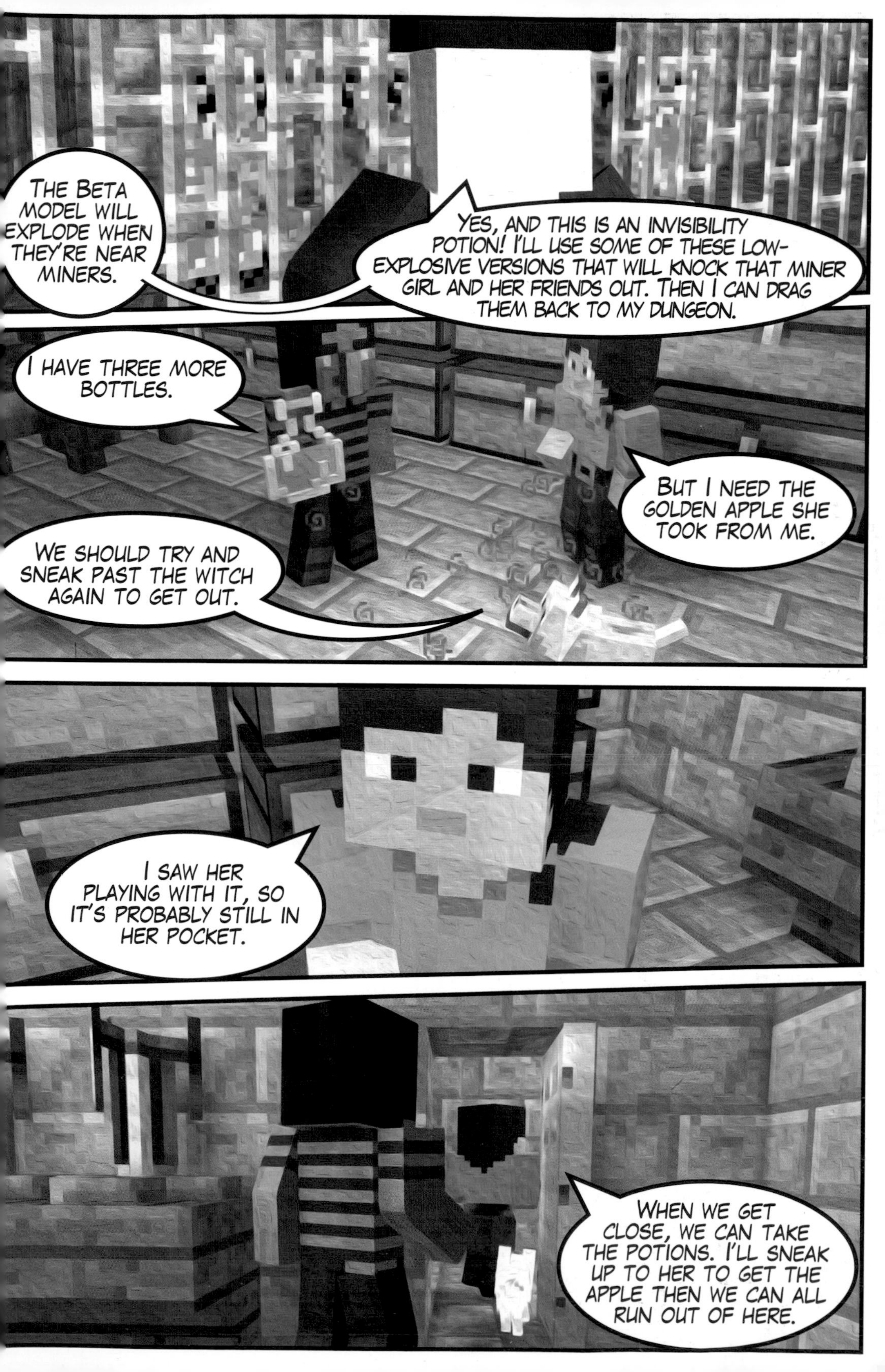
The Beta model will explode when they're near miners.
Yes, and this is an invisibility potion! I'll use some of these low-explosive versions that will knock that miner girl and her friends out. Then I can drag them back to my dungeon.
I have three more bottles.
But I need the golden apple she took from me.
We should try and sneak past the witch again to get out.
I saw her playing with it, so it's probably still in her pocket.
When we get close, we can take the potions. I'll sneak up to her to get the apple then we can all run out of here.

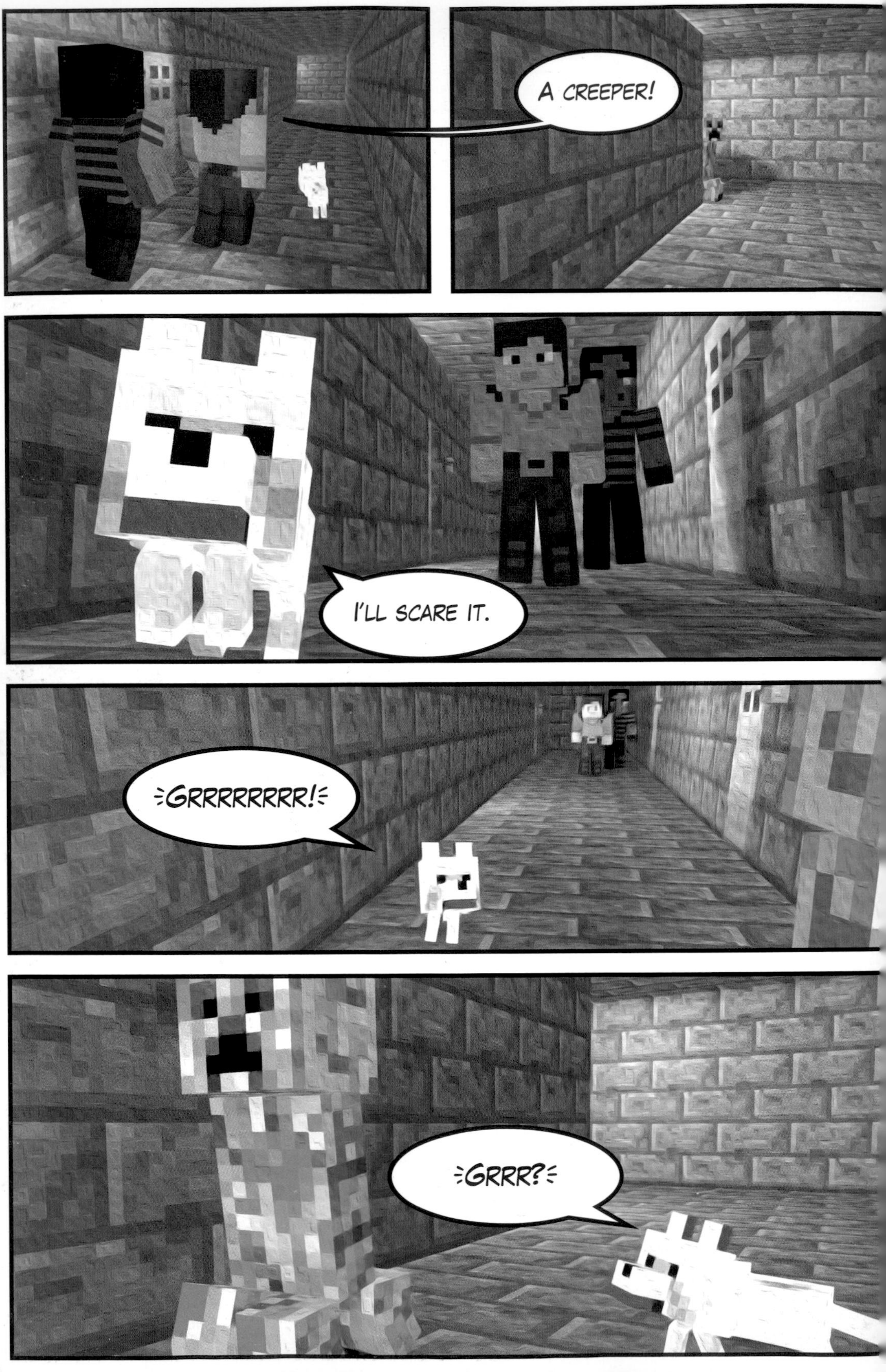
A CREEPER!
I'LL SCARE IT.
GRRRRRRRR!
GRRR?

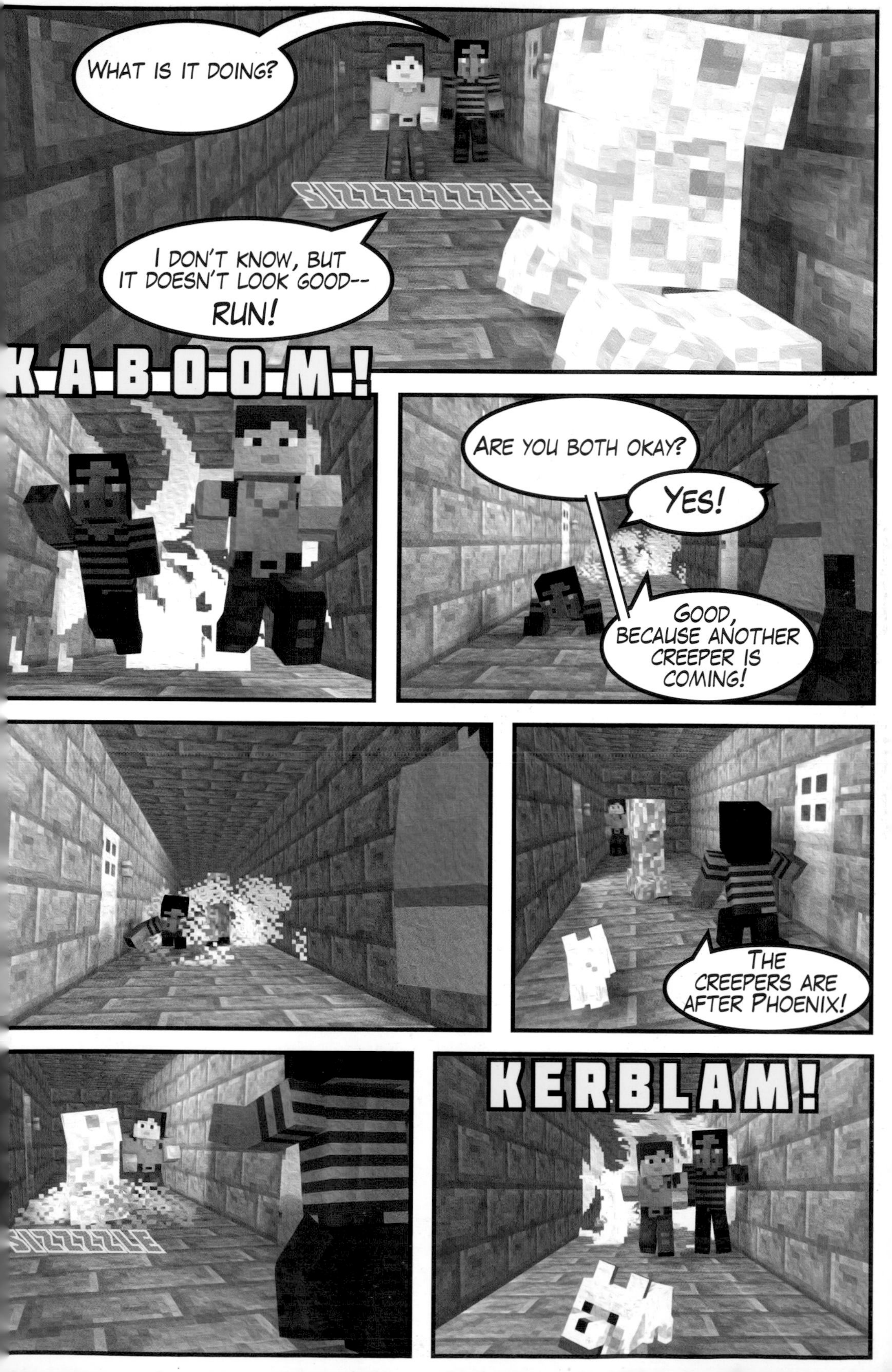
WHAT IS IT DOING?
SIZZZZZZZZZZLE
I DON'T KNOW, BUT IT DOESN'T LOOK GOOD-- RUN!
KABOOM!
ARE YOU BOTH OKAY?
YES!
GOOD, BECAUSE ANOTHER CREEPER IS COMING!
THE CREEPERS ARE AFTER PHOENIX!
SIZZZZZZLE
KERBLAM!

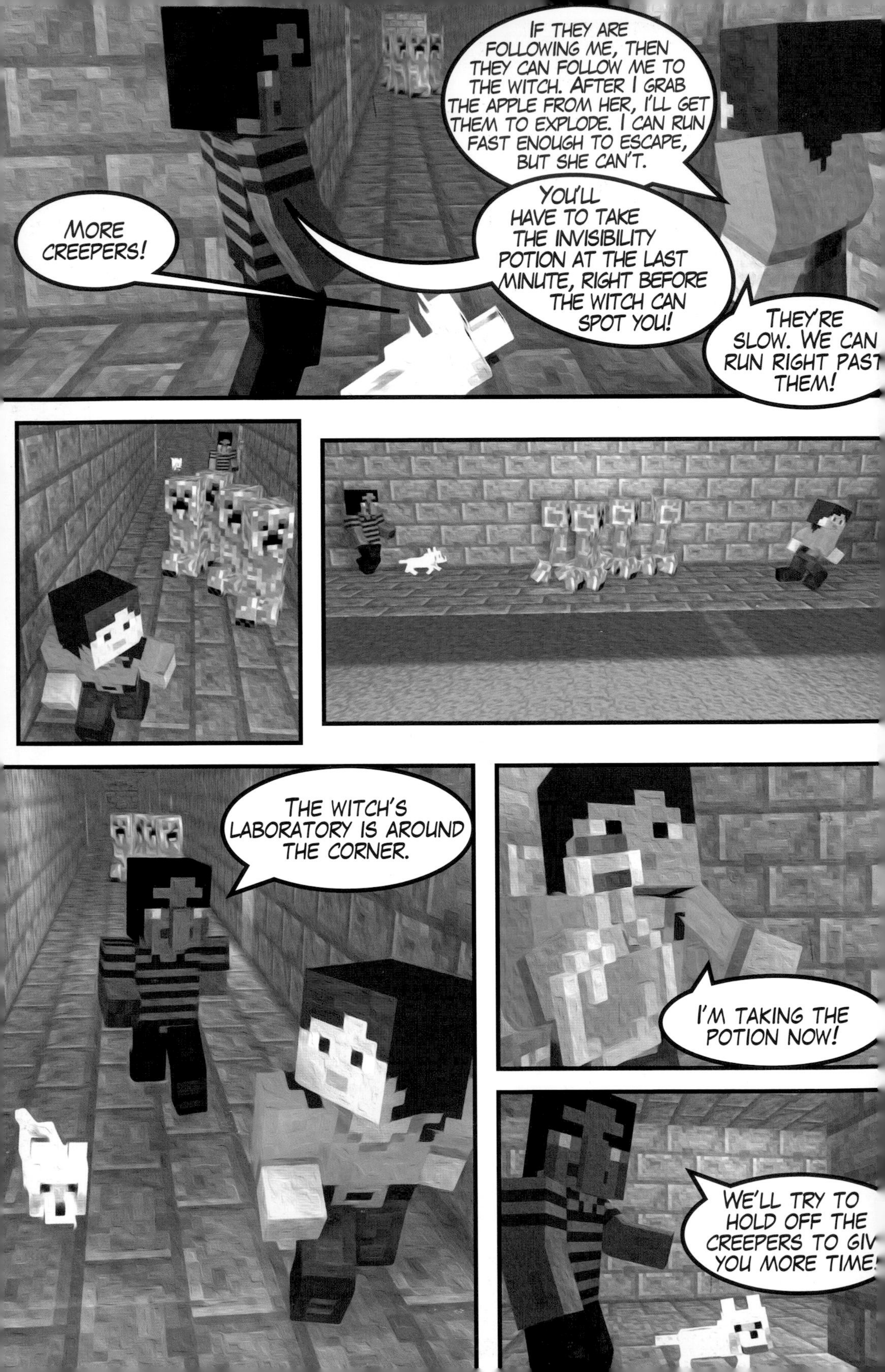
IF THEY ARE FOLLOWING ME, THEN THEY CAN FOLLOW ME TO THE WITCH. AFTER I GRAB THE APPLE FROM HER, I'LL GET THEM TO EXPLODE. I CAN RUN FAST ENOUGH TO ESCAPE, BUT SHE CAN'T.
MORE CREEPERS!
YOU'LL HAVE TO TAKE THE INVISIBILITY POTION AT THE LAST MINUTE, RIGHT BEFORE THE WITCH CAN SPOT YOU!
THEY'RE SLOW. WE CAN RUN RIGHT PAST THEM!
THE WITCH'S LABORATORY IS AROUND THE CORNER.
I'M TAKING THE POTION NOW!
WE'LL TRY TO HOLD OFF THE CREEPERS TO GIV YOU MORE TIME!

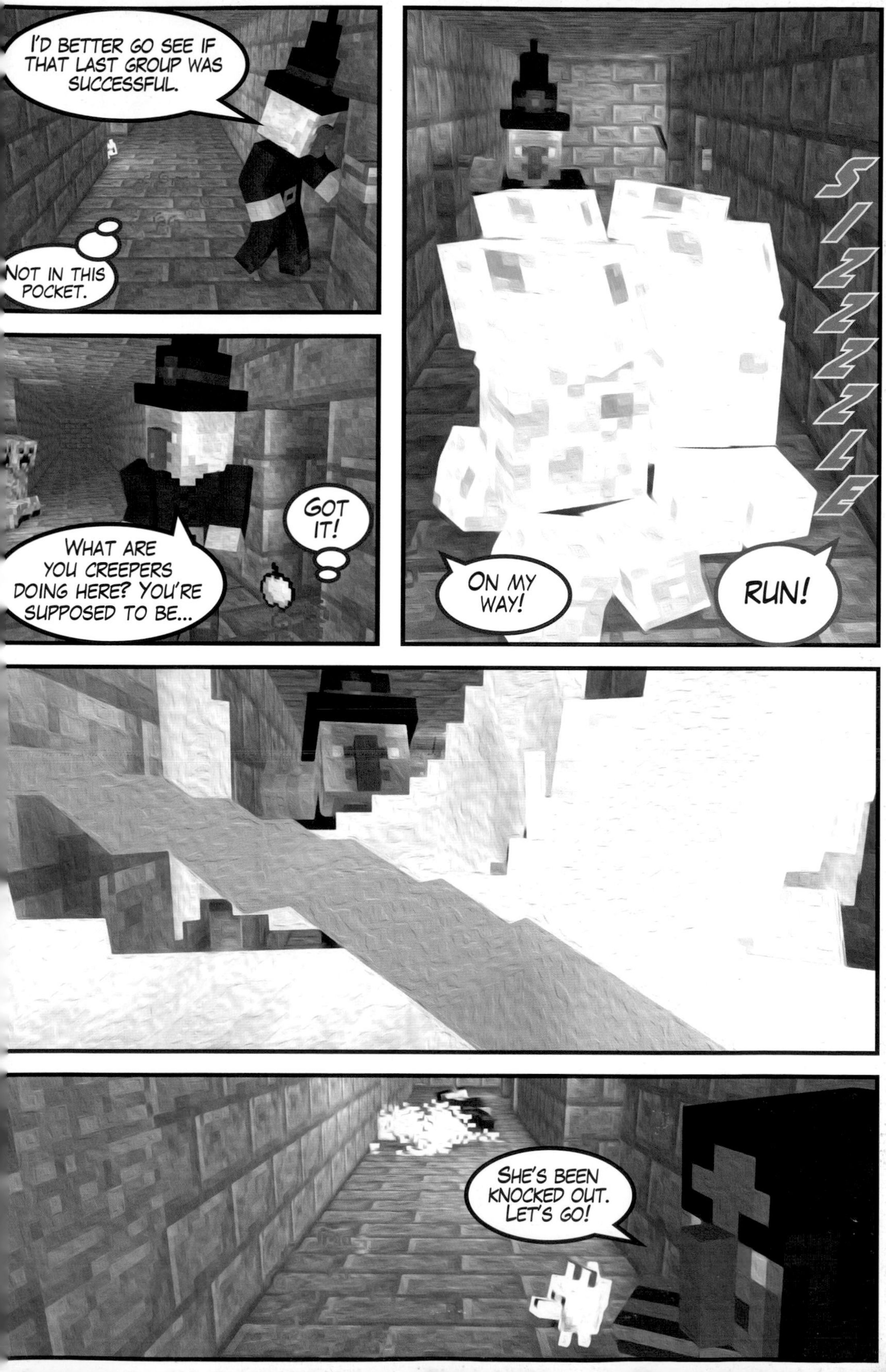
I'D BETTER GO SEE IF THAT LAST GROUP WAS SUCCESSFUL.
NOT IN THIS POCKET.
WHAT ARE YOU CREEPERS DOING HERE? YOU'RE SUPPOSED TO BE...
GOT IT!
SIZZZZLE
ON MY WAY!
RUN!
SHE'S BEEN KNOCKED OUT. LET'S GO!

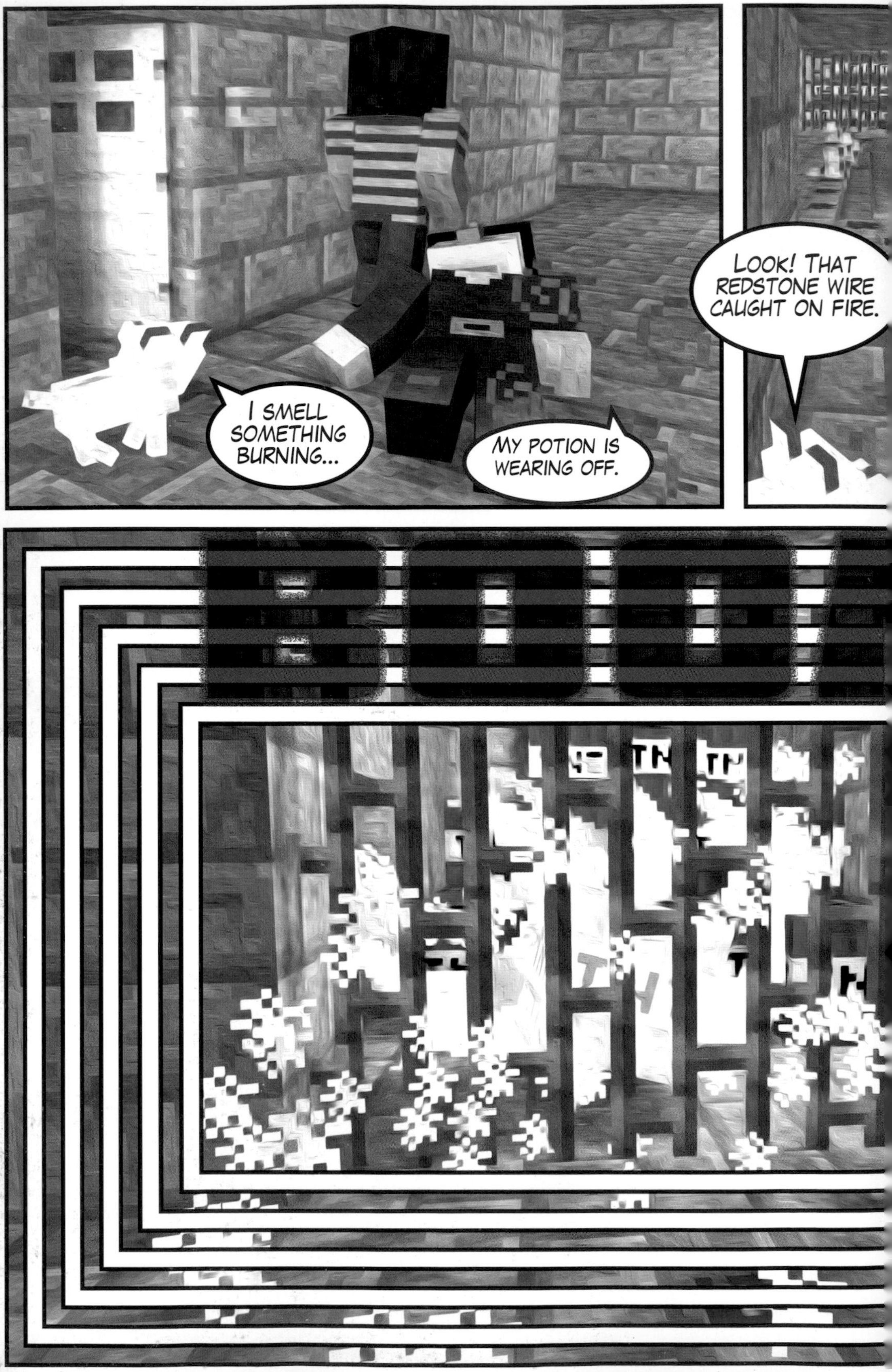
I SMELL SOMETHING BURNING...
MY POTION IS WEARING OFF.
LOOK! THAT REDSTONE WIRE CAUGHT ON FIRE.

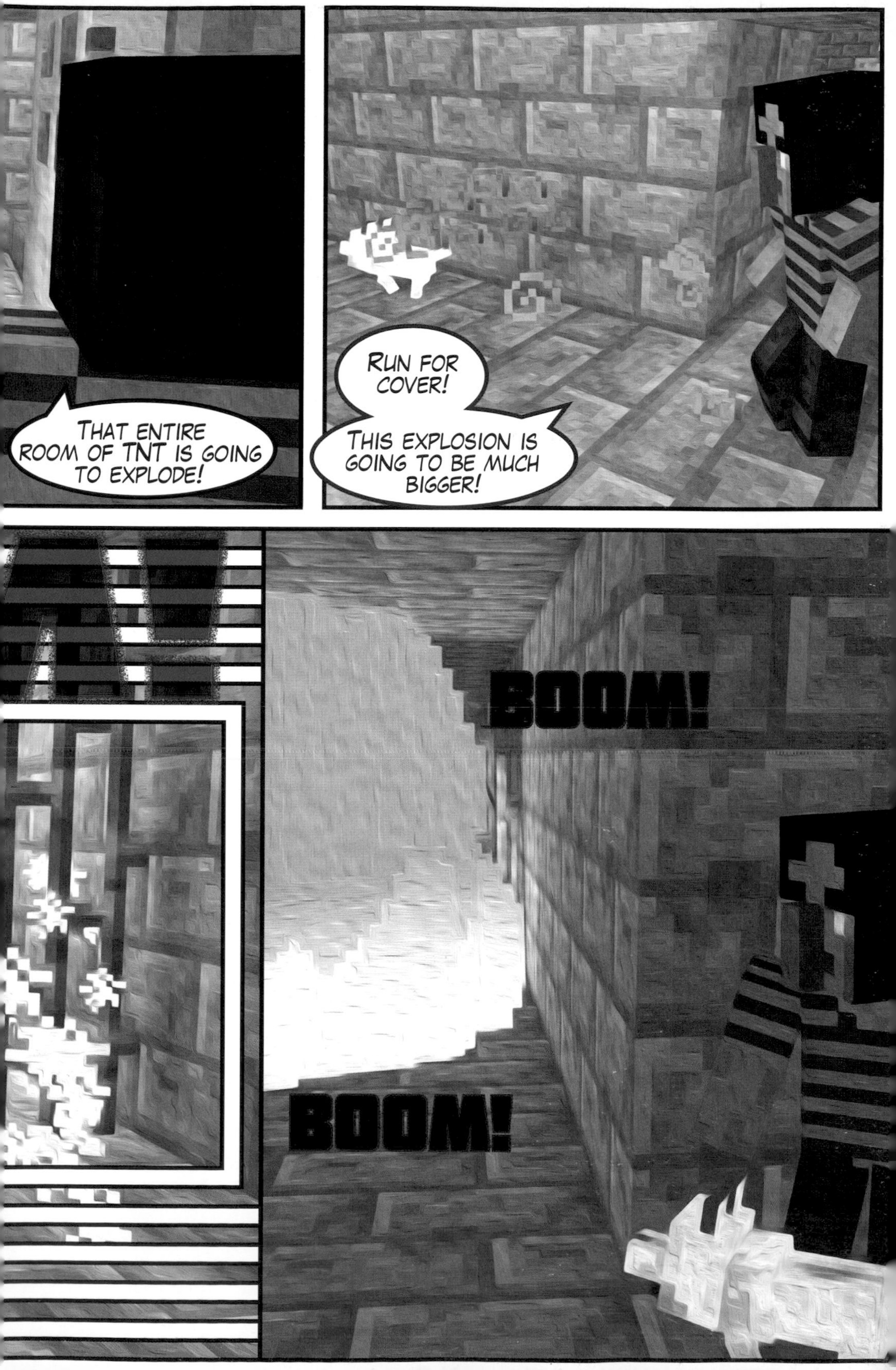
THAT ENTIRE ROOM OF TNT IS GOING TO EXPLODE!
RUN FOR COVER!
THIS EXPLOSION IS GOING TO BE MUCH BIGGER!
BOOM!
BOOM!

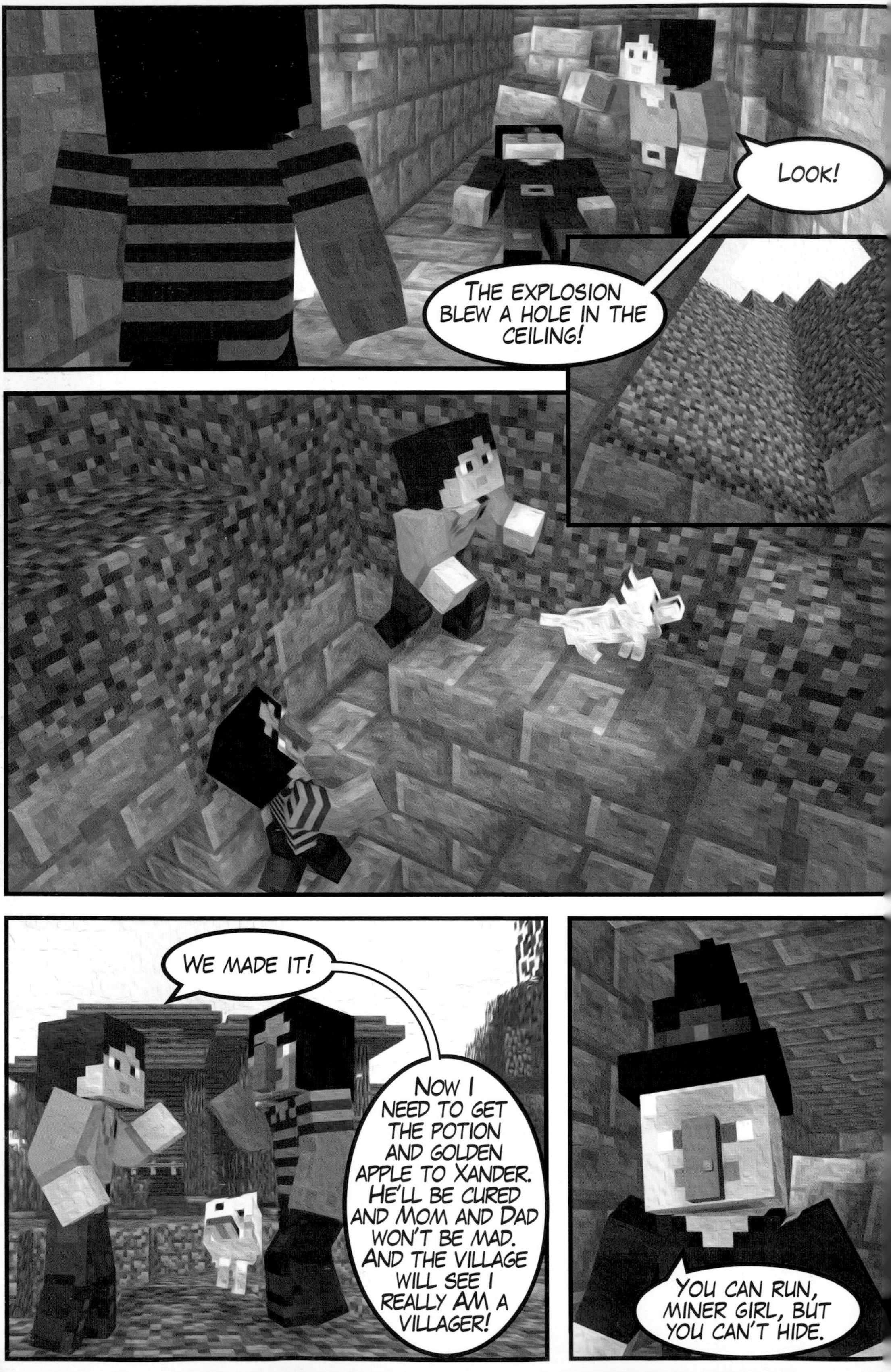
LOOK!
THE EXPLOSION BLEW A HOLE IN THE CEILING!
WE MADE IT!
NOW I NEED TO GET THE POTION AND GOLDEN APPLE TO XANDER. HE'LL BE CURED AND MOM AND DAD WON'T BE MAD. AND THE VILLAGE WILL SEE I REALLY AM A VILLAGER!
YOU CAN RUN, MINER GIRL, BUT YOU CAN'T HIDE.

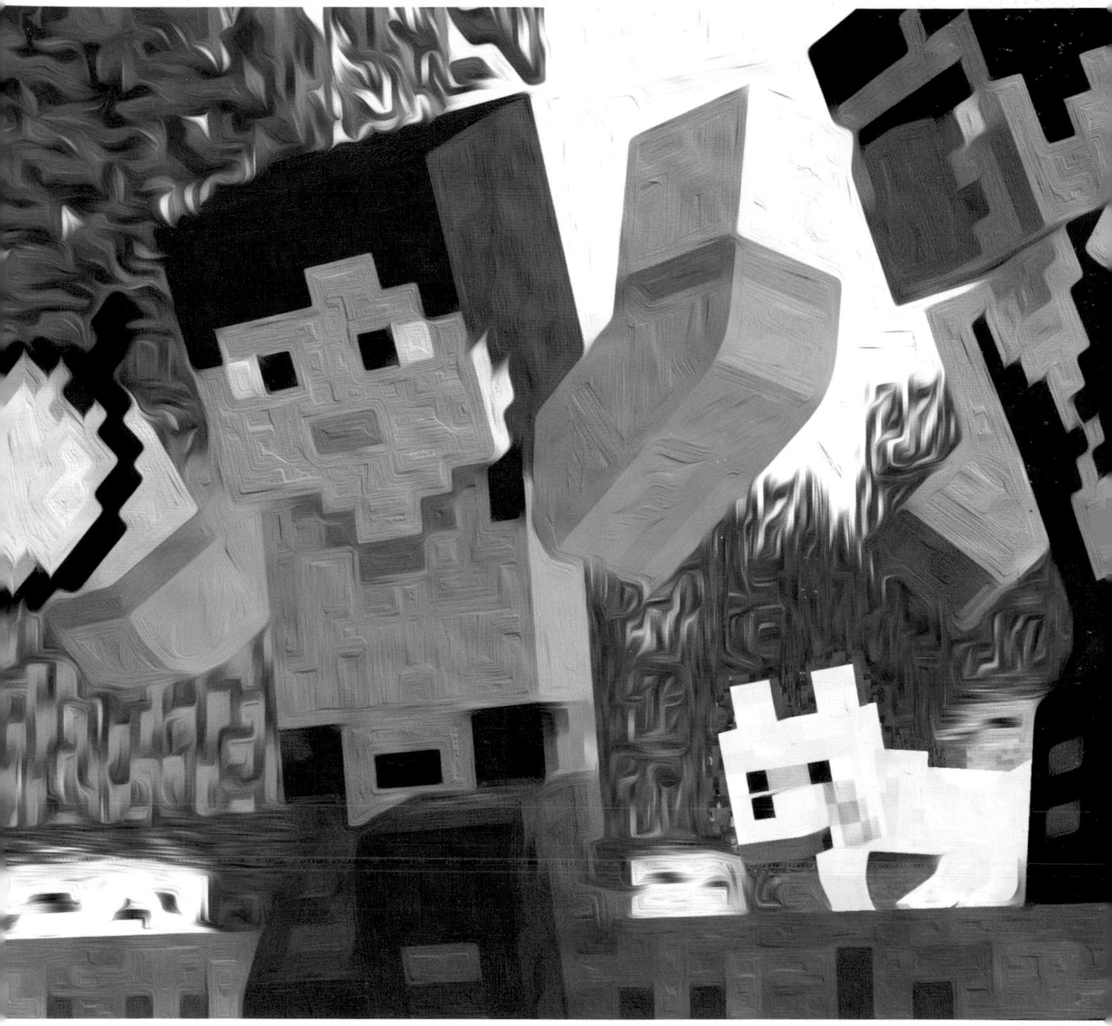

CHAPTER 11
XANDER

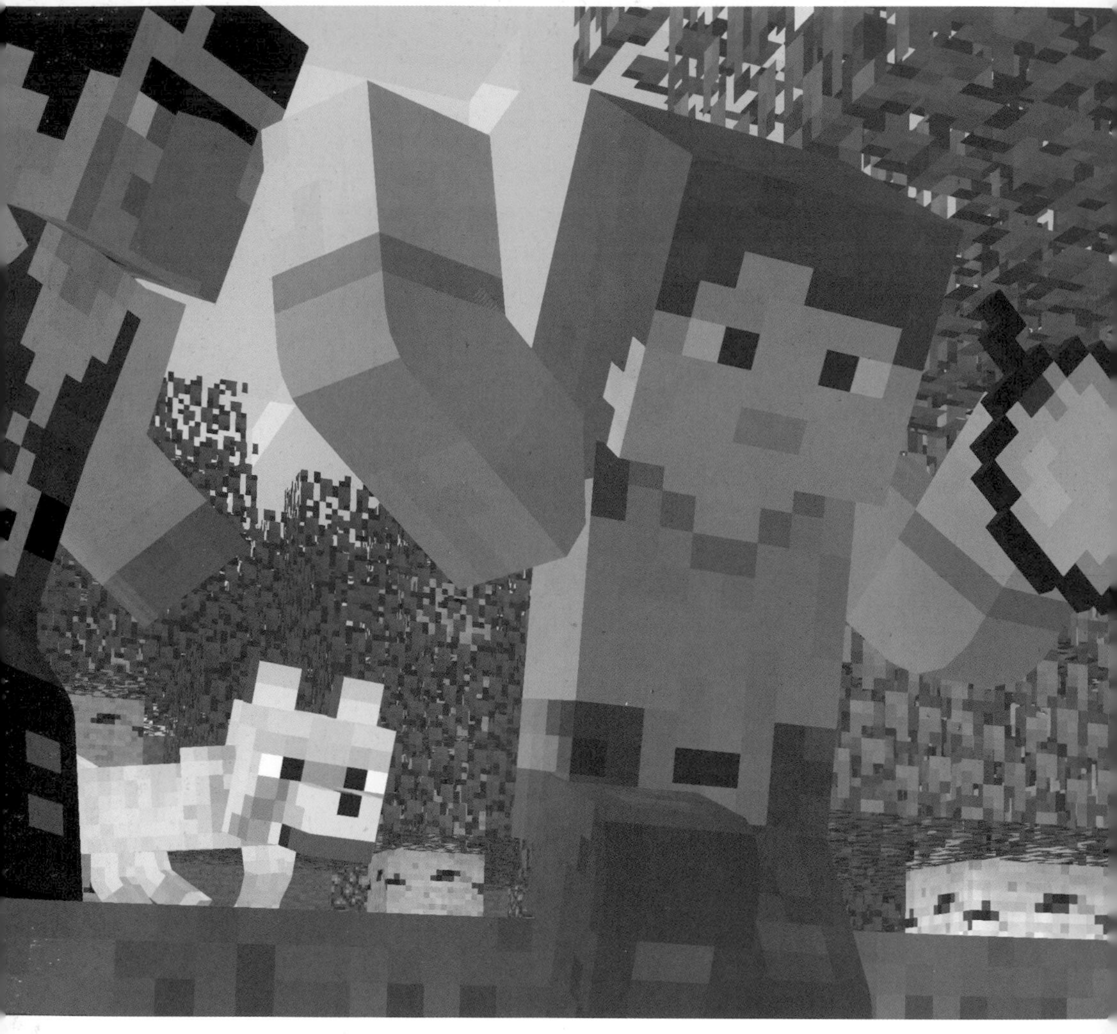

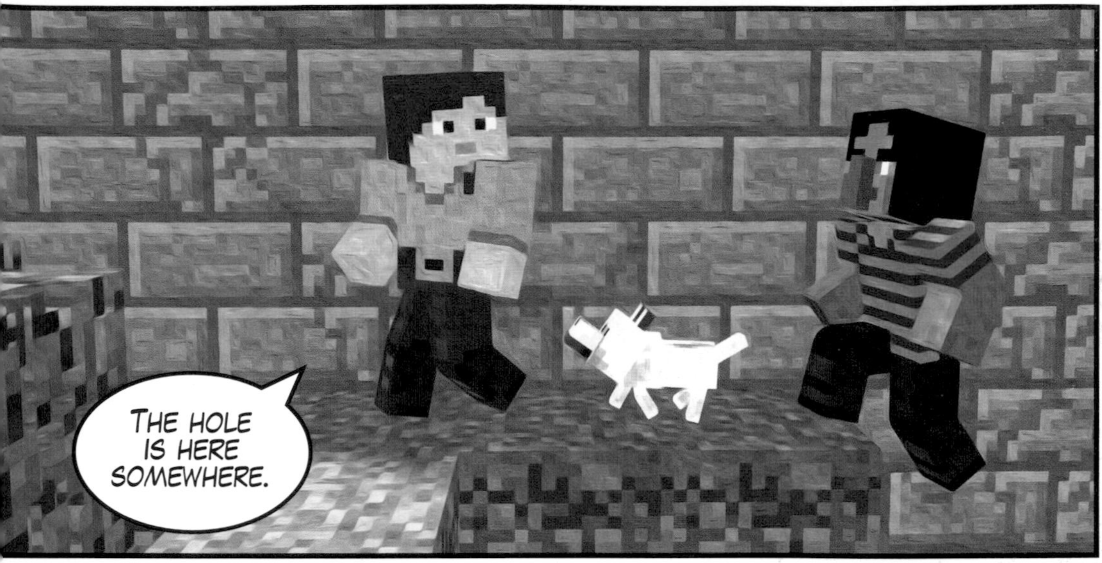
THE HOLE IS HERE SOMEWHERE.

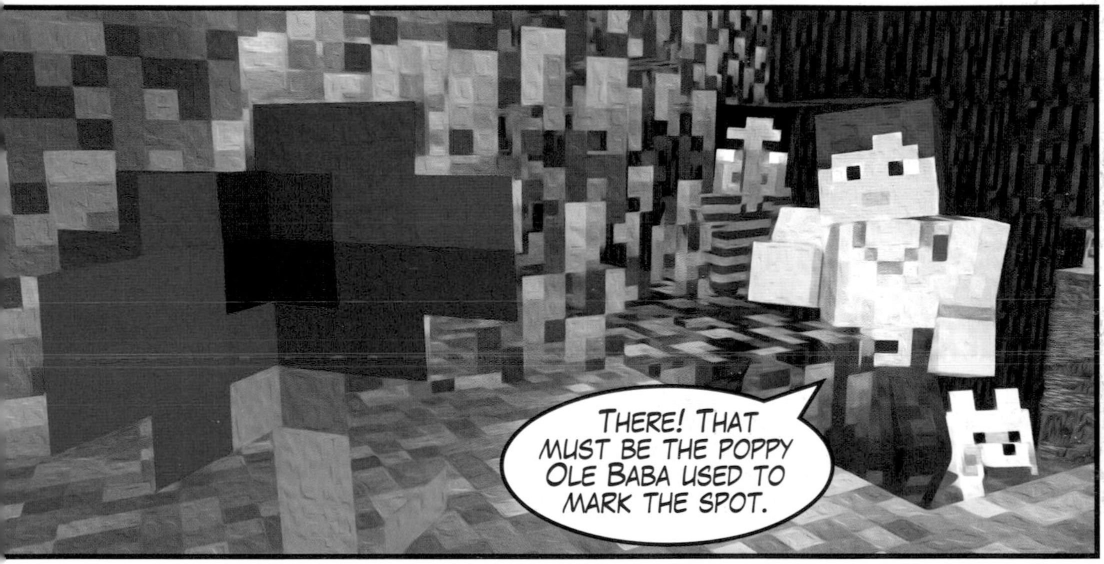
THERE! THAT MUST BE THE POPPY OLE BABA USED TO MARK THE SPOT.

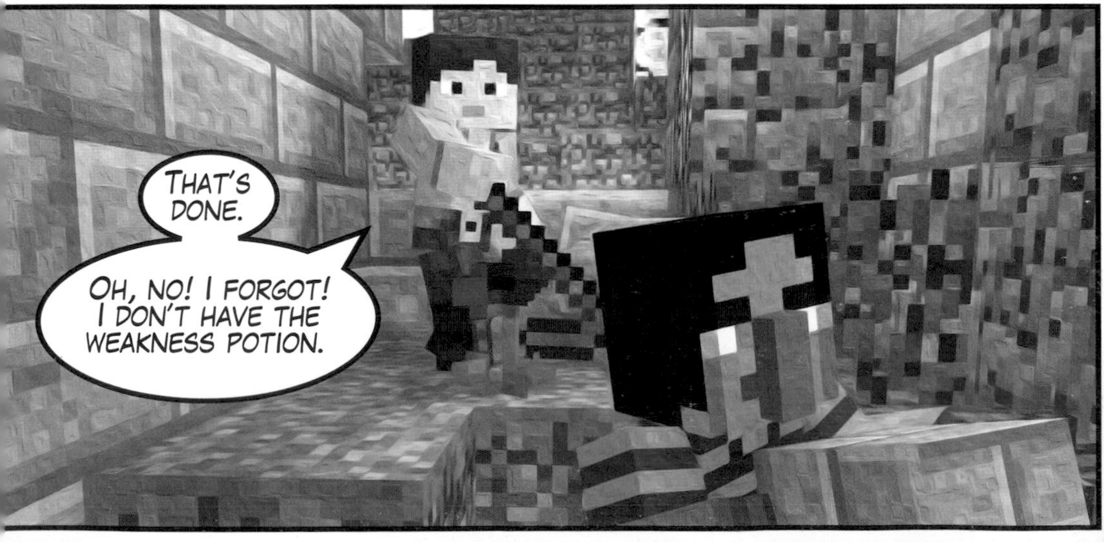
THAT'S DONE.
OH, NO! I FORGOT! I DON'T HAVE THE WEAKNESS POTION.

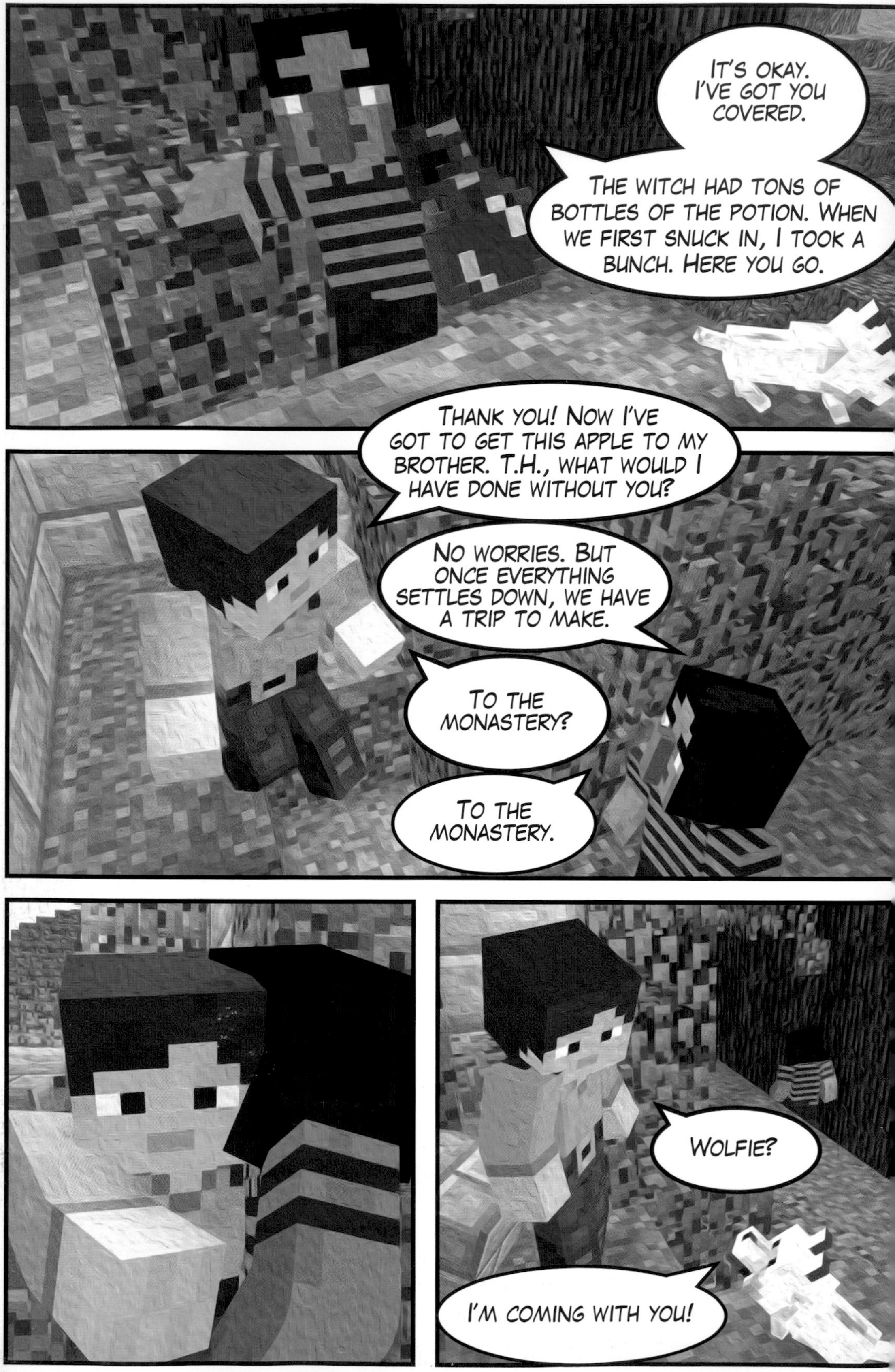

IT'S OKAY. I'VE GOT YOU COVERED.
THE WITCH HAD TONS OF BOTTLES OF THE POTION. WHEN WE FIRST SNUCK IN, I TOOK A BUNCH. HERE YOU GO.
THANK YOU! NOW I'VE GOT TO GET THIS APPLE TO MY BROTHER. T.H., WHAT WOULD I HAVE DONE WITHOUT YOU?
NO WORRIES. BUT ONCE EVERYTHING SETTLES DOWN, WE HAVE A TRIP TO MAKE.
TO THE MONASTERY?
TO THE MONASTERY.
WOLFIE?
I'M COMING WITH YOU!

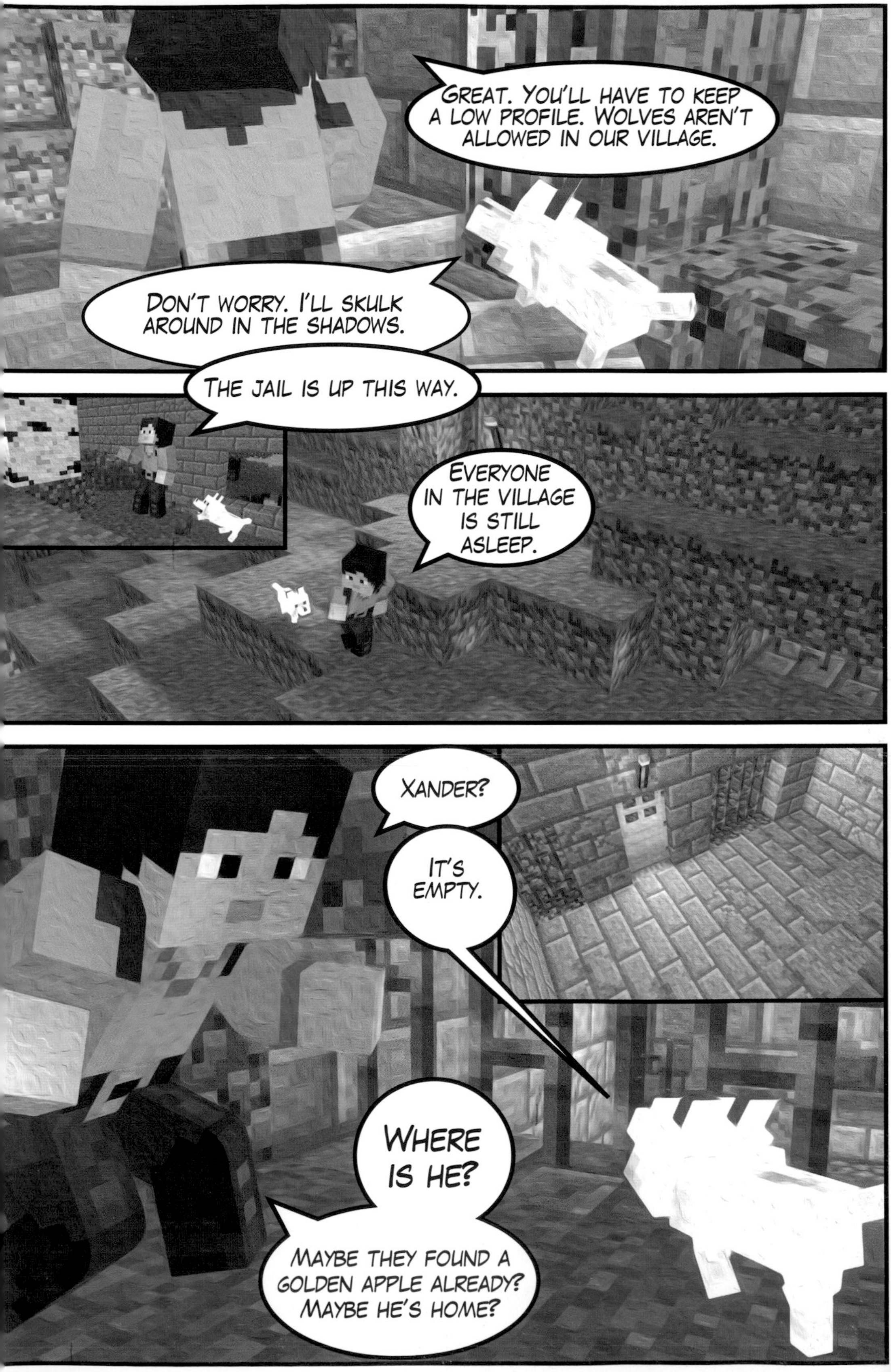
GREAT. YOU'LL HAVE TO KEEP A LOW PROFILE. WOLVES AREN'T ALLOWED IN OUR VILLAGE.
DON'T WORRY. I'LL SKULK AROUND IN THE SHADOWS.
THE JAIL IS UP THIS WAY.
EVERYONE IN THE VILLAGE IS STILL ASLEEP.
XANDER?
IT'S EMPTY.
WHERE IS HE?
MAYBE THEY FOUND A GOLDEN APPLE ALREADY? MAYBE HE'S HOME?

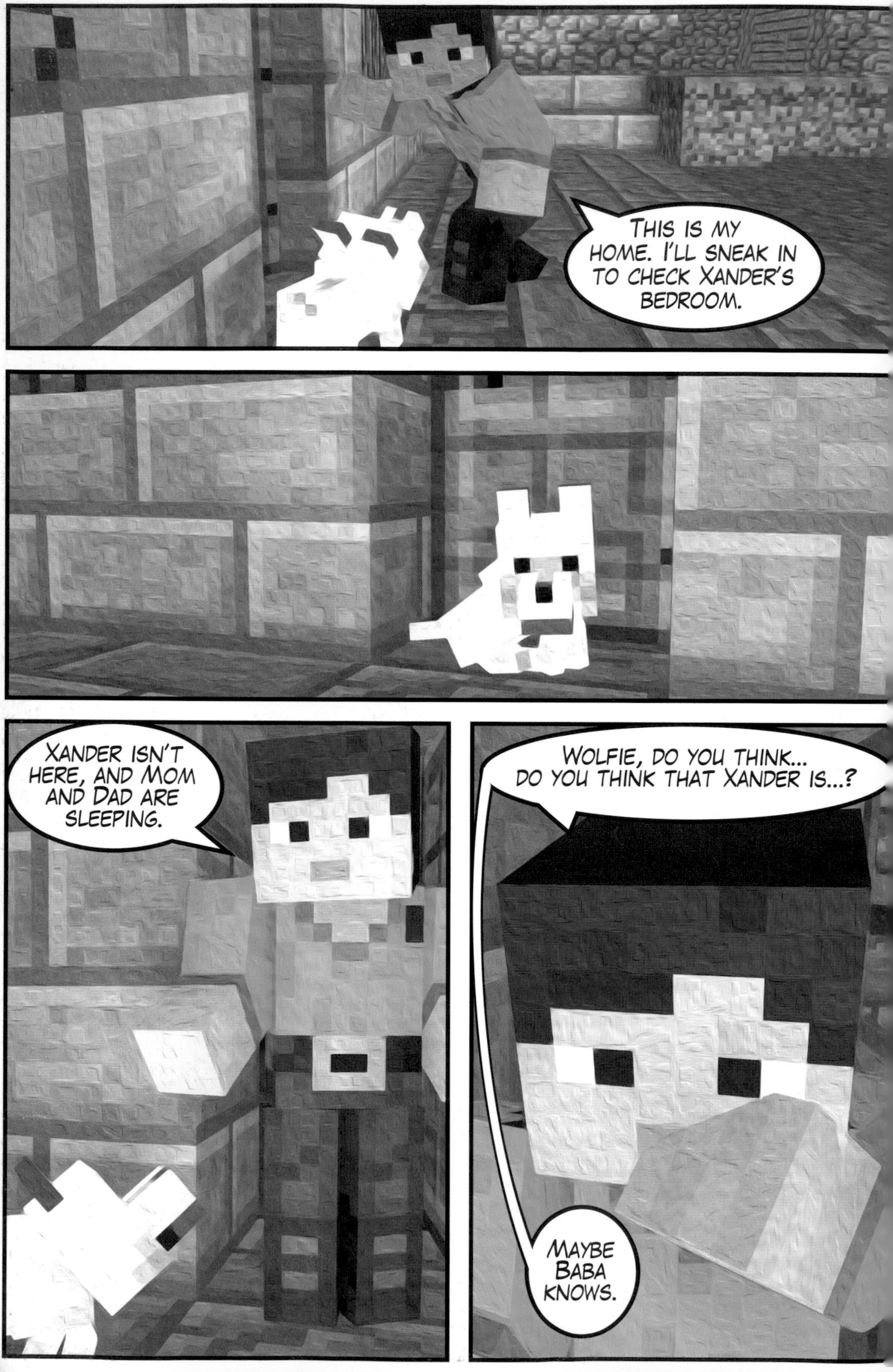
THIS IS MY HOME. I'LL SNEAK IN TO CHECK XANDER'S BEDROOM.
XANDER ISN'T HERE, AND MOM AND DAD ARE SLEEPING.
WOLFIE, DO YOU THINK... DO YOU THINK THAT XANDER IS...?
MAYBE BABA KNOWS.

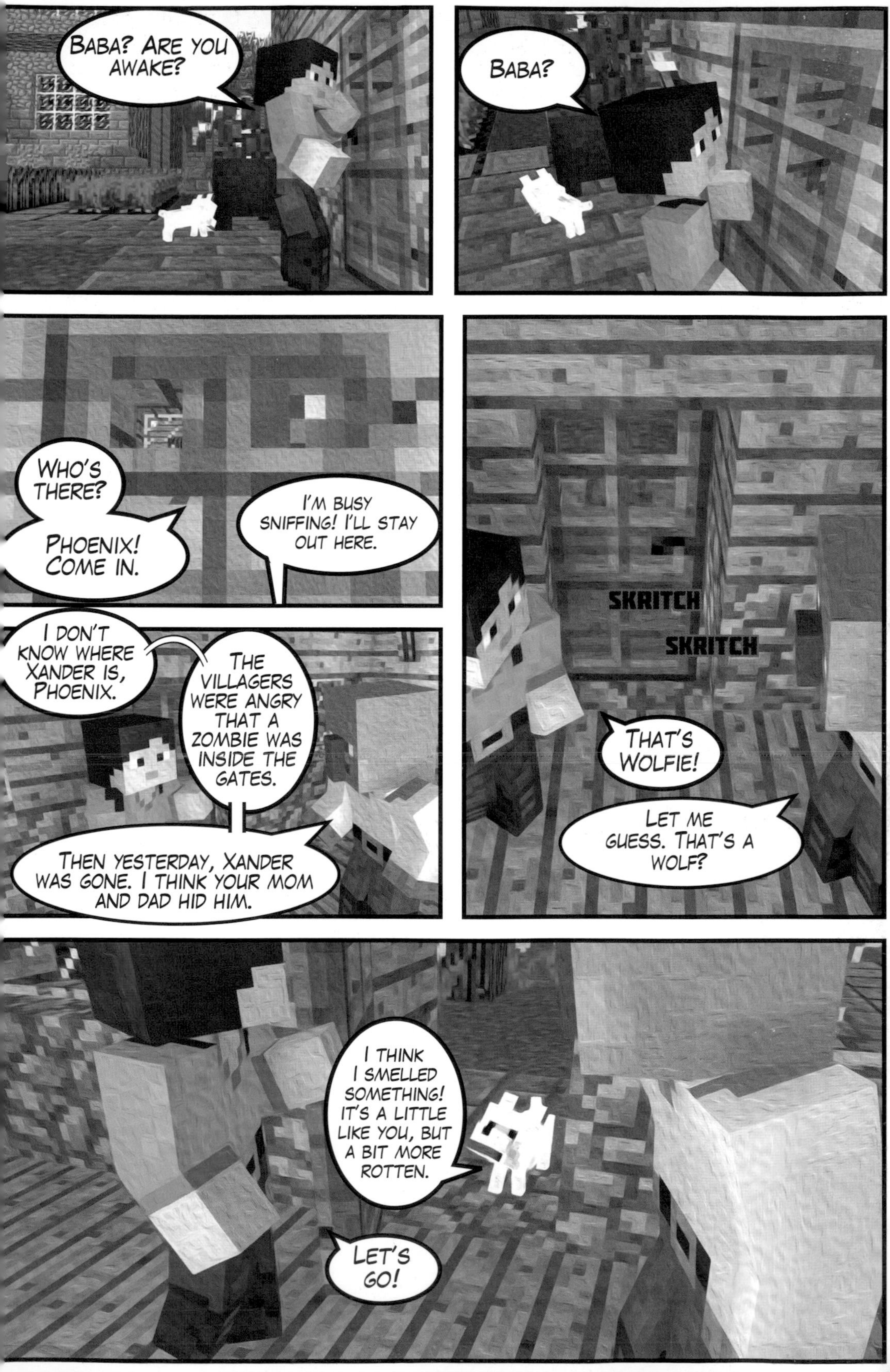
BABA? ARE YOU AWAKE?
BABA?
WHO'S THERE?
PHOENIX! COME IN.
I'M BUSY SNIFFING! I'LL STAY OUT HERE.
SKRITCH
SKRITCH
THAT'S WOLFIE!
LET ME GUESS. THAT'S A WOLF?
I DON'T KNOW WHERE XANDER IS, PHOENIX.
THE VILLAGERS WERE ANGRY THAT A ZOMBIE WAS INSIDE THE GATES.
THEN YESTERDAY, XANDER WAS GONE. I THINK YOUR MOM AND DAD HID HIM.
I THINK I SMELLED SOMETHING! IT'S A LITTLE LIKE YOU, BUT A BIT MORE ROTTEN.
LET'S GO!

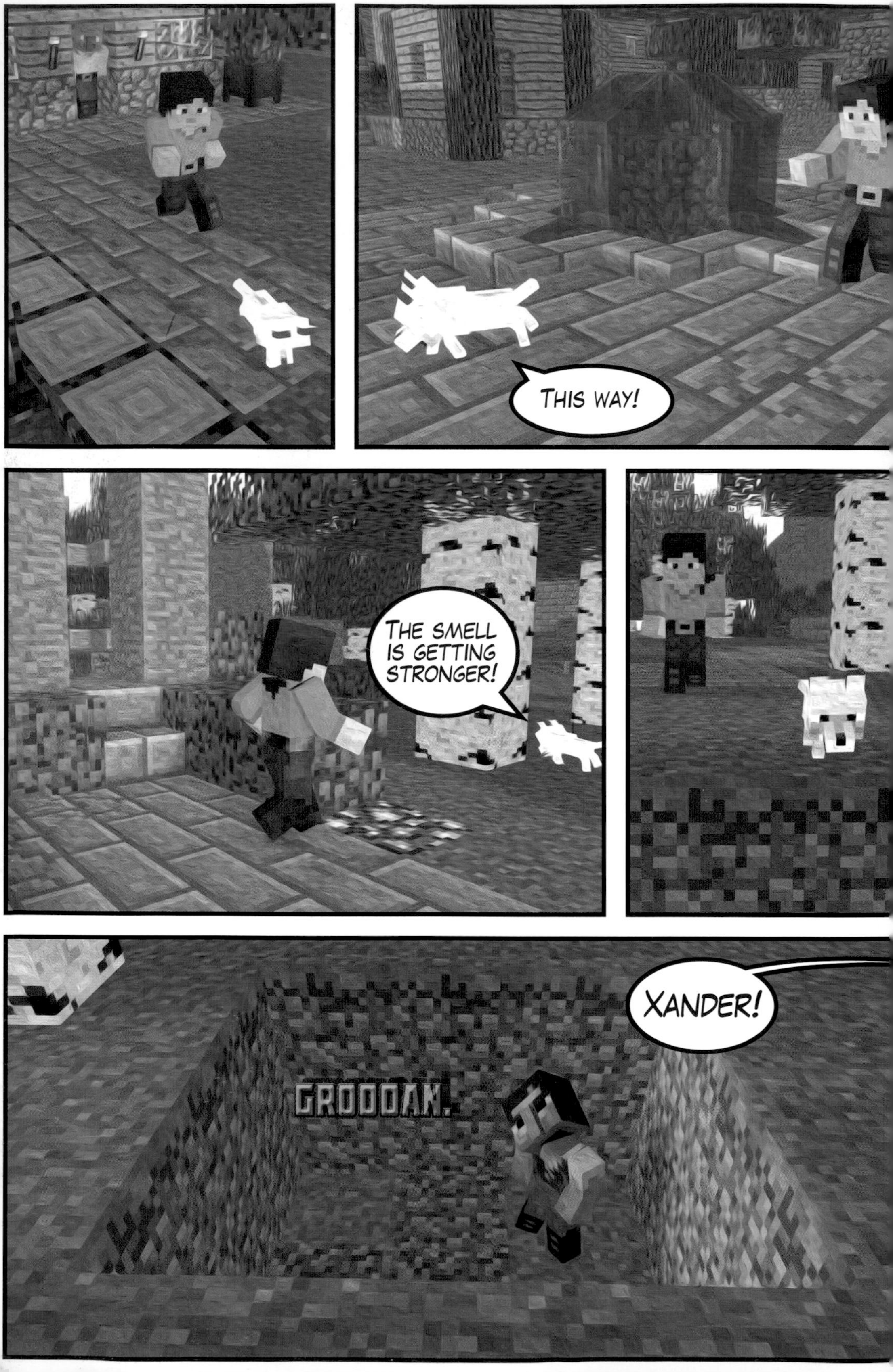
THIS WAY!
THE SMELL IS GETTING STRONGER!
XANDER!
GROOOAN.

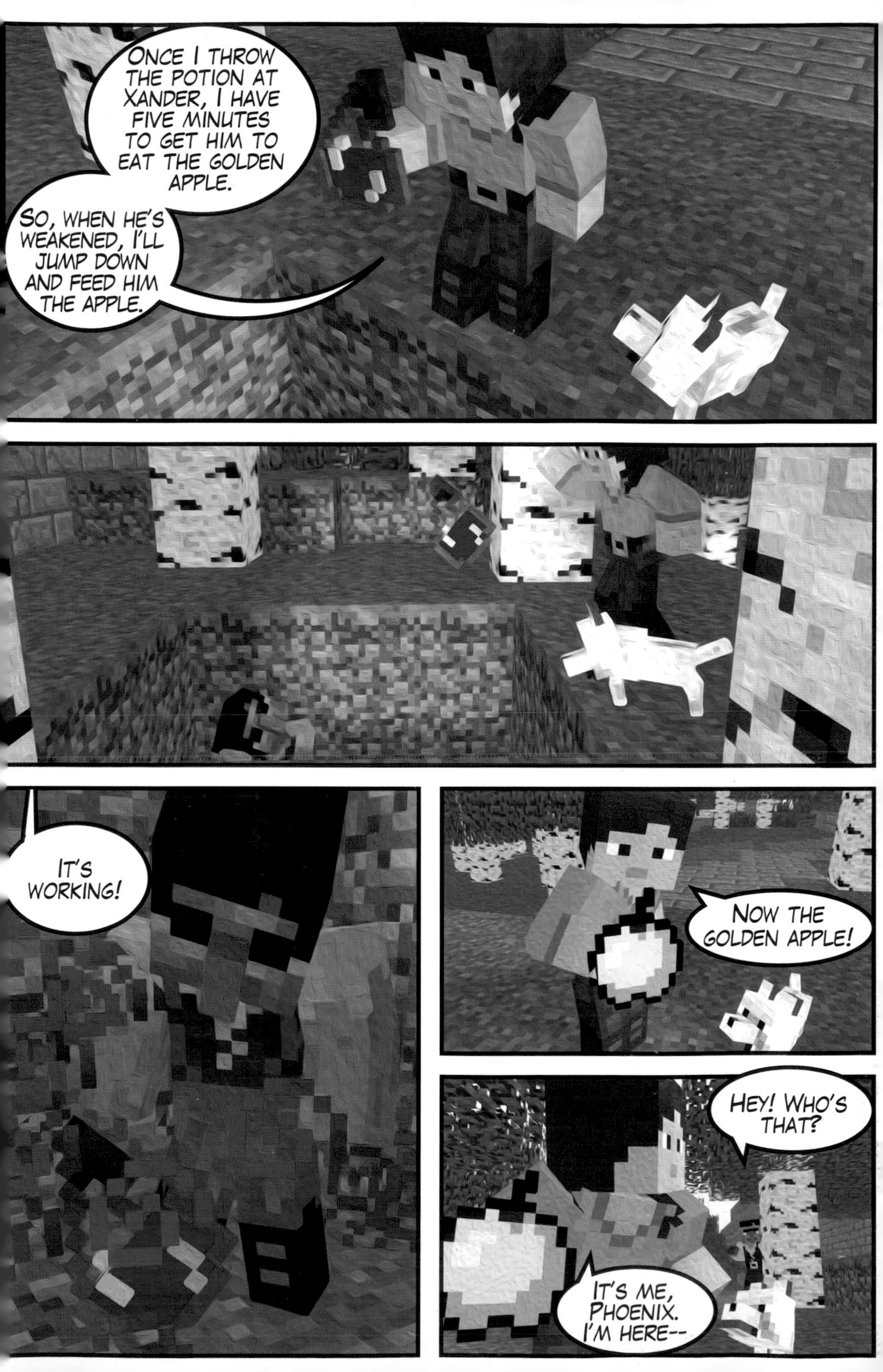
ONCE I THROW THE POTION AT XANDER, I HAVE FIVE MINUTES TO GET HIM TO EAT THE GOLDEN APPLE.
SO, WHEN HE'S WEAKENED, I'LL JUMP DOWN AND FEED HIM THE APPLE.
IT'S WORKING!
NOW THE GOLDEN APPLE!
HEY! WHO'S THAT?
IT'S ME, PHOENIX. I'M HERE--

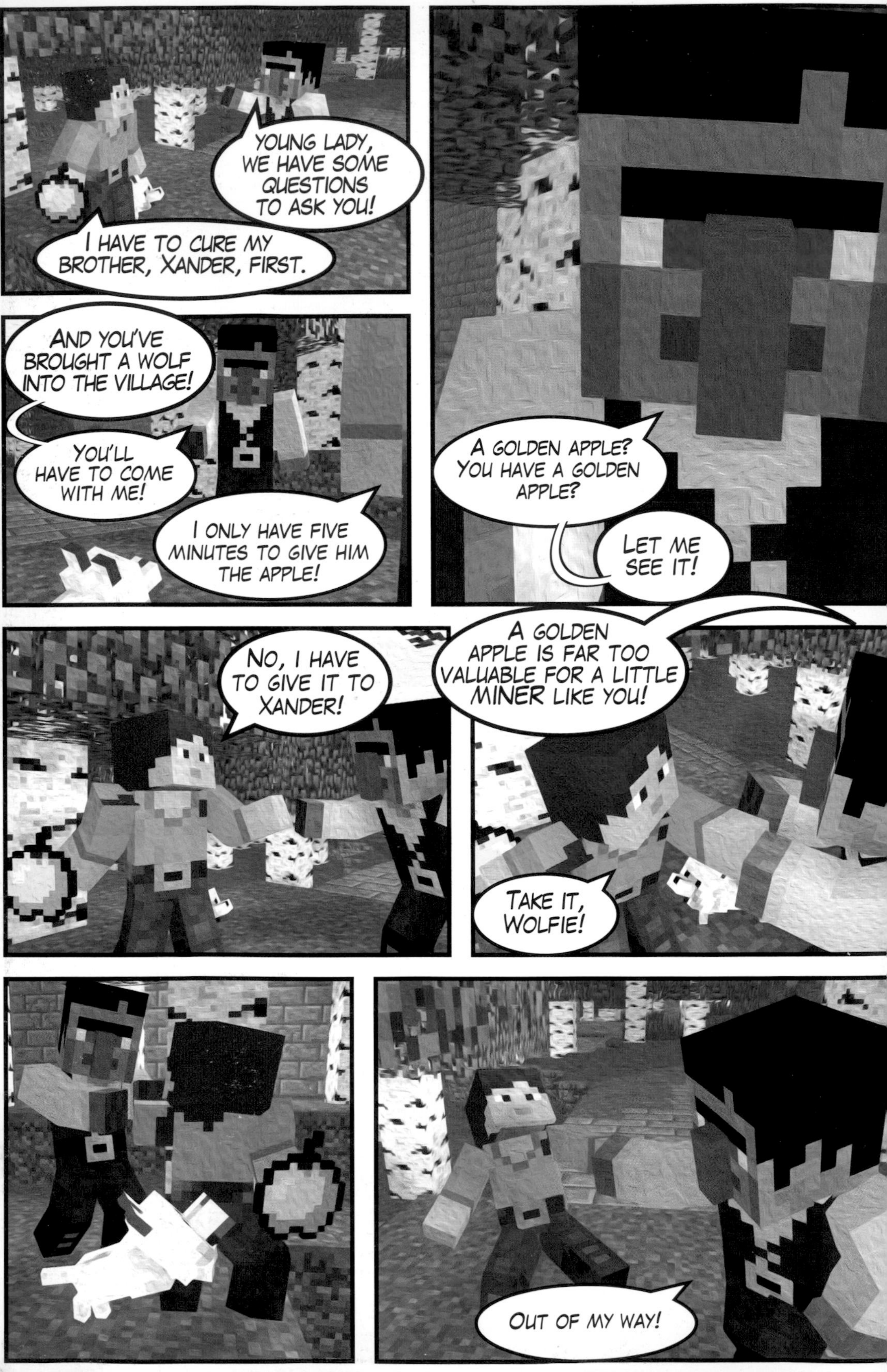
YOUNG LADY, WE HAVE SOME QUESTIONS TO ASK YOU!
I HAVE TO CURE MY BROTHER, XANDER, FIRST.
AND YOU'VE BROUGHT A WOLF INTO THE VILLAGE!
YOU'LL HAVE TO COME WITH ME!
I ONLY HAVE FIVE MINUTES TO GIVE HIM THE APPLE!
A GOLDEN APPLE? YOU HAVE A GOLDEN APPLE?
LET ME SEE IT!
NO, I HAVE TO GIVE IT TO XANDER!
A GOLDEN APPLE IS FAR TOO VALUABLE FOR A LITTLE MINER LIKE YOU!
TAKE IT, WOLFIE!
OUT OF MY WAY!

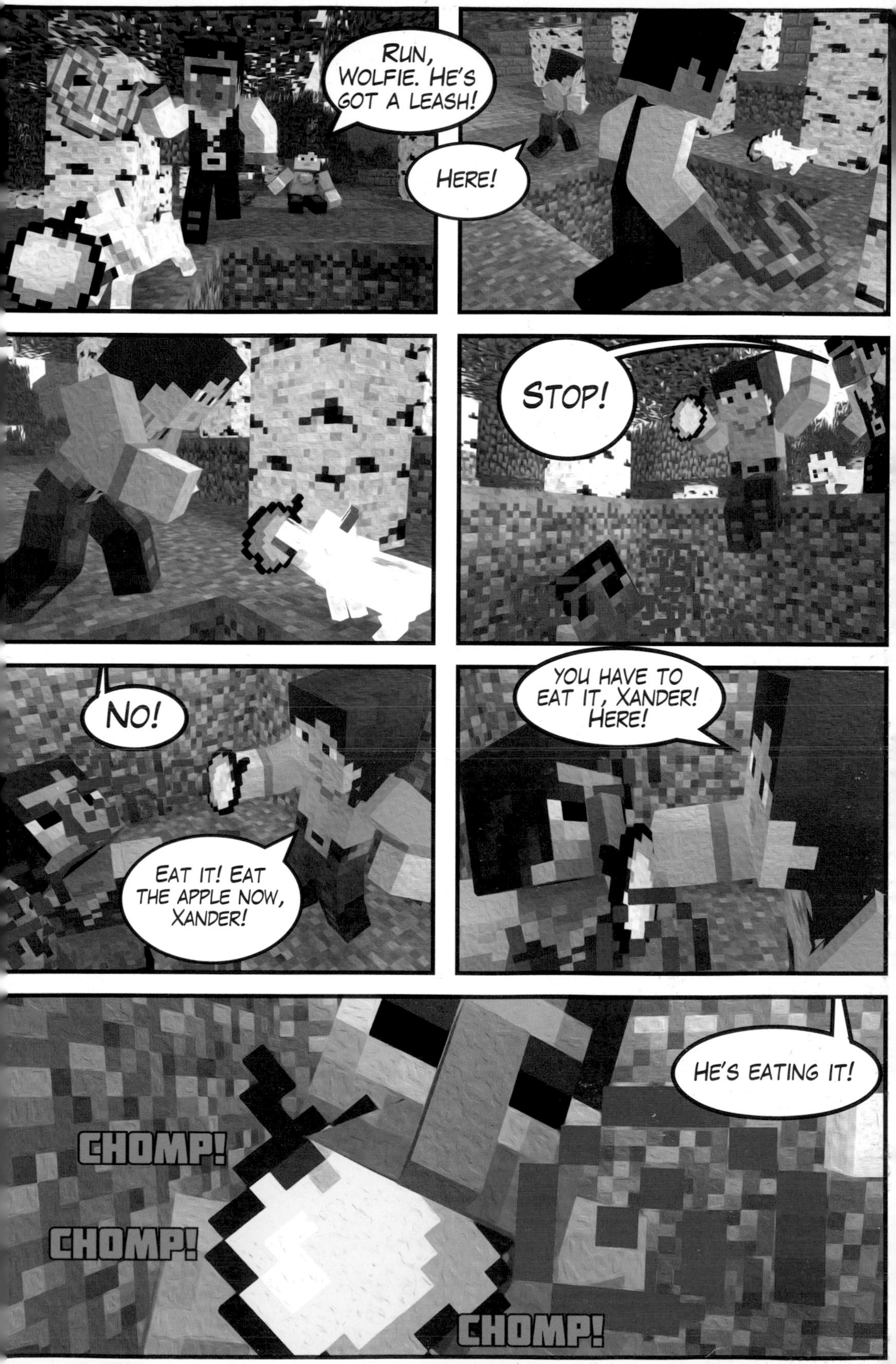
RUN, WOLFIE. HE'S GOT A LEASH!
HERE!
STOP!
NO!
EAT IT! EAT THE APPLE NOW, XANDER!
YOU HAVE TO EAT IT, XANDER! HERE!
CHOMP!
CHOMP!
CHOMP!
HE'S EATING IT!

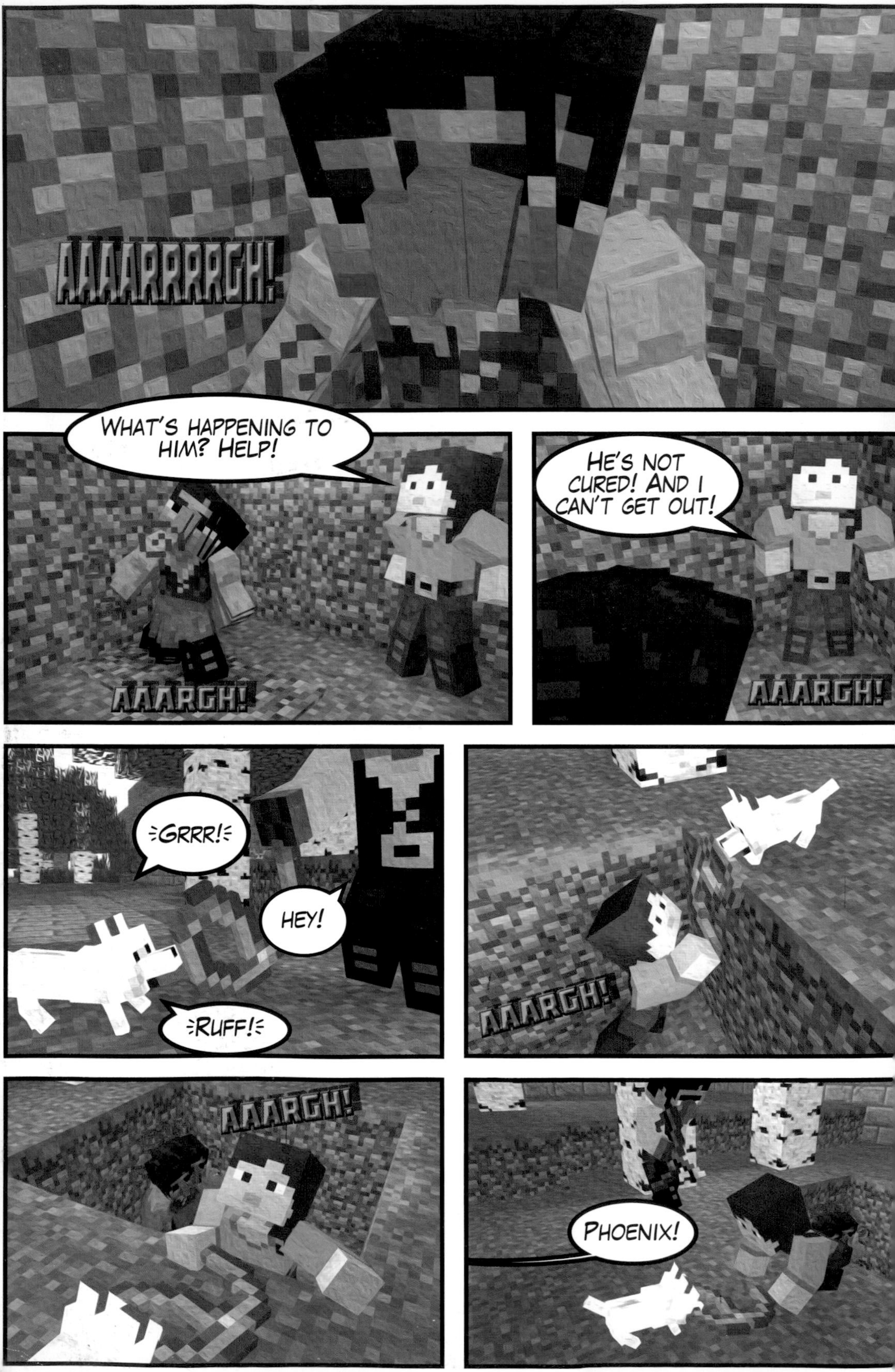
AAAARRRRGH!
WHAT'S HAPPENING TO HIM? HELP!
AAARGH!
HE'S NOT CURED! AND I CAN'T GET OUT!
AAARGH!
GRRR!
HEY!
RUFF!
AAARGH!
AAARGH!
PHOENIX!

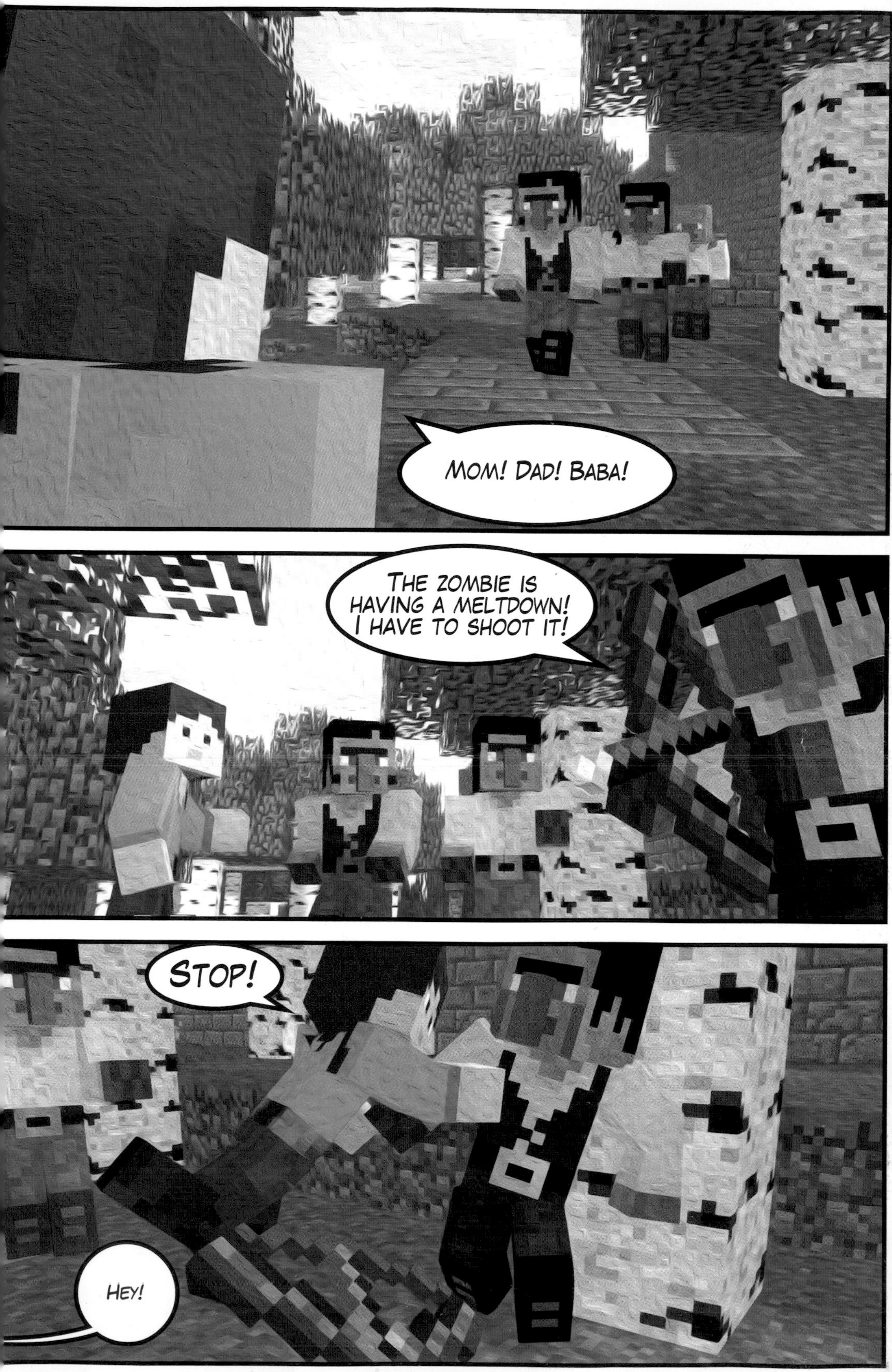
MOM! DAD! BABA!
THE ZOMBIE IS HAVING A MELTDOWN! I HAVE TO SHOOT IT!
STOP!
HEY!

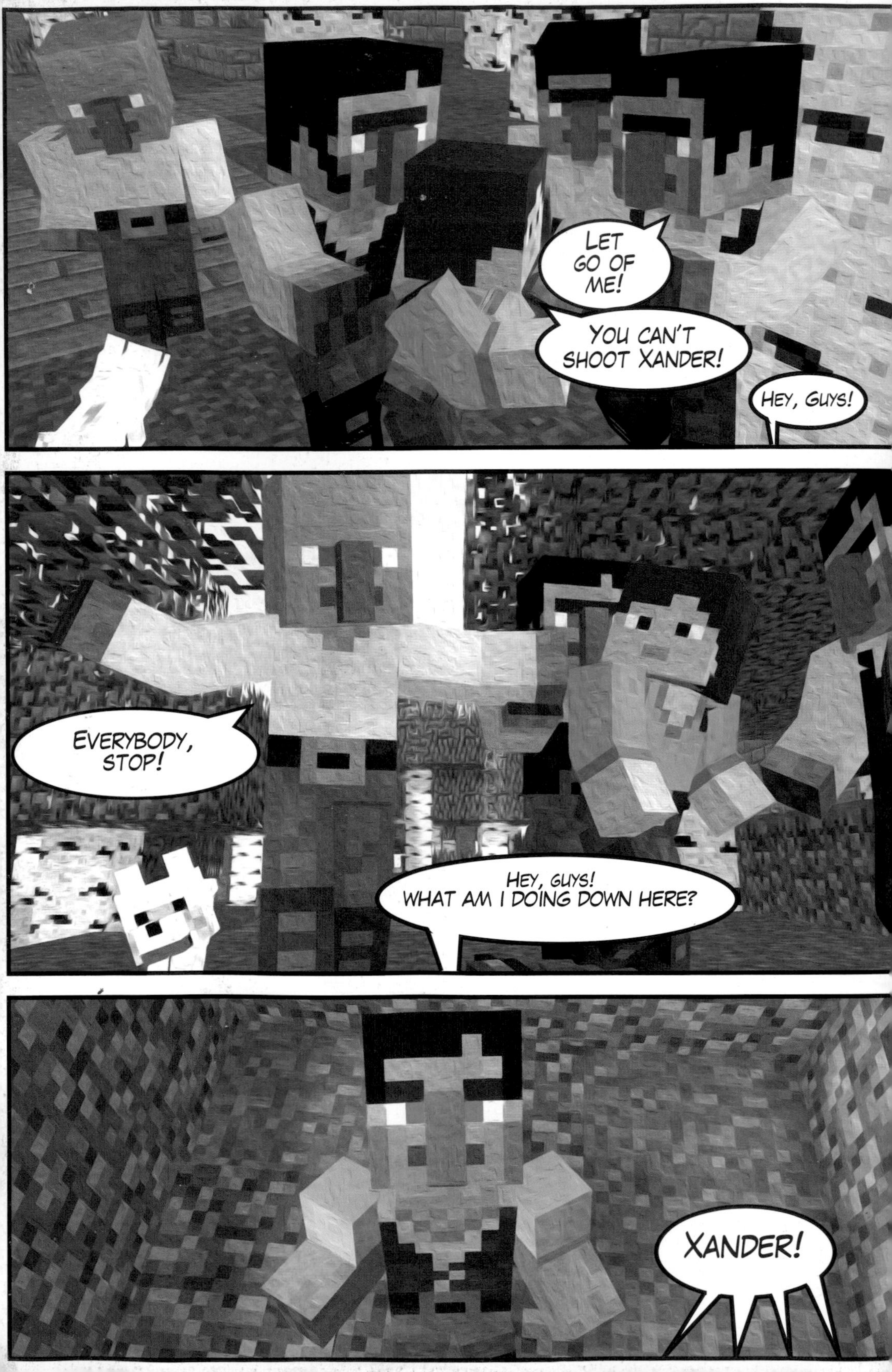
LET GO OF ME!
YOU CAN'T SHOOT XANDER!
HEY, GUYS!
EVERYBODY, STOP!
HEY, GUYS! WHAT AM I DOING DOWN HERE?
XANDER!

CHAPTER 12
TOGETHER

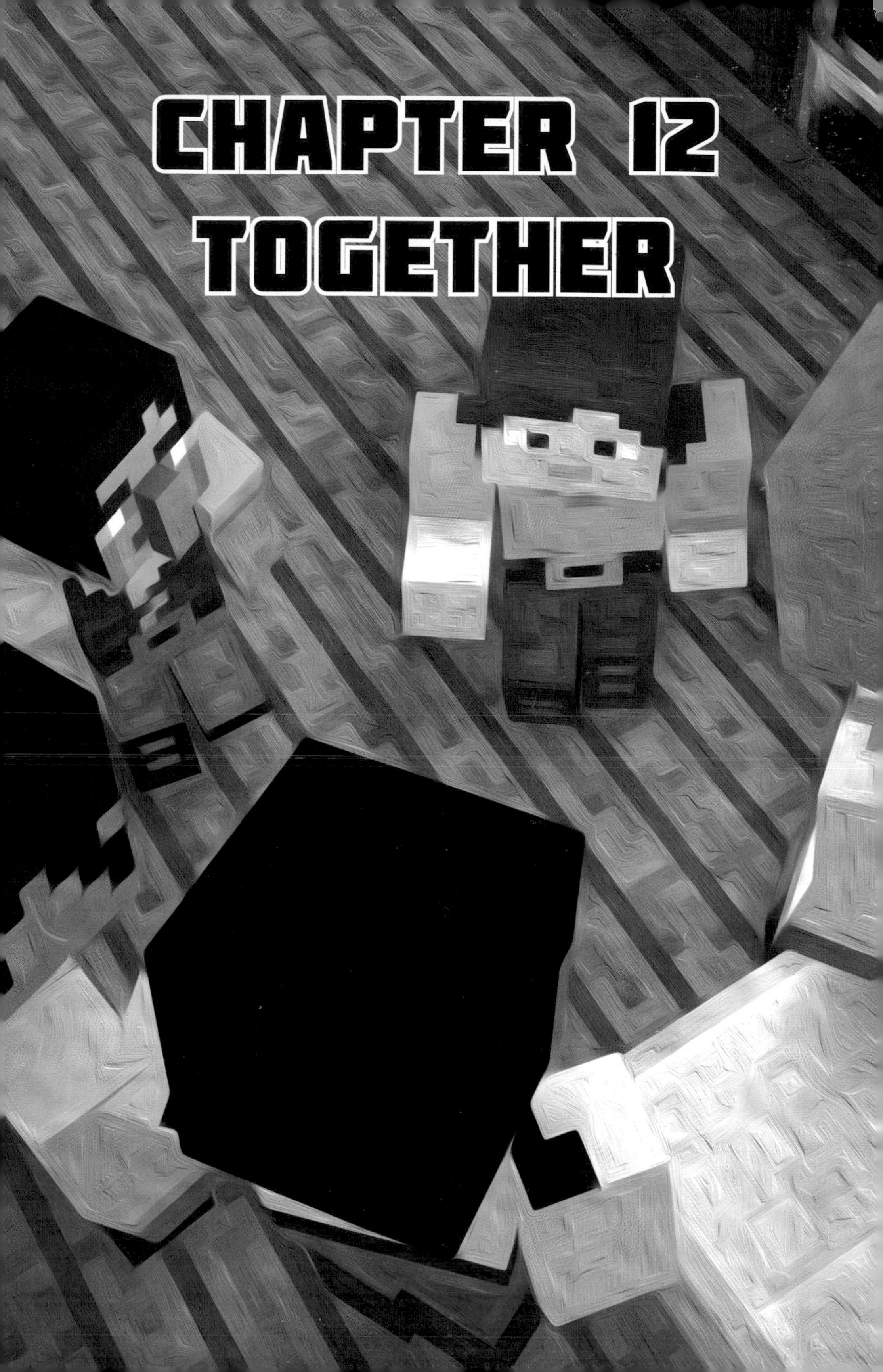

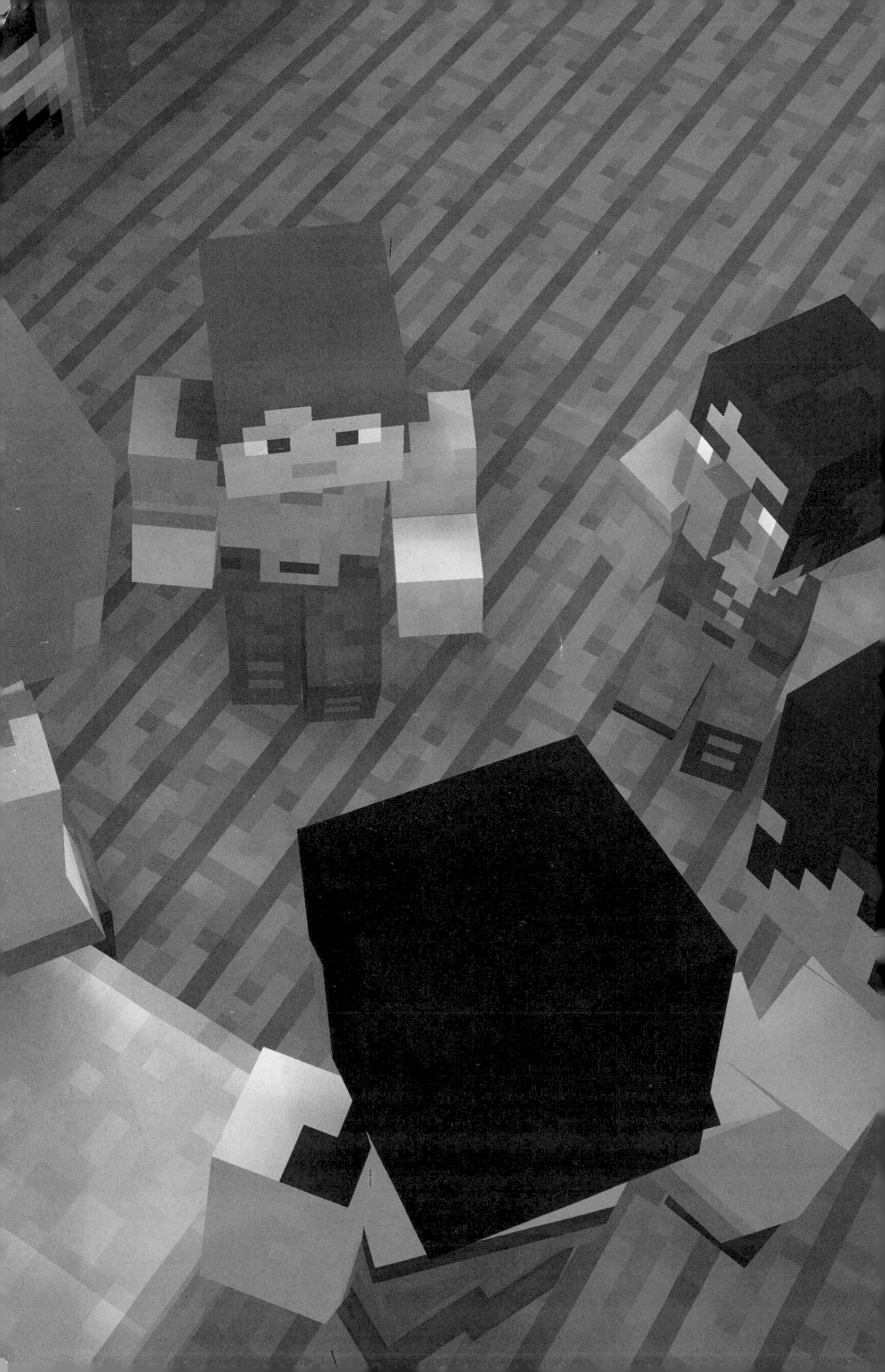

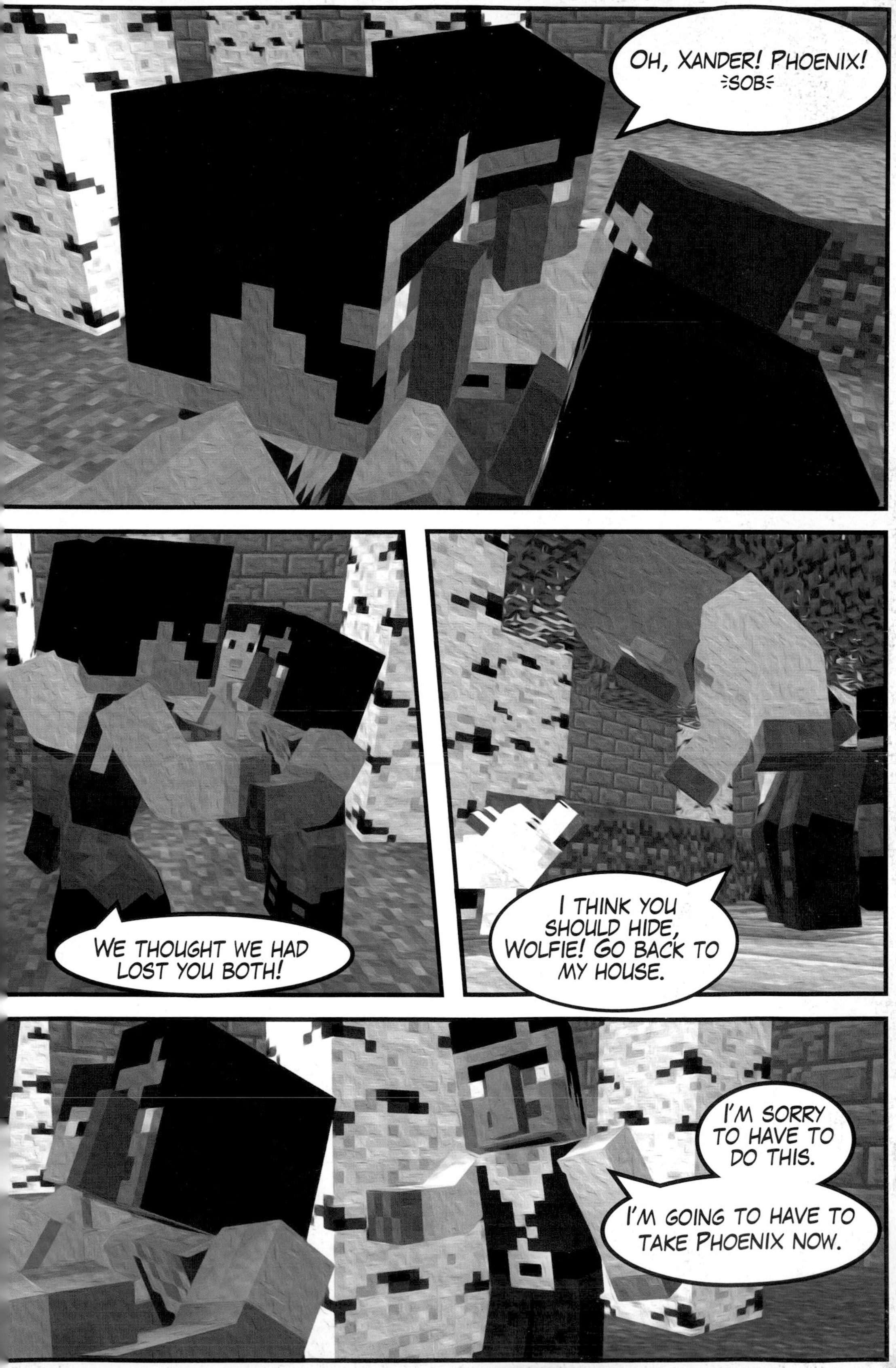
OH, XANDER! PHOENIX!
SOB
WE THOUGHT WE HAD LOST YOU BOTH!
I THINK YOU SHOULD HIDE, WOLFIE! GO BACK TO MY HOUSE.
I'M SORRY TO HAVE TO DO THIS.
I'M GOING TO HAVE TO TAKE PHOENIX NOW.

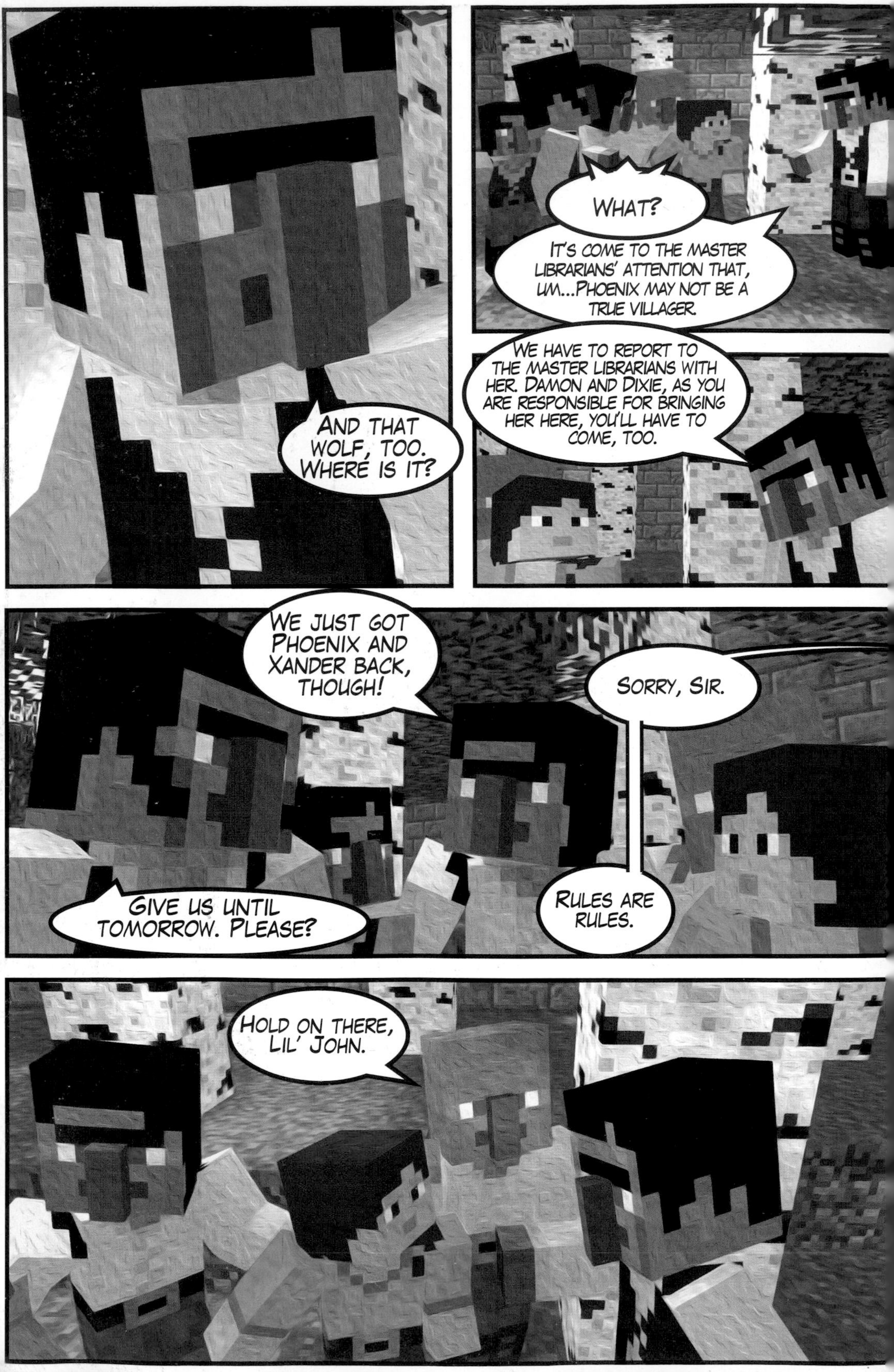

AND THAT WOLF, TOO. WHERE IS IT?
WHAT?
IT'S COME TO THE MASTER LIBRARIANS' ATTENTION THAT, UM...PHOENIX MAY NOT BE A TRUE VILLAGER.
WE HAVE TO REPORT TO THE MASTER LIBRARIANS WITH HER. DAMON AND DIXIE, AS YOU ARE RESPONSIBLE FOR BRINGING HER HERE, YOU'LL HAVE TO COME, TOO.
WE JUST GOT PHOENIX AND XANDER BACK, THOUGH!
GIVE US UNTIL TOMORROW. PLEASE?
SORRY, SIR.
RULES ARE RULES.
HOLD ON THERE, LIL' JOHN.

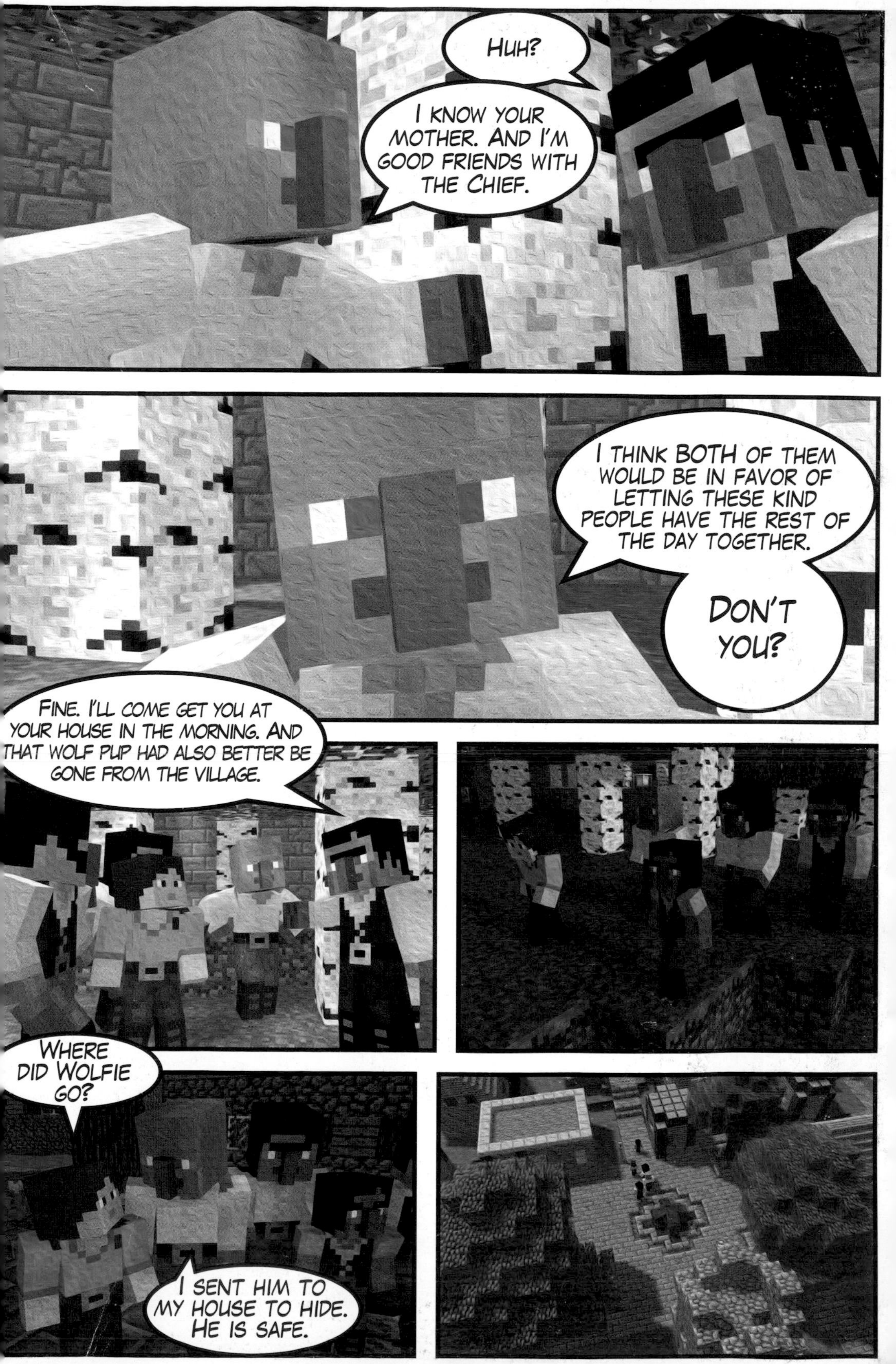
HUH?
I KNOW YOUR MOTHER. AND I'M GOOD FRIENDS WITH THE CHIEF.
I THINK BOTH OF THEM WOULD BE IN FAVOR OF LETTING THESE KIND PEOPLE HAVE THE REST OF THE DAY TOGETHER.
DON'T YOU?
FINE. I'LL COME GET YOU AT YOUR HOUSE IN THE MORNING. AND THAT WOLF PUP HAD ALSO BETTER BE GONE FROM THE VILLAGE.
WHERE DID WOLFIE GO?
I SENT HIM TO MY HOUSE TO HIDE. HE IS SAFE.

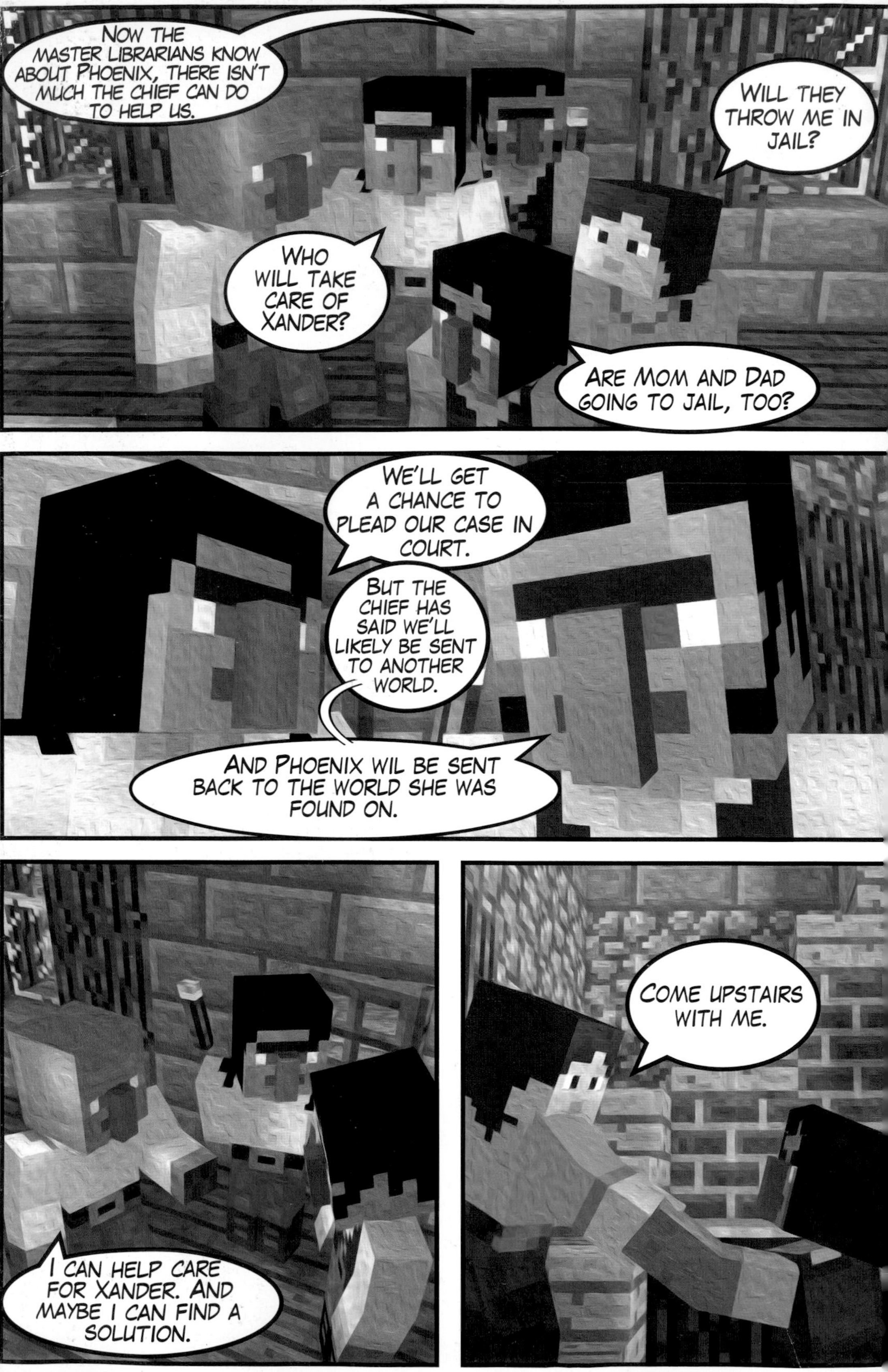
NOW THE MASTER LIBRARIANS KNOW ABOUT PHOENIX, THERE ISN'T MUCH THE CHIEF CAN DO TO HELP US.
WILL THEY THROW ME IN JAIL?
WHO WILL TAKE CARE OF XANDER?
ARE MOM AND DAD GOING TO JAIL, TOO?
WE'LL GET A CHANCE TO PLEAD OUR CASE IN COURT.
BUT THE CHIEF HAS SAID WE'LL LIKELY BE SENT TO ANOTHER WORLD.
AND PHOENIX WIL BE SENT BACK TO THE WORLD SHE WAS FOUND ON.
I CAN HELP CARE FOR XANDER. AND MAYBE I CAN FIND A SOLUTION.
COME UPSTAIRS WITH ME.

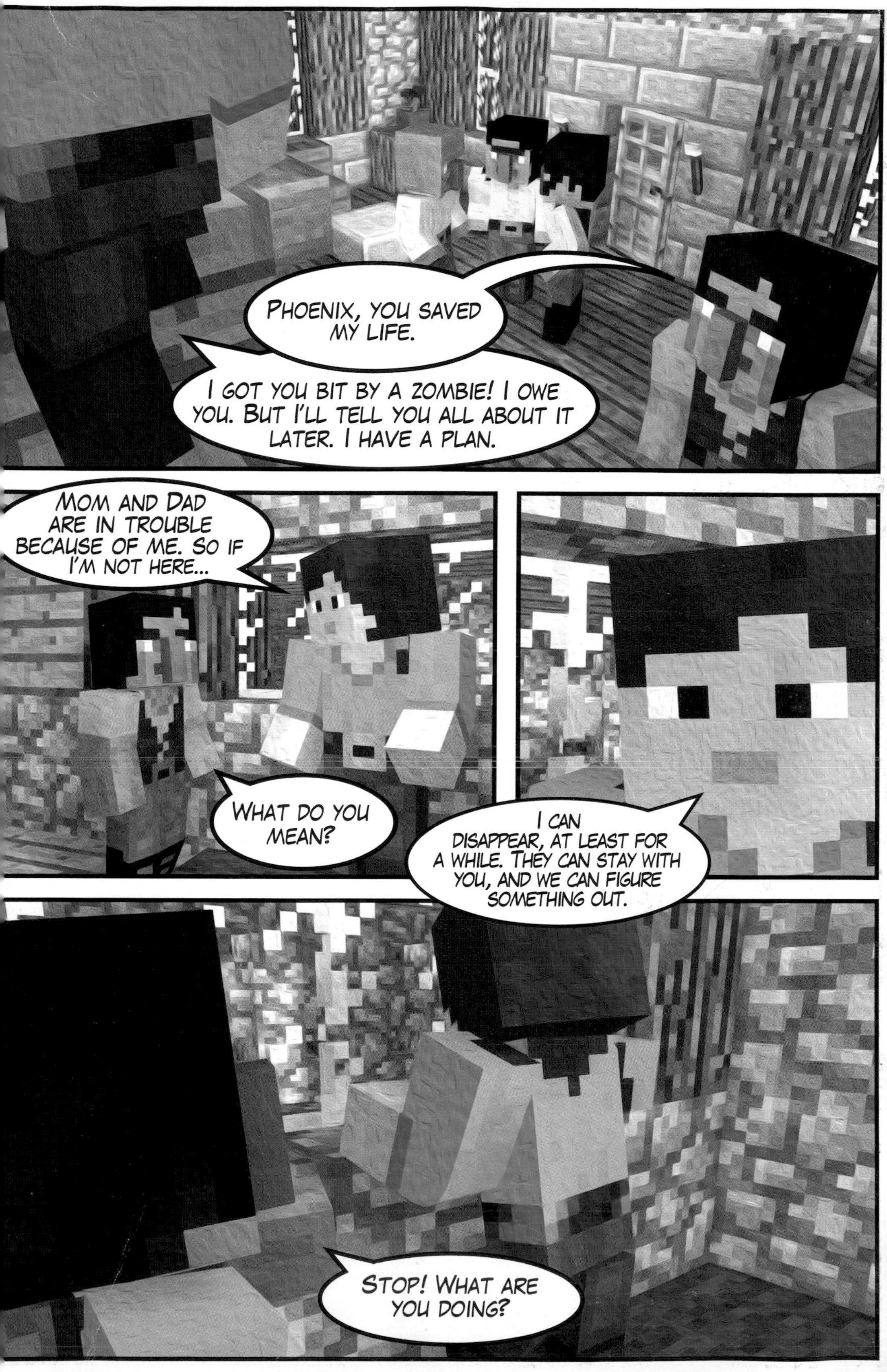
PHOENIX, YOU SAVED MY LIFE.
I GOT YOU BIT BY A ZOMBIE! I OWE YOU. BUT I'LL TELL YOU ALL ABOUT IT LATER. I HAVE A PLAN.
MOM AND DAD ARE IN TROUBLE BECAUSE OF ME. SO IF I'M NOT HERE...
WHAT DO YOU MEAN?
I CAN DISAPPEAR, AT LEAST FOR A WHILE. THEY CAN STAY WITH YOU, AND WE CAN FIGURE SOMETHING OUT.
STOP! WHAT ARE YOU DOING?

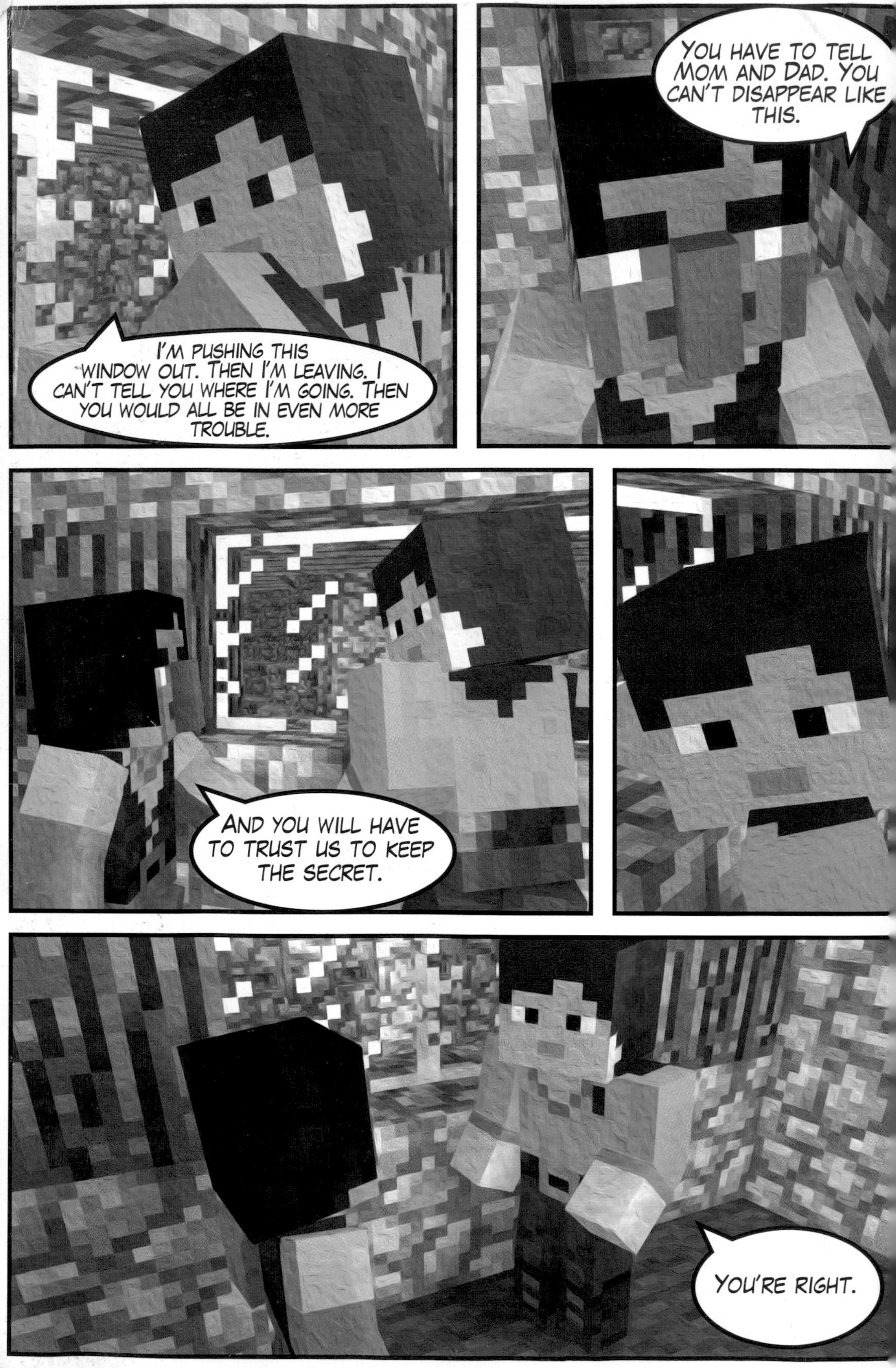
I'M PUSHING THIS WINDOW OUT. THEN I'M LEAVING. I CAN'T TELL YOU WHERE I'M GOING. THEN YOU WOULD ALL BE IN EVEN MORE TROUBLE.
YOU HAVE TO TELL MOM AND DAD. YOU CAN'T DISAPPEAR LIKE THIS.
AND YOU WILL HAVE TO TRUST US TO KEEP THE SECRET.
YOU'RE RIGHT.

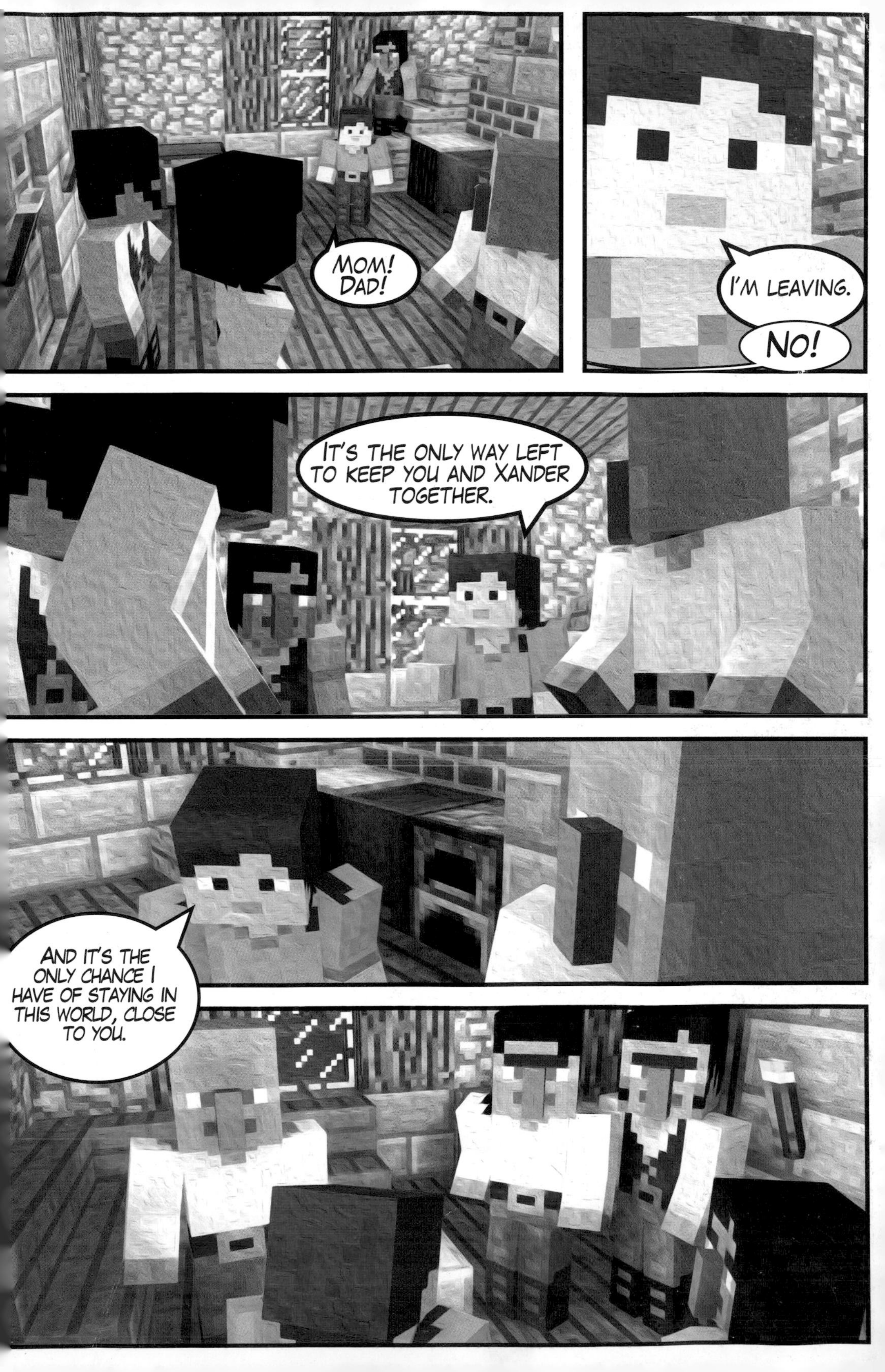
MOM! DAD!
I'M LEAVING.
NO!
IT'S THE ONLY WAY LEFT TO KEEP YOU AND XANDER TOGETHER.
AND IT'S THE ONLY CHANCE I HAVE OF STAYING IN THIS WORLD, CLOSE TO YOU.

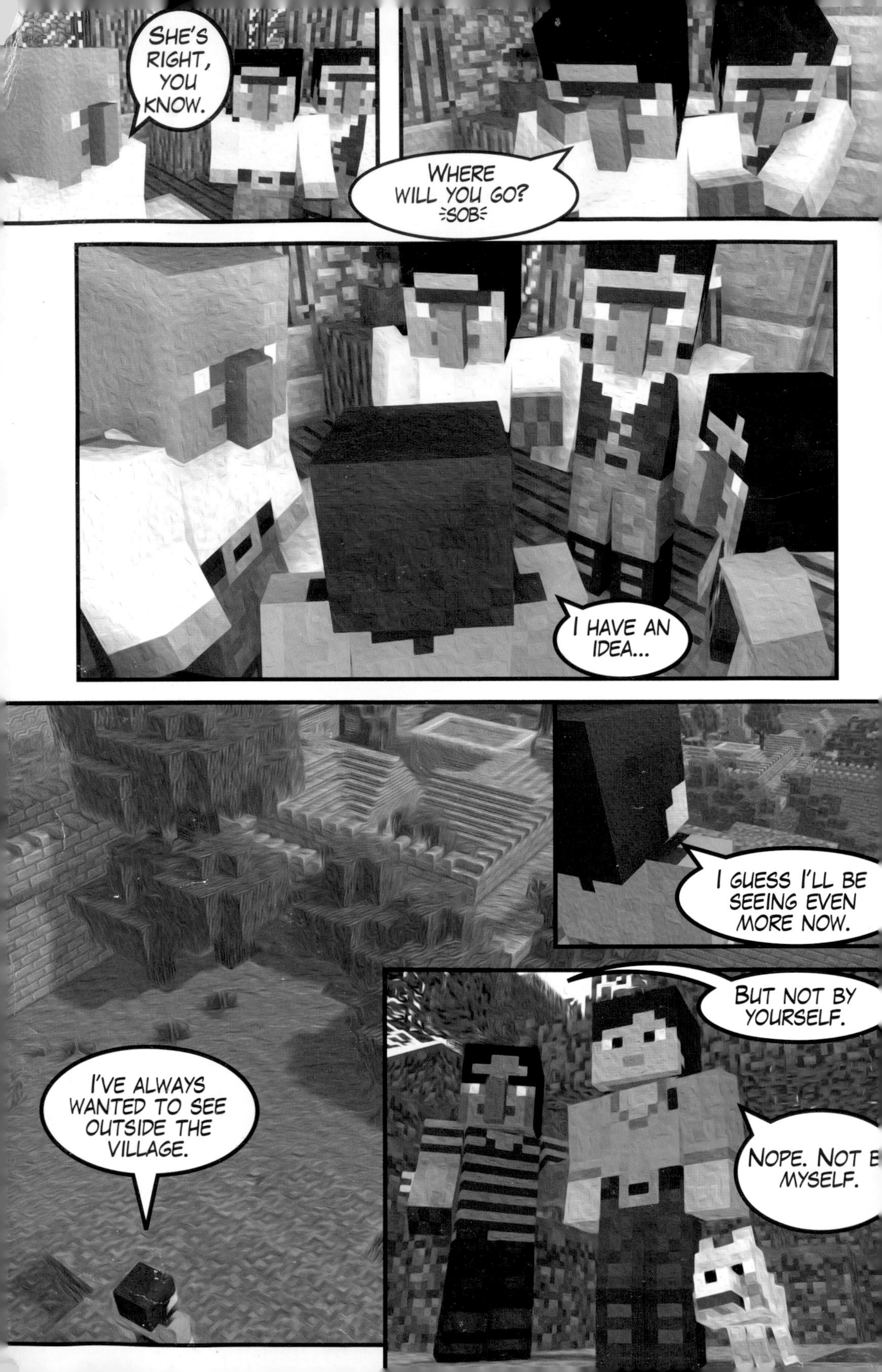
SHE'S RIGHT, YOU KNOW.
WHERE WILL YOU GO? ≡SOB≡
I HAVE AN IDEA...
I'VE ALWAYS WANTED TO SEE OUTSIDE THE VILLAGE.
I GUESS I'LL BE SEEING EVEN MORE NOW.
BUT NOT BY YOURSELF.
NOPE. NOT B MYSELF.